INIQUITY

THE ASCENT

MELODY WINTER

INIQUITY © 2016 Melody Winter.

ISBN-13: 978-153-9029755
ISBN-10: 1539029751

This book is a work of fiction. Any references to names, characters, places, and events are the product of the author's imagination, and any resemblance to actual events, or persons, living or dead, is entirely coincidental.

Cover art and design by Amalia Chitulescu: www.Amalia. Chitulescu.Digital.Art
Formatting by Stacey Blake at Champagne Formats: www. champagneformats.com

DEDICATION

To Barbara and Denise, for believing in me right from the
start.

PROLOGUE

TREPIDATION

"Paymon's coming," Gran warned as she stepped away from the window in our meagre, ramshackle house. "Hide that stupid book."

I lifted my gaze and huffed.

"I don't know why you waste so much time trying to read it," Gran scolded. "It's demon language. What do you expect? The words to jump out at you and suddenly make sense?"

"It might hold the secret to the darkness," I said, risking another argument with her.

She shook her head and hobbled toward the door. A hacking cough made her stumble, but she steadied herself with a hand on the uneven wattled wall and turned to glare at me.

"Hide it!" she snapped. "And make sure he doesn't see you."

I focused on my gran, concerned over the way she often became breathless and the cough that didn't sound as if it was getting any better. But when she pulled the rug back from over the door and took a step outside, I closed the book. I'd hide it, like I always did when Paymon visited the village. I understood her concern. She feared what he would do if he ever found out I had it.

Screams from outside switched my attention to the window. I rushed to the open space just in time to see Paymon shoot a ball of fire at one of the homes in our village. I froze for a second, gasping in air as the house caught fire. Transfixed by our village demon and his actions, he sent another three balls of fire at the house. I dropped the book and headed to the door.

"No," Gran said, blocking my exit. "You stay here."

"I want to help!" I said, angling my body toward the doorway. "Get some water from the lake."

"They'll manage. The fire will be out soon."

I widened my eyes at my gran. "But there are people in there!"

She nodded, but remained blocking the doorway. Her expression was steely. "You stay here. Have you hidden that book yet?" she asked, shifting her body so she could see around me.

"Not yet," I said, moving back to the table.

I dipped my head and glanced outside. The house was burning steadily, lighting the darkness that constantly surrounded us. Paymon was watching the unfolding event, his arms crossed over his chest as he grinned at the panic around him. Women were rushing from their homes, returning several moments later with buckets of water to dowse the flames.

Gran stood in the doorway, almost mimicking Paymon's stance as she too watched what was happening.

I picked the book up from the floor, wiped the dirt from the cover and traced the dimmed gold letters with my fingers.

'DNMGO'

What did it mean? Was it a person's name or the title of the book? I knew who it had belonged to—the only other demon who had been in our village. She'd treated the villagers far worse than Paymon ever had. She'd enjoyed torturing them for nothing other than entertainment. I was only ten when she'd arrived, and she'd secretly fascinated me. She looked how I imagined a princess to look. She'd worn beautiful embroidered dresses, and she walked with a grace I could only ever dream about. Whenever she came to the village with Paymon, I'd tried to follow them, watch their sinister interactions. And that one time . . . that one time they had argued. I could still hear her manic laughter—it ripped through me like a winter storm. I had frozen in my hiding place as Paymon turned on her. I still remembered the large ball of fire that he sent her way. When it hit her, she exploded in a bright blue flash that lit the world for a split second. I'd shielded my eyes, and when I had opened them, there was nothing but her smouldering dress crumpled on the floor where she had stood. Paymon had limped away from the scene, and once he had gone I crept from my hiding place and headed to the glowing embers. The book I now possessed had been lying only a short distance away from the remains of the woman. Charred around the edges, it carried the events of that day from four years ago, and I was convinced it was important—that it held the secret of how they'd hidden the light.

After tucking the book under the mattress of the bed I shared with Gran, I rushed back into the only other room in the house. Pulling one of the old wooden chairs away from the table, I settled it next to the window before sitting down. Resting the side of my face against the cold wall, I ensured I could spy on the strange and fascinating interaction between Gran and Paymon, just like I always did when he visited the village.

Fear prickled down my neck as Paymon turned away from the house he had set afire and limped toward Gran. I screwed my nose up as Gran hobbled to meet him, and then I huffed as she bowed. Paymon was no king, and he didn't deserve a greeting that was suited for one. I'd never bow to a demon. Never.

Paymon's cloaked figure towered over Gran, but then she was an old woman, shrinking every day before my eyes. I sighed heavily, biting my lip. She needed to step down from being the village elder; her health was suffering. She needed to rest more. She wasn't the only old woman in the village, and there were several who were younger than her who could step up to deal with Paymon and his demands.

Paymon leered toward Gran as his voice rose, and I took several deep breaths. He held an air of authority that I never saw in any of the men from the village. There was something about him that made the hairs on my neck rise and my heartbeat race whenever he came to the village.

He prowled around Gran, circling her as he spoke, and I wished more than ever that I could hear their exchange. What was he saying to her? What was she saying to him? When he stopped in front of her, he placed his hands on his hips. His cloak slipped away from his arms, and I caught a glimpse of what he was wearing. A dark jacket, trousers and knee-high boots. They were like clothes from a by-gone era, one from over a hundred years ago, one Gran had told me about.

My mind raced with the stories of what the world was like when I was a child. It had been a better place before the demons ascended. There was sunlight, freedom, and all sorts of machines. Now, there was a blanket of suffocating darkness covering the land. There was no freedom and no electricity. The demons' arrival had destroyed all sources of power and forced the humans out of the cities and into the forests. With no sun lighting the world, a mind-numbing cold sliced into our pale skin. It cracked blisters open and reached into holes in dull clothing. Everything was done by hand. We'd stepped back in time. Life was hard.

Paymon's raised voice snapped me from my thoughts. They were arguing, and I shrank away from the window, fearful of what would unfold. I rubbed my clammy hands on my tatty dress and licked my dry lips. Gran said it was never a good thing to annoy a demon, yet she was obviously not heeding her own advice.

The shouting became louder, but the words were still incomprehensible. My stomach churned, but when Paymon grabbed Gran's hair and pulled her head backward, I forgot all my fear and sprang into action. I shot out of the chair and across the room, reacting instinctively to protect my only living relative.

The coldness of the morning nipped at my skin, but I charged toward them. "Leave her alone!" I shouted.

Paymon was bending down to Gran's height, whispering something to her, but he stopped as soon as I shouted at him.

His withering gaze settled on me. Running on pure adrenaline, I stepped up to him, swallowed my fear and stared him right in the eye.

"Let. Her. Go."

He smiled, and it unnerved me, but I returned his stare, focusing on brown eyes that gradually darkened.

"Who are you?" Paymon said, releasing my gran.

I took a step backward, and Gran grabbed me. Her gnarled and wizened fingers tightened around my wrist, and I winced.

"You stupid girl," she hissed. "Why didn't you stay inside?"

Her face turned even paler than her usual deathly colour, and I froze. My mind raced, trying to find answers to her unexpected and hostile response. Had I done something wrong? I'd just saved her from the village demon. Why was she mad with me?

Paymon's smile grew even wider and his eyes even darker. "What's your name?"

His voice was nothing like I expected. It was too rich, too smooth, not what I imagined a demon to sound like. I glanced at my gran who refused to meet my questionable gaze.

I saw no harm in telling Paymon my name, so I said it, clear and confident. "Athena."

He nodded, his eyes narrowing as he drank in my appearance. I took another step backward, uncomfortable in his gaze. Relief flooded through me when he switched his attention back to Gran.

"Why have you kept her hidden from me?"

Gran closed her eyes before sighing. When she turned to me, she shot me such a fierce stare that in that moment I feared her as much as Paymon.

"Go back to the house," she ordered.

"But—"

"No arguing. Go. Now!"

I wanted to stay. Gran's age obviously wasn't a deterrent to Paymon's cruel behaviour. None of us knew how his mind worked, how he chose his next victim. He'd set fire to a house today, but would that be all he did? I stayed where I was, trying to balance my intrinsic fear to flee from Paymon with my overpowering need to protect Gran. But there was something about my gran's tone, a snippet of a warning in the way she spoke. I hated falling out with her, so I dipped my head before nodding.

I turned around and walked back to the house, ignoring the intense feeling of eyes following my departure. My body was heavy, each step was an effort, and I had a sinking feeling in my stomach. Something wasn't right.

Paymon's voice sounded out as he continued his chat with my gran, and I trudged back to the house and to the window to watch their continuing exchange.

Gran shifted from foot to foot, shaking her head as Paymon continued to shout at her.

But then he surprised me by placing his hand on her shoulder. She lifted her trembling hand to her forehead before looking down at the ground.

I groaned with frustration. What were they saying to each other?

Paymon rubbed his chin before speaking again, and when he did, Gran stumbled sideways. She dropped to her knees and pulled at his cloak.

I was on my feet, ready to charge from the house again. But as I stood up, Paymon tipped his head back and looked to the dark sky. When he dropped his gaze, his eyes locked with mine and a sinister grin twitched into place on his face.

I ducked away from the opening, sure he was about to engulf me in one of his balls of fire, but when the heated furnace never appeared, I risked another glance at him.

Gran was struggling to her feet. Paymon offered no

assistance, and when she eventually stood before him, he nodded toward me, speaking quickly, at a slightly higher pitch than before.

Gran's hands were shaking, and she lifted one of them to her throat before coughing. The hacking cough made her body convulse, and Paymon just watched as she took her time to recover.

When Gran had composed herself, she looked my way and then nodded at Paymon.

She began speaking fast, gesticulating with her hands, even stepping forward to continue her words when Paymon looked deep in thought. He only responded when she reached for his arm. He nodded and then closed his eyes.

I sighed. Whatever it was they were discussing, it looked like they'd come to an agreement. Maybe now she'd come back to the house, Paymon would leave us, and the danger he possessed would leave with him. Only then would my stomach stop twisting and churning.

But Paymon was grinning, and his relaxed expression made me even more anxious. Time slowed, and heat prickled at the back of my neck.

As if realising he was reacting in a way people were unaccustomed to seeing him behave, Paymon quickly recovered his malevolent composure. He shook his head before turning away from Gran, but when he was a few steps away from her, he suddenly stopped. His cloak billowed behind him as he spun around to face her.

With no warning, no exchange of any further words, he raised his arm. A ball of fire shot from his hand and engulfed my gran in flames.

CHAPTER 1

DREAD

A HIGH-PITCHED WAIL BLASTED THROUGH THE THIN wooden walls of my home. It was the familiar alarm for the start of another morning, the call for the men to rise and prepare for their day of work in the fields. The noise had the ability to wake the dead, not just the tired bodies that inhabited the village.

I drew in a shuddering breath as an arm tightened around my waist.

"Morning, sleepy." Thomas's whispered greeting was followed by a kiss to the base of my neck. I wriggled against him before turning onto my back.

He leaned over me, twisting my hair between his fingers. Familiar eyes searched mine in the false light of the morning.

"I have to go," he said softly, his words forming a white mist as his breath dissolved into the iciness of the air. "I've brought a lantern in for you, and I've lit the fire. I was as quiet as possible. I didn't want to disturb you. Not today."

He lightly brushed my lips with his own before sliding away. Standing tall, he stretched his arms above his head. His quietly defined chest muscles caught my eye, and he smirked when he caught me staring at him.

"Stop it," he said, reaching for his top. "If they saw you looking at me like that . . ." He shook his head. "We're already risking so much. You know the men of the village are forbidden to touch the women under twenty-one."

I huffed. "Stupid rules made by a stupid demon."

He sprang onto the bed, trapping me beneath the blankets. His tangled mess of hair dropped forward and tickled my forehead as he leaned over me and placed a finger on my lips. "Shhh . . ." His cheeky grin made another appearance. "Some say he has ears in every part of his kingdom. He could be listening to us this very moment."

I shook my head and spoke against his finger. "He may be powerful, but he's no magician."

"So you don't think he knows I took your virginity?" He removed his finger and pecked my lips before shifting away from me again. Swinging his legs over the edge of the bed, he reached for his boots.

"It was years ago," I protested, sitting up and pulling the scratchy blanket around my chest. "And what's done is done. I don't think Paymon cares about rules."

He scowled before turning away to pull his boots on. "It was three years ago exactly," he mumbled, struggling to fasten the fraying laces.

Three years ago—my eighteenth birthday. It was the best and most wondrous present he could have given me. A light in this dark, depressing world. My cheeks heated as I remembered our first clumsy attempts to familiarise ourselves with each other's bodies.

"So . . ." he drawled, leaning backward across my blanket covered legs, giving up on tying his laces. "Happy birthday, Athena."

I pushed him off my legs, my movements quick and agitated. "Why did you have to remind me?"

"Your twenty-first birthday won't disappear just because we ignore it." He jumped to his feet, slipping his arms into his mud stained shirt. "And look at it this way, you don't have to work today."

"Maybe if I was working, I could forget about all this."

He fastened the tiny buttons running up the front of his shirt. "Make the most of it. I would if the men were given the same privilege on their twenty-first birthday."

I narrowed my eyes. "It's only because we get summoned to see Paymon. I'd much rather work and not see him."

Thomas's shoulders dropped as concerned eyes met mine. "Maybe I can cheer you up."

"How?"

He rubbed his hand over his short cropped hair. "I've organised a small party for you tonight. Hannah's coming, James, Jacob . . . everyone."

I screwed my nose up, not replying. I didn't see any reason to celebrate my twenty-first birthday. I closed my eyes, pulled my knees to my chest, and wrapped my arms around them. "I don't want to be twenty-one."

"Hey." Thomas sank onto the bed next to me. He wrapped his arm around my shoulder and pulled me toward him.

"I don't want to be sent away. I want to stay in the village with you."

"You may not get sent away," he said, squeezing my

shoulder. "Not all the girls do."

"I will, Myrtle said I would."

I shifted even closer to Thomas, wanting to crawl onto his lap and never leave. He was the one person I trusted, the man who saved and protected me from this vile world.

He kissed the side of my head. "Well, she might not be right this time. She's got it wrong in the past. And let's remember that she's completely batty."

"You shouldn't talk like that about Myrtle."

He chuckled. "Athena, you've called her far worse."

I shoved him with my shoulder. He was right. I had called her a lot worse when she stepped up as the new village elder. It was a time when I was still raw, hurt from my gran's unexpected death. And it was Thomas who had come to my rescue, saved me from sinking into a depression even worse than the miserable darkness that surrounded us.

"Why don't you talk to Hannah?" Thomas said, reaching for my hand. "She was summoned to see Paymon yesterday. Haven't you spoken to her yet?"

I shook my head. I'd been so wrapped up in worrying about myself that I'd forgotten it was Hannah's birthday yesterday.

Thomas raised his brow. "Make sure you talk to her today."

"I can't believe I forgot."

He placed another kiss to the side of my head. "She'll understand." He released my hand and shifted to the side of the bed.

I picked at the fraying threads on the edge of one of the blankets. "Myrtle said that she'd be leaving the village. She'll be sent to the Master."

"Well, you need to talk to her. Find out if crazy Myrtle

was right." He sighed before standing up and reaching for his jacket. "She's your best friend. Ask her. I know Paymon scares you but he won't do anything to you, it's the Ascension Ceremony we need to worry about. That's when you'll be taken away, not today, and after all this worrying, you might not be going anywhere." His familiar dimple appeared in his left cheek as he smiled. "And like I said earlier, you've got a party to look forward to tonight."

I scowled at him. I wasn't in a party mood.

He pulled his jacket on before returning to the edge of the bed and grinning. "I wasn't going to mention it, but . . ."

"But what?" I said, trying pointlessly to hide my curiosity.

He shook his head. "No, no, I can't tell you. It'll spoil the surprise."

I shifted across the bed, dragging the covers with me. "Tell me," I said, reaching for his thigh.

He chuckled before tapping his chin with his finger. "What would you say if I suggested that your twenty-first party became slightly more than just a birthday party?"

"Explain."

"What about if it was also, oh, I don't know . . . say . . . your engagement party?"

"My what?" A lightness fluttered in my chest.

"Your, or rather, our engagement party."

"Really?"

He crouched at the side of the bed, never taking his eyes off me. "Athena, will you do me the honour of promising to be my wife?"

I stared at him. Thomas and I had been inseparable since Gran and I arrived in the village. We'd grown up together. He'd been the boy who stopped the other children picking on me, the boy who'd made me laugh through the dark days, and I wanted nothing more than to settle down with him in the village and have a family of our own.

"You gonna answer me?" Thomas said, tilting his head to the side, suddenly serious.

I nodded.

Thomas's lips lifted at one corner. "I've thought about it a lot. I don't want you to be sent away any more than you want to go. And if you are taken away from me then I want you to know that I'll be here for you when you get back."

"Thomas . . . I . . ." My words failed to form. I threw myself at him, and he stood up as I wrapped my legs around his hips.

"Hey," Thomas chuckled in between my fervent kisses. His familiar hands held my thighs. "Look at you, all naked and warm. I should be hung, drawn and quartered with the thoughts I'm having at the moment." He dipped his head and captured my lips. Stumbling forward with me still wrapped around him, we fell onto the bed. "Don't tell anyone we're engaged," he said. "Let's surprise them tonight."

I nodded before dragging him back for more kisses.

The holler of the village men trudging to the fields rung out as they passed outside.

"Shit," he mumbled. "I have to go."

I pouted and attempted to pull him closer for another kiss, but he straightened, pushing himself away from me. His eyes narrowed as they wandered over my body, and then he sighed. "You'll have to make your own porridge," he said, his eyes shooting to the heavy rug hanging at the window. "I can't be late again."

"Go then," I said, propping myself up on my elbows, and flashing him a flirtatious smile. "Don't let me keep you."

He shook his head, a grin pulling at the sides of his mouth. "I'll definitely see you later." He strode to the window and pulled the heavy curtain back. "Keep the bed warm," he said before throwing the wooden shutters open and jumping through the space. The rug swung back to its original position.

"Pig," I muttered under my breath. But I was glowing inside. We were to be married. We'd have children together. We'd have our own family.

Thomas had lost all his family when our village demon set fire to his house. He had as much reason as me to hate Paymon. His family survived the demons' arrival but perished soon after. My parents and sister presumably died when the demons came. They'd have been in a car travelling at speed when the world literally split open. Hardly anyone survived the carnage that occurred on the roads that day. I was eight when it happened—old enough to remember, too young to understand.

I sighed as I grasped the blankets and pulled them tightly around me. I didn't look to the window as the footfall of the passing men reached a crescendo. All the men who were fit enough to work trudged to the fields surrounding the village. It was a wonder anything grew under the constant heavy veil of darkness, but the fields around us were controlled by our village demon. He, and he alone, had the power to restore the light over the fields where the crops grew and the animals lived.

Yawning and stretching, I swung my legs over the side of the bed. I shivered when my bare feet touched the cold wooden floor and hurried to the chest of drawers containing my socks and shoes. My socks reached my mid-thigh, and my shoes, made from soft leather, covered the soles and sides of my feet. Laces threaded criss-cross over the top of my foot and around my ankle. They were comfortable to wear but offered little protection from the sharp stones and hard ground around the village. Only the men wore boots, the hardwearing thick leather was needed when they worked in the fields. The women were left with the flimsy coverings. I pulled my thin linen underdress over my head, wriggling as the coarse material scratched my skin, and then added my day dress over the top. I looked at the basic cut of what I wore and sighed at its simple box-like style. The underdress had long sleeves and covered my body from my neck to my ankles; the day dress laced up the front from my waist to my neck, and it also reached my ankles. It was brown and dull. Even the leather twisted belt I added did little to give the dress any defined shape. I vaguely remembered the clothes from before: bright colours, floaty skirts, jeans, thick coats to keep the cold out, proper shoes, underwear. We had no way of making those items in the village. In the thirteen years since the demons came, the clothes we brought with us had rotted, fallen to pieces or worn out. Gradually, we'd adapted to make the most basic of items.

I hated this monotonous, hard life. Gran told me what it was like before they came, and I always marvelled at how easy everything must have been. I longed for that life even though I only had vague memories of it. Electricity sounded like magic. There were computers, phones, televisions, engines, cars, and aeroplanes—machines that flew in the sky. I glanced toward the window, picturing the world beyond. The only things that flew in the sky now were the birds that surrounded our village.

Ravens.

Thomas had caught one once, pulled its neck and then

plucked it before roasting it on a spit over the central fire. But I'd refused to eat it. They were messengers of the demons, and I wanted nothing to do with them.

I yawned loudly as I picked the lantern from the top of the chest of drawers and stepped into the other room—the combined kitchen and living area. A fire danced within the central stone fireplace. It split the house in two, offering its welcome heat to both the bedroom and the living area.

This main room was bathed in a soft flickering orange glow from the fire. A lit lantern was situated on the large wooden table, and added another angle to the sinister shadows dancing on the walls. Four wooden chairs, all various designs, were tucked underneath the table. The only other item of furniture was a tall cupboard that kept all the pots and pans out of sight. I strode to the window and pulled the rug back before opening the shutters. The familiar smells—smoke, damp thatch, and stale cooking—and the sounds of a village waking up greeted me. I cast my gaze across the centre of the village and toward where Paymon lived. I squinted and was sure I could make out the fuzzy outline of his house through the dusty haze.

My house was set back from the centre of the village—one row of mismatched homes between mine and the bare earth around the large fire. All our houses looked like triangles from the front and back, the roofs sloped right to the ground. We lived simply, using the resources of the forest to build what we needed. Some people had brought, or stolen, items from the distant towns and cities where we used to live. Disease and the renegades, gangs of outlaws, that now lived there, and the dangers in between, made journeys back too perilous. A few houses had small windows with white plastic frames that rested in wooden low walls. They offered protection from the bitter winds that frequently rushed through the village. I had wooden shutters nestled against the open spaces, like the majority of people, and all of us had wooden doors, either made in the village, or once again stolen from the cities, but behind each one hung a thick rug to fight the chill.

"Athena!" Hannah waved as she strode toward my door. "The men have gone," she said, tucking her long blond hair behind her ears. "Let's get our jobs done, and then we can make you look pretty for tonight."

Her exuberance was difficult to ignore; she was like a whirlwind whenever she entered a room. But I nodded my reluctant agreement to her offer.

"What's wrong?" she said before linking her arm with mine and leading me to one of the chairs at the table. "You've got something on your mind. I can always tell. Sit and tell me what the problem is." She looked at the spluttering fire and tutted. "And I'll make the porridge seeing as you haven't."

I sat on one of the hard wooden chairs as she unclasped her cloak and threw it next to me.

"Do you ever wish it could be like it used to be?" I asked, placing my elbows on the table and resting my head in my hands. "Bright and sunny, magic homes, clean clothes?"

Hannah eyed me wearily. "We need to embrace our life as it is. Make the most of it, Athena. It's no good pining for something in the past."

"Maybe we can have it again." The light was the key—it wasn't the only thing that changed when they came, but it was the one thing I'd decided they couldn't tolerate. Why block the light and live in a depressing world? There was one reason and one reason only as far as I was concerned. They couldn't stand the light. Maybe it hurt them, burnt them, I didn't know, but I was confident it did something. That's why they hid it from us with the thick layer of grey clouds.

I sighed, sliding my hands to rub at the back of my neck as I looked toward Hannah. "It might not happen in our life-time, but eventually we'll become as wise and powerful as we were before they came. We'll find a way to get the light back and destroy them."

"Shhh . . ." she scolded. "They may hear you."

I raised my eyebrows at her statement. She sounded no different than Thomas.

"It's the light I miss the most," I mumbled. "I'm sick of all this gloom. Can you imagine what it would be like if it came back?"

"We'd probably all fry or be blinded by it." She scooped the oats that I'd left to soak overnight into a large black pot and hooked it over the fire. "Stop day-dreaming. It'll never happen, and it does you no good to obsess over it the way you do."

She usually humoured me when I started ranting about the dark, but I could tell that now was not the time. I knew we'd not fry, or be blinded by it. I'd stood in the light once, many years ago now, when Gran was alive. Inherent curiosity had pushed me forward to go to the beam of light that lit the sky above the fields, not just sit on the roof of our house and stare at it for hours on end. I'd followed the men one morning, sneaking away before Gran was out of bed. When they got to the fields I'd stayed along the perimeter watching them, en-suring nothing untoward happened. Gran always warned me that there were creatures in the forest that could attack and kill, and over the years several men had indeed disappeared, never to be found. But that day, I didn't care, and I longed to feel the heat of the sun, and see the true brightness of everything around me.

"Didn't Thomas have breakfast this morning?" Hannah asked, her back to me as she poured a jug of water into the oat mixture.

"No," I said, snapping from my memories. "He rushed off. We slept in. Which reminds me, I need to see Myrtle after we've eaten." Myrtle provided the women of the village with Queen Ann's lace, our only form of contraception.

I twisted a length of my dark hair, running its wild smoothness though my fingers. It was a nervous habit, one my Gran always scolded me for.

Hannah grinned. "I need to see her as well."

I chuckled. "Who is it this week?"

Hannah tapped the side of her nose with her finger. "Not telling."

"Hannah, I'm your best friend. You should tell me these things."

"Aren't you fed up of having to go to Myrtle for the lace?" she said. "She judges us every time we ask her for it. Does she glare and tut at you whenever you ask for it?" She wafting the smoke from the fire away from her face.

"No, not that I've noticed." I didn't have the heart to tell Hannah that it was probably because I was in a steady relationship with Thomas. Hannah wasn't in a relationship with anyone. But Myrtle wasn't stupid—she gave the Queen Anne's lace to those of us seeking its results. Even though it wasn't completely successful, it had always worked for me. Its side-affects were mild, a slight stomach-ache, perhaps a little constipation—both better than ignoring the situation and risking the alternative.

Hannah swung to face me, waving the wooden spoon in her hand. "I'm thinking of picking some of it myself, then I've got my own supply."

"No, you can't!" My heart lurched, and I sat straight in my chair. "It's too dangerous. Remember what happened to Charlotte?"

Hannah screwed her nose up. "I'm not stupid. I know the difference between poison hemlock and the lace."

"Promise me you won't," I said, appealing to her as I recalled Charlotte's agonising screams. The silence that followed was even more unsettling. "Hannah! Promise me."

She sighed and then nodded before turning back to the porridge pot. "We can take Thomas some food later seeing as he missed breakfast," she said, completely changing the subject. "Creep out when nobody's looking and surprise him."

I frowned, watching her as she continued to stir the porridge. She was acting so normal. Was she staying in the village or had Myrtle been right with her prediction that she'd be sent away in a few days? I shuddered and desperately tried to forget that today was my birthday. It was as unwanted as the stupid darkness.

"You know we can't take him anything," I said, pushing my nagging thoughts aside. "We're not allowed through the forest."

She turned again while still tending to our breakfast. "Don't be so boring. Where's your sense of adventure?"

"It's too dangerous." My thoughts drifted again to when I'd stepped out into the rays of light at the fields. My body had warmed as if heated by a thousand fires. Even my toes felt the tendrils of heat that melted the harsh bitterness of the soggy and cold earth. I'd narrowed my gaze, and tried to stare at the sun, but it was impossible. Years of gloom had diminished my tolerance to any form of natural light, and my eyes had watered and stung as I looked around.

My journey to the light over the field had been uneventful, but as I made my way back through the forest a loud howl had erupted in the distance. It echoed through the trees, before wrapping its sinister tone around me. I could still remember the putrid stench of rotting flesh. I could still hear my frantic loud heartbeats as I ran. And I could still hear the pounding footsteps of something chasing me.

I'd never stepped foot into the forest since that day.

"The men do it every day," Hannah said, as if her statement had a bearing on what we did.

"We're not men." I shifted from my chair to fetch two bowls and spoons from the cupboard. I placed them on the low bench next to the fire.

Hannah smiled her thanks. "Well, maybe we should both live a bit, have a last adventure. I'll not be here in a few days." Her voice faltered, but she quickly recovered. "I doubt you will either."

I slumped back into my chair and placed my shaking hands under the table out of sight.

"So Paymon confirmed that you're going to the Master's?"

She nodded, avoiding my gaze.

"Are you scared?"

Hannah stopped stirring the porridge. "No. I'm not scared. I'll miss my brothers when I go, but not my parents."

I widened my eyes at her admittance. "But your parents—"

"Interfere all the time. Restrict me. Tell me what I can and can't do." She tipped her head to each side as she checked off her list. "You know what they're like. They've been like it for years. There are times I wish they were dead. All they care about are my brothers."

I froze, my posture rigid with shock. I'd do anything to have my parents back. I'd never leave the house again if that was what they wanted. "How can you say such a thing? They love you."

"You think so? I'm not so sure anymore." Her shoulders dropped and she sighed. "Let's just say that I'm actually looking forward to getting away from the dreary life here . . . and them. It'll be amazing at the Master's home."

I gasped and jerked my head backward.

"I've heard it's a giant castle," she said, eyes wide as if she was actually imagining being there. "Tall turrets and a deep lake around it to keep people out."

"Or keep people in." Her positive outlook was one I didn't share. "And what about all the other things they say? The nasty things?"

She slopped two large ladles of porridge into each bowl and brought them to the table.

"Eat," she said, not answering my question as she plonked a bowl in front of me.

We ate in silence, both of us tucking into one of our two daily meals, breakfast and then dinner tonight, depending on what the men brought back from the fields.

Hannah shoved spoonfuls of hot porridge into her mouth, not pausing.

"Hannah," I said, placing my spoon on the table, the porridge forgotten.

"Don't," she said, her eyes glossy with unshed tears.

I reached across the table to rest my hand on her arm.

"I don't want to be sent away," she said as her tears broke free and her spoon slipped from her hand and clattered onto the table.

CHAPTER 2

UNEASE

hANNAH RECOVERED HER DEMEANOUR QUICKLY. SHE brushed my hand off her arm and picked her spoon from its dropped position before stirring her porridge.

She nodded at my bowl. "I haven't made it just for you to waste."

I narrowed my eyes at the girl sitting opposite me and duly did as she instructed. She refused to meet my concerned gaze, and concentrated on eating the bland oat mixture.

I hated what was awaiting us, and it seemed that Hannah did as well. Once a year there was an Ascension Ceremony. All the girls who had turned twenty-one between the ceremonies had to attend. Each girl was categorised on her twenty-first birthday by the village demon and either stayed in the village or left at the ceremony to fulfil her designated role. If sent away, she was allowed to return ten years later.

Gran never let me attend the yearly Ascension

Ceremonies, and since her death, I'd chosen not to watch them. But the screams and deathly wails that accompanied the ceremony crept into my nightmares for weeks after their occurrence. It was the same every year. Only this year it would be different. I'd see what caused the noise, I'd witness the horrors that I imagined—I'd be part of it.

"Did Paymon say what happens at the ceremony?" I eyed her wearily, unsure of how she would react to my mention of her recent visit to see him.

"He didn't tell me about the ceremony," she said, tucking her hair behind her ears. "All he told me was that I was suitable for the Master. He categorised me as a feeder."

"A feeder?"

She nodded, her eyes wide. "I mean, what's that?"

"I don't know." I paused, watching my friend. She was scared, and she was desperately trying to not let it overpower her. "Hannah, how did you know when to go and see Paymon?"

"He sent his raven . . . with a letter for me."

I shuddered. Damn ravens.

"He said I was ideal, that I would serve the Master perfectly." I detected an air of smugness about her as she smirked. "I wonder what you'll be selected as."

I shrugged, pushing my bowl aside, my appetite deserting me. "He's creepy," I said, recalling the last monthly village feast we held. I didn't always attend them; I preferred not to put on a show of thanks to a demon who was part of the reason for our miserable lives.

"Did he make you do anything?"

"No. He just invited me in and told me to stand in the hallway."

"And that's all?"

She nodded. "He walked around me a few times and then told me about my categorisation." Looking straight at me, she jutted her chin out and smiled. "I'm going to be a feeder for the Master."

"But you don't know what a feeder is," I said, shocked at her obvious pride.

"I think I'll cook, work in the kitchens. Maybe I'll catch the Master's attention if I'm really good."

I leaned back in my chair and sucked in a deep breath. "Seriously? You want to get his attention?"

"Why not?"

"I'd never want to get his attention. Gran told me he was evil, that he kills women. He uses them, gets bored, and then gets rid of them."

"He uses them?" She wiggled her eyebrows.

"I'm serious, Hannah."

"Maybe I can keep him interested. Demons are meant to be exciting lovers."

"Hannah!"

She shook her head. "Your Gran didn't know everything. I mean, come on. She was full of stories—and that's all they were."

"No, no, she knew things."

"How?"

I looked away and picked at the loose threads on my belt. "She just did."

"She was a dreamer, just like you. You go on about returning the light, but you have no idea that they've actually caused the darkness. Maybe it's just one of those things that happened when they came."

I shook my head. The darkness was all their doing.

"Perhaps getting sent away is the best thing at the moment," Hannah said. Her eyes danced with an excitement that didn't match my own. "Myrtle always said we'd both be sent away. It's not a surprise, is it?"

I shook my head.

"We'll be fine. We're survivors remember." She pulled me into an unexpected hug. "Remember what you always say? 'We lived through their arrival, and we'll live through their demise.' That Master Demon won't know what's hit him when we arrive."

I hugged her tighter. I needed to stay strong—for both of us. I didn't believe for one second that Hannah was as fearless as she was trying to make out.

Hannah shrugged away from my hold and smoothed her dress over her hips.

"Let's go see Myrtle and get the lace," she said. "And then I'll come back to see you when I have a break. I'll make you look pretty for your party tonight. It'll be fun. James has managed to get some mead."

I sighed. Partying was the last thing I felt like doing at the moment.

Hannah picked her cloak up and swirled it over her shoulders before heading toward the door. I reached for my dirty brown cloak and pulled it tight around my shoulders.

The warmth of the fire-lit room disappeared as soon as we stepped outside. The sooty smell of the inside fire left my nostrils, but the overpowering aroma of multiple fires sending their smoke into the air only replaced it. I glanced at the crackling central fire as it too sent unpleasant plumes into the darkness above. This fire was the life-force of the village and was always lit.

Lanterns lit the village, the false light of day swinging merrily on ropes strung between houses and across the central clearing. It was as if they were to remind us of what we'd all forgotten, although there was always the distant glow of the light over the fields, a tease for what we all craved.

Hannah and I walked to the large hall, which rested in the first row of houses. It was the only building with walls on four sides, and it was the biggest structure in the village, easily the size of ten of our homes. The older men shuffled around the village, feeding the animals and fetching water to the large hall where the evening meal would be prepared. They looked as miserable as I felt, trying to carry on as if all of this was normal.

As we strolled into the hall, Myrtle cast a smile my way, but I noticed it drop when she saw Hannah.

"Hannah and I need some lace please, Myrtle," I said, requesting the seeds that we'd need to chew to a mushy slime before swallowing.

She tutted, fussing with the grey hood of her cloak, before reaching into a black pouch tied around her waist. She dipped her head toward Hannah and glared at her before pouring out a small heap of the black seeds into each of my palms. "Who's she sleeping with now?"

"I don't know," I replied, placing my seeds in my mouth.

Not wanting to chat with her any longer than necessary, I walked across the room to Hannah.

"Lace?" she said.

I held my hand in her direction, palm upward.

"What was the old bag nagging you about this time?" Hannah said, reaching to take her lace seeds.

"Nothing. I didn't give her chance to start."

"She's crazy." Hannah shook her head before popping the seeds in her mouth. "Get out of here before she ties you to the loom and makes you work." She shooed me away with her hand. "And don't forget, I'll come and see you later, sort your hair out for tonight."

I nodded before striding out of the hall.

Hannah called to see me as she'd promised. She'd twisted my hair and secured it in two long plaits along the crown of my head. I'd remained quiet while she worked, letting her chatter and fuss over me. And when she'd left, I slumped in the chair, placed my arms on the table, and rested my head on them.

Just as the distant comfort of sleep beckoned, a fluttering of wings and a loud squawk broke me from my tranquillity. A raven perched at the window opening, its wings flapping. It didn't need to create such a commotion to announce its presence. I was aware of its sinister arrival without the waft from its rainbow oiled feathers. I eyed it wearily, trying to ignore the white paper in its beak. The letter stood out against the blackness of the bird's feathers, although a white streak on its breast merged effortlessly with the ominous envelope. I had no desire to rush and read Paymon's words. As far as I was concerned, he could wait all day, but I jumped at each unwelcome loud squawk the raven made. My skin heated and tingled, and I pulled at the neck on my smock. I was hot, sticky hot. I hated ravens.

"Stupid bird," I muttered.

It stilled, watching me with as much interest as I was

trying not to show it, and then I noticed something else in its beak—a red rose. I frowned trying to understand why I'd not seen it earlier. The raven squawked and my heart pounded as we stared at each other, eyes locked as if daring the other to make a move.

"It's a bird, Athena," I whispered to myself. "Just a bird."

It squawked again, tilting its head to the side, angling the letter, tempting me with the contents of its beak. I swallowed and ran my tongue over my dry lips. Ignoring my raised heartbeat and my shaking hands, I stepped toward the raven. It dipped its head, and then turned it sideways, its beady eyes staring back at me. I'd never seen a raven close up and its size added another shudder to my movements.

But I pushed through my fear. This was the start of a journey I'd always known would happen. As my fingers touched the edge of the paper, the raven closed its eyes but remained in its strange position, tipped forward. Only when I removed the envelope and the rose from its beak did it straighten. It cawed noisily before flapping its wings and flying away.

I slammed the wooden shutters together, blocking its return. Grabbing one of the lit lanterns I placed it on the table with the envelope and rose. A black embossed seal greeted my weary eyes. It had the indent of a pentagram with a circle surrounding it—a pentacle, the demons' symbol. I'd seen it once when I was little, drawn into the ground behind the lake. There were wooden posts situated at each point of the pentagram. Long ropes were threaded through the posts, and I often wondered what they were for. It was Thomas who'd told me that Paymon tortured one of the old men in the village. He'd tied his hands and feet with the ropes, before burning him alive. An unwelcome tremor ran from the bottom of my spine to my neck, and I took a deep breath to steady my rising panic. This was their symbol, nothing more.

I pulled the lantern closer to the envelope before opening the letter.

Athena,

Congratulations on reaching your twenty-first birthday. I wish to speak to you regarding your suitability for the Master Demon's household. It is an honour and a great privilege for a girl of your low breeding to be given the opportunity to serve Him.

Come to my house on the outskirts of the village on receipt of this letter. I shall be awaiting your arrival.

Paymon

I read it once, twice, and then again.

He'd called me a girl of low breeding. How dare he? My mother had been a physician and my father a professor. I huffed as I reread each word. *An honour and a privilege?* Who was he trying to kid? I reached for the rose, frowning at the stem, which was devoid of any thorns. As I lifted the delicate red bloom to my nose, the sweet aroma caressed my senses. I closed my eyes as the scent became deeper—it reminded me of the perfume my mother used to wear. Grabbing the lantern from the table, I jumped to my feet and rushed to my bedroom. There were only two items of furniture in here apart from the bed— my Gran's old wooden chest of drawers and a wooden wardrobe with two ill-fitting doors. I headed to the chest, balancing the lantern on the top. The drawers never opened easily, and as I rattled the middle one, the dirty, scratched mirror balanced on top wobbled.

"Come on, come on," I muttered, yanking the drawer.

It opened, but the force of my gesture sent the unlevelled mirror and the lantern crashing to the floor. I groaned as the only light in the room extinguished. As if I needed anymore bad luck.

I groped around the drawer, rummaging through the haphazard jumble of knitted socks and shawls. Feeling each bunched up item, I systematically felt for the one hiding my secret treasure—my mother's perfume. The gold topped, slim, smooth bottle was labelled with the branding of what used to be a popular perfume maker, and there was still an inch of the amber coloured scent inside. I'd never sprayed it onto my skin, but often sniffed at the bottle top when I wanted a deeper connection to my mother. The scent brought memories of her laughter, singing, and bright, sunny days outside. It also reminded me of the love I had felt—the safe, unquestionable love of a mother for her daughter.

Refusing to let my memories bring on a full blown crying session, I took a deep breath before spraying the perfume on both my wrists and at the base of my neck. I knew, without looking in the shattered pieces of the mirror, that I would pass as presentable. My hair was still held securely in place from Hannah's earlier ministrations, and my cheeks were still red from the nip of her fingertips.

I wanted to postpone my meeting with Paymon for as long as possible, but I knew it would only increase my worry and feed my fear. I lifted my chin, defiant to my inner emotions. I was strong; I was a survivor. I would go and see him. Now.

After lighting a fresh candle with a splint from the fire and placing it in a lantern, I grabbed my cloak from its hanging place and swung it over my back, pulling it tight across my chest.

As I strode through the centre of the village, the wind brushed against my face, and I couldn't help but think that it was a warning for me to stay. Several women looked up from their tasks as I passed them, and others peered out from behind their doors.

"Good luck, Athena," a woman called.

"Be careful!" another warned from her doorway. "You know he'll take it out on the whole village if you upset him."

I took a deep breath and carried on walking. Their concerns weren't needed; they weren't welcome either. I'd make sure I was the same categorisation as Hannah—a feeder. We'd get through the next ten years together. We'd look out for each other like we always had.

Leaving the village behind, my bravado deserted me. My heartbeat raced, and I clutched my free arm across my chest, pulled my cloak even tighter and curled my shoulders forward. The wind was even wilder outside of the village. It whipped its sharp tongue of icy breath across my face as I trudged forward with no haste to reach my destination.

The path to Paymon's was near enough hidden. Piles of pine needles covered the earth and obscured what lay beneath, but the blurred outline of Paymon's house loomed before me like a dark foreboding beacon. My walk led up a slight incline bordered with nettles and weeds, beyond which grew the monstrous pine trees that surrounded the village. I couldn't see into the crowded trunks and thick growth of bushes; the constant gloom ensured the forest was a solid black mystery. I hunched over even more, trying to make myself small, invisible even, to the unknown creatures that lived there. My misted breath blew from my mouth, each short burst coming in rapid succession as my heart rate accelerated. I increased my pace, eyes forward, fixed on my destination. I kept the lantern as steady as possible in my knuckle white grip so as not to shine its flickering light into the forest.

As I approached Paymon's house, I gasped. The building had always been a mystery to me, its blurred outline only occasionally visible from the village, but now that I was here, it was impossible not to notice the narrow beam of light that shone from the sky and disappeared into the centre of the house. Why had I never seen it before? Surely I should have seen the light, even if I couldn't see the house. I frowned, confused and even more curious.

Paymon's house was dark and mysterious, like an angular monster waiting to devour me. I stepped forward as if invisible ties had wrapped around my legs and moved them without my agreement.

"Stupid demon," I muttered, and not for the first time, I cursed their very existence and the day they crawled from the earth below us.

When I placed my hand on the lopsided gate, the damp

cold wood forced another unwelcoming shiver from me. I breathed deeply, trying to steady my nerves as I looked up at the house. All the windows were dark or had curtains pulled shut. But these windows had proper fitted glass, small rectangular panels—physical barriers against the cold we all suffered in the village. Two storeys tall, large chimneys, and ivy covered walls helped paint it perfectly as the demon's home— it was creepy, sinister, and cold looking—a house you'd run away from.

I narrowed my eyes as I caught sight of a flickering light from an upstairs window, but as soon as I focused, the light was gone. Shadows clung to the walls as I followed the line of windows upstairs, but there were no other lights to see.

With nerves jangling and my hands shaking, I shuffled along the short path to the wooden door—the final barrier between me and my future.

Holding my head high, I lifted my hand to knock on the door.

CHAPTER 3

CONFLICTION

J UST AS MY KNUCKLES WERE ABOUT TO MEET THE WOOD, the door creaked open. I stepped back, quick to retreat from the tall, shadowy figure who stood before me.

Paymon.

He wasn't wearing his cloak, and from this close, it was clear to see his short black hair shot with streaks of grey. He had a darkness under his eyes that hinted at many sleepless nights—if indeed demons slept.

"Athena." His voice was rich and deep, reminding me of the only other time he had spoken to me. He peered behind me before opening the door wider. "Come in."

I took a deep breath and steadied myself before stepping into the hall. I kept my gaze fixed on Paymon, not trusting him.

"I've been keeping a very close eye on you these last few years," he said.

"Me?"

He nodded, his parted lips curled into a smile. It didn't seem genuine, like it hurt to move his muscles.

Just before he closed the door, a raven flew inside. It soared high into the hall before swooping low and settling on the balustrade of the staircase. I recognised the bird as the one that brought me the letter—it had the same single white feather in its chest. I backed away from its presence, as unsure of the raven as I was of Paymon.

"Lantern," Paymon said, holding his hand in my direction.

I unwrapped my fingers, one by one, from the cold handle and handed him the light that had guided me to this house.

He blew the candle out and placed the lantern on the floor next to the door.

"And your cloak." He waited for me to part with the tatty covering. "You don't need it here."

His black cloak hung on a hook next to the door, and after I'd shrugged out of my dirty brown one, he placed it over his.

"Follow me." He strode past where I was standing and headed across the hall.

I frowned, noticing how he walked with ease. The ungainly limp he displayed when I'd seen him come to the village wasn't present. I glanced quickly around the hall, familiarising myself with as much of the layout of the house as possible.

There were two doors to my left and one to my right. All the walls had wood panelling. Sconces hung on every other panel and held candles that flickered with varying brightness. A grand staircase rose toward the back of the hall before flowing into a sweeping curve and disappearing from view.

"Where are we going?" Hannah told me she stood in the hall. She didn't follow him further into the house.

He stopped walking and turned to face me. His forehead

creased with lines as he spoke.

"Is there a problem?"

"Hannah—"

"Has been discussing what happened while she was here? It doesn't surprise me." He took a step toward me, and even though I wanted to back away, I held my ground. "What did she tell you?"

"That you stayed in the hall." My voice quivered. He was too close. I could feel the heat radiating from his body. The evidence of his power seemed to resonate around him. I swallowed as he leaned forward, and prayed he couldn't hear my racing heart.

"There was no need for me to discuss anything with her," he said. "Her categorisation was set several weeks ago, unlike yours, which was set years ago." He spun around and indicated for me to walk in front of him along the dark corridor.

I didn't move. The decision was meant to be a recent one, one that was based on our current suitability.

"Athena, I understand your hesitancy, but I wish you no harm. I merely feel you would be more comfortable having a conversation whilst sitting. We have a lot to discuss."

"We do?"

He nodded, indicating with a sweep of his arm for me to start walking. When I still didn't move, he sighed. "Your obstinacy is charming, but I will soon tire of it. And I won't keep repeating myself." His brown eyes darkened but caught the reflection of the flickering candles. "Follow me. Now."

As he walked, he clicked his fingers several times. I flinched when small balls of flame shot to the candles. He must have noticed my unease.

"Don't panic, Athena. I'm only lighting the way for us to

walk. Or would you prefer the dark?"

I took a deep calming breath.

"It's an ancient power," he said, as if discussing an every-day occurrence.

I didn't care that it was ancient. I'd seen what Paymon did with fire.

I trudged behind him, determined to keep my distance. "Can all demons do that?" I asked. The woman demon he had incinerated didn't appear to have any power. If she had, I was sure she would have attempted to defend herself when he attacked her.

Paymon shook his head and stopped walking. "No, but we all have some sort of power, all different."

"What other powers do demons have?" I breathed heavily.

He fixed me with his gaze. "Why do you want to know?"

I stepped back, he was too close again, drinking me in with his piercing eyes.

"I'm interested," I managed to say, although my words were barely a whisper.

"Really?" His brow rose and the corner of his mouth twitched into a tiny smile. "Then you need to keep listening."

He turned his back to me. My posture stiffened and I pinched my lips together.

Paymon stopped next to a large wooden door. He pushed it open and waited for me to enter. I hesitated before stepping inside, startling when flames shot past me to light the group of candles on the table. The room was small; it smelt stuffy and old, and I wondered when it had last been used.

"Sit." His tone was sharp.

As I moved to sit on the chair, he closed the door behind him and made his way to the opposite side of the table.

"Before we begin with your categorisation, I need to tell you a few things."

I nodded, torn between taking in my surroundings and not taking my eyes off him. But my eyes were glued to his, like I'd been hypnotised. I blinked rapidly, fighting the overpowering sensation with the urgency to look away.

"First, you need to know that you will not be returning to the village tonight." His face held no flicker of emotion. He was delivering an order with no room for discussion. He grinned salaciously as he lowered himself into a chair opposite mine. "You will stay here."

The wood of the chair dug into my skin as I squeezed the edge of it. My chest tightened and it became difficult to take a breath. "I'm not willing to stay here," I gasped. "I'll be returning whether you want me to or not."

"Silence!" he roared, banging his fist on the table as he jumped to his feet.

My heart leapt into my mouth and I shook as he glared at me, shrinking into my chair.

He drew in a breath before returning to his composed, seated position. "When I am speaking, you remain quiet. And when I tell you to do something, you will do it. Understand?"

I nodded, assuming it to be the only safe way to response.

He leaned across the table and tapped his fingers on the wood. "I have no need to interview you today." His tongue licked his lips. "I can taste you. Oh, the Master would love you. What he would do . . ." He closed his eyes and drew in a deep breath. "He would be pleased with me for presenting him with a girl like you."

I immediately grasped his inference. My pulse raced and I shifted in my chair, choking down an audible whimper. All the rumours I'd heard in the village became a frightening reality. I stared wide-eyed at him, unable to look away.

Paymon's eyes snapped open. Black orbs met mine. Even though there were no pupils to see, I knew he was staring. The shadows cast around the room set his facial features as an eerie effigy, a frightening reminder of the true creature before me.

Panic shot through me, and I backed away from the table, the legs of my chair scraping on the wooden floor. A slow grimace pulled at the corners of Paymon's mouth. Gone was the old man. I was now witnessing the true demon that lurked under the surface.

I sprung to my feet. The chair tipped over and crashed backward. I had to get out of here.

"Athena!" Paymon shouted.

I rushed to the door and pulled at the handle.

"Athena. Sit down."

I turned the handle, rattling it up and down, but it wouldn't open.

"Don't make me compel you to sit down!"

I stilled. I'd heard rumours of the way demons could compel humans. I turned to face him. My breathing was short and shallow, and tears flooded my eyes as I looked around the room for another way of escape. I didn't want to stay in here with him. All the stories I'd heard rushed through my mind. This is what they meant. I was going to be a sacrifice to the Master.

Paymon rose to his feet, and my attention swung to him as he walked around the table.

"Stay there," I mumbled, waving my hands in front of me. "Don't come near me." My voice was weak, pathetic.

"Athena, I have already promised I will not hurt you. Why have you reacted so strongly?"

"You said . . . the Master . . . what he would do to me . . ."

He offered a strained smile. It looked surreal with his black eyes. "We need to carry on our conversation."

"But you said . . . and your eyes?" I pointed at the greedy, guilty orbs.

"I suspect they've changed colour. They're black."

"Yes."

"A demon's eyes change colour depending on their mood and their hunger." He narrowed his gaze. "You will need to get used to my eyes being black. It is your fault they are this colour."

"What you're saying is ridiculous," I said.

Paymon replaced my upturned chair.

"I can't change people's eye colour."

"Yes, you can." Paymon returned to his side of the table. "Demons gain strength from emotions."

"What? How?" I waved my hand in the general direction of his head. Was this common knowledge? Why hadn't I known this before I came here? Why hadn't Gran told me?

"There's a lot for you to learn," Paymon said, watching me with an un-nerving steadiness.

Turning away from his gaze, I looked around the room. It was small, the table and two chairs the only furniture. The five flickering candles on the table cast unworldly shadows across the walls, dancing devils that never stilled. The door was to one side of me and a long patterned curtain to the other. It wasn't a rug like the ones at home, but a proper curtain— one that draped and tumbled onto the wooden floor. Three walls were panelled in wood and held no decorations, but the lower wall behind Paymon had a large stone fireplace, sitting dark and cold. Hanging above the unlit fireplace was a single framed picture of the head and shoulders of a man.

"Who's that?" I asked, inclining my head to the picture and sliding back into my chair.

Paymon raised his brow before answering me. "The Master," he said without even looking at the painting.

I narrowed my eyes, trying to take in the detail of a man I would soon see first-hand. He looked normal, a bit old, but not as old as Paymon. His hair was dark, short, and he wore stubble where his beard would have been.

"So that's who you're going to send me to?" He didn't look evil, far from it. He actually looked quite handsome, although there was something sinister about his deep-set hazel eyes.

Paymon tapped his fingers on the table, diverting my attention back to him.

"If I categorised you, I should send you to him." He kept his gaze on me, then sighed deeply and closed his eyes. "My recommendation is that you should be wed to him. He would appreciate a woman like you as a wife."

"A wife?" I leaned back in my chair and bit back the rising nausea in my stomach. I'd visualised that I'd be a sacrifice, and now I was to be a wife . . . of a demon? "I don't want to be married to him. I don't want to be married to anyone."

His eyes narrowed. "Not even Thomas?"

I crossed my arms over my chest and didn't reply. Paymon's jaw tightened and he leaned forward.

"He has nothing to do with this." I smoothed my shaking hands over the skirt of my dress.

He increased the drumming of his fingers on the table.

"So you're categorising me as a wife for the Master."

I straightened my back and swept my arms in front of me. "That's it. No choice?"

"I decide your categorisation—no argument, no discussion, but this time . . ."

I was prepared to ask him to let me be a feeder. It was what I'd promised Hannah. We could spend our ten years together, help each other survive, but I held my question.

He ceased tapping his fingers. The warm air in the room turned cold. "I would like to ask for your hand in marriage."

My stomach churned and then tightened. "You?"

"Yes, me."

"But you're . . . you're . . . old." I shuddered, thinking of what Hannah had said. Demons were highly sexed, demanding. Is that why he wanted to marry me? He wanted my body to play with.

Paymon laughed, the sound eerie and distant.

"Why me?" I asked, covering my chest with my arms. "Why didn't you want to marry Hannah?" She'd be willing, she'd welcome a demon lover—she'd admitted it just this morning.

His laughing immediately stopped. "Hannah is not worthy of marrying anyone. Why on earth would I want her?"

"She's pretty," I replied. Her long blonde hair always ensured she was the centre of attention. I also knew she'd had a secret relationship with one of the more mature men in the village. Age didn't bother her.

"Pretty? You think I'm bothered about someone being pretty?"

"She's popular, a good cook," I continued.

Paymon shook his head.

"Athena, ever since you turned sixteen, I have waited for

you."

I shuddered again and leaned back in my chair, putting as much visible distance between him and me.

"Do you recall the time I came to the village and set fire to one of the houses?" He had a lightness about his question, one that was glaringly out of place as he spoke about a fire he had intentionally started.

"You constantly set fire to the houses," I said, moving my hands from my knee to the chair. I sat on them to try to stop their constant shaking. "You'll have to be more specific."

"It was the first time I saw you. When you shot out of your house to rescue your grandmother."

A lump built in my throat, and I stared at the table, not looking at him. I remembered that day all too clearly. "That was the day you killed her." I sounded like a man, my voice raw and deep.

"That's when I felt you making me strong. I latched on to your emotions." He spoke quickly, his enthusiasm brimming away like a pan of boiling water. "It's rare that it happens, that a demon finds a human who he can latch onto so strongly. And just because I find your emotions particularly strong doesn't mean that another demon will."

"You killed Gran," I repeated, not interested in his theories on my emotions. "Why? She was no danger to you."

"A gossiping old woman who knew too much and was no use to the Master was of no use to me."

I placed my elbows on the table and covered my face with my hands. He didn't have any remorse about murdering her. And here he was, wanting to marry me. I would take no part in it.

"You could have left her alone. Told her to step down as

the village elder. You had no need to kill her."

He lifted his chin and smirked. "Now, now, Athena. I am a demon, a man with no morals. She wasn't needed. The village shouldn't have to support the weakest." He paused, and smoothed the front of his shirt before clearing his throat. "I also struck a deal with your grandmother that day."

I slid my hands from my face and hugged myself. I knew they'd been talking about me, but I thought it had been about serving him at the village feast. Apparently not. I clenched my jaw, preparing for the revelation. "What was the deal?"

"Your grandmother knew how strong your emotions were in feeding me, she'd witnessed it." He stopped talking, his mouth twitching at the side. "She asked me what I would categorise you as when you turned twenty-one. You are suitable for the Master, as one of his wives."

"But you just said you wanted to marry me."

"That was the deal. She asked me to save you from the Master, to take you as my wife instead. I wanted to take you there and then, but she persuaded me to wait until you turned twenty-one. And twenty-one is an age when all females blossom from a child into a woman."

I stared at him, open-mouthed as he talked with unabashed glee and excitement.

"I should send you to the Master," he said. "But I am going keep you for myself and uphold my end of the bargain with your grandmother."

I shivered as the cold hard truth hit me. Gran had promised me to a demon, and he was about to claim his prize.

"She's dead," I said, seeing a slight glimmer of hope in the tragedy. "It's not as if she'll know whether you marry me or not."

"I am aware of that." His voice held no emotion. "But I still intend to honour my side of the deal."

I lowered my head, and rubbed my arms. "Can I refuse to marry you?"

"I have left you alone for the last five years. You could at least show some gratitude."

I narrowed my eyes. Did he really expect me to be grateful? "If you really care about me then just send me back to the village. Say I wasn't suitable. Let me live in the village as a free woman."

"A free woman?" He snorted. "You're never free, Athena. You know the women who stay in the village are expected to breed."

"Seems a better alternative than marriage either to you, or him." I nodded at the portrait on the wall.

He studied me for a few moments.

"Let me explain the situation you face if you stay in the village." He leaned forward as if he was about to share another great secret. "It's not the nice alternative you seem to think it is. I grant my villagers the privilege of one year to produce a child before I intervene." He sighed again and rubbed the back of his neck. "I presume you would be planning on Thomas being the father of your children?"

When I didn't respond, he continued with his view on the situation. "Do you seriously think that the girls I allow to stay in the village have an easy life?"

I nodded. Veronica had been allowed to stay. She'd had three children over the last four years. She seemed happy . . . well as happy as you could be. There was Sally. She had only recently given birth. How many children did she have? I ran through their faces in my head. Five—she had five children.

And then there was Tracey before her, although she'd died whilst giving birth to her fourth child.

Paymon raised his brow. "The Master doesn't like us to keep the females away from him, he forgets that women need to stay in order to provide him with future generations to select from."

"So you'll not let me stay?"

He shook his head and lowered his gaze. "Not in the village." He looked straight at me. "Athena, have you given any thought to what would happen if Thomas failed to impregnate you? And even if he did, you know that the risk of death in child-birth is high."

I closed my eyes and nodded, digesting what he said. I hadn't thought about Thomas and me not being able to have children or about the danger of dying like Tracey.

"Why are you saying all this?"

"Because it's what your life would become. Sex wouldn't be pleasurable, it would be a chore, and it would be constant—several times a day. And every month you'd live with the question of 'what if it doesn't happen?'"

"And . . . what if it didn't?"

"I've already told you. I'd have to intervene."

I screwed my nose up and clenched my hands around the base of the chair. "As in, you'd—"

"No, no, no. You have me all wrong. I would not attempt to impregnate you. I would select a man from the village to do so." He smirked. "It would most likely be the man who had the most children, the most virile amongst you. Who would that be, I wonder?"

I gritted my teeth as I realised who it was Paymon would select. Hannah had six brothers. It would be her father. "You wouldn't. He's my best friend's father."

Paymon grinned and straightened, folding his arms. "I would. I wouldn't care who impregnated you, as long as someone did, and quickly. And Thomas would be killed. No point in him living if he can't provide the future generation."

I closed my eyes and breathed steadily, calming myself as much as possible. The happy, smiling family life I'd always imagined was ripped from my mind. Paymon was right. I would become a breeding machine, the only concern being that I had children—girls. And when each of my daughters turned twenty-one they too would be summoned by Paymon and he would send them away or leave them with the same miserable life I'd faced.

"And as soon as you'd given birth, I'd insist you were on your back and trying for another. You'd have no choice in the matter. You'd be constantly pregnant by any man who could successfully impregnate you. The Master needs females. His demand is insatiable." Another sigh left him as he placed his hands palm down on the table. "I would like to marry you, uphold my end of the bargain to your grandmother. But I also want to save you from the miserable life the village would offer you, and save you from the Master. Living as his wife would grant you a life of luxury, but I fear it would not be one you would tolerate. Once his wife, you would be his property, and he would compel you to obey him." He shook his head as if thinking and picking his words carefully. "He has no conscience, and he can be brutal."

"So what would the difference be being married to you?"

"I am old, at the end of my days, and contrary to what you may think of me, I am not cruel unless provoked. If you marry me, I would not need to inflict pain or cause fear within the village ever again. You would keep me fed, just with your presence. If your own future holds no importance to you then maybe that of your fellow villagers should."

I studied his appearance for a few moments. Without the cloak he appeared normal, smart and distinguished.

"What if I say no?"

Paymon stood before answering me. "If you refuse to marry me, I will send you to the Master, with my recommendation that he marry you."

"So, either way, I'm forced to marry a demon?"

"So it seems." His black eyes met mine, and I shifted in my chair, uneasy in his gaze.

"What about the other positions within the Master's home?"

He folded his arms across his chest, his eyebrows arched. "Those are not fit for you."

"I might want to be something else." Anything was better than being married to a demon. A cook, a cleaner. Anything.

Paymon stilled before eying me cautiously. "You don't ever get the choice. I chose for you."

"But what do you select from?"

He frowned at me, "Why do you want to know?"

"There must be something else I can do for the Master. You selected Hannah as a feeder, why can't I be the same as her?"

Paymon widened his eyes and then smirked. "You will not be a feeder."

"Why not?"

He unfolded his arms and rubbed his chin, seeming to observe my request with some amusement. "I'm not discussing this with you. Not now."

"But—"

"No!" He held his hand up, the signal to match his word. "Now, either you marry me or you are sent away to become one of the many wives of the Master."

"Neither is acceptable," I said, shooting him as fierce a stare as I could manage.

"One of them is your future."

"I don't want either."

Paymon scratched the side of his neck. "Think about it. What could you cope with? The Master will use you, break you and then dispose of you. He has no soul, no heart, and no sense of right and wrong."

"You mean other demons have a heart, a soul?"

Paymon grinned before leaning against the mantelpiece, one elbow resting casually on the stone ledge. He laughed quietly.

"We're not all as bad as you seem to think."

"Do *you* have a soul?"

Paymon grinned even more.

"A heart?"

"I most definitely have a heart," he answered briskly, as if I'd offended him. "If I didn't, I would be sending you to the Master and reaping the reward for finding you. I would have also whisked you away from the village when you were sixteen years old."

With a sinking feeling pulling deeper in my belly, I realised I had no escape from my forced categorisation. Paymon appeared the safest option, but his confidence ate away at my usual bravado. "So what exactly do you expect of me . . . if I agree to be your wife?"

He straightened. "There is a ceremony I must conduct

between us to seal our marriage, and it is necessary to protect you from the miscreants. I am sure it will not be pleasant for you, but, as I said, it's necessary."

"Miscreants?" I asked, but he held his hand up like before, indicating my silence.

"This ceremony will mark you as mine, every demon that comes near you will know that you are tied to me, and as such, you will be untouchable. And I will protect you from anyone and anything. No harm will ever come to you."

He smiled, satisfied with his assessment of my future. But I was still curious. Words were all well and good, but I had no knowledge of anything he was telling me. I knew it could all be lies.

"I want to know what happens at this ceremony."

Paymon tapped his fingers on the mantelpiece. "Of course you do. But your decision needs to be made first."

I crossed my arms over my chest. "That's hardly fair."

Paymon raised his brow. "Life isn't fair, Athena. Not for humans and not even for demons. Now, as my wife you will need new clothes, you need to be dressed appropriately, not in those rags."

I glanced at my attire; I would hardly call them rags, but they were dirty, dull, with several holes in them. Paymon's clothes were smart, clean, and his jacket buttons shone as they caught the flicker of the candles.

"And cleanliness. You will bathe every day."

I shivered. Although it was wonderful to feel clean, the cold water and the harsh soap we used in the village hardly made the experience pleasurable. I only bathed once a week, although I washed daily.

"I will provide you with everything you need," he

continued. "If you require anything else, you will only need to ask me."

"And what do you get from all this?" He was too calm. I was waiting for the great revelation, the true meaning behind marriage to a demon.

Once again, he smiled. "I get the pleasure of your company and your emotions."

My hand flew to my chest and my breath hitched. "And that's all?"

He nodded, chuckling quietly.

"So, Athena, you need to make a decision. And that decision must be made before tomorrow evening. The day of the Ascension Ceremony will be too late. Whatever you decide, though, you will stay here tonight. You will also stay here tomorrow night. You may return to the village during the day, but you will be back here at the call of the raven."

I frowned. "So even though I've not made my decision, I still have to stay here? Why?"

"Because I say so." He resumed his pattern of tapping his fingers on the mantelpiece.

"And what's the call of the raven?"

"It's when Odin will come for you. He brought you the letter and the rose earlier today."

"I don't like ravens," I said. "And why the rose?"

"Odin is my raven. He does as I command, I suggest you tolerate him and perhaps even get to know him. And the rose . . ." He sniffed the air. "Perhaps it reminded me of the scent you are wearing."

I gasped. All luxuries were taken away from us when we came to the village. "How did you know?"

"I know everything about my villagers. Even you, hiding

your mother's perfume in an old sock in your chest of drawers." He tutted and shook his head. "I decided to let you keep it. Perhaps it is an item you would like to bring with you. You can collect it tomorrow along with any other items of sentimental value. I promise not to dispose of anything you bring, unless it's to remind you of Thomas." He frowned, a challenge for me to select carefully. "And another thing. Your relationship with Thomas must cease to exist. Neither the Master nor I will be married to a whore. Do not seek him out."

I bit my lip, remembering the party he'd organised for me tonight.

"I have no doubt that he will find you tomorrow, but you must not make any effort to find him. I will know if you do." He straightened in his chair. "And I may retract my offer of marriage. The Master can have you as his wife."

"I don't think you'll do that."

I sat high in my chair, but my throat was bone dry when I went to swallow. I could see how much he wanted me to stay with him. He wouldn't send me away.

"Really?" His brow rose as he strode around the table toward me. "Don't test me, Athena, or try to get the better of me. The fight you put up would be most dangerous for you and those you care about. And it would only increase my strength."

Any bravado I'd had seeped away with each step he took. The hairs on the back of my neck stiffened, and a warmth flooded through me. I tried to move, but couldn't. My feet remained firmly fixed on the floor, and my arms rested unresponsive in my lap.

Paymon stood behind me as I pointlessly fought against a paralysis that rendered me a prisoner in my own body.

"Sweet, sweet Athena," he said, running his fingers along

the side of my face and under my chin. "I have waited a long time for you. I knew you were special when I first met you, but to be this close to you, to feel the strength you give me. It's remarkable."

I desperately tried to shrug away from his presence. I whimpered as any remaining energy left me. Threads of colour binding me together frayed and split, diminishing, floating away—all collected by Paymon. As I became weak, he grew strong.

"You are a beautiful woman. It would give me great pleasure to have you," he whispered, nestling the side of his face against mine.

From somewhere deep inside me came a force so powerful it left me breathless.

"Stop!" I shouted, springing to my feet. I breathed heavily as Paymon remained standing behind the chair, staring at me with black eyes even wider than before.

"What did you just do to me?"

He smiled and nodded.

"So strong," he said. "So very strong."

His gaze drifted to the back of my vacated chair, and he ran his finger across the top of it as if removing imaginary dust.

"I compelled you to stay still," he said, lifting his blackened eyes to mine.

"You compelled me? Why?"

"I wanted to be close to you without feeling your unease. It worked, for a moment. Tell me, how did you break free?"

I shrugged, frowning.

He sniffed, patting the back of my chair. A silent standoff developed. Both of us watched the other, assessing the next move. I wanted to flee the room, run straight to the front door and back to the village and to Thomas. But I knew I couldn't. Paymon would compel me to stay if I tried to leave.

Paymon cocked his head, his jaw twitching. "Seems we have nothing more to say to each other."

I had plenty to say, and a mountain of questions to ask, but now was not the time.

"I'm tired," I said, looking to the door.

"Then I shall show you to your room."

"My room?"

"Yes, or do you want to stay in my room?"

"I . . . I . . ." After everything he'd said, I'd presumed I would be in his room, in his bed. Was this a temporary measure—one that would change if we married?

Paymon laughed, a sound I was becoming quickly used to. It wasn't like the laugh of a normal person—it sounded distant, as though someone else was laughing inside of him and Paymon only acted the accompanying actions.

"Athena, I jest with you. I shall sense your presence, your emotions. It is all I ask. It is how it shall be if we marry. The room you stay in tonight will be yours permanently."

"I really don't want to stay the night. I was—"

"Going to meet Thomas. Tell him of our chat?"

I narrowed my lips before nodding.

"You can tell him in the morning. I have no issues with you telling him what we have discussed. Find Hannah if you must, but be careful what you say to her. She has a nasty side; one you could well fall foul of."

My frown deepened.

"In time it will all become clear. As my wife, I will be willing to discuss anything with you. I rather enjoy intelligent conversation. It's something that can't be replaced by a raven." He smiled again, the gesture appearing more natural than when I first saw him smile. "Would you like some food, a drink, before you sleep?"

"No, I'll be fine." I'd not be able to keep anything down. When Paymon left me alone, I knew I would be attacked by every perceivable emotion known to mankind. I fought to keep from screaming—or bursting into tears. Once I was alone, the enormity of my situation, of my decision, would consume me.

"There's fresh water in your room to drink if you change your mind. And if you'd like to bathe—"

"No," I interrupted him. I would not be undressing while I was here.

"Athena, I will give you the key to your room. You can lock me out if you so wish. I will not stay where I am not welcome."

I breathed deeply, prepared to verbally attack his reasoning, but he looked away, and I momentarily caught a glimmer of something I struggled to place—sadness, regret?

"I shall show you to your room," he said, and instantly the look disappeared.

Traipsing after him, I kept quiet, not wanting to annoy or aggravate him further.

As Paymon approached the bottom of the staircase, the raven cawed loudly. It flapped its wings several times before jumping into the air. With several hard beats of its black feathers, it flew in front of Paymon.

"Follow Odin," Paymon said. "He wishes to show you the way. It seems he has taken quite a shine to you."

"Is he feeding off my emotions as well?" I snapped before walking up the dimly lit stairs.

"I doubt it. He much prefers scavenging for scraps of food in the forest, although he is rather fond of cheese."

Odin landed on the floor at the top of the stairs and ruffled his feathers before strutting along the corridor. Tiny balls of fire flew past me as Paymon lit the sconces on the walls.

Odin stopped in front of a door, turning to face it.

"No, Odin," Paymon said, shaking his head. "Not my room. Show Athena to her room."

He tipped his head sideways, and then fluttered to the next door along the corridor.

Taking a candle from the sconce outside this room, Paymon handed it to me before opening the door.

"Your room, Athena."

I lifted the candle high, trying to light the hidden corners of the room. It was five, six, maybe seven times the size of my house in the village. Beautiful heavy curtains hung at the window, and a large four-poster bed dominated one wall.

"This is mine?" I asked, my mouth dropping open. I stepped further into the room, ignoring the flights of fire as Paymon lit the candles dotted around the surfaces.

"Carpet," I murmured and handed the candle back to Paymon before sinking to my knees. I ran my hands over the rich softness, and a huge smile spread across my face.

"I trust you will be comfortable. If you need anything, just ask, you have seen where my room is. Do not hesitate to come and get me."

I nodded, too in awe of my surroundings to verbally respond. After everything I'd heard and now this, I was shocked into silence.

Paymon stood in the doorway, hovering.

"Good night," I managed to say, looking his way, hopeful

he would take the hint.

His eyes darkened, and a wide smile pulled across his face.

"Good night, Athena, sleep well. Remember, none of the other girls were given a choice in what happened to them when they turned twenty-one," he said, each word sounding as if it were selected carefully. "You have been given one. Choose wisely."

He placed a key on the sideboard next to the door before backing out of the room.

CHAPTER 4

REGRET

As soon as Paymon left the room, the expected crash of emotions careered through me. Tears, so near to spilling since I arrived, burst forth as I sat on the edge of the bed. I let them fall. What sort of world was I living in? Demons, forced marriage, secret deals, depressing darkness. Was there any end to this living nightmare?

When I was a child, I promised my younger friends that I would make the light return. They had no need to be afraid of the constant darkness. And now? I was just as afraid as those friends I'd tried to comfort. Not from the oppressive dark, but from what it contained—secrets—a life I had no idea about, a life to be feared. I didn't want to marry Paymon or the Master Demon. But marriage to Thomas wasn't an option anymore. Paymon had made it quite clear.

I rubbed my eyes and sniffed loudly. He'd said I had a choice, but it didn't seem like one.

I glanced around the room, taking in the luxury that

surrounded me. The hall had been simple, bare wooden floors and walls, matching the initial room I'd been taken into, but this room was grand and ornate. The walls were covered in patterned paper, and the rich purple curtains that hung from each of the four tall windows tumbled to the floor—a carpeted floor. I quickly untied my scruffy shoes and rubbed my feet back and forth across the soft carpet. I moaned in pleasure as the fibres tickled the soles of my feet.

The room was a strange shape, angular like the curves of a circle had been sliced away. Each window was at a different angle to the world outside, and only two walls were free from a window—the one the bed was against, and the one with the door. A tall wooden screen divided one area of the room and, curious about what was behind, I made my way toward it. I couldn't contain my high-pitched shriek when I saw what was there—a pristine white bath-tub full of water. I dipped my hand into the waiting water. It was warm, more than warm—hot. Bathing here wouldn't be an ordeal like it was in the village. A white, solid rectangle laid across a smooth piece of wood that stretched across the edges of the bath. Soap? I picked the item up and sniffed it.

"Oh my, oh my, oh my," I mumbled. It smelt of how I imagined summer meadows to smell—fresh, sweet, the scent of long-forgotten memories. Next to the tub was a roaring fire, heating the secluded space with a warmth that had wrapped itself around me since I entered the house.

Was this the life Paymon was offering? I wasn't a person who placed personal comfort over the need of others, but others weren't an option at the moment. My decision was becoming clearer.

I walked to the bed, stunned by its grandeur. There were

four tall pillars, one at each corner, and pale blue swaths of material dipped between each pair. I threw myself backward onto the deep pile of blankets, revelling in the ensuing bounce. Everything was so soft, so welcoming, so . . . right, just right. But it was also unnerving. Had Paymon prepared this room for me? With a racing mind and an equally racing heart, I strode to the door before peering into the darkness of the corridor. The silence hinted that there was no one around; perhaps Paymon and Odin had settled downstairs in one of the rooms I had yet to see. Satisfied that Paymon wasn't creeping around outside my room, I debated whether to bathe. Seeing the key on the sideboard, I quickly picked it up and locked the door.

I undid my fraying leather belt while crossing the room, but stopped when I saw another door at the far side of the bed. I needed a key for this door as well, and I wondered why Paymon hadn't offered one to me if he really wanted to allay all my fears about his intentions. I stepped to the door and pulled on the handle, not sure what to expect. The door opened toward me, and I was greeted with a cupboard full of women's clothes. Swallowing my apprehension, I ran my hand across the fabric of one of the dresses. I'd never felt anything so soft, and the colours were brighter than any I'd ever seen in the village. They were like the clothes the female demon had worn—the one I'd viewed as a princess. As I ran my fingers against the softness of the fabric the hairs on the back of my neck bristled. Were they hers? The thought made me shudder, and I closed the cupboard door, locking away their secrets. Unsettled, I decided not to bathe. And after washing my face and feet, I lay on top of the bed, not prepared to soil the blankets underneath.

I slept fitfully at first, my mind refusing to shut down, but after a while the soothing crackle of the fire and the warmth of the air lulled me into a deep sleep.

Morning came, signified by the distant siren from the village. It sounded different from here, like an eerie call for demons to rise. I stayed on the bed, enjoying the ever present warmth of my surroundings. It was a stark contrast to the freezing cold that I'd woken to for the last thirteen years of my life.

I sat upright, my cheeks burning as I remembered my friends in the village. My shoulders hunched and I dropped my chin to my chest. What about Hannah, Janine, Sarah and Ellie? Hannah was already selected to be sent away to the Master tomorrow, with the other girls following over the next few years. What future did they all have? After what Paymon told me yesterday, I doubted that they'd be treated to any luxuries at the Master's. Life would be more difficult than it was in the village, and living in the village wasn't easy. And what about Thomas? I'd hardly given any thought to him as I drifted to sleep last night. Any plans we'd had were well and truly ruined. Would I still be able to see Thomas whilst I lived here?

I brightened thinking about him. I could visit him, sneak out at night for snatched moments of kisses and whispered words when Paymon was sleeping. We could still be together. Creeping around behind Paymon's back had the potential to be thrilling. I bit back a smile and swallowed the laugh that had built inside. He would not control me the way he thought he could. I'd still see Thomas, and I'd still see my remaining friends.

Another thought sprung into my head almost secondary to everything else: the light. Maybe I'd be able to find out about the light. Not immediately; Paymon would sense what I was doing and why I was asking, but maybe after we'd been together a while and I got to know him better, I could sneak it into conversations. I brightened even more as I planned out the next few months of my life. If I married Paymon, I'd be able to ask him all sorts of questions.

A sharp knock switched my attention to the bedroom door, and I jumped, startled by the sudden noise.

"Athena, time to get up. You need to start your day." Paymon, calling for me through the door. I smoothed my hands over my dress, tied my shoes, and ambled to the door. After unlocking it, I pulled it only slightly ajar and peered through the narrow gap.

"Ah," Paymon greeted me with one of his customary unnatural smiles. "I see you are already awake. I trust you are well rested."

I nodded, slightly taken aback by the sight of him. All the strange conversations from yesterday ran through my head as I stood facing him. His eyes were not black this morning; they'd returned to their normal brown colour, and they sparkled with amused curiosity. His skin crinkled at the corner of his eyes, and he chuckled.

"My, my, Athena, you look at me as you would a potential lover. What's happened to you overnight?"

I snapped from my stupor and looked to the floor. "Sorry, I'm just reminding myself of why I'm here," I said, embarrassed to have been caught looking at him so intently.

"And the decision you need to make when you return later today." Paymon straightened before turning away and marching along the corridor. I followed, trotting to keep up with his sudden burst of speed. As I reached the top of the stairs, Odin made an unwelcome appearance, swooping so low over my head that I had to duck to avoid him crashing into me.

"Odin!" Paymon shouted. "Do not tease Athena. She is not used to your playful ways and needs time to adjust." He stopped walking and inclined his head, fixing me in his gaze. "That is if she intends to stay."

"I haven't decided yet." All my well thought out reasons for marrying him disappeared now I was in his company. It had been too easy to forget he was a demon, to compartmentalise him as just another man. He was far from it, and I felt increasingly nervous in his presence. How would he react if I told him I wouldn't marry him and would prefer to take my chance with the Master Demon?

I followed his descent down the stairs and waited in the hall for further instructions.

"I said I'd let you go back to the village for the day," he said, walking to the hook where the cloaks hung.

"I can go back?" I hadn't truly believed him last night. This was great news I'd be able to explain everything to Thomas. With a lightness in my limbs, I practically skipped to the doorway.

"Only for today. When Odin calls for you, you must return immediately. I want your decision as soon as you return."

My shoulders dropped. I'd had a fleeting second of hope, of my former happiness returning, but the reality of the situation hit me. I wouldn't be staying in the village.

"Say goodbye to your friends. You'll not be able to talk to them again."

"I can, if I stay here with you."

"You think I'll let you?" He prowled toward me with his cloak. "When you're my wife you'll have nothing to do with any of them. And if you try to continue any kind of relationship with Thomas, I will kill him. Don't dare seek him out today. I will know if you do."

I took a step backward, and shifted away from Paymon's heavy stare.

"If you decide to take your chances with the Master, then I will take my anger out on the village and its inhabitants. Thomas will be at the top of my list. But I doubt that will concern you. You'll be too busy entertaining the Master and his chosen cohorts."

I clenched my hands, desperately trying to keep a hold of my anger. My flesh was hot, sticky with perspiration.

"What about my friends?" I wasn't prepared to lose everything I knew.

"What about them? I've already told you, you'll not have anything to do with anyone from the village." He tutted and stepped closer, reaching for my arm. "Am I not making myself clear?"

His hand grabbed my wrist. His grip was firm, and unwelcome. I shrank away from him just as an uncomfortable heat snaked its way through the place where he held me. Every muscle ceased to move, and I couldn't respond. My tongue felt heavy, as though it was stuck to the bottom of my mouth. Whilst I remained fixed in place Paymon shifted his hand to my shoulder and lifted my hair away from my neck. The warmth of his cloak flowed around me as the fabric fell into place.

"Your clothes," Paymon said, releasing me from whatever

hold he had momentarily cast over me. I took a deep breath as if gasping new life into my lungs. Compelment—I knew without asking what he had done. I narrowed my eyes at him and lifted my head high. I wouldn't let him think he could intimidate me so easily.

"What about my clothes?"

"I will burn them. There are replacements in your room. I'm sure you saw them whilst you explored. I do not want any part of your past life in my home."

"What about my personal belongings?" I ignored my basic demand to ask why the clothes were there in the first place. It didn't seem as worrying as it had last night.

"I told you yesterday that they were acceptable."

Paymon stepped to the door before lifting my lantern from the floor. Snapping his fingers, his customary flame appeared, and he blew it onto the wick of the candle. Handing me the lantern, he offered a smile.

"Remember, the wedding ceremony must take place tonight, otherwise I will have no choice but to send you to the Master."

"I know," I muttered.

Paymon unlocked the door. I didn't move toward it, instead I shifted from one foot to the other.

"What's wrong, Athena? Do you not want to leave?"

I took a deep breath and looked at the lantern. "This will be the last time I can go to the village. Things will be different after today."

"They'll be different from today, Athena, not after today." Paymon focused on the darkness and unwelcoming cold outside. "You can always come back before Odin calls you. I will welcome your early return."

Not willing to stay in his company for a moment longer, I stepped out into the world I'd come from only yesterday.

The door slammed behind me. My skin rose in goose bumps, and I shivered again. The warmth from the house deserted me, and the sinister tendrils of a cold, dense fog weaved around my feet.

The flapping of wings diverted my attention to the gate. Odin, I presumed. What was he going to do? Lead me back to the village? Keep an eye on me so he could report back to Paymon? Check that I didn't go looking for Thomas? Even if I didn't seek out Thomas, I knew he'd find me. He'd be out at the fields today, but he'd return later this afternoon wanting to know where I was last night. And what about Hannah? What would I say to her?

Odin cawed loudly before flying into the air. I took his call as a command to keep moving. As I walked further away from Paymon's house, he followed me, swooping low and clicking his beak. By the time I arrived at the edge of the village, I was smiling at his insistent game.

My smile soon disappeared when one of the older women of the village saw me. She ran forward, shouting and alerting the other villagers to my return.

"Someone go and fetch Thomas from the fields." Her words were rushed, panicked. "Quick. He must return, Athena's back!"

She took the lantern from me, her cold, leathery skin brushing against mine, and led me to the clearing at the centre of the village. Guiding me to one of the logs we used to sit on around the fire, she quickly made me a hot brew.

"Oh, child, what did he do to you? Look at you, shaking like a leaf."

Other women surrounded me, ones my gran had been friends with. They all stated their concerns. I examined each of them in turn, wondering whether they'd known about the deal Gran had made with Paymon.

"I'm fine," I said, ignoring my churning stomach. "He didn't do anything to me."

"Then why did he keep you there all night?"

"You look terrified."

My stupid hands refused to stop shaking, and I spotted concerned glances between the fussing women. Were they worried I'd upset him? That he'd take his anger out on them, on the village? Was their worry for themselves, not for me?

"Is that his cloak?" one of the women said.

I nodded before sipping at the herbal infused hot drink.

"Burn it," she demanded, reaching for the warm covering.

"No!" I slapped her hands away and jumped to my feet. The mug crashed to the ground, breaking and spilling its contents on impact. "I need to return it this evening. If you burn it, he'll punish all of us."

"You side with a demon?" she said, gripping my shoulders and shaking me. Her eyes were wide, fear clouding her judgement.

I shifted backward, releasing myself from her hold. "No, all I meant was the cloak was his and he expects it back."

"Why do you have it then?"

"To keep warm."

The women's hushed chatter stopped.

"He gave it to you to keep warm?" another woman asked. "What else did he give you?"

"Nothing." I shook my head, trying to assess their mood and their reasoning. What was wrong with them?

The women suddenly parted. Myrtle came through the space they'd created. She hobbled toward me, leaning on the stick she used to help her walk. She was with her daughter, Bessie, a sickly woman in her forties who'd never had any children.

Bessie stayed back whilst Myrtle approached. She lifted her gnarled hand and pointed her finger at me.

"You," she said, her voice raspy. "You, Athena. He has chosen you."

The women around us didn't speak, but I sensed the shift in their mood. The air became thick with unspoken whispers and superstitions.

"You are to be wed to him." She turned her face and spat on the ground. "I knew this day would come. Your Gran foresaw it."

I stepped toward her, angry. "She never foresaw anything," I snapped. "She made a deal with him. And I bet you knew."

Myrtle gripped my chin with her fingers and pulled my face to the same height as hers. "I knew no such thing. I have no idea what you're on about."

I widened my eyes. "You're lying."

"Prove it."

The old women of the village stepped closer, but as I glanced around at them, I recognised their overly bright eyes, their trembling lips and the way they gripped each other. They were scared, scared of something they knew nothing about.

"I have a choice," I said, quiet and calm with my delivery of the words.

"You do?" A deep frown settled across Myrtle's forehead.

"I can either marry our village demon or be sent away at the Ascension Ceremony to marry the Master."

An audible gasp rattled before all of the women backed away, but Myrtle stayed next to me. "And what have you decided?"

"I . . . I'm not sure yet."

She smiled, gaps where teeth used to be making the gesture strangely grotesque. "There is only one acceptable decision, isn't there, Athena?"

I focused on her eyes, ones that held so much wonder and unspoken knowledge. "Paymon told me I could choose."

She held my arm, her grip strong and uncomfortable. "But what is there to choose between when you either marry Paymon or enter the Master Demon's world?" Her voice lowered to a raspy breath. "If you don't marry Paymon, we will all suffer. Do you think he will leave us alone if you disappear to the Master?" Tightening her grasp on my arm, she turned to the side and spat onto the ground again. "He will torture us. Did you never wonder what happened to Arthur's hand?"

Arthur didn't have a right hand, just a blackened stump that often flared up with infection.

Myrtle patted my arm before reaching for the small black pouch tied to her belt. "Here," she said, "you best have some now. You'll need it after last night." She lifted my hand and placed the pouch onto my palm. "Take it with you."

"Lace?"

"Keep it hidden from him." She scratched her nose, and pushed her grey hair away from her face. "Don't let him find it."

Closing her hand over mine, she squeezed it tightly.

My face heated and my skin felt like a thousand ants were crawling over it. Myrtle thought that Paymon had slept with me last night and obviously expected him to continue doing so. I caught my bottom lip between my teeth and looked at the ground. This was always the deal. Not just marriage but everything that came with it. My mouth moved, but no words came out. Had Gran given any thought to what Paymon would do to me?

"Athena!"

Thomas raced across the central opening in the village. His body slammed into mine, and his dirt-covered hands grabbed my face holding me close enough to smell the morning of hard labour on his clothes. I squirmed in his hold and tried to push him away.

"Don't," I said, hooking the pouch of lace onto my belt as he released me.

Myrtle stepped closer. "You know what choice to make. Don't be a fool and risk it all. Don't sentence us to his anger."

She hobbled away, and her departure led to the other women leaving. Not one of them stayed to talk to me, or offer any support. Only Thomas remained. He dipped his head, trying to make eye contact with me, but I couldn't bring myself to look into his soft, loving eyes, not now.

"What happened? Are you okay?" He rubbed the top of my arms with his hands. "Why didn't you come home last night?"

"Please, don't touch me."

A frown pulled across his forehead. "Why not? What's wrong?"

I backed away.

"Athena, I need answers here. What's going on?" His words were clipped, edged with frustration.

I sank onto the log and stared at the dwindling fire. Aware of Thomas shuffling to sit next to me, I shifted away from him, ensuring a significant gap was created between us.

"I couldn't come back last night. Paymon made me stay with him at his house." I twisted the end of my hair around my fingers, unwilling to face him.

"Why? Why did he make you stay?"

I shrugged my shoulders. I didn't really understand his insistence that I stay. The only reason I could think of was to keep me away from Thomas.

"We were going to announce our engagement. I could hardly do it with you not there." His voice rose, his frustration brimming over. "You could at least have made some effort to get back."

I rubbed my hand over my forehead. "I couldn't," I repeated. "I wanted to come back, but he wouldn't let me."

Thomas huffed. "So the demon who killed your gran and my parents is more important than me?"

I sucked in a deep breath. "No, of course not. Do you think I wanted to stay with him?"

"So he tied you down, physically stopped you from returning?"

"No." I wanted him to understand, but couldn't think how to explain everything that had happened. Even though Paymon hadn't forced me to do anything, the threats he had carefully wheedled into our earlier conversations made me too afraid to even think about disobeying him. Guilt suddenly swept over me, and I dipped my head, shying away from any eye contact. I'd spent the night in a large comfy bed, warm and dry. I'd not given any thought to our engagement party. I released a long drawn-out sigh and shifted further along the log.

"I have to go back to the house tonight," I said, my gaze downcast. "Paymon won't let me stay in the village."

Thomas kicked a stone into the fire. "So when will you come back?"

I shook my head, swallowing the lump that had risen in my throat. "I won't."

Thomas reached for my hand, his demeanour changing to that of the man I knew and loved. "So Myrtle was right. He's sending you away?"

I didn't pull my hand away from his. The comfort it offered was welcome, reassuring and familiar, but I knew it was short-lived. This would probably be the last time I spoke to him. I chewed my bottom lip, uncertain how much to tell him. "He's not sending me away," I muttered.

"What do you mean? Either he is, or he isn't." He squeezed my hand. "Athena look at me, please. Explain what's happened."

The dwindling flames of the fire spluttered. I saw their pathetic attempt to burn brightly as a direct comparison to my relationship with Thomas.

"Paymon's asked me to marry him," I said.

"What? I hope you told him what to do with his stupid proposal."

I didn't reply. I couldn't bring myself to confirm the situation, but my silence said more than words ever could.

Thomas sat upright, his hand releasing mine. His gaze followed mine into the fire.

"I have to marry him," I eventually said. "If I don't, I'll be sent to the Master and married to him. If I don't marry Paymon, he'll come to the village and torture you all. People will die . . . and it will be my fault."

"What about our plans? We were to be married, stay in the village, and have children together." His eyes held mine, an accusing stare that he had no right to cast my way.

I closed my eyes, but the life I'd envisioned with him had already been snatched away by Paymon.

"You can't go back to Paymon. Why don't we run away together? Spoil his stupid plans."

"What?"

"Run away with me. We can go now or this afternoon. Let's get away from here."

"We can't," I said, shaking my head. Running away wasn't an option. I slid my feet back and forth in the dirt. "I have to go back to Paymon."

"To marry him?"

I nodded.

"So you'd rather marry a demon than run away with me?" His voice was raw, choked, threatening to spill over into anger.

"If we ran away together, we'd be found. He'd find us," I said, understanding the true horrors of what would come. "Believe me, he'd find us. He's already warned me not to be around you. Running away with you would seal our fate. He'd kill you, and me . . . well, I'm not sure."

"No demon will ever kill me." He puffed his chest out, an action so comical but tragically unfounded.

"You don't know Paymon. By not running away with you, I'm saving your life and probably many others in the village."

I didn't know what else to say. The silence was uncomfortable, rising around both of us and wrapping us in its unnerving cold grasp.

Thomas stared into the flames of the fire. The crackling of the wood was the only sound. I followed his gaze, wishing more than ever that he'd tell me it would all be okay. Everything would be fine.

When he jumped to his feet, the move was sudden and unexpected. The iciness of his stare pierced every part of me.

"Go, then!" he shouted. "Go and marry your demon."

"What?" I understood he was hurt, angry, and desperate, but to turn on me like this was cruel. "Haven't you heard anything I've said?"

He pointed an accusing finger at me. "If you go back to him, I want nothing more to do with you."

"Thomas—"

"No, forget it, Athena. Forget about us, forget about our engagement. There is no us anymore. Go and marry Paymon. Maybe he'll share his secrets about the light, whisper it in your ear when he's screwing you."

My gaze hardened, and I gritted my teeth.

"The truth hurts, doesn't it?" he said before spinning around and storming away.

How dare he speak to me like that? I was about to shout after him, ask him to come back, not to end things this way, but I stopped myself. What was the point?

I slumped onto the log and stared at the fire for several minutes. When I lifted my head and systematically focused on every house within view, doors were suddenly shut, a barrier between them and me. No one was around.

A fluttering of wings to my side shifted my attention. Odin had landed and was strutting toward me.

"Now what?" I asked him as he fluttered onto the log beside me.

He cawed, not loud and brash like he usually did, and tipped his head sideways.

"You coming with me?" I said as I stood.

I wandered to my home with Odin hopping alongside

me, but once I pushed the door open, he flew away.

I moved the rug aside and stared blindly at the room. I couldn't help but compare my simple home with the luxury of my surroundings last night. The bed at Paymon's was soft, not lumpy and itchy, and the water was warm, not cold enough to form goose bumps. I pulled his cloak even tighter, welcoming its warmth.

The table was littered with pots and mugs of mismatched shapes and sizes. It seemed that even though I wasn't here last night, the party celebrating my twenty-first birthday had still been held. The room smelt of stale body odour, and an underlying waft of spilt mead drifted in the air. I ignored the mess and walked into my bedroom. The multiple blankets were neatly folded across the bed, and I half-smiled at an action I had never known Thomas to complete before—he wasn't the tidiest of men.

I needed to pack for when I returned to Paymon's later today. I pulled the book, containing all its secrets, from under the mattress and stuffed it in an old fabric bag. The only other items I wanted with me were my mother's perfume and a faded photograph of my parents and sister. I wrapped the bottle of perfume and the photo in layers of socks before stuffing them in the bag on top of the book.

I ambled back into the kitchen and placed the bag on the kitchen table. I huffed. The main room was in such a mess after the party, and a trip to the village well was necessary. I wouldn't leave my house like this even if I had no idea when or if I'd return.

I called for Hannah on my way to collect the water. Her mother came to the door when she heard me calling, but her usual friendly nature had disappeared. She was brisk with her response, telling me that Hannah was in the main hall, working, and I was not to disturb her. There was no further small talk, and she shut the door on me.

I kept my head down as I trudged to the well, not wanting to make eye-contact with the few people that were around. Each step I took seemed to take me further away from the only family I'd ever known. My stomach twisted, uneasy with the emptiness of food and now with the ache of losing Thomas in all this madness. Who'd comfort me this time? Paymon? I doubted that he'd know how. He'd probably just feed from my upset and confusion. I wiped my eyes with the back of my hand and kept walking, ignoring the silence that hung around me.

Once at the well, Odin made another appearance. And when I walked back through the village, water slopping over the sides of the buckets as I struggled with their weight, he fluttered along the thatched roofs of the houses, following me.

I pushed the heavy rug to the side when I arrived at my house. Stepping sideways through the doorway I placed the buckets on the floor, groaning as the water spilt over the sides. Straightening up, I rested my hands on my hips and leaned backward, stretching out the knots in my back.

The fluttering of wings caused my attention to swing to the open window. Odin stood proud on the wooden ledge and cawed loudly at me, not quietly like earlier. Was this the call of the raven, the sign to tell me it was time to return to Paymon? It was earlier than I expected, not even midday.

Odin cawed again, impatiently waiting for me—flapping his wings and hopping back and forth on the windowsill—but the noise wasn't loud enough to disguise a stifled moan that came from my bedroom. With no locks or other ways to secure our homes, the villagers adhered to a high level of trust, but other's bedrooms were not privy to the same level of openness. Another muffled moan urged me forward.

I moved quietly and only inched the rug away from the side of the doorway. The silent gasp that flew from my mouth was immediately covered by my hand.

Even in the subdued light cast by a solitary flickering candle, I could see exactly what was happening. Bending forward over my bed was a woman, her skirts pushed up around her waist. A man was behind her. He still wore his shirt, but his breeches were around his thighs. The woman's long blond hair was wrapped around his fist, and he was pulling her head backward. She moaned encouragingly, alternated with a sharp breath forced from her body each time he thrust his hips to her raised bottom. So shocked by what I was seeing, I only registered the overall image of two people having sex. It took several long moments before the painful truth seeped into my recognition. The two people on my bed, lost in their wild guttural actions, were Thomas and Hannah.

CHAPTER 5

RESIGNATION

I BACKED AWAY FROM THE DOORWAY. EVERY PART OF ME wanted to scream, run into the room and drag them apart. But I didn't.

I turned around, picked up my bag from the table, grabbed a lit lantern and headed outside. I moved slowly, my steps short and unsteady. Once I reached the path that led to my destination, Odin flew alongside me before hopping onto the ground.

"He's got what he wanted," I said to him. "I'll marry him."

Odin cawed and then took off into the sky.

My short journey gave me too much time to mull over what I'd witnessed. My mind unkindly pasted a detailed image of what I'd seen. How could Thomas do that to me? How could Hannah betray my friendship? We were best friends. Well, not anymore. Thomas could mess with her all he wanted between now and tomorrow evening because she'd then be sent away. I couldn't feel sorry for her, not at the moment.

And Thomas—the one man I had trusted above all others. Had he been seeing Hannah behind my back, or was this the first time? I tried to fight the tears that were so near to falling. All the times when Thomas had been late back from the fields, running off to sort something that couldn't wait . . . was he with Hannah? When he came home drunk from the feasts I didn't attend, had he been with her? I groaned and clutched my stomach with my free hand. Leaning over, I spat out the bile that had risen in my throat.

Then the tears started. They flowed as fast as the stream that bordered the south of the village. No wonder Hannah didn't want to tell me who she was sleeping with.

My unwelcome tears rolled down my cheeks, and I sniffed loudly. I didn't want to cry over what I'd lost. We wouldn't be together again anyway. I was to be married to someone else. I looked ahead, facing the imposing house in the distance— facing my future. There was no turning back, not now. I had a new life to start living. I needed to leave the village girl behind. I was going to marry a demon.

With a renewed determination to be brave and strong, I walked briskly. I focused on the one potential good thing to come from all this—information. I would use my time with Paymon to find out why we were in constant darkness. And maybe, just maybe, I'd find out how to get the light back permanently.

Approaching the house, I untied the pouch of lace from my belt and slipped it into my bag. When I looked up, Odin had settled on the gate. He leaned forward, repeating the action he'd demonstrated the first time he appeared at my window. It was a strange gesture, and I was still convinced that he was going to topple forward.

"Stupid bird," I muttered. "You'll do that one day and end up on the ground."

He flapped his wings and returned to a normal standing position before turning and facing the door.

"I know," I said, watching him. "He's waiting for me, yes?" Just as I was about to tut at myself for thinking a bird could understand me, Odin dipped his head several times in quick succession.

"Athena?"

I spun around. Paymon was standing at the door.

"You're upset." He stayed in the doorway, arms folded as he observed me. "What's happened?"

I shook my head. I couldn't tell him.

"I didn't expect you back until later," he said, moving aside as I stepped into the warmth.

"You sent Odin for me," I said, catching sight of him as he flew onto the same perch in the hall as when I arrived yesterday.

"I can assure you I didn't. I wanted to give you as much time as possible in the village so you could say your good-byes." He tutted and then continued, "Is that why you're upset, because you're leaving them?"

"No." I felt my tears building again.

"Tell me what's bothering you. Take the cloak off and extinguish the lantern. I'll be in the lounge." He swept away, striding to the doorway across the hall.

When he disappeared from view, I blew out the candle in the lantern and placed it on the floor with my bag. I shrugged his thick cloak from my shoulders and hung it up before pausing and taking several slow calming breaths.

When I entered the room, I immediately focused on

Paymon. He was sitting in a chair, his back to me.

"Come in, Athena. Don't linger in the doorway."

I shut the door before turning around and inspecting what was another amazing room. Candles were situated on several surfaces, lighting the space in a comforting, warm orange glow. A fire blazed away in the fireplace giving off so much heat that I could feel it from the doorway. There was a large comfy looking chair, big enough for four people to sit on, positioned across from the fire. Other chairs filled the room, all of them covered in fabric. There were no wooden seats here.

"Warm enough?" Paymon asked, turning to face me.

I nodded.

"I noticed you seem to struggle with the cold. You'll have no need to worry about that whilst you are here. Now, sit down." He gestured toward the large chair with a sweep of his arm. I duly did as he'd requested, convinced that this chair was what my Gran had referred to as a sofa.

"Books," I gasped as I saw the rows of neatly arranged spines upon four shelves. Books were a luxury in the village. I'd only ever seen a dictionary and the secret book I possessed.

"Yes, I like to read. I have a library—the room next to this one. Perhaps you'll read to me sometime? You can read, can't you?"

I nodded before lifting my gaze to his. When our eyes met, he smiled.

"Athena, tell me why you're so upset."

I took a deep breath, and then gritted my teeth. "Thomas," I said, as if that one word would suffice.

Paymon's eyebrows lifted at the same time that Odin squawked.

"He was with Hannah," I added.

Paymon sighed heavily before addressing Odin. "Did you try to stop Athena seeing them? Is that why she's back early? You called her before I asked you to?"

Odin made a clicking sound in his throat and fluttered across the room to perch behind me on the back of the sofa.

Paymon chuckled before turning serious. "Odin's actions are most peculiar. I have never known of a raven becoming so attached to a human."

I sat upright and leaned away from Odin, unsettled by his proximity. Even though I was becoming used to him, I was still uncomfortable around him. Birds were not an animal I had ever been close to.

"So Odin called for you just before you saw Thomas and Hannah?"

I nodded again, unsure of my voice.

"And what exactly were they doing?"

I frowned at him. He knew, surely he knew. It didn't take much guessing.

"Athena?" he encouraged. "Tell me."

My body became uncomfortably warm and heavy. I recognised the feeling immediately. He was compelling me. This wasn't fair. He had to stop doing this to me.

"Stop it!" I jumped to my feet before the loss of movement took control. "Don't compel me."

"Then tell me."

The heat left me and I sunk onto the sofa again. "They were having sex!" I blurted out.

Paymon smirked. Black eyes met mine. "And did it excite you? Seeing them together like that?"

"What? No. It upset me."

He closed his eyes, a serene smile tugging at the corners of his mouth. He didn't speak, and I realised that my angry reaction had been like a bolt of lightning to him—he was feeding from my heightened emotions.

Eventually he opened his eyes and drew in a deep breath.

"It seems you've had an upsetting morning. If I was a gentleman then I would offer you sympathy and apologise for my somewhat unorthodox response to your anguish, but I won't do either. Selfishly, I am enjoying your turmoil. Your emotions are incredible at the moment. I only wish you could feel their strength in the way I do."

I turned away from him, willing myself to be calm. Odin hopped from the back of the sofa onto the seat beside me. He made a clicking noise in his throat before settling against my thigh.

Paymon shook his head but grinned at Odin before rising to his feet. He stood in front of me, only a few steps away.

"So, Athena, are you ready to make your decision? I told you that I expected you to tell me as soon as you returned. I've already humoured your arrival for far longer than I intended. Will you agree to be my wife, or do I send you to the Master?"

The decision, so easy to make after seeing Thomas and Hannah together, stuck in my throat. It wasn't that I was undecided, but part of me was still struggling to come to terms with the life I would be leaving behind. I hoped Paymon would understand and give me time to mourn what I had lost. My lover, my best friend, and the trust and friendship of everyone in the village.

"Your decision?" Paymon prompted, leaning forward.

I looked to him, black eyes bearing down on me, waiting, and anticipating my answer.

"I'll marry you," I said. "I accept your proposal."

His eyes widened and another smile crossed his dark features, but he immediately regained his composure.

"Then the ceremony must take place immediately. There's no point in waiting any longer." He looked around the room before returning his gaze to me. After shooing Odin from the sofa, he sat next to me. "You need to know that the bond created when a demon marries is unbreakable. Most of us are completely honourable in our relationships." He reached for my hands before continuing. "The ceremony is sealed by the union of the bride and groom's bodies."

"You mean sex?" His words did not surprise me. I'd always assumed he wanted more than my companionship. This was his way of getting what he always wanted.

"I mean more than sex, Athena. It's a sharing of so much more. I can compel you to stay calm, but the ceremony would have more intimacy for me if you were free to feel."

"I don't want to be compelled, and I don't want to have sex with you." I frowned and fidgeted on the seat. "I hardly know you."

"And you think you would have sex with me if you knew me?" He cleared his throat and then continued. "So I find myself giving you another choice. Do I have your permission to join with you completely by the sharing of our bodies during the marriage ceremony?"

I shook my head, no doubt about my answer. "If it's my choice, then I choose not to."

"And what about compelling you? Think carefully. It would be easier for you."

I glanced at his face, trying to work out whether this was some sort of trick. If I was compelled, he'd be able to do whatever he wanted to me.

"No, I don't want to be compelled."

Paymon nodded. "For what it's worth, you have my word that I will not force myself upon you or compel you during the ceremony." He released my hands and stood. "I can be most trustworthy when required."

I snorted at his declaration.

"So what else happens at the ceremony?" I tilted my head to the side. "You said you'd tell me when I'd agreed to marry you. You told me it wouldn't be pleasant."

"It's old magic," he said, his words rushed, excitable. "Once we enter the room where the ceremony takes place, I will not be able to offer you any verbal reassurances. I will be chanting spells and incantations in my own language."

"Demon language?" I sat on my hands to hide their shaking. Unfortunately, I could do little to hide my inner emotions. Paymon was in his element.

"Yes. You will not understand me, and I will not be able to stop and explain. Once again, I ask you to trust me."

"I can't trust you. You're a demon."

He took a quick stride forward and pointed his finger at me. This time his tone was sharp. "If you were to be married to the Master, he would have insisted you had sex with him."

I snapped from my reverie and jumped to my feet. "And you weren't prepared to tell me that before I made my decision? Don't you think it was important information? What if I'd decided to be married to him and not you?"

He closed the gap between us, our chests beating against each other's. I refused to show any sign of weakness.

Paymon sneered. "If you had chosen the Master, I would have cut all ties with you and your emotions. I would have let him have you as the worthless whore that Thomas left behind."

I backed away from him, my bravado and anger slapped aside by his cruel words. Once again I saw the true demon spring to life from under his calm and controlled façade.

"I think I prefer you better when you act naturally," I bit back at him. "There's no surprises when you talk to me as your true nature dictates. It helps me remember that you're not human, that you're a demon who crawled out of the centre of the earth."

He smiled at my outburst. "All your anger does is feed me, Athena."

His words made me stop any further sarcasm.

"A feeder," I said, Hannah's categorisation sprung to the front of my mind. "That's what the categorisation is. Hannah will feed the Master through her emotions."

Paymon nodded, his coal dark eyes seemingly sparkling with new excitement. "It is the worst categorisation I can give of the three. She will not be well looked after. In fact, the more pain and humiliation she receives, the more the Master will feed. Seems fitting for her after she deceived you in such a way."

"That's so wrong," I said, looking to the carpet. The swirls of dull browns and reds diverted my attention from his eyes. Even though I was angry with Hannah and doubted I'd ever forgive her deceit and betrayal with Thomas, I couldn't wish her any harm at the hands of demons.

I held my hands up in front of me, stopping any further revelations.

"I need some space," I mumbled before turning to the door.

"You'll stay here."

I shook my head. "I'm going to my room. I . . . I can't think straight."

"No, you're not. We need to be married."

"It can wait!" I snapped before running from the room.

"You'll take your belongings and then come straight back," Paymon shouted. "The ceremony must happen immediately, and I can't marry you without you being there."

I picked my bag from the floor in the hall and trudged up the stairs. Odin followed, bouncing alongside me.

"You should stay with Paymon," I snapped. "You're his bird, not mine. I don't want you with me."

He ruffled his feathers but stayed at my side. When I reached my room, I crept through as narrow a gap as I could manage and kept him out by waving my foot around so he didn't get close.

Once in the room, I leaned back against the door and breathed heavily. All my emotions hit me at once: Hurt ripped at my heart, tugged and stamped on it after seeing Thomas with Hannah. Disappointment and bewilderment that my best friend had lied to me so easily. Anger at both of them for deceiving me. Frustration for not doing anything when I saw them, for just standing there silently, disbelieving what I was witnessing. And most of all, fear—fear of what was to come.

"Athena!"

I quickly opened my bag and pulled out the book. I also searched for the pouch of lace. Grasping both of them tightly, I slipped them into the drawer at the side of my bed. I hadn't needed the lace yet, but I still wasn't convinced about Paymon's assurance that he was only after my companionship.

"Athena!" Paymon was outside my room. I ambled to the door, not willing to rush the impending event, but also not wanting to anger my future husband.

On opening the door, Paymon greeted me with a false smile. Odin was nowhere to be seen.

"Ready?"

I sighed, doubting he wanted my true response.

He offered his hand and waited for me to hold it before leading me along the corridor and down the stairs. I bristled at the unwanted contact. His skin was warm, uncomfortably so.

I didn't speak, and neither did Paymon, but the quietness was false. It was full of unanswered questions, nerves, and my very obvious fear. There was no need to keep checking Paymon's eyes to know what colour they were.

He led me to the same room he'd taken me when I first arrived at the house.

"Take a seat," he said, releasing my hand and wandering around the table that our conversations had taken place at only yesterday. He waited for me to sit before pulling his own chair to the table. He drummed his fingers on the wood before speaking. "Each house that a demon resides in has a secret room. You will only be allowed to cross into it with me today. But after this first visit, it will also let you enter whenever you please."

"I doubt I'll ever want to," I said. Why would I need to visit the room where I was begrudgingly married?

Paymon raised his brow. "It's a safe room for you if ever you need it, not just a place for us to marry."

"What's in this room?"

"Not much. It's a room of purpose rather than a room to live in. Now, before we enter, I must remind you that no harm will come to you, but the things that happen whilst in there may frighten you and cause you distress. It will all be temporary."

I inhaled a deep breath, desperate to control my panic.

"How long is the ceremony?"

Paymon smirked. "Long enough."

I widened my eyes at his response.

"Remember, I will not be able to talk to you once we enter the room. Any questions you ask will go unanswered."

"Just like normal then," I muttered.

"Athena, I will talk to you properly, but not before we are married." He stood, his tall frame rising above me. "After all, I wouldn't want to scare you away, would I?" The edge of his mouth twitched, and he turned away before indicating, with a wave of his hand, for me to join him on his side of the table.

Fighting every bone in my body as it begged to stay where it was, I forced myself to my feet and walked toward him.

"This is how you open the entrance," he said as he tilted the picture of the Master. Once he replaced the portrait to the correct position, a click sounded out from the right-hand side of the fireplace, and a panel of the wooden wall slid to the side. Paymon stepped to the revealed opening and nodded at me.

I followed his silent instructions but paused at the doorway, staring into a dark void.

His hand rested on the small of my back, and he gently pushed me forward.

"Down the steps," he said. "The room is at the bottom. There'll be no more speaking from now on."

As soon as Paymon moved behind me, the wooden panel that had revealed its secret passageway closed. His warm breath blew across the top of my head, and he placed his hands on my shoulders, pushing me further into the unwelcoming darkness. His proximity made me anxious, and I was uncomfortable with his overheated body touching mine. The enormity of what I was about to face was too apparent, and I fought the tightness in my stomach and the need to run screaming. My breaths caught in my chest, and I swallowed several times, suddenly thirsty. I was trapped. There was no turning back.

"I'm here. Don't worry." Paymon said as he squeezed my shoulders.

I pushed my hair away from my face and took a deep, calming breath. This was necessary; it would save me from a life with the Master. It would ensure the villagers were safe and not subjected to Paymon's torture.

Sliding my left foot in front of me, I searched for the edge of the step. When I found it, I moved forward. A candle on the side of the wall sprung to life, lighting the way. Each hesitant step I took, another flame ignited. The stairwell was straight, and as I reached the bottom step, Paymon released my shoulders. He chanted words in an unfamiliar language and the room became lit in an orange glow. The room was circular, high stone walls with five narrow recesses in which a candle brightly burned. The floor was also cold, unforgiving stone. There was no furniture.

I stepped further into the room, and Paymon pointed to the floor. My racing heartbeat accelerated even more as I noted the lines etched into the stone, ones that created an all too familiar shape: a large circle, with a pentagram drawn in the middle of it. At each point of the pentagram, where it touched the circle, a metal ring was fixed to the floor. Each point aligned with the flickering candles.

My feet refused to move; they stuck to the floor like glue, dead weights unable to be lifted, but Paymon led me to the circle before moving behind me. His hands pushed down on my shoulders, and I took his action as a sign to sit.

"Bee-enn-el dee-ay," he said.

He crouched behind me and, supporting my shoulders, pulled me backward onto the floor. He took his time laying me out, placing each limb in a point in the pentagram and my head in the remaining one. I suddenly understood the position of the metal rings—they were to hold my wrists and ankles. Another crippling wave of fear washed through me. I was going to be restrained.

Paymon stepped over to one of my hands and bent down before closing my fingers around the metal ring. He squeezed my clenched fist before repeating the same procedure with my other hand. I swallowed hard, fighting the rising unease in my stomach. I kept my gaze on Paymon but didn't move away from the position he had put me in. If I kept hold of the rings, I hoped he wouldn't restrain me with ropes or chains.

Paymon moved around the room, circling me five times before standing between my feet. A whispered chant left his lips as he closed his eyes and raised his hands to his sides.

My eyelids became heavy, and I dropped my head back onto the ground. For one brief moment, I thought he was compelling me, but as I twisted my foot to the side, I realised there was no accompanying paralysis of my limbs. So what was this strange, soothing calmness that had taken a hold over me?

Paymon's chanting continued, a jumble of mismatched words. The tiny flames from the candles appeared to glow brighter and then fade again. When the chanting stopped, I lifted my head to focus on Paymon. He had his arms raised above his head and a large circular bowl in his hands. He stepped forward before sinking to his knees between my spread legs.

"Ef-eh-el eye-hu-enn-bay."

I didn't move. The calmness that had flooded through me was replaced by uncontrolled fear. My chin trembled and my throat restricted. My breathing became shallow and fast. I wanted to jump to my feet and run from the room, but I gripped the rings in my hands tighter and forced myself to take deep, slow breaths. I didn't move my gaze away from Paymon as he stared at me. When he began chanting once again, the familiar calmness returned.

He reached into the bowl and lifted a knife into the air. I concentrated on the surreal way the flames danced in the reflective blade. They were beautiful, each one licking the shiny metal as Paymon turned the blade to point downward. His action should have made me scream, and a split second image of the blade being thrust into my chest coincided with Paymon's chant becoming louder and faster. He lowered the glistening blade toward me and sliced my leather belt. His chanting stopped, and as soon as it did, I whimpered. My previous panic spread through me as the fast thump of each heartbeat echoed in my ears. I willed him to start the chant again.

I fought back tears as Paymon cut my dress at the hem and placed the knife back into the bowl. He tore my dress and ripped open my under-dress. I squirmed on the ground, exposed, vulnerable, desperate to cover myself, but not daring to move my hands from the metal rings. I was racked with a sudden heat and then a frigid cold. My body shook, my skin bristled, and I struggled to catch my breath, but I stayed where I was. Paymon would compel me if I didn't behave, and I had no doubt that behaving meant I didn't move.

Several further rips ensured he released me from the covering of all my clothes, and he calmly collected the tattered pieces of material and placed them in the bowl. I paid great attention to what he was doing. It helped keep my mind preoccupied and away from the fact that I was naked and spread out on the floor before him. I turned my head to the side when he sought my eyes with his own. I couldn't look at him, not when I was this vulnerable.

He slipped away from between my legs and removed each fabric shoe and long sock before placing them in the bowl with my clothes. Standing, he held the bowl in one hand and produced a flame from the fingers on his other. He blew the flame to the bowl and watched as my clothes burnt with flames. I focused on them, seeing them change from orange and red, to blue and white. The flames died and Paymon placed his hand into the bowl. He retrieved a white bundle of material which he immediately unwrapped and held in front of him. It was a dress, plain white fabric—my wedding dress.

"Eye-eh-em-jad." He indicated for me to stand, a curl of his finger.

I looked at my hands before frowning at him. Did he mean for me to release my grip on the metal rings?

He curled his finger at me again, and I stumbled to my feet. Acutely aware of my nakedness as I stood before him, I covered my breasts with my arms. Paymon shook his head and stepped forward. He grabbed my arms and positioned them by my sides before manoeuvring me into the centre of the circle. He was so much stronger than me, and the power that I'd felt flow from him when I first arrived seemed even greater at the moment. My limbs began to shake again, and I feared how much longer this would continue.

He placed a kiss on my forehead and resumed his chanting, this time louder than before. I welcomed his mysterious words and the accompanying loss of my crushing fear. Hopefully this would be the end of the ceremony, a final chant to seal our marriage, and then we could leave the room.

Paymon placed the white dress over my head, and I slipped my arms into the sleeves, grateful of the soft covering of fabric, regardless as to what it stood for.

Once the dress was in place, Paymon closed his eyes. I stared at him, trying to work out what would happen next.

My eyes widened as another glint of the knife caught my eye. Paymon cut the palm of his right hand before taking hold of my right hand. In an action so quick I didn't see it happen, he sliced my palm with the knife. Pain—searing, screaming pain spread through my hand as blood oozed from the deep cut. Paymon pressed his cut palm against mine. My vision clouded as our blood mixed. My mind failed to function, and my mouth moved of its own accord. Words I never knew to exist sprung from me as I wavered between consciousness and unconsciousness. My voice wasn't my own, and I was speaking in a language I had no knowledge of, matching Paymon's chant word for word.

When our synchronised chanting stopped, a renewed pain skewered my hand. I screamed and tried to pull my hand away from Paymon's. The icy, sharp, stabbing pain wasn't from the cut, though—it was from the back of my hand. It felt as if shards of glass were being drawn across it. Like an insect crawling between layers of my flesh, the skin on the back of my hand lifted in a red, raised pattern. Paymon held my hand tightly, refusing to let go as the mark continued to grow.

"Please," I said. "Please, it hurts . . . so much."

I slumped against Paymon, but he still refused to relinquish his hold. Time held no meaning as I whimpered and begged against his chest.

When Paymon scooped me into his arms, I curled into him, welcoming his hold. He moved forward, entered the circle and stopped in the centre of the pentagram. The edge of the circle burst into flames, and I clung even tighter to him, burying myself in his jacket. The flames roared and crackled around us; their heat licked my flesh and overheated my body, but Paymon held me securely against him.

When the roar of the fire stopped, the ferocious flames disappeared. The light in the room restored to the recessed flickering candles. Paymon kept me in his arms as he crossed the room and carried me up the stairs. I was grateful that he didn't make me walk. I had no energy left to even stand, and my limbs shook and ached. My skin prickled with beads of sweat, and my stomach heaved. I turned my head to the side and groaned as my stomach tried to empty itself.

"Stop it. We'll have none of that." Paymon's stern voice broke through my stupor. But as I tried to focus on him, my peripheral vision spun. I closed my eyes, too dizzy to keep them open.

A familiar squawk signified Odin's presence.

"She'll be fine," Paymon said. "The ceremony has exhausted her. She'll need time to recover."

I was placed on a comfy surface, and a soft blanket was thrown over me.

"Odin, go fetch some soup from Myrtle." His footsteps brushed across the carpet. "Take this note with you, she'll know who it's for and why it's needed." More footsteps, fading, quieter. The front door was opened, a welcoming blast of cold air kissed my overheated skin. Another loud squawk sounded before the heavy beating of wings gradually faded. The click of the door closing was quickly followed by Paymon's return to the room.

"Sleep, Athena. I'll sit with you whilst you do. You'll come to no harm now we are married."

Aware of the rustling of clothes as Paymon fidgeted in his chair, I tried to block out the imagery of what had just happened.

I was a married woman.

Married to Paymon.

Married to a demon.

CHAPTER 6

GRATITUDE

"**E**AT," PAYMON SAID.

I opened my eyes. He was holding a bowl in one hand and a spoon in the other.

"You need to eat. You're exhausted," he said, lifting the spoon to my mouth. "You've been asleep for several hours."

He pushed the spoon gently against my lips, and I opened my mouth. The broth was warm and smooth—a velvety texture that slipped easily down my throat. I focused on Paymon whilst I ate. His normal brown eyes stared back at me, although the iris was outlined in a thick black line.

Another spoonful pressed against my lips.

"Chicken soup," Paymon announced. "It should help ease the tiredness."

"Chicken?" I asked after swallowing another mouthful of the tasty liquid. "We're not allowed chicken." In the village we only ate chickens on the night of a full moon when the feasts were held.

"Athena, remember who you are married to. You can have chicken everyday now if you wish." He offered the bowl to me to hold.

I gripped the bowl with one hand, but a mark on the back of my other hand caught my eye. It resembled the markings on the floor in the room we'd been married in. The lines were black, raised, with an angry redness still evident underneath. As I took the spoon from Paymon, I winced. My palm stung, and I turned my hand over to inspect it. The single cut Paymon had made during the ceremony was very prominent.

"The cut will heal quickly, and the mark of marriage will not be sore for long," Paymon said, guessing my concerns. "In fact, yours will heal quicker than mine." He held his right hand toward me, palm upward showing the single cut, and then turned it. He had exactly the same mark as I did on the back of his hand.

"Why will mine heal faster than yours?" I asked as Paymon nodded at the bowl reminding me to eat.

"You're young and not a demon."

I frowned as I swallowed.

Paymon pulled his chair closer to where I was sitting.

"I'm old, Athena," he said as he sat down, "although your emotions are feeding me and giving me a new lease of life. Have you noticed that I don't limp anymore? That happened as soon as you arrived yesterday. I was surprised by how quickly I reacted to your presence."

"I did that?"

Paymon grinned. "You did so much more. Now, you can't reverse time, make me younger or revive me if I die, but I am stronger and feel like I did thirteen years ago when I came to live on this world. But I am also a demon, not that you need reminding, and we heal slowly. A cut can take weeks, not days to heal. Many demons can die from injuries that humans simply endure."

I eyed him suspiciously. As interesting as this was, I couldn't understand why was he telling me. I nodded, storing the information for future recall.

"Obviously, I have an immunity to fire, and most other demons have some sort of tolerance for it."

"You told me that other demons have powers," I said, focusing on the only other piece of information I had about their secret lives.

Paymon nodded.

"What power does the Master have?" I guessed it would be something really powerful or a mix of several different ones.

Paymon smirked before replying. "He can take the form of anyone he touches."

His words made me freeze.

"As long as he has touched the flesh of another. It could be your face, your hand. And he need not touch you with his hand. His cheek against yours, his arm brushing against you. It's a gift that gives him ultimate power."

"Can he only change into another demon?"

Paymon shook his head. "No, he can change into anyone, anything, male or female."

I shuddered.

"I've never met him, but I believe his normal appearance is the one in the portrait." He smiled again, reaching for my right hand. "This mark proves to others that you are married."

"It hurt," I mumbled, pulling my hand away from his and continuing to eat the soup.

"It must have been incredibly painful for you. I thought for a moment I had lost you—you nearly fainted." He shook his head before looking at me. "I have never been stronger than I was when we were experiencing the full force of the marriage ceremony. But the ceremony, the stress of what has happened since yesterday—it's all taken a toll on you."

"So why didn't you stop?"

"Stop? I didn't want to. I took every emotion you gave me, more than necessary, but . . . Athena, I live for that feeling every day. And I will continue to seek it from you."

I widened my eyes. "You mean you enjoy my pain?"

He frowned. "No. I enjoy your heightened emotions, be it fear, pain, jealousy, hate. But I would like to feed from your positive emotions." He reached his hand to the side of my face and rested it against my cheek. "Joy, happiness, contentment, perhaps even love."

I froze, a reaction I was becoming accustomed to in his presence.

"You can feed from positive emotions?"

He nodded. "I feel too much fear coming from you, Athena. What can I do to change that?" He removed his hand and leaned away from me. "I promised you I would look after you. I will also provide you with whatever you desire, as long as it is within my powers. You have already done more for me than I could've ever wished for."

"Why are your eyes not black?"

"They are, around the edges."

"What does that mean?"

"That I am full. A stuffed, overindulged, fed demon." He chuckled quietly. "Talking of food, have you had enough, or do I need to send for more?"

"I'm fine. A bit thirsty, though."

"I always have water to drink," he said, striding to a long table at the side of the room. He poured me a glass of water. "Unfortunately it will always be warm."

"Like the water in my bath?"

"Not quite. I ensure that is kept at a temperature that will be most comfortable for you." He handed me the glass of water, and I sipped at the liquid—warm, as he said.

"Perhaps you would bathe tonight and dress in something more suitable for our day tomorrow? You have a cupboard full of dresses. Each one was made especially for you. Wear one of them."

I spluttered but managed to swallow the water. The dresses were mine? Those beautiful, soft dresses belonged to me?

"I can't wear them. They're too grand for me," I said. "I'm just a village girl."

Paymon narrowed his gaze. "No, you are not. You are no longer the village girl. You are my wife." He paused for a few moments. "Anyway, what else do you have to wear?"

I glanced at the dress I was currently wearing. "What's wrong with—?"

I stopped my sentence as I saw the trails of dark crimson on my white dress.

"That is your wedding dress. It's not suitable for tomorrow and definitely not suitable for the Ascension Ceremony."

My curiosity rose. Paymon was chatting away, quite unassuming about the information he was giving me. "Why not the ceremony?"

"Because both Hannah and Julie will be wearing white, you must not. It dictates that you are to be taken to the Master. It gives the illusion of cleanliness and of purity. Traits that the

Master adores. Although they will not arrive as pristine as they look when they leave here. And, as you well know, white is the last colour Hannah should be wearing." He smirked as he returned to the counter at the side of the room and poured himself a drink.

I didn't like the reminder of Hannah's infidelities and decided that today had been long enough. I wanted to have a soak in the warm water upstairs.

"Do I still have the key to my room?"

"Of course," Paymon said, lifting his glass to his lips, an amused look pulling across his face.

"Then may I go to my room?"

"Athena, you have no need to ask my permission to go to your room. And if I recall correctly, you never asked my permission earlier when you practically ran away from me."

I looked to the floor, embarrassed.

"I'm sorry," I said. "I shouldn't have done that."

"Really?" Paymon frowned as he marched across the room toward me. "You feel the need to apologise to me for your behaviour?"

I nodded, keeping my gaze on the floor.

Warm fingers nudged under my chin, and I lifted my face to be met by Paymon's puzzled expression.

"You are the first woman to ever apologise to me," he said.

"Then you haven't met many decent ones."

He narrowed his gaze and then chuckled.

"No, I don't think I have." He held my chin, his fingers light in their touch as his eyes bore into mine. And then his demeanour altered. His eyes widened, and he practically snarled. "I bid you good night, Athena." He removed his fingers and turned his back to me.

"N . . . night," I stuttered. I didn't wait for him to say anything else and fled the room as quickly as I had earlier today.

Odin was nowhere to be seen as I climbed the stairs, and I found myself missing his encouraging squawks and flapping of feathers.

When I entered my room, I immediately locked the door. Even though Paymon had seen me naked, I didn't want him barging in on me whilst I bathed. I shuddered when I recalled the wedding ceremony. My fears had somehow guided me through the bulk of it, my heightened emotions suppressed whilst in the room. I stared at the back of my hand and traced the pentagram with my finger. The redness was fading faster than the memory.

I pulled all the curtains shut before turning to the bath. Someone, and I had no doubt who it was, had scattered red rose petals on the surface. My skin prickled, and I leaned away from the water. This was something I imagined a lover would do, not a carer. The rose petals threw numerous doubts into my head, nagging ones that I kept trying to suppress.

I stood tall, peeking over the screen that divided the room, checking to see if Paymon had magically walked through the door. He'd said he was a fire demon, but I had no idea if he had other powers as well. The air hung thick and heavy as a chill of realisation shot through me. I knew nothing about this new life, nothing at all.

Glancing back to the tub I tried to ignore the overwhelming desire to soak in the hot water, to scrub myself clean from the feel of his hands on my naked flesh. But after several nervous glances to the door, the pull of the warm water was too great. I lifted my dress over my head and stepped into the waiting tub. I sunk onto my bottom and let the heat of the sweet smelling liquid surround me.

It didn't take long for the relaxing warmth of the water to lull me into a peaceful state of mind. Was this my life now? I felt like the lady of the manor from hundreds of years ago, when large houses had servants and maids to look after them. I'd been born way after that period in history. Gran said I'd been born in 2035, on the twenty-fourth of February. Back then, people lived in large houses, with glass windows and heat, and even items that kept you cool when it was too hot. So many everyday items needed electricity to work. I could hardly believe the things Gran had told me about: communication through tiny metal things called phones, boxes that connected you to instant information, moving pictures, music, you could even communicate with other people around the world. To me, it seemed we became too clever, ignoring the forces around us—the natural occurrences. We somehow upset the balance. We weren't completely blameless in the demons' ascent. They had waited for an opportune moment to rise from the depths of the earth, and our self-centred way of life, our selfish actions to those around us, had given them the perfect opportunity. Gran had said that the natural disasters started to increase in frequency when she was a child. Earthquakes rocked cities that had never experienced their frightening power. Large waves travelled across the oceans, killing thousands of people who lived along the coast. Volcanoes, dormant for thousands of years, began spewing lava and clouds of dust. And all of these events were warnings, warnings of what was to come.

I closed my eyes and sank under the water, letting the sound of this new world drift around me. Paymon was a demon, but he was also my husband. He had already introduced me to a life with more luxuries than I would have ever had in the village. He'd also saved me from a life with the Master Demon.

Lifting my head free from the water, I breathed in the scent of the roses before reaching for the soap. I let out a low moan of happiness when I rubbed the smooth, silky texture against my skin.

I stopped my action and dropped the soap. How could I think like this and accept all this luxury? It wasn't my life; it wasn't who I was. My friends were still in the village where the cold tore at their skin, where warm water was a far-flung dream. This life may be luxurious, but what had I unwillingly traded it for? Marriage to a demon who fed from my emotions. Trapped in a house with him? I'd not been free in the village—confined by its borders, too scared to roam into the forest that surrounded it. And I wasn't free here. I lifted my hand from the water and turned it so I could see the mark, their mark, my marriage mark. I was no freer here than in the village. I dipped my hand back into the water and sunk under the surface again.

I was worried about my friends; what awaited them when they turned twenty-one? What life were the girls who'd already been sent away enduring? Were any of them worried about me, here, married to Paymon? I doubted that they'd give me a second thought. They'd already shunned me, decided I wasn't one of them anymore. And what about Thomas? We'd been through so much together, and even though I'd never forgive him for his betrayal, I couldn't hate him. I missed him. But I also questioned whether he'd ever loved me like he said, or was I just a convenience for him? Had he slept with other girls, not just Hannah? And Hannah, what would become of her at the Master's—it didn't sound good.

I pushed myself into a sitting position in the water, the depth still high on my chest. I couldn't do this, punish myself with thoughts of what I'd left behind. It wasn't as if I'd any choice in the matter. If I hadn't married Paymon, I would be marrying the Master. My life in the village would have ended one way or another.

With my mind jumbled and my emotions swaying, I stayed in the bath for a long time. The water remained the same temperature, and it was only when my fingers and toes started to wrinkle that I moved from the comforting warmth. I dried myself in front of the fire with a large fluffy piece of cloth that had been hanging over the edge of the screen and marvelled at how absorbent it was, nothing like the rough linen we used in the village.

I crossed the room to the cupboard full of dresses to see if there was anything suitable for me to sleep in. I quickly flicked through the rail and stopped when I saw a dark red dress. Pulling it free from the others, I held it against myself. I marvelled at how soft the fabric was—a brushed, risen fabric. As I looked back to the row of dresses, there was a dark green one in exactly the same type of material. Paymon said they were mine, made especially for me. I had no choice but to wear these dresses or wander around naked. His claim of ownership, of the fact I was married to him, was gradually fitting into place. He was moulding me to be the wife he wanted.

But I wouldn't be the victim in all this. Gran may have made the deal with Paymon, but neither of them knew how strong I could be. I'd never forget where I came from, and I would never stop hoping that one day the light would return to the world.

I slipped the dress back into the cupboard and pulled out a simple white tunic that hung on the end of the row of colourful dresses. It was the nearest thing to a nightgown, and I certainly wasn't sleeping naked.

Yawning loudly, I settled myself in the centre of the bed, once again frowning at the luxury surrounding me. I should have felt like a princess, but I didn't. I was under no illusion why I was here. Paymon had plans, ones I still didn't know about. I wasn't a princess—I was a prisoner.

The mouth-watering smell of fried bacon drifted under my nose.

Dreaming, I was still dreaming. Bacon was never allowed for breakfast.

I turned over and pulled the warm covers further up my body. I was comfortable and didn't want to move.

An insistent scratching noise followed by a squawk had me wide awake.

"Odin?" I said, jumping out of bed and heading to the door.

His noise became louder as I turned the key in the lock.

"What are you doing here?" I said as I peered out into the dark corridor. He ruffled his feathers before bowing at me and moving toward the gap in the door.

"Hey," I said, waving my foot around at him. "You shouldn't come in here. You'll make too much mess."

He watched my foot as it stopped him from entering the room, but when he realised it wasn't a game, he sprung forward and pecked my toe.

"Oww!" I shrieked and backed away from his sharp weapon. He took that moment to sneak into my room. I sighed in defeat and shut the door before turning to him. He'd already chosen his position—the top of the screen that divided the bathing area from the rest of the room. He chattered away, the noise rumbling in his throat making his feathers ruffle.

"Where were you yesterday?" I asked. He clicked his beak several times before turning to face one of the windows. Curious as to whether he was responding to me, I crossed the room and opened the curtains at the window he'd turned toward. I could just make out the glowing lanterns that lit the village.

"Didn't Paymon want you around when he married me?" I said. He didn't reply and walked sideways along the screen, his talons clicking on the wooden frame as he flapped his wings. "Guess not," I said, noting his silence.

I wandered to the cupboard and pulled out the first dress I came across. I laid it out on the bed and stared at it. It was gorgeous, made from a soft risen material and deep red in colour. Was it suitable for today? Was it too grand?

Odin fluttered across the room and landed on the end of the bed. He looked at the dress and then at me before squawking loudly.

"This okay?"

He nibbled at the dress, pulling the ties that fastened it. I grinned, realising that the leather must look like worms to him.

"Turn away then," I said to him. "Raven or not, you're a male, and you shouldn't watch a lady undress."

I grinned as Odin took off across the room and landed on the screen again, although this time he faced away from me.

I watched him for a few moments, ensuring he didn't turn around, before slipping out of my nightgown and putting the dress on. He only turned when I sat at the dressing table and brushed through my knotted hair. There were three jewelled hair clasps on the table. I picked each one up and decided to wear the one set with red glistening stones. With a few quick twists of segments of my hair, I secured it through the clasp and in a high ponytail.

"Will I do?" I said as I approached Odin, beginning to feel a little more confident around him.

Once again, he did his strange manoeuvre where he looked like he was going to topple forward.

"One day," I laughed, "one day you will fall over."

He straightened and flapped his wings before dropping onto the floor and leading me to the door.

I watched him with curious amusement and recalled what Paymon had said yesterday. He'd never known a raven take to a human as Odin had to me. Maybe we could be friends, but I could never see him as my bird—he belonged to Paymon. As I walked down the stairs, Odin flew into the air, and as if to confirm my earlier thought, he swooped low and onto the arm of Paymon, who stood waiting for me.

"Good morning, Athena," he said. "I sent Odin to wake you. I assumed you would prefer him to rouse you from your sleep rather than myself."

I was about to answer but stopped myself when his black eyes locked with mine. They momentarily shocked me. I'd got used to seeing his brown eyes yesterday, even though they were edged with the black rim.

"Don't you look beautiful this morning." He inclined his head to one side. "The colour red most definitely suits you."

"Thank you."

He waved Odin from his arm and held his hand toward me.

"I've organised some breakfast for you. I took the liberty of selecting bacon. It always smells divine and will go well with the fresh bread and eggs."

"Seriously? Bacon, bread and eggs?" I near enough skipped at his side as he led me to a doorway across the hall from the lounge.

"It's all for you," he said, indicating with a tilt of his head to the steaming plate of food on the table. "I presume you must be hungry. Yesterday was quite a draining day for you."

I nodded before sitting down to eat. Paymon sat on the chair beside me.

I picked my knife from the table and stabbed one of the eggs. The creamy yolk burst into a river of yellow as it snaked its way onto my plate and pooled next to the bacon. Cutting into the egg, I scooped a quarter of it onto my fork along with some of the thick cut bacon, the edges of which were crisp. I inhaled deeply, savouring the tingle of decent food about to unleash itself on my taste buds.

Just as I was about to place the first loaded fork of food into my mouth, I realised there wasn't a plate for Paymon.

"Are you not eating?" I asked, looking away from my feast and concentrating on his bemused expression.

He laughed, leaning back in his chair. "Athena. I feed constantly with you here."

I frowned. "I meant proper food. Don't you eat?"

He shook his head. "Demons have no need to eat. I can eat, but it serves no purpose."

"Really? But bacon, you said it smelt divine. How can

anyone resist eating it?"

He laughed even louder. "You smell divine to me as well, but I doubt you would like me to eat you."

I grinned. "No, I don't think I'd taste very nice."

His laughter raised another notch, and he lifted his hand and rubbed his forehead. I quickly ate what I'd cut up, holding back a moan of pleasure as I chewed.

"You need to eat more than you did in the village. You're underweight, and you're too pale. It's too easy these days for humans to become ill and not survive. I don't want that happening to you."

"I'm not sick very often. I'm pretty healthy, considering."

Paymon lifted his hand. "Ah, that's what I mean. There should be no need for you to add the 'considering.' You need to think about what your favourite meals are, and I shall make sure you eat them." He leaned forward, his marked hand patting my arm. "I want to look after you. And as long as it is within my power, I will not deny you anything."

I stopped eating, my fork poised in mid-air as Paymon's eyes locked on mine.

I broke his stare, looking away and tearing a piece of bread from the loaf and shoving it in my mouth.

"It feels wrong, me eating whilst you just sit there," I said, covering my mouth as I chewed.

Paymon straightened his back and tapped his fingers on the table. "I can assure you I am not just sitting here. Whilst you eat, I get fed."

"My emotions?" I wiped a crust of bread through the yolk of the second egg.

He nodded. "You're enjoying your food. You're happy. It's not as strong as other emotions, but it's enough. You were very emotional last night after you went to your room."

"I had a soak in the tub. It relaxed me."

He frowned and cocked his head. "It was a strange emotion, are you sure you were just relaxing?"

I swallowed my food and nodded.

"I see you need lacing up." He dipped his chin and raised his eyebrows as he caught sight of my bare back. "Finish your breakfast and then I'll fasten it for you."

I continued eating, trying to ignore his insistent stare. He seemed as intrigued by me as I was wary of him.

"So what would you like to do today?" he asked.

I had no idea what things a demon normally did or whether Paymon would limit my free time. Was I expected to be with him all day? "What can I do?"

"Anything you want, within reason. And you must stay in the house."

I nodded, it was what I'd expected, what I'd considered last night. I was a prisoner here—this was my life now, confined to these impenetrable walls. My muscles tightened and I straightened my back. This wasn't what I wanted. And, given time, I would find a way to leave. I refused to become anyone's prisoner.

"I'll need to leave you for a while this morning, but Odin will stay with you." He looked briefly to the hallway where Odin sat preening himself.

"Where are you going?"

"Only to the village. I need to round up the girls for the Master."

"What for?"

He rubbed his forehead and sighed. "I need to put them into a trance. It will calm them and ease their worry about the ceremony tonight." He paused for a moment. "Can't have them running off at the last minute with one of the boys from the village, can I?"

I dropped my fork on the table. "You knew?"

"Of course I knew. Don't treat me like a fool." He banged his fist on the table and jerked to his feet. The demon had returned. "I knew exactly what Thomas suggested, and believe me when I say you did the right thing in not running away with him. You wouldn't have got far."

I recoiled, and placed my hand to my chest. "We might have."

"No, you wouldn't!" Paymon paced the end of the room, glancing at me intermittently. "You'd have enjoyed one night of freedom. Last night would have been a celebration of your escape with your lover. He knows of the dangers out there yet he was willing to lead you into those dangers for his own selfish desires."

"What dangers?" I turned in my chair to face him. He had all my attention. Maybe this was when I found out what had chased me all those years ago.

He returned to his chair and sat down. "The beasts that roam the land away from the village. There are many creatures eager to snatch a human and take them away to their lair and do unspeakable things to them. And there are just as many longing to tear them limb from limb and eat them."

"What sort of creatures?"

"Wolves, bears, other demons . . ." He shook his head. "As your village demon, I keep these creatures away from the village. It's surrounded by many charms and protective spells. Have you ever seen a wolf or a bear?"

"I haven't, but the men who work in the fields have."

"That's because they step out of the area of my protection when they go to the fields."

"So Thomas would have been risking his own life as well, not just mine."

Paymon reached out and patted my shoulder.

"If you had missed the Ascension Ceremony, then the miscreants would have come looking for you."

"What are they?"

He rose to his feet. "You really don't want to know."

I pushed my plate away, not willing to eat anymore. My appetite deserted me.

"Let me lace you up," he said, gesturing with his hand for me to stand.

"The miscreants, what are they?" I repeated as sure hands tugged on the laces on the back of my dress.

"They work for the Master. He has them under his control. You'll see them tonight at the ceremony."

"Are they evil?"

"Evil?" He chuckled; his breath warmed my neck, and I fought the urge to shiver.

"Some say demons are evil, Athena. I'll let you be the judge." He stepped away from me, the dress fastened, and walked toward the door. "If you've finished breakfast, perhaps you'd like to see the library?"

I nodded, rushing to catch up with him.

"It's the one room I tend to not let Odin enter," he said as he crossed the hall. "He once destroyed a favourite book of mine, *How to Tame a Wild Bird*." His ensuing laugh continued until he clicked the door handle. Stepping back, he allowed me to enter first.

I blinked several times at the darkness but didn't flinch

when Paymon shot flames across the room, lighting the strategically placed candles. It seemed I was already becoming used to his tricks.

All four walls had book shelves reaching from the floor to the ceiling, and each shelf was full. There were no spaces that I could see.

"What do you enjoy reading?" He walked into the middle of the room to a large desk piled high with even more books. "History, politics, inventions, gardening, mythology? What about fictional stories, the classics that humans fought so hard to hang on to? I have Shakespeare, Austen, Dickens."

I stood open-mouthed as I turned on the spot. My feet bounced on the carpet, and I stifled a giggle. My mouth became dry, and I felt breathless. This was amazing.

Paymon was grinning so wide that he looked fit to burst. "I would have brought you in here earlier if I'd known it would make you feel like this," he said, extending his arms toward me. "Look at you!"

I cleared my throat and stared at row upon row of books. "You mentioned that you'd like me to read to you," I said, remembering Paymon's declaration. "What do you have in mind?"

He chuckled. "My choice of reading material may not be suitable for you to read out loud. You select. I'm sure I will adore anything you read to me."

"Tell me. What do you read?"

"I have many books depicting our rise to power. The plans that were put into operation thousands of years ago. Demons have a history as well as humans. I find it fascinating learning about my past, but I'm sure you won't. And it's written in my language, not yours."

"You could teach me your language," I said, stepping over to the desk. This was an opportunity I wasn't going to miss. If I learnt to read demon language, I could read the books depicting their arrival and the book I kept hidden. Surely there'd be something in one of them about the light. There had to be. "I'd quite like to learn another language."

"Then try French or German."

I shook my head. "No, I want to learn your language. When will I ever get the chance to speak to a French or German person? But if I learn to read and speak your language, I'll be able to talk to you."

He pursed his lips. "That's a very nice gesture, but I promise you, you have no need to learn my language."

I huffed under my breath.

"Find a book, see what there is," he said.

I dawdled to the first wall of books and set about trying to find one of *his* books.

He sat on the edge of the desk, watching me for several moments before saying, "What books have you read?"

"Just an old dictionary." I ran my fingers across the spines of the books. It wasn't just the books that I was in awe of, it was the smell of the room. Old paper, glue that bound the pages together, even the tang of leather from some of the older books.

"You'd like a fictional story then, something different, something to escape into."

I shrugged. "I'd like to learn your language."

"I assure you, it would not be of any interest to you even if you could read it. Why don't you read about your history?"

Historical books sounded amazing. Gran had told me a lot about the history of mankind, but to read about it, see pictures of what she described would be opening up a whole new world to me.

I imagined myself sprawled out on my bed surrounded by numerous books, educating myself with the history of the world. "Can I take books to my room to read?"

"Of course, but you can read downstairs as well. You've no need to hide in your room."

"Are there any books about here?" I turned to face him, and expanded my sentence when he frowned. "Anything about what it was like before you all came."

"For this area?"

I nodded.

Paymon walked toward the wall opposite the door and began looking along a line of books.

"Do you even know where you are?"

"England," I said. "I was born in York."

"And where are you now? England is a significant sized country, or rather, it was before the coastline moved inland."

"I know I'm somewhere near York. Gran didn't move us far."

"You're in a wood just outside what was the village of Buttercrambe. Here." He pulled a book from the shelf and took it to the desk.

I joined him as he flicked through the pages. Once he found what he was looking for, he placed the book open on the desk.

"Here's a map of England, Scotland and Wales. This," he said, pointing to an area half way up the right-hand side of the irregular shape, "is York. Buttercrambe is just to the east."

I pulled a chair to the desk and sat down, devouring the information.

"Does this show where the sea used to be or where it is now?" I asked.

He rummaged around on the disorganised desk, finally finding a piece of discoloured paper. Quickly drawing a copy of the image on the page in the book, he shaded in the sea surrounding the land.

"This is how it was," he tapped the pencil on his drawing, "and this will be where it is now." He drew another line inside the outline of the other. "The sea covers all the low lying land that used to be around the coast. In some areas it remains the same, but people will not go back for fear of another great wave coming." He quickly shaded in the area between the old outline and his new one. "The coast is nearer to York than it was before, the river runs through it at a higher level."

I studied his drawing intently. "Will I ever be able to go back?"

Paymon shook his head. "The cities are not safe." He pushed his chair away from the table. "Not for any of us."

I frowned as he wandered away.

"Find a book, Athena, and don't take too long."

"Why's it not . . . safe?"

He was already out of the room, his shoes tapping on the wooden floor in the hall as he left me alone.

I looked at the map in the book and Paymon's drawing. Things had definitely changed—so much land had disappeared. I suspected it was the same across the whole of the world. And what did he mean that the cities weren't safe for anyone?

I turned the book to see the front cover. Simply titled *Maps of the World*, it contained a treasure of information about different countries and their climates and people. I wondered how much of it was relevant now. I flicked through the book, staring in wonder at the buildings and technology that had been prolific in various parts of the world. It was difficult to visualise a world any different to what I knew. Paymon had mentioned finding a fictional book, and as I flicked through the images on the pages in front of me, I realised that this book was as fictional to me as others would be to Paymon.

I closed the book of maps and their corresponding information before searching out one of the names he had mentioned earlier. With so many books to look through, I found it impossible to locate any of the so called classics he'd suggested. I decided to close my eyes and simply pull a book from a shelf.

The thick book that presented itself to me was an anthology of stories, fables from times gone by.

I took another lingering look around the room before blowing the candles out and heading to the living room. Paymon was sitting at his desk, writing notes at an alarmingly fast rate. I settled on the sofa and Odin fluttered into the room, silently landing next to me. He leaned against my thigh, his beard fluffing as he croaked quietly in his throat. As my confidence around him grew, so did my curiosity about his actions, and without pausing for thought, I reached out to touch him. I rubbed my finger back and forth on the top of his head, creating a ruffled hairstyle. He didn't move away or try to peck me; he turned his head sideways as if to give me a better angle. I subdued a giggle as he closed his eyes and appeared to take a deep breath.

"Most unusual," Paymon said.

I looked up to see him watching Odin and me.

"The only person he has ever let touch him is me. Seems

you have made as much an impression on Odin as you have on me." He smiled before standing. "Ahhh, I see you've selected a book."

I held the book so he could see the cover.

Paymon clicked his finger, and Odin immediately flew onto his shoulder.

"I need to go to the village to compel Hannah and Julie," he said, his words a whisper as he spoke to Odin. "You will stay with Athena. Perhaps she'll read to you while I'm gone." He strode across the room and out into the hall.

I shuffled after him, undecided on whether I wanted to be left alone in this strange house. When he opened the door to the darkness outside, a chilling cold swept inside. I shivered, backing away from the icy blast. Paymon turned his head slightly, gave me a crooked grin and then pulled the hood of the cloak over his head. The door slammed shut and every candle in the hall extinguished.

CHAPTER 7

CURIOSITY

I STARTLED AT THE SUDDEN LOSS OF LIGHT. IT DIDN'T frighten me—I was more than used to the dark—but I couldn't help but wonder what had caused it. Had Paymon somehow extinguished the candles? And if so, why? To frighten me, to show he was still in charge and powerful? I didn't need his reminder.

Odin squawked, and I followed his call back to the room. As soon as I stepped inside, he flew toward me and landed on my shoulder. I tipped my head away from him.

"What's wrong? Do you not like it when he's gone?"

He croaked in his throat and padded his feet on my shoulder.

"Hey," I turned to give him a sideways stare, "you'll have to get down if you keep doing that." He remained still but continued with his throat noises.

I bit down a smile at the unexpected situation I was now in. This was the perfect opportunity to try and discover more.

I crossed the room to Paymon's desk, my focus on the drawers. Odin dropped onto the mess of papers and busied himself pecking and playing with a pencil. I lifted the lit lantern from the top of the desk and lowered it to the drawers.

The first drawer was full of papers, some with symbols surrounded by writing. I took the top piece of paper and held it near the lantern. I couldn't make anything out—the writing was impossible to read. It was the same strange arrangement of letters that were in the book I'd brought with me.

"Stupid demon language." I didn't just want to know what was written in my book; I wanted to know what he was writing and researching. Perhaps his notes would give me information about this life I'd been traded in to, and I could gain some understanding of what lay ahead.

The pentacle symbol, the same as the mark on my hand, was drawn in various places on the page, with other symbols joining it: a spiral, and what looked like a double-headed axe. I turned the paper over, eagerly searching for anything that made sense. There wasn't.

"Stupid, stupid language." I placed the paper back on top of the other haphazardly arranged ones.

The next drawer proved to be just as messy as the first. My heart sunk, and I slammed the drawer shut. There was nothing here that could help me.

"Time to explore." I smoothed my dress with my hands and walked to the door. "Are you coming?" I said, looking back at Odin as he threw a pencil across the room. "You look bored. Why don't you show me around?"

He flapped his wings and squawked at me but didn't move from the desk.

"I'll explore by myself then." I headed into the hall, and

peered past the library doorway. "What's down here?" I followed a narrow corridor that ran to the back of the house. Odin must have changed his mind as he appeared behind me, bouncing along the wooden floor. I smiled, enjoying his company, and held the lantern high, lighting the unknown.

The corridor turned to a sharp right under the stairs, before a further door presented itself. But my attention was drawn to a brightness shining through the window to my left. Through the panes of glass was a rosebush with dark red flowers. It was highlighted in a ray of light. The blooms ranged from small and tight to large and full. I'd never seen anything so beautiful. I pressed my nose against the cold glass eager to take in every detail of the lit bush. I didn't move until the glass became misty from my warm breath. This must be the rosebush from which Paymon had selected the rose for me and where he had got the petals for my bath. It was also the beam of light that I'd seen when I had first arrived at the house. But why hadn't I seen it before, from the staircase above that overlooked the same courtyard?

I stared upward through the window, following the seemingly random beam of light. I had no doubt that this was a spell of Paymon's—parting the darkness, like he did over the fields. No other plants grew in the courtyard, just the solitary rosebush, but there was an archway leading out of the stone walled courtyard. I couldn't see what lay beyond.

Odin cawed at my feet, and I lowered the lantern before stepping to the door in front of me. There was a key in the lock, and with a quick turn, the mechanism clicked. I wriggled the handle and edged the door open.

"Wow . . ." My eyes widened and a rush of heat radiated through my chest. I bounced on my feet as I looked around. It was a kitchen: a huge kitchen, dimly lit by three hanging lanterns. A large wooden table that near enough filled the room was in the middle. A cast iron stove, one like we had in the main hall in the village, filled a wide chimney breast. The fire in the stove burnt brightly, throwing its impressive heat into the room.

There was no sign of any pots or pans, even though the smell of bacon still hung in the air. I wandered further into the room, moving clockwise around the table. Odin fluttered onto the far corner of the table but didn't make any vocal sounds as he stared at the floor.

"What is it?" I asked, unable to see what he was staring at.

A soft snore sounded from the area of the room where Odin was, and I stilled. My fixed smiled slipped away and I held my breath. My gaze flitted between Odin and the corner of the room where the snoring came from. I tightened my shoulders and approached the area Odin was staring at. When I lowered my lantern the light illuminated a white creature in a basket on the floor. I cocked my head sideways, trying to make out what it was. Was it a large dog, curled up, asleep? My heart raced at my unexpected discovery, but then I frowned. There was no hair on its body—just deathly white skin covering angular bones. Whatever it was let out another soft snore, and then uncurled from its sleeping position. The head of whatever was in the basket was covered in jet black hair.

It wasn't a dog.

I swallowed, but my throat was dry. Whatever it was, I didn't want to wake it.

I stepped backward on my tiptoes, and moved with a deliberate slow pace, not taking my eyes off the basket. I froze when my leg brushed against an object, and waited for the inevitable noise that would follow. As soon as the deafening crash sounded out, I sprang into action. I shot toward the doorway that led back to the hall, but tripped over the bucket and mop I'd knocked over.

Odin squawked, and from the urgency of his call, I had no need to look toward the basket.

A sinister hiss exploded from the corner of the kitchen, and I scrambled to the door on my hands and knees. My heart thumped wildly as I caught a glimpse of movement from the corner of the room. I staggered to my feet, but a sickening thud made me turn my head. Crouched on skinny feet, with razor-sharp angled bones and lanky fingers scratching the table top, was the creature. Sunken eyes shone through a layer of long, black hair, and it hissed. I whimpered and turned my attention back to my escape.

Odin took to the air and created so much noise that I could hardly hear the snarling that came from the awakened beast.

I reached for the doorknob, but my sweaty hand slipped on the metal. As I dared to glance back into the kitchen, I screamed.

The creature was advancing across the table. The glow from the fire reflected in its eyes. I saw pain, anger, and death. My death.

It crouched low on its back legs, knees bent, prepared to launch itself at me.

Odin attacked—a flurry of squawks and black feathers, mixed with snarls and pale, waving arms.

I wiped my sweaty hands on my dress, focused on the door, and reached for the handle again. This time I kept hold of it, turned it, and pulled as hard as I could. Amid all the squawking and snarling, the door swung open.

"Odin, quick!" I called as I slipped through the opening.

He left his attack and flew to the door, flying past me and into the hallway.

The creature sprung from the table, arms reaching for me. The door blocked its body but not its hands. Claw-like fingers stretched over my hold on the handle. Blood sprung from the puncture wounds. I pulled the door hard, trapping its arm against the edge, but it still didn't release me. A loud hiss, a pull on the door by my attacker, and the kitchen was in full view again—so was the creature. It bared its sharp teeth and tightened its hold on my hand.

I screamed and attempted to release the door handle to shake its hand off mine, but its hold was too tight. I scratched wildly at it, but it wouldn't let go. Wide-eyed and furious, it took a step toward me, snarling louder than any beast I'd ever heard.

Then, with no warning, it released me. It turned away.

I didn't wait to see what else it was going to do, and with a snarl of my own, I pulled the door shut and locked it with the key.

I stumbled away from the door and leaned against the wall. My heart was racing and my chest heaving. I lifted a trembling hand to my forehead and tipped my head backward. Tears welled up behind my eyes as I tried to make sense of what had just happened. Were there any other dangerous creatures hiding in other rooms? And why hadn't Paymon told me about what he kept in the kitchen?

As my breathing became steady, sharp stings of pain pricked my hand. I was bleeding. The creature had sliced my skin several times with its claws. I needed to stem the blood, bandage my hand.

"What the hell was that creature, and why was it in the kitchen?" I snapped at Odin who was nonchalantly preening himself on the bannister. He offered no response.

I slumped onto the step at the bottom of the stairs and yanked at the hem of my dress. Within moments I had a strip of material to bandage my bleeding hand. I didn't move into the room for a more comfortable seat. I chose to stay where I was and wait for Paymon in the gloom he'd created when he left. As soon as he came through the door he could see what had happened.

How long would he be?

What would he say to explain the creature?

I huffed and folded my arms, staring at the doorway. Highly alert, each creak, each small sound made my chest tighten and my heart thud erratically. Time drifted on, and I shifted on the step, my bones aching from sitting on the hard wooden ledge.

Odin cawed loudly, several times in succession, and within moments, Paymon's hooded figure entered the hall.

He looked at me and frowned before removing his cloak and hanging it up. Flames shot from his hands to light the candles in the sconces.

"Why are you sitting in the dark?"

I shrugged before responding, "Someone made the candles go out when they left. And I'm sitting here because I'm waiting for you."

He smiled, but the expression was quickly gone as he spotted my hand. He crossed the space between us with two long strides. "What happened?"

"I found the kitchen."

His black eyes widened, and he drew in a sharp breath. "You're lucky to be alive."

I jumped to my feet. "What the hell have you got in there? You gave me no warning about exploring, and you certainly never told me to keep out of the kitchen. Don't you think that would have been a sensible thing to do considering what's in there?"

Paymon huffed before walking to the lounge.

I followed. "I mean, what is it?"

"Sit down, Athena, and I shall explain. I can bathe your injury first, or would you like to know what attacked you?"

"I want to know what it is," I said, sitting on the edge of the sofa.

Paymon paced the room, blocking the fire each time he passed it.

"She is an infernal," he eventually said as he stopped at the side of the fireplace.

The creature was female?

"I should have told you about Bia, but I didn't expect you to be running into her so quickly."

"Bia? It has a name? Is she some sort of pet?"

Paymon chuckled, his black mood lifting slightly.

"I suppose you could call her my pet, she has lived all her life with me—the one below and the one above. She is an infernal, the lowest of the lowest creatures from our world. They hate everyone other than their own kind but harbour the most hate for demons."

"And humans," I added, glancing at my hand.

"She will be punished for attacking you." He tapped his fingers on the mantelpiece.

"But you must have known what she'd do if she saw me.

If she hates demons even more than humans, then why keep her? Surely she'll attack you."

Paymon grinned. "She is compelled not to attack me. She is usually quite docile."

"Docile, you're kidding me."

"No, actually. I'm not." He stepped away from the fire and rubbed his hands together, smiling. "If she wasn't compelled, she would be a danger to both of us, not just you. She is a form of vampire, a primitive one, but still, a vampire. She would not have been trying to attack you to kill you, she would have been trying to immobilise you so she could latch onto you to feed." He paused. "And then she'd kill you. You're lucky she was under my compelment. She would have been slower than normal because of it. Usually they are very fast."

My mind was filled with the image of Bia when she attacked me. She was so angry and wild, and that was under Paymon's compelment. I didn't ever want to see her when she was free from his control.

"She might have got me if Odin hadn't attacked her. I was lucky he was with me."

Paymon turned to look at Odin who had made his way behind me onto the sofa.

"He is a very intelligent bird," he said. "Now, are you going to let me look at what she's done to your hand?"

I lifted a single eyebrow. "Seriously? That's all you have to say? I could have been killed."

"But you weren't."

"And that's it?" I searched his face for any understanding of how dangerous it had been to have a creature like that in the kitchen.

He frowned. He obviously didn't see her as a danger.

"What do you want me to say? If you want an apology, you'll be waiting a long time. You shouldn't have gone snooping around the first opportunity you got. I know I never told you not to, but honestly, what did you expect to find?"

I pulled my legs underneath me. "I was curious, and you should have warned me."

"If I'd known you were going to go into the kitchen then I would have."

I folded my arms across my chest and huffed.

Paymon headed to the door. "I shall fetch some boiled water to clean your hand. I'll not be long. Do you think you can stay where you are until I return?"

I didn't turn to face him as I nodded my response.

"Stupid demon," I said as Odin hopped next to me on the sofa. He repeated what he had done the other day and leaned against my leg, croaking quietly in his throat. "And thank you," I said as I rubbed his feathered beard. "You saved me from her. I probably wouldn't be here if you'd not attacked her."

Paymon's booming voice carried from the hall and into the room. "And you will behave around Athena. No more attacks, you will treat her with respect!"

I sprung from the sofa when the white creature fell into the room. As she attempted to stand, Paymon kicked her in the back and she stumbled forward again.

"Athena is my wife," he shouted, "and you will never harm her again. Understand?" He placed a bowl of water on the sideboard, but never took his eyes off Bia.

She slowly crawled to her feet, watching Paymon as if fearing another attack. Her shoulders were hunched, and for the first time, I noticed just how tiny she was. She only reached the height of Paymon's thigh. When she turned to face me, her large, dark eyes widened.

"Welcome," she said, the word soft, soothing, and nothing like I expected after hearing her spits and snarls earlier. "My Master tells me you are to be trusted, you are his chosen one." Her pale grey lips moved as she spoke, showing a top and bottom row of many tiny pointed teeth. Beyond the teeth was another black void. She had no discernible features that enabled me to recognise her as a female. Her chest was flat, and she wore a simple black cloth around her waist. Paymon pushed her in the back with his foot again, and she stumbled nearer to me.

"I promise not to attack you again," she said as Paymon rounded on her.

I cringed and leaned backward.

She shuddered before hunching her shoulders even further forward and dipping her head to the side. "My Master's last chosen one was evil."

With no warning at all, Paymon kicked her again, but with much more force than earlier. She fell to the floor but urgently attempted to scramble to her feet. Before she could stand, Paymon grabbed one of her skeletal legs.

"Watch your mouth. You're nothing but vermin!" he snarled, lifting her from the ground.

"Master, please, I was only fearing another chosen one like your last. She hated me, please, release me, pleeeeease!"

Her wail was long and loud, and when it finished, she tried desperately to escape from Paymon. He sneered, shaking her as she hung upside down.

"Paymon," I implored. "Please let her go."

"She needs to be reminded of who is in control around here." He shook her again, and her arms flailed in the air. "Do

I need to remind you?" he roared at her.

"Master, please!"

He grabbed one of her swinging arms and released her leg.

As he stared at her, a slow smirk spread from one side of his mouth to the other.

"I should have left you under-land, thrown you to the proper vampires, let them feast on your rancid blood."

He laughed, but the sound made me shiver, and I took a step toward the door, ready to flee the room.

He clicked his fingers, a usually harmless gesture. Harmless from anyone but Paymon, a fire demon.

The scream that erupted from Bia reminded me of a child crying. A cold sweat erupted all over my skin, and my mouth dropped open.

"No!" I shrieked as I saw the cause for her scream. The hand holding her was engulfed in flames. Fire didn't bother Paymon, but it obviously bothered Bia. She wriggled frantically and continued to scream. Her flesh was burning where Paymon held her, the putrid stench quickly filling the room.

"Paymon!" I shouted, crossing the room in fast strides. "Stop it! Stop it, right now!"

"She needs to be taught a lesson!"

"Not like this. If you keep torturing her, I'll go to the Ascension Ceremony and willingly go to the Master. Leave her alone!"

My words must have hit a nerve, perhaps the bursts of kindness I had witnessed from him suddenly rose to the surface, because the flames extinguished, and he released her. She dropped to the floor and scurried to my feet.

"You'll not be so disloyal again, will you?" he snarled at

her.

Her bony fingers wrapped around my ankles. "Thank you, thank you, thank you," she whispered.

Paymon sighed before glaring at me. Black eyes, yet again, focused on me.

"Why did you ask me to stop? She attacked you earlier—she would have killed you if she had the chance. You just saved her miserable life."

"She didn't deserve to be set alight," I said, glancing at the sniffling creature at my feet.

"And did you seriously think I believed your little tantrum about going to the Master?" He crossed the room toward the fireplace before shooting several orange flames into the grate.

"It made you stop," I said as Bia released my ankles and straightened.

He spun around. "Athena, I wouldn't allow you to go to the Master. We are married, or did you forget that? You belong here with me. You won't be going anywhere."

Bia took a few steps away from me before smiling, a strange gesture considering what had just happened.

After a small bow in my direction, she turned to Paymon, her smile turning into a grimace. "May I return to the kitchen?"

"I will punish you again if you don't behave. Understand?"

She nodded.

"And I won't only set fire to you next time, I'll throw you out of the house."

She stilled, her hands wringing together as he spoke to her.

Paymon raised his brow as if waiting for her to react.

"Will you call me when food is required by your chosen

one?" she said, dipping her head.

"Yes. But get out of my sight." He pointed to the doorway. "I don't want to see you again today."

Bia bowed deeply at Paymon and then left the room. I grimaced as I caught sight of the arm that he had burnt. Her pale skin was blistered and black, a marked contrast to the whiteness of the rest of her body.

I turned to Paymon, still angry with him. "You didn't tell me she cooked my meals."

"You didn't think I prepared your breakfast this morning, did you?" He sank into his usual chair and leaned back.

My silence confirmed my answer. I had thought that he had cooked my breakfast. The gesture had reassured me that he cared.

"Bia keeps things tidy around here," he said, leaning forward and placing his hands together. He looked like he was praying, which was kind of ironic. "She will change the sheets on your bed, wash your clothes, cook for you—"

"Put rose petals in my bath water," I added as sarcastically as I could manage.

"No, she didn't do that. I did. It seems you still doubt my intentions. You need to try harder to trust me."

I sat on the sofa, not interested in his pleas for my trust. Trust had to be earned, and he wasn't doing a great job of it.

"The light, on the rosebush?" It had puzzled me from the moment I saw it. "Why can't I see it from the stairs?"

"You can, but only when I part the darkness. It takes a lot of my energy to part the sky over the fields, to keep enchantments in place to protect the village. I tend to light the rosebush every other day. Although now you are here, I should be able to keep it constantly lit."

"Because I feed you with my emotions."

Paymon nodded.

"Why did you threaten to throw Bia out of the house?" I asked, twiddling with the cuff on my sleeve. "That's not a threat. You'd give her freedom."

Paymon rubbed his forehead. "Freedom, yes, but you have to understand that every infernal is obsessed with owning their own house. They love cleanliness and order. Everything has a place, everything is clean, tidy, sorted. She hates my desk." He grinned at the untidy arrangement of papers on top of it. "She would also be branded. It is the worst thing I could do to her."

"Worse than death?" I turned my hand, seeing my own branding—the one that tied me to Paymon in marriage.

Paymon caught my action and closed his eyes momentarily, as if realising the truth of what he said. Once he opened them, he raised his own hand and showed me his identical mark.

"Sometimes a branding is worn with pride and love." He rose from his chair, collected the bowl of water that he'd brought in earlier, and came to sit next to me on the sofa. "But to brand an infernal is a sign of ownership, and no infernal wants to be owned."

A heavy silence hung between us. He obviously viewed the marriage branding completely differently than I did.

"Do all demons have infernals?"

"No, not all of us. Many escaped when we came above land."

He swiftly grabbed my hand and removed my makeshift bandage. He tutted when he saw the deep nail marks that Bia had left me with.

"So where are they now?"

"There have been many sightings of them in the abandoned cities. Another reason why we encouraged the humans to move to the safety of a village."

Heated fingers brushed against my hand as he dabbed the blood with the cloth that had been soaking in the bowl of water. Its warmth instantly soothed the sharp stings that had existed since Bia's attack.

"I located this house and set about finding my villagers," he continued. "I offered them protection from the wild creatures many of them had seen. The city is no place for anyone these days. The homes where the humans lived serve no purpose now. Nothing works in them, and the people have no resources to fix or create replacements. Disease killed many, but so did the infernals. Your grandmother made a good decision when she moved here with you."

"Her decision certainly worked out well for you." I controlled my sarcasm as best I could, but I was sure Paymon noticed.

He didn't shift his gaze from my hand as he answered. "Yes, yes it did."

His fingers continued to generate an incredible amount of heat, soothing the sting as he worked systematically around my hand, inspecting it from all angles.

"Would you care to read to me when I have cleaned your hand? If not for me then perhaps for Odin. He likes to listen to stories, and I'm sure he'll be very keen to hear you read."

I turned to Odin. He was perched on the back of the sofa overseeing Paymon's ministrations. "How can I refuse?"

"Somehow, I think you could, very easily."

The atmosphere changed, and for a split second I relaxed.

But as Paymon finished cleaning my hand, the tense atmosphere returned.

I remembered his visit to the village. "How were Hannah and Julie?"

"Not as frightened as they were when I arrived," he said, reaching for the book I'd brought into the room earlier.

"Is compelling them the only way to help them?" I shifted on the sofa, uneasy with the enthusiasm Paymon showed about his compelment.

Paymon narrowed his gaze. "I've noticed you don't like being compelled. You even asked me not to do it during the marriage ceremony. It would have helped, you know."

I shook my head. "I want to feel my own thoughts, control myself. Not have you or anyone else control me."

"Well, it's a very useful way to alleviate someone's fears, which is why I compelled Hannah and Julie. Unfortunately, it will leave them as soon as the carriage arrives at the ceremony tonight."

Having never seen what happened at the ceremony, I was more than willing to miss this one as well. How would I react to seeing my friends dragged away?

"I will be with you, Athena. You'll come to no harm. There'll be no need to be afraid. Now," he patted the book in his hands, "I would like to sit in my usual chair whilst you read to me."

He handed me the book then moved to the single chair. Shifting his legs to the side, he pointed at the floor.

"You can sit there," he instructed.

I followed the line of his arm and then glanced at Paymon. "On the floor?"

"Yes, Athena. At my feet."

CHAPTER 8

TERROR

W ITH HEAVY, SHUFFLING FOOTSTEPS, I WANDERED to the window that overlooked the distant village. Through the thin veil of darkness, it shone like a beckoning light, offering a welcoming and friendly arrival. I sighed—it didn't offer either of those to me now, and I doubted that it ever would.

I stared out of the window for a long time, not really seeing the village, just gazing, unfocused, with my hands clasped tightly together. What would happen tonight? What caused the noises I was so used to hearing but never witnessed?

It was only when Paymon knocked on my door that I moved.

"Time to go," he said as he stepped into the room. "We don't keep the Master waiting."

I was unwilling to rush to a ceremony that I'd feared for years. The fact that I wasn't to be taken away didn't do anything to slow my racing heart or calm my fluttering nerves.

Paymon followed me along the corridor and down the stairs. He didn't speak to me, probably well aware of my heightened emotions. He insisted I wore his cloak over my dress for warmth as we prepared to leave the house. He wore a thinner looking one, reassuring me that he didn't need the cloak for warmth—he was already running at a temperature far above what was necessary to withstand the cold.

Odin flew above us as we walked to the village. He joined a few other ravens as they swooped and glided across the sky.

"Does he have a family?" I squinted into the dark, trying to follow his movements.

"Probably. But his real family is here, isn't it? You and me. He views himself as one of us, not a bird."

As we neared the edge of the village, Paymon's stride became unsteady.

"Why are you limping?" I asked. His eyes informed me he was full, therefore strong.

Paymon scowled before replying, "What would the villagers say if I seemed to have been miraculously cured of my limp? I can't have them sensing the importance of your presence to me. It would show a weakness, and that's something I will never let them see."

He viewed the village with narrowed eyes before pulling the hood of his cape over his head.

"You never did tell me what caused you to limp."

"No, I don't believe I did."

"Will you tell me?"

He turned his head to face me. "Not tonight. There will be more than enough happening to keep that curious mind of yours occupied."

We stopped walking when we reached the centre of the

village. There was no one around, not even at the fire, which was usually overseen by the older men. It was only just alight, the embers coughing out their last remnant of heat and struggling to glow.

I swallowed nervously as the people drifted from their homes into the central area of the village. Faces I'd known all my life stared back at me, fear etched into their darkened, dirty features. My heart was screaming, telling me to insist they understood that I was still the same person they had always known, that I'd never change. But as I glanced at my luxurious dress and shoes, I saw what they did. I was married to the village demon, dressed in clothes they could only ever dream of. I was clean, my face free of smudges of ash and dirt. I'd already changed. I wasn't one of them anymore.

"Don't let them worry you," Paymon said, bending to whisper the words in my ear. "Their emotions run higher than normal tonight. They fear everything about this ceremony."

As if to wake them from their trance, Paymon clicked his fingers. He blew the resulting flame into the dying fire, and it roared to life, burning brightly and lighting the open area in its warming glow.

The villagers were silent. Usually they chatted, joked and laughed, but not even Paymon's trick of relighting the fire stirred them to speak.

"When does it all start?" I whispered, not wanting to break the silence that surrounded us.

Paymon lifted his gaze to the sky. "They are almost here."

He took a few steps forward, nearer to the fire, and began to chant in his language. Everyone in the village froze, like pillars of stone, and I cautiously wiggled my fingers before taking a step closer to Paymon. Whatever he had done to the villagers hadn't affected me.

I took the opportunity to look through the extended family I'd always been welcomed into, searching out an all too familiar set of eyes. They were the ones I'd fallen in love with, the ones I'd given myself to. Thomas's eyes. But I couldn't see him.

Paymon's chant became louder, and as he held his hands out to his sides, both Hannah and Julie walked from the communal hall and into the clearing. They were dressed, as Paymon had said, in white flowing dresses. The thin material wrapped around their bodies before floating to the ground. They each carried a single candle, shielding it with their hands from the blustery breeze that drifted through the village. The gusts of wind caught their hair, loose and teased into curls that skimmed their backs. Each of them had markings on their faces, a band of black running across their eyes from one side of their faces to the other. Above their noses was a thumb print in the same smudging of black—this continued along their noses to the very tip. I stared, seeing the design as a symbol of the cross or a beast with wings—I couldn't decide. But the strangest thing about them was the way they walked; unhurried, lethargic, looking straight ahead but not focusing on anything. They were under Paymon's compelment. Was that the reason Bia was so calm this afternoon? She'd moved in exactly the same way. Had Paymon strengthened his compelment over her? I screwed my nose up, more certain than ever that I would never willingly let him compel me.

Once the girls had stopped where Paymon wanted them, near to the fire—near enough to feel its heat, but not to burn—his chanting stopped.

He turned to face me, his eyes alive with what I assumed

was excitement. I looked away, hating that the people's fears were a feast to him, one that made him strong and increased his power.

"Don't turn away from me, Athena. You need to accept what I am, what I do, not hide from the truth."

I lifted my gaze and narrowed my eyes. Accept what he was? Never. He didn't belong here, none of them did. This was our world, not theirs. I lifted my head to the blackened sky above us, wishing more than anything that I could see the stars. If I could see the stars, I'd make a wish on every single one of them, beg them to end this miserable life we all had to endure. And I'd wish for all the demons to disappear back to below, or even better, that the light would kill them, shrivel them up, burn them, whatever it was they couldn't stand.

"They're so close," Paymon said. Lifting his nose into the air, he inhaled deeply. "I can smell them."

The atmosphere became thick, touched with a sickly sweet aroma—a smell I couldn't identify. The trees ceased their gentle sway in the breeze, and the silence yawned before us with a deafening urgency. The air hung with unpalatable foreboding, a sense of what was to come—the anticipation of evil arriving in the village.

A distant rumble gradually increased in volume. Beating hooves, shouts and howls of laughter disrupted the stillness. I looked to Hannah, dressed in her virginal white gown, and was met by bright, shiny, fear-filled eyes. She may have been under Paymon's compelment, but her fear shone from within. My own fear held me in a cocoon, a trance of unplaced calmness.

As the approaching noise became deafening, Paymon grabbed my hand. Warmth charged across the flesh of my palm when he tightened his fingers. He stepped in front of me as an unkindness of ravens burst into the clearing. Their wings beat furiously as they circled above the fire, squawking and screeching.

Their unholy noise was quickly drowned out by four large horses, blacker than the sky that surrounded us, as they charged out of the forest. Behind them was a small carriage, pulled along so fast it threatened to overturn on every bump in the uneven ground. Paymon stood still as they crashed past us, but the rest of the villagers ran and hid—all except Hannah and Julie who remained frozen in place.

"Move!" I shouted as the horses thundered toward them.

"They can't," Paymon said. "The Master's power has already caught them."

A shrill noise drew my attention to the back of the carriage. A tall female was laughing, a red cloak billowing behind her as her white hair whipped about her head. The lanterns that lit the carriage accentuated the woman's wild features as she clung to a high rail that ran around the top of it. She never blinked, and I was sure, even from this distance, that her eyes were red. She wasn't a demon—she was something else.

The carriage came to a sudden stop, and the horses reared onto their hind legs. The mysterious looking female continued to cackle manically. As she jumped from her high vantage position, her cloak unfurled behind her, and she landed gracefully on the ground. With her sinister red eyes fixed on Paymon, she walked toward him. She moved with a grace that didn't befit her crazy, manic expression, and I shrunk behind Paymon, wanting to tuck myself into the darkness of his cloak.

"Well, well, well, Paymon," she said, her voice smooth, sweet and sultry.

"Livia." Paymon nodded his head in response.

"So, you've selected a wife after all these years?" Her gaze flickered to me.

Paymon nodded once again. "I have."

"Who'd have thought? Paymon and a human."

She moved, without noise and without warning, beside me in an instant. Fear crashed through me, a fear even stronger than the one I'd had when I had first met Paymon. Her deathly-cold fingers touched my skin. Ghostly hands drew my hair away from my neck. Desire glowed in her fiery eyes as she closed in until her nose pressed against my skin. I wanted to run, but my legs wouldn't move. I whimpered as she inhaled deeply. She pulled my hair tight, forcing me to twist, exposing my neck to her, and then licked my skin from collarbone to jaw. A soft purr swept from her throat.

"Livia!" Paymon spun around, his eyes wide, black. "Step away!"

She huffed but didn't move.

"Now!"

I was released, and immediately reached for Paymon. He held my arm, keeping me upright, but didn't take his eyes off Livia.

She kicked at the dry earth and sauntered back to the carriage. Leaning on the side of it, she inspected her nails.

"Only two for me to take back to our Master?" She nodded in the direction of Hannah and Julie. "He will be disappointed, Paymon."

"His greed for all the women turning twenty-one has depleted the village," Paymon said bitterly. "What does he expect?"

"He can have any woman he desires." Livia stopped

picking her nails and viewed Hannah and Julie.

"He desires too many."

"What he wants, he gets."

"A child by a union with a human? It has never worked and never will."

I listened, once again privy to an exchange between creatures that knew more than me. So the Master wanted children with a human. Was that why the women were selected for him? I swallowed hard, realising what my life would have become with him. A breeding machine disguised as a wife.

"His seed lies within his selected wives." She straightened and glared at Paymon. "He has two spawn expected over the coming months."

I held my breath at the confirmation of my thoughts.

Paymon shrugged. "That is if they survive the birth. No child has ever lived more than a few minutes, and all the women have died."

I tightened my hold on Paymon. I'd wanted to learn more about the demons, understand how they lived, and know what my life would have been if I'd not chosen to marry Paymon. The facts were horrendous. Not only would I have been married, raped and impregnated with the Master's child, I would also die whilst giving birth.

"How many attempts have failed?" Paymon asked.

Livia hissed and stepped up to Paymon. "Are you challenging our Master?"

Paymon didn't flinch. "Your unrequited love blinds you to all sense. I am not challenging our Master, only questioning his robust selection of young women from the villages."

"It's a challenge!" She moved her face against Paymon's. They stood nose to nose. I slipped behind Paymon, not wanting to be anywhere near the angry female.

He snarled. "Step back, Livia. I may be old, but I still have my powers."

Livia sneered but stepped away before turning her eyes, as red as the roses in Paymon's courtyard, to me. "So, this pretty one is yours? The ceremony complete?"

I nodded as Paymon answered. I didn't want any confusion about my category. I was married to Paymon. I was not going away with her. I was staying here.

"Yes," Paymon said, "and if you were a demon, you would have no need to ask." His gaze followed Livia's stroll to my side. "My scent is all over her, my blood runs with hers."

Livia grabbed my hand, wrapping my wrist in a vice-like grip. I squirmed, trying to alleviate the pressure of her hold, but she only gripped me tighter. She held the healing scar across my palm to her nose and inhaled deeply.

"Fresh." She dropped my hand and glared at Paymon. "A last minute decision?"

"I selected Athena many years ago, not that it's any business of yours." Paymon near enough growled. "But the timing to seal our union was only justifiable recently."

Her brow lifted before she stalked toward the carriage. "Saving the best for yourself?"

"No, not at all." Paymon refused to look away from her. I tried to work out the powers at work between them. They obviously knew each other, and Paymon didn't seem intimidated by her. But he was a demon, and even though he was old, he was powerful, and she'd stepped away as soon as he threatened her.

"Your classification, if she wasn't yours?" Livia spun on the spot, her white hair falling perfectly as she stilled.

"Marriage."

She hissed and sank into a crouch that could only be described as one an animal would make before killing its prey. Her blood-red eyes fixed on me once more, and I whimpered as two sharp fangs became visible at the side of her mouth.

"Enough!" Paymon bellowed, stepping between us, shielding me from her.

She either didn't hear him or ignored him. Her advance was slow, predatory.

"Do not make me kill you, Livia." He pointed a finger at her. "You forget whose presence you are in."

She growled before straightening up. As I peered around Paymon's tall figure, she flicked her lustrous hair behind her head, her gaze still on me.

"Do not forget that the demons saved your kind, and we can just as easily destroy you. Do you understand?"

She didn't respond, but her intense gaze switched to Paymon. Was Paymon's threat enough to make her back down? Why did he have the upper hand? Faced with Livia by myself, I had no doubt that this meeting would have ended very differently.

"Let me put this another way," Paymon sneered. "I will kill you if you threaten Athena again."

Her mouth pulled into a pout, and she moved to the back of the carriage. I didn't shift my attention away from her, and my mouth dropped open as she leapt from the ground onto the top of the carriage in one smooth movement.

She stamped her foot, and as if breaking a trance, moans and sobs sprung from inside the carriage. White clothed arms reached out into empty air from a foot-wide barred opening at the back.

It was then that I understood. The carriage was a prison on wheels. Girls were locked away, trapped, on their way to the Master.

A coldness swept over me, chilling the air around me even more. My mouth was dry, and my stomach twisted with a new fear.

Livia laughed, a sinister edge to her high-pitched trill. "They would have been your companions on the journey to the Master," she said, her attention back on me. "Care to join them?"

I shook my head, grabbing hold of Paymon's cloak. Ridiculous as it was, he was the only person I trusted at the moment. This is what he had saved me from.

"We keep them chained. It helps remind them of where they are heading," Livia said, her voice now monotonous, bored.

"How . . . how many?"

"Six feeders." She stamped her foot again before glancing at Hannah and Julie who were still standing completely still. They should have been shuddering with fear and the cold— their thin dresses offered no protection against the bitter nip of the air. "Another feeder and a servant here?" she asked.

Paymon nodded.

"Lanim, Lucan!" Livia shouted, although her attention was on Hannah and Julie.

The sweet scent that had accompanied the carriage's arrival grew in strength and became pungent, sickly. I leaned against Paymon, steadying myself from a sudden weakness. Livia laughed again and looked toward the front of the carriage. Two large black shadows slid from the high driver's seat and onto the ground. Crossing the dry earth like a liquid, fluid and quick, I wouldn't have known they were there if it hadn't been for the moans and high-pitched wails accompanying their otherwise silent journey. Paymon manoeuvred me in front of him, pulled me against his chest, and wrapped his arms around me.

"Don't watch," he said, resting his hand on the back of my head and gently pushing my face onto his cloak.

But I needed to see what was happening. I wanted to understand exactly what I'd been saved from. I turned my head sideward and watched, hypnotised, as one pool of liquid travelled to Hannah's feet, the other to Julie's. Blackness climbed into the air behind each girl and then morphed into the most grotesque creatures I had ever seen. My stomach flipped, tightened, and threatened to spill the contents of this afternoon's meal. It should have been me in a white dress, under the Master's spell. I should have been standing with Hannah and Julie. One of those creatures should have been behind me, swallowing me into its terrorising pit of darkness. I glanced back to the carriage as Livia jumped to the ground, and I once again caught sight of the arms of the girls trapped. All this had been waiting for me.

But what shocked me the most was that Myrtle and my gran knew this happened. Why did they allow it? Why didn't they save the girls? We were young, many of us innocent. The life that awaited all of us when we turned twenty-one was horrendous. Why did no one stop it?

A moment of clarity swept over me as I realised what Gran had done. In making the deal with Paymon, she had saved me from this. She had stopped it for one girl at least. She stopped it from happening to me. My eyes glossed over with tears. Did she sacrifice herself as part of that deal as well? Is that why Paymon killed her? Did she promise me to Paymon in exchange for her life?

I swallowed a shaky breath and turned back to the creatures behind Hannah and Julie. My muscles trembled and gave way to defined shaking. Paymon's hold on me tightened, offering reassurance. I should have turned away from the evil creatures, but they transfixed me. They towered above the girls. Resembling humans in their overall shape, their faces had no discernible features—no eyes, just deep, black holes where their cheeks should have been. Their foreheads were wide and long, continuing down the front of their faces. I saw no mouth, though the creatures had ears, and both of them wore several hooped piercings through the lobes.

Loud, high-pitched screeches rang around the clearing as they lifted their arms away from their bodies. Dull, dirty, leather looking membranes unfurled between their arms and waists. And as they wrapped their arms around the girls, they became encased in the rotting black skin. The noise the creatures emitted reached an even higher ear-hurting level.

Then silence.

As quickly as the imposing figures had formed into physical creatures, they shrank to the ground into pools of black liquid. Hannah and Julie dissolved with them. Horrified, my shaking increased. The black shadowy pools crept across the ground before slithering around the wheels of the carriage and onto the top of it. Two loud thuds and then screams came from the enclosed prison before the black masses shrank away and moved to their original positions at the front of the carriage.

The ravens that swept through the village heralding the arrival of the unwelcome visitors made their appearance yet again, swooping low and creating an ear-blasting collection of squawks.

"Time to go!" Livia snarled as the ravens vacated the area. She leapt onto the back of the carriage, reclaiming her centurion position. A sickly sweet smile spread across her face, and she bared her fangs at me. The horses reared their front legs into the air, whinnying noisily. Their hooves stamped the ground before the carriage clattered forward, continuing its journey, taking the selected girls to the Master.

Cold fear tapped its skeleton fingers across my chest as the burning fire at the centre of the village died. Paymon tutted before clicking his fingers and blowing the ensuing flame onto the half–burnt logs. As the fire burst to life, the villagers emerged from their homes. Paymon looked around at the frightened faces, seeming to take each and every one into his memory.

"There will be another ceremony next year. I suggest that you all behave, keep your precious children under control, or I will send for the carriage again. If any of you value your daughter's future, I suggest you keep her pure. I will decide her fate, and the Master has no time for whores. Warn your daughters, save them from a fate that should be viewed as worse than death."

He held his arm toward me. "Athena, time for us to go home."

His voice was gentler than I'd ever heard before, and his eyes held mine with a softness I'd never witnessed from him. How could he just switch from being the threatening demon to the caring one beside me now?

I took a lingering look at the familiar faces of my former family before grasping Paymon's arm and turning away.

"Damn vampire," he muttered as we began to walk, him limping at my side.

"Livia was a vampire?"

Paymon nodded. "Did you not guess what she was? Red eyes, her speed, her agility? Livia's always on the lookout for blood, the sweeter the better. She has a distinct lack of respect for following rules. I have no idea why the Master tolerates her."

"Maybe she's really emotional."

Paymon laughed. "Livia, emotional? Never. And, just so you know, demons can't feed from a vampire. They are a closed book to us in that way."

"Not at all?" I pulled the cloak tighter around my neck. A bitter cold wind blew along the track toward us, unsettling leaves and overhanging tree branches. Paymon didn't seem to notice the increased breeze.

"They block us," he said. "I'm pretty sure it's unintentional, otherwise one of them would have slipped and let their guard down. And Livia's desperate to please the Master, so I'm sure she'd be willing to feed him with her emotions."

I kicked at a stone as we walked, thinking through what I had seen tonight. "Is that why she reacted so fiercely to me, when you told her you'd have recommended me as a wife?"

Paymon pulled his hood away from his face. "As his wife, you would give him everything she can't. Her jealousy was quite entertaining until she threatened your life."

"She stopped when you threatened her. Why? What would you have done?"

"Set her alight and watch her burn. I have no time for vampires. Not many demons tolerate them. Although I am told they make excellent lovers." He smiled briefly and then sank into his more customary seriousness. As we continued walking, he stopped his pretend limp.

"What were those creatures, the ones that took Hannah and Julie?"

"They were the miscreants I told you about. The ones who would have found you if you'd ran away."

"They'd have come looking for me?"

"Yes." He squinted into the distance. "If you'd missed the Ascension Ceremony, they would have set about finding you."

I frowned. "But how would they know?"

"What? That you were missing? I would have told Livia, and she would have told the Master. If he knew you were suitable as his wife, he would have sent them to find you immediately."

"So, if I'd been a feeder or a servant, he'd not have bothered?"

Paymon chuckled. "Oh, he would have bothered, with the instruction for them to kill you. But as a potential wife, he would have urgently sought your deliverance unharmed . . . well, to a certain degree."

"What—?"

"The miscreants are not known for their ability to keep people uninjured whilst travelling back to the Master. You saw them, once you are in their grasp, there is no escape until they choose to release you."

My shuddering fear from when they wrapped their arms around Hannah and Julie drifted through me, and I shook my head to rid myself of the vision that formed.

"Now, are you glad you married me or would you rather have gone with them or risked running away with Thomas?" His eyebrows rose as he asked me a question that there was really only one answer for.

"I made the right decision considering the limited options." But how I would have loved another option, one that would have let me live as a free woman in the village with no demands to procreate.

"Yes, you did."

Paymon's eyes flickered toward the house, and he grinned. "I see Odin is waiting for us."

He was perched on the gate post. "Was he with the ones that flew in front of the carriage?"

"No. He would never allow himself to fall to their level. He's an intelligent bird. He used to get my attention by tapping on the door. He became quite a nuisance until I let him into the house. But I wouldn't be without him now." He nodded toward Odin. "He is most trustworthy, unlike Bia."

I inhaled deeply. My thoughts on the way he treated her were not ones I wanted to dwell on. Unfortunately, I didn't trust her enough to befriend her in any way. Even though Paymon had compelled her not to attack me, I didn't fancy testing the strength of his compelment.

Odin flew toward us and settled silently on Paymon's shoulder.

"Are you hungry?" Paymon asked as he held the gate open for me. "Bia can prepare some supper for you."

I shook my head, unsure as to whether I'd keep any food down. The stench of the miscreants lingered in my nostrils, and I could still sense Livia's cold fingers crawling over my skin. My warm and comfortable bed was too much of a temptation—a refuge to hide in, somewhere where I could crawl into a ball and let my fear run free. I doubted I'd get much sleep. I was sure the very real nightmare of what I'd witnessed wouldn't leave me.

Once we were inside, cloaks hung up, warmth surrounding us, Paymon sighed.

"You're tired," he said.

I nodded, stifling a yawn as he lit the sconces on the walls with his flying flames.

"Go straight to bed. Hopefully you will be fully recovered in the morning. And don't worry about Livia, she'll not come near you now." He held his hand up, showing me his marriage mark.

I gazed at the back of my hand and nodded. I was protected from her, this was my protection—the mark of ownership, of marriage to a demon.

"Bed," Paymon repeated before turning away and heading to the lounge. "Good night, Athena."

I walked upstairs in a trance, slow and lethargic, as if all energy had been drained from me. By the time I reached my room, I was fighting to stay awake. Had Paymon compelled me? Had the miscreants done something to me? Had Livia's touch poisoned me? I fought with my own personal demons, images of what I'd witnessed flashed through my mind as I fell onto the bed.

That night I dreamed of beasts tearing me limb from limb, vampires sucking my blood, and miscreants wrapping their rotting bodies around me.

CHAPTER 9

ANGUISH

OVER THE FOLLOWING WEEKS, PAYMON AND I managed to slip into a tense but somewhat easy routine. He had many dark moments and excelled in rousing my emotions. Those moments were thought out, planned, and orchestrated to garner the strongest of emotions. Anger and fear were the ones he resorted to when he needed a quick fix, and he was getting sneaky in the way he instigated them. But he also looked after me, made sure I ate, and revelled in my company. He seemed content and happy, and whereas I was growing fond of him, I never allowed myself to forget he was a demon. I viewed him more as a father figure, a role that had been lacking in my life for many years. And as the days went by, I relaxed in his company, not fearing that he was my husband. True to his word, he expected nothing sexual from me; all he wanted was my company.

There was a full moon three weeks after the Ascension Ceremony. We couldn't see it through the dense clouds of darkness, but it signified the monthly feast in the village. Paymon was excited about the pending meal; I was nervous.

As we stepped out of the house, I swallowed my apprehension. At the last feast, days before the Ascension Ceremony, I'd been scared by Paymon's constant stare and his increased attention on me. Now I understood why he'd singled me out at the feasts—he was keeping an eye on his future wife.

Tonight, Paymon carried the lantern to the village, his familiar limp when out of the house returned, and he hobbled beside me, grinning whenever I caught his gaze. Music and laughter rose from the village centre, and it didn't quieten when we arrived. Myrtle stood in the doorway of her home, leaning on the frame for support, her face strained. Having not seen her for three weeks, she looked tired and paler than I remembered. She didn't take her eyes off me as Paymon led the way to the logs set aside for us near the central fire.

As soon as we were seated, others took their place on various logs or boulders. None of them sat near us.

Mead flowed freely at these monthly occasions, and a pig or lamb was slaughtered for the feast. Vegetables and potatoes were cooked and shared with everyone who attended, and also sent to the ones who couldn't or didn't want to partake in the festivities. The whole village enjoyed what was the best monthly meal they ever ate.

Paymon's hood was pulled over his head, hiding his eyes in the darkness of its shadow, but he nodded at Sharon and Fiona when they presented him with food. I spoke my thanks, knowing how much time and effort went into providing the feast—I usually helped prepare it.

Families huddled together, groups of teenagers spoke loudly whilst the elderly spoke in hushed whispers. I sought out Thomas, seated by himself as he stared at the flames of the fire. As if knowing my gaze was upon him, he lifted his head. There was no smile, no hint of an apology, just a vacant, accusing gaze that pinned me to the spot. I looked away quickly as Paymon moved his head next to mine.

"Ignore him, Athena," he said quietly. "The emotions he unleashes in you are not ones I wish to feed from."

I turned to Paymon, noting the large piece of meat he held in his hand.

"Why are you eating?" I asked as he took a bite out of the tender meat.

"I don't want to insult them. Tell me, Athena, when you lived in the village, what was the reason given for these feasts?"

"To thank you for protecting us."

"So I would be insulting each and every person gathered around this fire if I refused." His gaze travelled around the groups of men and women before settling on Thomas. "Although there are some who I'd take great pleasure in insulting. You must tell me if he's bothering you."

"You mean Thomas?" He sat in a hunched position, poking the ground with a stick. "I think he's miserable enough." I looked away, still angry with the deceitful way he'd behaved.

"Oh, I can make him even more miserable, trust me." The glint I often saw in Paymon's dark eyes returned for a split second, and the corners of his mouth twitched.

"Leave him," I said.

Paymon slid his arm around my back and held my waist, pulling me toward him, reminding me who was in control. He laughed, although I suspected that I was the only person who heard it.

I peered through the flames of the fire, seeking out the

older girls in our village. Caroline and Emma were twins, only a year younger than me. Jet black hair swung around their shoulders, and their dull plain clothes hinted that they wanted nothing more than to disappear into the darkness around them. Their parents never let them out of their sight, even now they sat on either side of them, talking in whispered voices.

"What's wrong, Athena?" Paymon reached for my hand and squeezed it.

I sighed. "I'm looking at the girls in the village, seeing who you'll send to the Master next year."

"You say it as if I enjoy sending them to him. Remember, I have no choice."

"Some of them won't cope." I inclined my head toward Caroline and Emma.

"They are not your responsibility, but it may satisfy you to know that neither of them will be going anyway. They'll be staying here."

"But they don't even have boyfriends. You'll expect them to get pregnant."

He nodded. "I have already selected the man who will impregnate them."

"One man?"

"Yes. One man is capable of impregnating the whole village if he is fertile enough."

I flinched and swallowed hard before questioning who the man would be. But I already knew—the most fertile man in the village. "Hannah's father?"

"No, he would have been suitable for you, not them." He turned to face me, his mouth slightly raised at one side. "When I select a man for the women, I oversee the act of impregnation." He sneered and narrowed his eyes at me. "I would have fed voraciously from your emotions when Hannah's father took you. It would have brought every single one of them crashing to the surface. Imagine—your best friend's father defiling you."

I recoiled and pressed my knees together. My hand came to my mouth as I fought the primitive urge to empty my stomach. Once again he was showing me the true demon that hid so close to the surface.

"That's disgusting." I shifted further away from him, and pulled my cloak tighter around my neck. "How can you do that? Why? As if the act itself isn't forced, vile and disgusting. You pick a man who you know would cause the most distress. And you'd watch!"

He grinned widely. "I'd like to take part, not just watch, but we need human females to be born, not half-breeds that won't survive for more than a few minutes. It would be a waste of a pregnancy and potentially kill the woman if I impregnated her. And the emotions you females release when making love are the pinnacle of emotions. I can't even begin to explain what they feel like to a demon." He licked his lips, and I shrank away from him once again.

"You're talking about a woman's emotions when she's enjoying herself. I can assure you that no woman will enjoy being forced to have sex with any man." I shot an accusing stare at him, but he didn't react. "It's nothing but organised rape, approved by you."

Paymon shook his head. "I only approve what is necessary to keep the Master happy."

I stared into the fire, confused by the man who sat next to me. One minute he seemed to revel in the suffering he caused, the next he seemed to only be following orders.

"So who have you selected for Caroline and Emma?" My voice sounded distant, detached, as if it wasn't my own.

Paymon shifted on the log before angling his body toward mine. "Samson. He's from a neighbouring village. He's young, smart, and desperate to work with any demon."

"I bet he is if he gets free rein to have sex with everyone."

Paymon chuckled. "Would you like to meet him? He is most handsome. Perhaps I can arrange for a little private party between you both."

"No!" I attempted to jump to my feet, but Paymon had second guessed my intention and a wave of calmness swept through me. I remained where I was, unable to direct my limbs to do anything.

"Calm yourself, Athena. I don't mean it. I will not allow any man or demon to touch you now that you are my wife. If I'd wanted to see you with Samson, or any other man, I would have kept you in the village, wouldn't I?"

His compelment lifted, and my former panic returned for a brief moment before vanishing. He wouldn't do that to me. He would keep his promise. Yet again, this had been a test, a play on words to enable him to feed from my emotions.

"It may comfort you to know that I won't invite Samson to the village and immediately expect him to perform. He will have a month to get to know the girls. He is a handsome and quite charming young man. I'm sure both of them will crave his attention when the time comes."

I closed my eyes and breathed deeply. I didn't think comforting me was the right phrase, but Paymon's reassurance of time for them to get to know the man who would sleep with them was a welcome one.

"Can you only have one wife?" I asked.

"Demons tend not to marry. They are not usually faithful." Paymon switched his gaze from the fire to me. "Many demons prefer the easy company of vampires."

"Like Livia?"

Paymon nodded. "They are always keen to please us . . . but I hate them." He looked around at the people feasting with us. Some of the men were already becoming merry, drunk on too much mead as they sang and danced. "Demons are strong creatures who often forget their own strength and power. A vampire can deal with the intensity of loving a demon. Humans, unfortunately, can die."

I wet my lips with my tongue and asked the question I needed to know the answer to. "Have . . . have you—"

"No," he said. "I've never killed a woman whilst having sex with her." He smiled. "I prefer the warmth of a human rather than the deathly cold of a vampire. But I don't have much of a track record with human females. Only one."

He took the last pork chop from the tray that was presented to him. I offered a half smile at Janine, a former friend, but she didn't acknowledge my greeting and walked away.

"So you didn't force her?" I had to know. Somehow this conversation had taken on a different meaning. I wasn't just finding out about his past, I was finding out about my possible future.

"No, I didn't. She was a willing participant." He closed his eyes and smiled before taking a bite of the pork.

"What happened?"

He opened his eyes and frowned. "She died, but it wasn't my doing."

I wanted to ask what happened, but didn't. His complexion had taken on a grey tinge, as if the memory was painful.

Had he really loved her? Was it even possible for a demon to love a human?

"She was called Amber," he said. "A beautiful name for a beautiful woman. I saw her for many months before the day we officially came above land."

"You mean you could come here before then? What about the light?" This didn't fit with what I'd always assumed. The light would kill them, wouldn't it?

"The light?"

I nodded, waving my hands around to aid my descriptions. "I didn't think you could stand the sun, the brightness it created. I presumed you hid the light because it harmed you."

Paymon chuckled and shook his head. "Athena, the light does not harm us in any way. If I'm completely honest with you, I much preferred this world when the sun was present. I miss the colours—bright reds, yellow, pinks, oranges. The heat was never an issue for me, but I saw how much happier people were in your summertime when the sun was shining."

"Bring it back then."

"It's not that simple."

Surely he wasn't the only demon who felt like that, others would miss it. "So why take it? Why leave us like this?"

"The Master is the only one who can answer that question. He controls the darkness that surrounds us."

"It's the one thing I'd change," I said. "I'd bring the light back instantly if I could. I'd do whatever I had to for it to return."

"Even if it wasn't pleasant?"

I snapped from my day-dreaming and looked to Paymon before nodding.

He chuckled before patting my hand. "Sometimes we all

wish for things we can't have."

"What do you wish for?" I asked, suddenly nervous about his reply.

"The return of Amber. You remind me of her a little, perhaps that's another reason why I was willing to strike a deal with your grandmother."

"There must have been others," I said. I didn't believe that a demon of his age had only ever had one lover. And I remembered the woman who had lived with him in the village—the one he killed.

"When I came to land to live here, I met a demon." His voice was quiet and tinged with sadness. "I thought I loved her. We appeared to be kindred spirits, like-minded souls."

I snorted, quite unladylike, and quite rude considering his upset. "There you go again, mentioning souls," I said. "I've told you, I don't believe demons have them."

He raised his brow and then frowned at me.

I inwardly scolded myself for interrupting him and offering no sympathy to his memories.

"I think it's time we went home," he said before standing and waiting for me.

I shuffled to my feet, all too aware of the dismissive nature of his statement.

"Sorry," I said, trying to catch his gaze. "I shouldn't have said what I did."

"Your apology is not necessary. You believe I don't have a soul, and I quite like that thought. But for your own well-being, you need to cling to the hope that I do have one, that I am driven by some semblance of need to be good. Demons, by nature, are not good, they don't care, and they certainly wouldn't treat you the way I'm treating you."

I looked away from his gaze, but in doing so caught Thomas's concerned expression. I looked to the ground, shocked by both Paymon's words and by Thomas's sudden concern.

Paymon held out his hand for me to take. I risked another glance in Thomas's direction, and this time he attempted a weak smile. I gave him no visual acknowledgement.

"Home, Athena. Now," Paymon said, reaching for my hand as he limped alongside me. Today had been another long day, and I was tired. I was looking forward to tomorrow and searching through the selection of books I'd picked out earlier. The library was my favourite room in the house, and I spent most of my days browsing the hundreds of books on offer. And today, I'd come across a book written the year I was born. It was titled *The Book Every Modern Woman Should Have,* and promised an explanation of what everyday life was like before the world was sent hurtling into what it existed as now.

As we strolled back to the house, Paymon was decidedly quiet, and I didn't interrupt what I imagined to be his thoughts about the women he'd once loved. His pace was slow, awkward with his limp, but necessary to fool the villagers. I thought nothing of it until we reached the gate and he stumbled, groaning as he leaned against the gate.

"Are you okay?"

Odin circled above us before swooping toward Paymon.

"Let's get inside," he said. "I'll be fine. I'm tired, that's all."

His face was significantly paler than normal, and he seemed to be struggling with each step he took toward the door. Odin voiced his own thoughts by squawking.

Once inside, Paymon stumbled again and reached for the wall to steady himself.

"You're not okay," I said. "What's wrong? Tell me, I can help." I unfastened my cloak and hung it up before turning to him.

He was breathing deeply, laboured gulps of air that made his face twist with pain. He scrunched his eyes shut before letting his cloak fall to the floor.

"Is it your leg?" I asked, resting my hand on his arm.

He shook his head before looking toward Odin who was on his usual perching place at the bottom of the stairs. "You know what's happening," he gasped.

"Tell me," I said, moving to block his vision of Odin. Why did his raven know more than me?

Paymon closed his eyes again, and I glanced at Odin who was uncharacteristically still and silent.

"Is this some sort of demon thing? Something you do regularly?"

"I can assure you I have never done this before, nor will I do it again," he said before staggering forward. He used the wall to guide his unbalanced and weakened body.

I tried to help him, offering my arm, but he pushed me away, fighting my assistance.

"Come with me, Athena." He stopped outside the room where we'd had our first discussion. "Open the door to the safe room."

I pushed the door open, and Paymon staggered inside. I duly did as he'd requested, moving to the portrait of the Master and tilting it to the right. The secret door opened, and a blast of cold air flooded into the room. I shivered before turning to Paymon.

"Will you please tell me what's going on?" My worry was building faster than I would have ever thought it could concerning Paymon. He slumped against the wall, clutching his stomach, and then sank to the floor.

"Paymon?" I gasped, rushing to his crumpled body.

"Get me to the room." He pointed his shaking hand toward the entrance to the room where we were married.

He groaned loudly, a shuddering sound of terror.

"Quick, Athena," he rasped.

I wrapped my arm around his waist, and he hooked his arm over my shoulder. But he was too heavy, and without any assistance from his weakened body, I couldn't move him.

I took his hand in mine, our matching marked marriage hands, and willed him to feed from my emotions. There were plenty charging through me at the moment.

"Feed, Paymon," I said. "Take all you can so you can get to the room."

"Athena . . ."

"Feed!" I demanded as his eyes locked with mine.

"I can't." His voice was a whisper, a hushed sigh of air. He moaned loudly, a direct contrast to his words.

"You can. Do as I say. Feed from me." I was desperate. I had no idea what was happening to him, but I had a frightening thought that if he couldn't feed from me, it was something very serious. "There are plenty of emotions for you to take. Just do it!"

"Athena . . . it's too late."

"It's not, please, try again." I squeezed his hand between both of mine. I knew he didn't need contact to enable him to feed from me, but I somehow felt that it should.

"I'm dying. . ." he said, his voice failing as he struggled to breathe.

"No. No, Paymon, you're not. You can't." Tears sprung

into the corners of my eyes as I searched for his pupils. Our eyes locked, but there was no black pupil to see. Just his normal chestnut iris.

"Feed from me, damn you. Please, feed." He couldn't die. Demons didn't just die like this. I knew he was old, but this was so sudden. Had he known this would happen? Had he picked me as his wife so he could enjoy his last few weeks alive? No. I shook my head, Paymon intended to live longer than this.

He lifted his hand to his neck.

"Do you want water?"

He shook his head and tried to unbutton the top of his shirt. I immediately assisted as his hand fell away. Paper thin, pale skin was revealed.

"Take it."

I dipped my head closer. "Take what?"

He pulled at his shirt, and a silver chain became visible.

"It's yours now. Use it well." He managed a smile before his face contorted with pain. "Take it!"

Doing as instructed, I pulled on the chain, lifting it as gently as possible over his head. Unseen until it was removed was a pendant that hung from the chain. A plum-sized pendant, it looked like bright blue glass encased in an intricate design of open silver leaves.

Shocked by its beauty, I stared at it for several moments.

"Thank you," I offered through tear-stung eyes.

"I need to tell . . . you," he said.

I leaned closer to catch his words.

"Your gran."

"What about her?"

"She . . ." He coughed and his face scrunched up. "She . . .

was dying. She asked me to end her life."

I froze. A surge of emotions hit me. I slumped forward as waves of sadness crashed over me. My tears broke free, and I bowed my head. I'd had Paymon wrong, so wrong. I thought he'd killed her, struck down an elderly woman for no other reason other than because he wanted to.

"She made another deal with me, years before that day." His voice was becoming quieter, and I struggled to hear every word. "She was in pain. I promised I'd end her life when she asked me."

My tears continued to flow.

"Do you forgive me?"

I bit my lip as I looked him in the eye and nodded. "Yes."

He smiled. "Look after Odin." His voice was disappearing as fast as the life was draining from him.

"I will." I concentrated on his eyes, unwilling to look away.

He shivered, and once again, I took hold of both his hands and held them in mine. He was cold, not warm.

"Paymon," I sniffed, the tears falling uncontrollably, "don't leave me."

His eyes closed, and his usual silent breathing became a strained gasp for air.

It was his last living action.

His face relaxed, and his head lolled to the side.

A loud hissing noise sounded from the doorway of the secret room, and as I turned to see what was making the noise, ribbons of red and amber air swirled through the doorway toward me and Paymon. I jumped away from his body, confident that the swirling coloured mist was meant for him, not me.

I stood, wide-eyed, as the mist wrapped itself around his

body and lifted him from the floor. Demon magic. It was powerful. It was also beautiful.

The swirling mist carried Paymon toward the door it had emerged from, and I followed, not willing to just hand Paymon over to whatever forces were at work.

Once in the safe room, the images of our wedding flitted through my head. He had been so powerful that day, so full of energy and excitement about what our life would be. It felt wrong to be back here now, only a few weeks later, with his still and lifeless body.

I focused on him as the mist gently released its hold, laying him on the pentagram on the floor. It arranged his limbs into the same position Paymon had placed me in. The candles that were gently flickering when we entered the room flared several times and then burst into ferocious heated flames. I stepped back toward the bottom of the steps, sheltering myself against the stone wall as the heat built in the room.

A low mumbled chant began. Demon language bombarded me from all sides. And as the chanting became louder, as if spoken by many people, the flames from the five burning candles rose high into the room before arching into the middle of the pentagram—straight toward Paymon's body.

I released a loud sob, knowing that the flames were going to take him. This was the ceremony that would take every last part of him away from me. I looked away, not prepared to see the image of him burning.

Crackles and snaps of burning flesh assaulted my ears, and I cried freely, mourning his unwanted departure.

A loud roar filled the room, and I startled, switching my gaze back to the centre of the room. The flames swept high and then instantly died.

Focusing on where Paymon's body had been, nothing remained. He'd gone, whisked away by demon magic. The pentagram was drawn out on the floor, as if awaiting another person. The candles around the room were flickering innocently, not as if they had just incinerated a man.

My vision blurred, and I was suddenly cold. It was as if a part of me had died with him. How strange that I'd grown so attached to him in such a short amount of time. I took a deep breath and tried, unsuccessfully, to control my tears.

I trudged up the stairs and back into the room. Passing through the hallway, I caught sight of Odin silently strutting across the back of the sofa in the lounge. I sniffed loudly before calling him.

He flew to my side, and we climbed the stairs together.

My bedroom was cold, and once the door was locked and Odin settled on the end of my bed, I turned my attention to the fire. It usually burnt brightly, but now it was nothing more than a pathetic splutter, the embers fading fast. I trailed my hand through the water in the tub—cold. And as I lifted my hand, I noticed my marriage mark was fading.

Not only had Paymon gone, but everything about him, everything controlled by him had also gone—died when he did. The warmth that had constantly surrounded me since I arrived in the house was now replaced with a cold synonymous with the temperature in the village.

I threw myself on the bed and wrapped my hand around the pendant Paymon had given me.

There was no ceremony to celebrate the end of his life, no one to reminisce about his time alive. I knew so little about him. A few weeks of knowing him was nothing compared to a lifetime of memories.

What happened now? Was I free?

I jolted when a loud, slow scratching noise sounded out.

Spinning to the source of the sound, I stared at the bedroom door and clasped my hands to my chest.

The scratching stopped for a few moments but then started again, only this time it was more insistent, demanding my attention.

"Atheeenaaa."

My eyes widened and I gasped.

Bia.

CHAPTER 10

DESPAIR

ODIN SQUAWKED. HIS WILD FLAPPING OF WINGS knocked my hairbrush and perfume from the dressing table.

"Atheeenaaa."

More scratching.

Since the time I'd discovered Bia, I'd kept away from the kitchen. I'd left her alone, scared of another attack. Paymon had compelled her not to harm me, but he wasn't here anymore, and just like all the other things he'd controlled, his magic had died.

I glanced around the room; the door wasn't an option. The windows were my only way of escape.

"Atheeenaaa . . ." A loud thump hit the door. The noise was too solid to be her hand. Was she actually throwing herself at it?

Odin was cawing and flitting from one vantage point to another.

I rushed to the window at the end of the room and fumbled with the unfamiliar lock. My hands shook as I slid the metal catch to the side. I pulled at the window, but it wouldn't budge. Mustering all my strength I strained against the stiffness of the wooden frame, and little by little it eventually slid open. Once the first few centimetres of outside were revealed, the frame shot up. The bitter sting of wintry air rushed into the room, and I hunched my shoulders against the freezing temperature.

There was another thud, and then silence.

"Come on, Odin," I whispered. "We've got to get out of here."

He fluttered to the floor next to my feet, and I nodded at him before hitching my skirt up and lifting one leg out of the window.

"Let me in." Bia's tone was more insistent, annoyed, and I ducked my head under the window, shifting the bulk of my body outside. I couldn't see the ground below me. Shadows and the darkness hid my landing spot. I swallowed, ignoring my intrinsic desire to go back into the room. Bia was still calling my name and charging at the door. Injury from a fall seemed a small price to pay when the only other option was Bia attacking me. I glanced at the forest sprawling out in front of me like a sinister, frosty unknown. And in the distance, the warm flickering glow of lanterns in the village beckoned. I took a deep steadying breath. I had to jump.

As another thud hit the door. Odin squawked, and my instincts kicked in. Shifting my other leg through the window, I didn't pause. I twisted on the thin ledge and fixed my hands firmly on the wood before letting my arms take my full body weight. I hung for a split second before letting go.

Pain shot through my ankle as I landed, but as Odin flew out of the window above me, his calls of alarm had me hobbling toward the surrounding trees. My ankle jarred on each step I took, and needle-like jabs twisted up my leg. I winced each time my weight fell on my ankle, but managed to stumble forward. Each step took me nearer to the forest and the safety of the cover of the trees. Odin landed beside me and then hopped ahead, silent as he guided me away from the house.

I pressed my lips together, gritted my teeth, and began to run.

Only when I was under the cover of the trees, hidden behind a trunk, did I sneak a look back at the house. Bia was standing at the window I had jumped from. Her ghostly pale skin was highlighted against the darkness behind her, and I momentarily panicked that she would follow me.

My stomach twisted with a heightened fear when she leaned out of the window. She scanned the surrounding forest, slow and methodical with her sweeping eyes. When she started to laugh, my skin prickled with nervous anticipation.

"Go!" she hissed into the darkness. "Go! Run away. I will find you, Atheeenaaa."

I looked around for Odin. He was perched on a nearby branch, his all-knowing eyes also watching Bia. I waved my hand in the air, taking care that my action was completed behind the tree so Bia couldn't see. He turned his head toward me, and I pointed in the direction of the village.

He dipped his head before turning to look into the oppressive darkness of the forest.

I glanced back at the window seeing Bia disappear into the darkness of the room, and with no further thought, headed into the forest.

Damp, cold moss wet my fingers and sharp angular branches scratched my hands as I blindly staggered forward. Freezing air nipped at my flesh, and the wind that rustled branches carried the cloying scent of pine. Odin flapped a short distance in front of me, and I followed, trusting him to guide me to the village.

A distant howl sounded out, and I stopped moving. My breaths were coming short and fast, the air in front of my face misting as soon as they left my mouth. Odin stilled as well, and we both stared at each other. After a few moments, there was another howl, only this time it was nearer. With a nod of my head at Odin, we began moving again. I didn't walk this time, I ran. My heart thudded, and my senses became fine-tuned. Every snap of a branch, every rustle of leaves, and every shift in scent hit me. We weren't alone. We were being chased.

"Keep moving," I called to Odin, ignoring the throbbing pain in my ankle.

An overpowering stench of rotting food replaced the scent of pine, but I carried on running.

There was a flicker of movement to my right. The undeniable crash of footfall behind me.

Heat exploded on my back, and I screamed as I fell.

My attacker was revealed as I looked up. Standing far higher than me was a creature that resembled the docile deer I had once seen enter the village. Only this one was demonised. Its snout was elongated, and as it snarled, it revealed a row of sharp teeth. A large set of antlers were on top of its head, and small, piercing yellow eyes surveyed me. It stood on its hind legs, although its front ones, each with four large claws, grazed the muddy ground. Its large pulsing heart was visible through exposed ribs.

It tipped its head back and howled. The sound sent shock-waves of terror running through me, and I whimpered when another distant howl responded to the creature. I grovelled amongst the leaves and dirt on the forest floor, searching for anything that could be used as a weapon. A stick, dirt—something to throw at the beast or defend myself with. My fingers wrapped around a rock, large enough to inflict injury, but easy to lift in one hand and throw with accuracy.

With a deep breath, I pushed myself up from the ground and stood on shaky legs. As the creature held me in its slit-eyed stare, I threw a handful of dirt toward its face. It recoiled, staggering backward and rubbing at its eyes. Only when it stilled did I step forward and throw the rock at its head. My aim was good. The rock hit its snout, and it yelped in pain before crouching away from me.

I took the opportunity to run. I headed deeper into the forest, the tree trunks larger and more spaced out.

Just as I was beginning to think I'd escaped, the creature stepped out in front of me. I had no time to change direction or even slow down, and I crashed into its putrid chest. My whole body shook as I staggered backward.

Its snout was bleeding, the result of my attack, but it was also dribbling drool and saliva. It snarled. Rancid breath and spittle blasted into my face, and I whimpered. I took another step backward and squeezed my eyes shut, trying to block out the reality of what was happening. But when I opened my eyes, the creature seemed even larger.

Odin chose that moment to make an appearance. He let out a rabbling chatter as a large stick dropped from the foliage above. I glanced at the stick as it lay on the ground to my side. It was solid, thick, and pointed at one end.

As the beast approached me, swinging its head from one side to the other and scratching its claws in the ground, I flung myself toward the stick. Gripping it tightly, I held it in both hands, the sharp end pointing at my attacker. As it raised one of its arms into the air, Odin flew at it, causing a moment of distraction. I charged at the beast and thrust the pointed end of the stick through its rib cage and into its monstrous beating heart. The pulsating muscle exploded, covering me in warm sticky blood. But the beast still didn't stop. It roared and reared up to its full height. I twisted my weapon, ensuring it would not survive.

Odin was still making a nuisance of himself, flying at the beast, his claws reaching for its eyes. The beast continued to try and catch him, but its movements became slow, its life-force spilt all over the forest floor. When it eventually fell to the ground, its body twitched for several moments before finally stopping. I leaned against a nearby tree trunk and wiped my face with my sleeve. Tears crept into the corners of my eyes as I breathed heavily, trying to calm my galloping heart.

I'd killed it. I'd actually managed to kill it.

Odin fluttered to the ground and hopped around at my feet.

"Thank you," I said, sniffing. "If you hadn't dropped that stick . . ." I shook my head, refusing to think of the alternative. "We need to keep going. Come on." A chorus of howls rang out in the distance. I pulled the stick from the dead beast's chest and set off running. Once again, Odin led the way.

I listened for the panting breath; I waited for the pungent stench of another of the creatures. But I refused to look back. I had to get to the village.

It wasn't long before I caught the glimmer of distant

lanterns. And, as if sensing that I was at my destination, Odin cawed and then flew away. Tears welled up behind my eyelids. Only a few more steps.

The relief that had flooded through me was short-lived. Numerous ravens suddenly flew into the village, and a familiar cackle ricocheted through the trees.

Livia.

The few women who were around fled into their homes, and I rushed to a nearby tree and hid behind it.

The carriage had returned. Why? For me? Was this what normally happened? When the village demon died, his wife was returned to the selected categorisation for the ceremony?

Panic disorientated my vision, my palms sweated even though my skin was cold.

"Where is she?" Livia's voice rang out clear and melodic. "Where is the little whore who murdered Paymon and thought she could get away with it? No one gets away with killing a demon."

No one replied.

"Is no one prepared to tell me?" she roared. "Maybe you need persuading."

Pots clattered as they hit the ground, followed by a loud scream.

"I can take this one instead," Livia screeched. "A young girl for the Master. He'll enjoy playing with her!"

"No," I muttered, seeing that she'd grabbed hold of Susie. She was only fourteen.

"I hear you." Livia giggled, and I clamped my hand over my mouth. Vampires—not only equipped with speed, but with an acute hearing ability as well. "You'd better come out, Athena, or I will take this pretty young thing back to the

Master. I may even find some others to accompany her."

I remained where I was, trying to alleviate my fear of Livia and what would await me at the Master's with the need to do the right thing.

Livia laughed. The sound ran through me and made my every nerve rattle with agitation. I'd just escaped from an infernal and whatever that creature was that stopped me in the forest, and now I had to face a vampire.

I hobbled out of the forest, leaving the covering shelter of trees behind, and focused on Livia as she spun around to face me. Her white hair rippled in the breeze, and her vivid red eyes bore into me. The red cape that she'd worn at the Ascension Ceremony pooled at her feet like a puddle of blood. She was holding Susie with a vice-like grip around her throat, but she flung her to the ground as soon as she saw me. Instantly she stood beside me, the scent of death in her wake. She snarled in my ear, grabbed both of my hands and pulled them behind my back. I held back a scream as her nails dug into my flesh. What was she going to do to me? Take me to the Master? Kill me? I desired neither outcome, but with one certain to be my fate, I was strangely undecided as to which was the better option.

"You look disgusting," she said. "Dirty and covered in blood." She licked her lips before marching me into the centre of the village. Her cold breath ghosted across my neck, and she yanked my hair to one side. She licked my neck and pushed her nose against my skin. A quiet hiss filled my ear moments before my neck erupted in a burning heat. I screamed and twisted in her grasp, but couldn't escape. The pain in my neck intensified, red hot pokers sunk deep into the flesh—a localised agonising pain that spread further and further away from its source of puncture. A noisy slurp sounded out, and a surreal groan of contentment was uttered.

I stumbled against my captor as she drew from my life force. Was this how I was going to die? After everything Paymon had said, that I would be safe when we married, had it all been lies? I closed my eyes, not willing to fight the pain any longer. If this was my fate, my life was over.

"Athena!" It was Thomas, shouting from the edge of the village clearing. "Athena!"

Something inside me clicked. No, this was not my time. I wasn't just going to become this vile vampire's next meal. I'd face the Master; I'd survive my years with him. I'd come back alive. I couldn't just give up. I'd fight whatever was thrown at me—starting with Livia.

Gathering all my weakened strength, I twisted sharply, determined to force her away from my neck, but she only held me tighter. My strength was nothing compared to hers.

"I'm sure the Master won't be happy if you kill his potential wife," I rasped.

Her lips shifted on my neck, but she only sucked harder, the skin tearing where she had hold of me.

I continued to twist and turn, but Livia moved with me. I couldn't shake her off. But as I fought to release her grip, I spotted Thomas charging toward us. He held a spade, carrying it high in the air as he ran. I prayed his aim was accurate as the metal plate swung toward the back of Livia's head.

Before the expected blow struck, I was released and thrown to the floor. Livia effortlessly caught the swinging spade.

"You fool!" She pulled the spade toward her, and in doing so, brought Thomas within her grasp. She swung at him with the back of her hand and connected with his face. He flew backward before landing several metres away on his back.

I shifted onto my knees but lurched to the side. "Thomas!"

Livia stood between us, her rapacious feeding of my blood evident on her red smeared face. I lifted my hand to my neck before inspecting my fingers. Blood, and plenty of it. I ripped a length of fabric from the sleeve of my dress and pressed it to the open wound. If the lack of blood didn't kill me, infection surely would.

Livia had moved sideways and seemed content on prowling around Thomas. She licked her lips and drew her hand across them as if sizing up her prey. Several of the villagers tended to him as he groggily sat up. But no one came to my assistance, not even Myrtle who stood in the doorway of her home staring off into the distance.

At least Thomas's attempted attack on Livia had stopped her gluttonous feeding on my blood. As if knowing I was thinking about her, she spun to face me, her lips still stained a dark crimson. Smirking, she sauntered toward me and crouched over my crumpled body. I backed away from her, too fearful of what she now intended. I flinched when she grabbed my right hand.

"No mark," she said, quickly inspecting the back of the palm. "I wonder why he didn't complete the full ceremony with you. The bond would've remained unbroken if he had."

I frowned, trying to determine what she meant.

"Lanim!" Livia called before hissing against my ear. "If you had not been selected as a wife for the Master, I'd drain you until nothing remained but a corpse."

"And now?" I pushed myself away from her cold hands and lips.

"I'll let Lanim take you to the Master. He's not the gentlest of miscreants, but you will still be of use to the Master when you arrive." She sniggered as she stepped away. "The Master will complete the full marriage ceremony as soon as you arrive. There'll be no doubt as to who you belong to for the rest of your pathetic life."

In a repeat of what had happened at the Ascension Ceremony, one of the shadows sitting at the front of the carriage slipped from its seat. It moved as pooled liquid, moaning and whining with the painful echo of distant voices. The sickly sweet aroma that I'd smelt at the ceremony grew in intensity as the miscreants headed toward me. Livia hauled me to my feet, but my legs had no strength in them, and I fell against her. She held me still, upright, ensuring I saw the approaching dark void.

Only when it touched my feet did Livia back away. My knees didn't give way as I expected; they remained locked in place. I couldn't move, not only were my feet stuck to the ground, but my arms were locked at my sides. I was nothing but a statue. The liquid reverted to the shadow, and a painful cold crept through me. I clenched my jaw, determined to fight off the debilitating hold the creature had, but as black spots appeared in front of my eyes, I understood it was pointless. I was no match for the miscreant, or Livia, or any demon. This world wasn't ours anymore—it was theirs. They were in control.

When the moaning shadow crept over my face, my world was plunged into complete darkness. My pulse raced, and the sound of my own heartbeat thrashed loudly in my ears. I felt sick, dizzy, and disorientated, but with my lack of sight, my hearing became fine-tuned.

"Athena!" Thomas shouted, but I couldn't respond. My

muscles ached with the will to move, but with no control to do so.

"You are mine to take to the Master," the miscreant hissed in my ear. Its voice was scratchy, low and terrifying.

A leathery creaking signified the unfurling of the winged membrane. But, as the stench of the miscreant became over-powering, I became aware of another sound, one I'd not heard for a long time—the distinctive strike of a set of hooves upon the hard ground. The sound gradually became louder and then stopped. A horse snorted. Not only did the snort hint at the horse's agitation on its arrival in the clearing, the rider who spoke out, didn't sound any happier.

"Livia," a man roared. "What is Lanim doing with that woman?"

CHAPTER 11

RELUCTANCE

"Erebus?" Livia's voice was sweet and soft, nothing like the tone she'd directed at me.

"I believe that's my name," he said, sharp and concise.

"To what do I owe this pleasure of your visit?" Livia sounded as if she were singing. "You have no need to be in this disgusting village with all these peasants."

The man sniggered. "I have every right to be here. But you? You have no right to be anywhere near this village. Not unless I send for you."

"You've been given this village? Since when?"

"I was summoned several hours ago when Paymon died. I've been travelling constantly. Seems I got here just in time."

A breeze brushed against my skin and a raven cawed overhead.

"Call that filthy beast off that woman," the man said. "If you have no need to be here, it certainly doesn't."

"Lanim," Livia snapped. "Back to the carriage without the girl. It seems Erebus wants to save her."

There was a creak of movement, and the sickly aroma surrounding me lost intensity.

When moans and wails filled the air, I knew the miscreant was returning to the carriage, but the frightening blindness didn't leave me. My hands and feet tingled as some feeling began to return to them, but the little strength I had in my legs wasn't enough to prevent me from falling to the ground. I landed on my side and was unable to find the strength to sit. Footsteps approached. After a rustle of clothing, I was pulled against warmth.

"Athena, can you hear me?" It was Thomas, his voice strained, breaking.

I nodded. As the oppressive cold snaked away from my limbs, every muscle hurt, throbbing with a dull numbness. But it felt good to be in Thomas's arms. He was warm and familiar.

The darkness that had surrounded me clouded and then dispersed, and I focused on the man who had arrived. He was seated on a large black stallion, but his facial features were hidden by the hood of his cloak. When he dismounted his horse, his cloak swirled behind him in an elegant flourish.

He prowled toward Livia. "So, you didn't explain. Why are you here with the carriage? Has this woman done something to upset you?"

I drew in a sharp intake of breath and placed my hand over my chest as he pulled the hood of his cloak way from his face. He was young, much younger than Paymon. He had stubble, and where the beginnings of a beard ended, streaks of dirt were smudged across his face. The dark shadows beneath his eyes hinted at his tiredness and possible frustration. A deep scowl pulled across his forehead, and Livia backed away from him.

"Such a pity I can't feed from your emotions, Livia. I'd be having my own private party if that were the case. But I can sense your fear—it's quite disturbing, but also deeply satisfying. Something worrying you?" His brow lifted, and he shot a sideways glance at me. "And you. Paymon's wife, I suspect? About to be claimed by the miscreant."

"She killed Paymon." Livia pointed at me, her hand movement wide and exaggerated.

"I didn't!" I stood on shaking legs as Thomas held my arm, supporting my dizzy body. "He died in my arms. I never wanted him dead."

"You killed him!" she roared.

Erebus spun to face Livia, and she immediately froze in place, like the statues that the girls had been when the carriage last came. He walked to where I stood, his steps slow and predatory.

Thomas backed away, leaving me alone. I glanced quickly at him, shooting him a disgusted frown.

Erebus scanned my bloodied and ripped dress. "So you didn't kill him?"

I shook my head.

"Are you sure?"

I nodded.

Now he was next to me I could see his eyes. They were black, no doubt feeding from my racing emotions. His dark hair was tied away from his face, and he stood a head taller than me. He was also dressed similarly to Paymon, old-world clothes, but his were worn with the simple adornment of belts.

"You can speak, you know. Livia will stay where she is. I've compelled her." He leaned toward me and whispered, "I hate vampires."

I managed a small smile at his shared confidence.

"What's your name?" He seemed genuinely curious and there was no sign of the former annoyance in his tone.

"Athena."

He reached his gloved hand toward my face and lowered it to my neck. When he lifted his hand away he looked at the blood staining the black leather and tutted before striding back to Livia.

"Get on your knees!"

She immediately sank to the ground, no choice under his compelment. With no words uttered and no warning issued, he kicked her in the chest. She flew backward before slumping to her side. She didn't look up as Erebus strode to her crumpled body. He grabbed her hair before wrapping it around his hand, pulling it and forcing her to look at him. "You're a worthless whore," he snarled before placing his spare hand around her neck and lifting her to her feet. "How dare you feed from her?" he shouted only inches away from her face. "You have no right to even be here. Athena was Paymon's wife, and now she will be mine. You will not touch her ever again." He threw her to the side and then added another kick to her stomach.

I looked away, shocked and outraged by his violent attack on Livia. No man should ever treat a woman like that. And he thought I was going to be his wife? No, no way at all. I wouldn't marry any man who'd raise a hand to me. And I'd just got my freedom back; I wasn't losing it again.

"Worthless, stupid vampire!" He kicked her again as she

lay on the ground. "I shall inform the Master of your greed to collect Athena when she should have been left alone. How dare you break the rules that are set out before all of us who serve him? You forget your place in this world, do I need to remind you?"

Livia hissed and turned away from her attacker. Her white hair hid her face as she remained crouched on the ground.

Erebus resumed his observation of me, his eyes dancing with secret amusement. "You look worried, Athena."

"You . . . you attacked her."

"Vampires do not feel pain. Their subservience to demons overrides their basic instinct to attack. They know their place, but I like to remind them who exactly is in charge." He switched his gaze briefly to Livia. "Look at her, not a mark on her, only her pride is bruised, and believe me, that's even worse for Livia. I'm sure she'd like to be bruised and battered rather than have her pride damaged, especially in front of you."

Livia hissed again, baring her fangs at me.

I stepped backward.

Erebus chuckled. "Now, now, Livia. Remember whose company you are in."

She ignored him and sprung to her feet before heading to the back of the carriage. Even though Erebus had pulled her hair and attacked her, she moved gracefully.

Erebus followed her to the carriage and roughly grabbed her arm. "If I ever see you again, it will be too soon. You leave now, and never return. Send someone else with the carriage at the Ascension Ceremony next year."

Livia's bright-red eyes burned at Erebus who refused to look away. Only when he released her arm did she move. She jumped onto the back of the carriage, and as if knowing she was there, the horses snorted their approval. The ravens swept into the clearing, their noise deafening as they departed. Livia kept her eyes forward as the carriage charged away.

The villagers stepped out from their homes, and Susie ran to me before flinging her arms around my waist.

"Thank you, Athena, you saved me." Her eyes were pooled with tears. "You saved all of us."

"Hey." I crouched to her level and softly nudged her chin with my fingers. "Don't cry. She's gone now."

She hugged me even tighter as tears crept down her cheeks.

"Go to Myrtle," I said, gently pushing her away as Erebus approached.

Her eyes widened as she saw him, and as if understanding that she was best hidden, she ran to Myrtle.

"Come along, Athena. Time we left," Erebus said.

I shook my head.

"I'm staying here in the village. It's where I belong." Even though he said he hadn't physically hurt Livia, I feared the violence that he'd unleash on me.

"I say you're coming with me." He strode to his horse and patted the magnificent beast on its neck.

"She said she's staying here." Thomas sidled next to me.

"I suggest you back off. Leave Athena to me. I'm sure I'll cope." Erebus's glower confirmed his agitation.

"You can't just drag her away from the village!" Thomas shouted.

"I can. And I will." He beckoned me toward him with an incline of his head.

"She's not leaving," Thomas repeated as he stepped in front of me. It reminded me of when we were young and the times he stopped the other children teasing me. I fleetingly felt the twinge of regret, of my love for Thomas resurfacing, but quickly brushed it aside. I wouldn't let myself forget what he did. If I stayed in the village, I wanted nothing to do with him. I reached for his arm when he took a step forward as if prepared to challenge Erebus. I'd seen the power Paymon had, I wasn't willing to see Thomas get hurt by whatever power Erebus had.

Erebus stopped concentrating on his horse and faced Thomas. "Don't mess with me, boy. Back off. That's your one and only warning."

"You don't frighten me," Thomas said.

"Really?" Erebus chuckled.

Thomas immediately sank to his knees, shouting and groaning as his body twisted and turned, each limb shaking uncontrollably.

"Stop it," I shouted, rushing to Erebus. "Stop it. Leave him alone!"

I stood in front of him, blocking his focus on Thomas. Erebus snarled and grabbed both of my wrists. I wriggled in his grasp, but his hold only tightened.

"Don't be difficult," he snapped.

My body flooded with heat, my limbs became heavy.

"Stop it!" I immediately recognised the sensation. "Don't you dare compel me."

He yanked me closer, and his eyes bore into mine. "Then do as I say. I won't put up with this behaviour."

"I've told you I'm not coming with you."

The familiar trait of compelment hit me again, only this time I got the full force and swayed with the intensity of it. Before I had time to react in any way, the world around me began to spin. Thomas called my name, but I slumped forward against Erebus's hard chest.

"You'll learn," he whispered against my ear, "to do as I say."

He lifted me in his arms, handling me no better than a worthless belonging, and bundled me across the horse's back.

He jumped into the saddle behind me, and within moments we were moving. He sighed as Thomas continued to shout my name, but as we rode further away from the village, heading to the house I had fled from only a few hours ago, everything around me faded. I didn't have enough strength to fight his compelment as it drew me deeper and deeper into an unsettling nightmare.

Bright flickering flames danced around me.

My hands were tied with rope to metal rings.

My legs spread apart and my ankles bound to two further rings.

Fear.

Chants spoken in a language I had no understanding of.

The removal of my clothes, cut from my body.

A man's naked body lying over mine.

Confusion.

Need.

Kisses to each shoulder, to each breast, my stomach, each hip, each knee.

Lust.

More flames, more chants.

Pain.

Blood.
Sparks lighting the room with a white light.
Tiredness.
Lifted in a man's arms.
Whispered words.
Sleep.
Sleep.

I awoke with a start. A loud rumbling shook the bed. I stared at the canopy above me. Flashes lit the room, eagerly illuminating everything in a surreal brightness. More loud bangs and rumbles. More flashes. My heart calmed as I realised there was a thunderstorm, although it sounded as if it was directly overhead.

Relief flooded though me as I recognised that I was alone, back in my bedroom at Paymon's house. But the numbness of my nightmare returned as I sensed that under the bedsheets I was naked. I lifted the sheet up.

Completely naked.

My right hand burnt with a pain I'd experienced only a few weeks ago, and I lifted my hand, not wanting to see confirmation of what I was sure had happened, but needing to see the proof.

My palm was cut, the wound sore and angry looking. And the back of my hand showed the red raised mark of marriage that would eventually leave me with the same black-lined design as before.

Even more memories—for that's definitely what they were, not a nightmare but my subconscious during the marriage ceremony—came flooding back.

Erebus, tying me to the rings on each point of the pentagram, his chanting in demon language as he stood between my parted legs. The flash of the blade and the jewelled handle as he cut me free from my dress. The heaviness of his naked body as he pressed against me. His kisses, tender, on my exposed body. The feel of his hips pushing against mine.

Had he had sex with me whilst I was under his compelment? Paymon had told me it was a usual part of the ceremony—he gave me a choice on whether it happened or not. There had been no choice with Erebus.

Lace, I needed the lace. I'd left it when I'd fled from Bia.

I reached into the drawer in my bedside table. My fingers wrapped around the dark pouch, and I tipped a small handful of the dark seeds onto my palm before slipping them into my mouth and chewing.

My ankle peeked out from under the blankets and I frowned. It was bandaged. I lifted my hand to my neck, and timidly touched the side where Livia had fed from me. It too was bandaged. I pulled one of the fur skins from the bed before wrapping it around me and rushing to my dressing table. My reflection in the mirror confirmed that I was also clean. There was no dried blood or dirt on my face, hands or arms. My hair was loose, but clean, freshly washed. So he'd bathed me, washed my hair, tended to my injuries and then married me? Or had he married me first, completed the full ceremony before tending to my injuries and dirty body?

An insistent tap at the window caught my attention, and I hobbled across the room and pulled the curtain back.

"Odin," I shouted, seeing his bedraggled feathered body. He'd obviously got caught in the storm.

I slid the latch holding the window shut, and just as I opened the heavy frame, another flash of lightning lit the world in front of me. The forest flared a ghostly white, and the scent of damp pine wafted in the air, reminding me of what had occurred before Livia had arrived with the carriage. Odin shuffled past me and hopped from the window ledge into the room. He was on edge, like a secret lover calling on me during the night, and I laughed as he squawked and fluttered before settling on the bed. After pulling the window shut, I joined him on the bed as he hopped across the blankets.

"Where did you go?" I asked, reaching to rub his ruffled beard.

He leaned into my touch, a throaty gonk greeting the attention.

"Well, you're back now," I said.

I rolled onto my back, and Odin hopped onto my stomach, picking at bits of fluff from the fur I was wrapped in.

"It's a pity you're not human," I said, reaching to the back of his head to scratch him. "What do you think?"

"I think it's a very strange and somewhat disturbing idea."

I sat upright, spinning to face the door where the voice had come from.

Erebus.

He walked into the room, eying Odin suspiciously.

I pulled the fur tighter and crossed my arms over my chest.

"There's no need to cover yourself," he said. "I've already seen what you have to offer, and I'm not impressed."

I glared at him as he strode past the screen that divided he room.

"I want some answers," I said, shifting to the edge of the

bed.

Erebus halted his stride and turned to face me. "To what exactly?"

"You've obviously completed the marriage ceremony." I lifted my hand and showed him the stinging mark.

"Likewise," he said, lifting his matching hand, although it was covered in a black leather glove. "How very astute of you."

I stood but didn't walk any nearer to him. He was too imposing, standing there fully clothed whilst I was wrapped in a fur that only just covered what it needed to. He also alluded a power that I couldn't place. I'd caught ripples of it with Paymon, but it was more powerful from Erebus.

"At the ceremony. Did you . . . I mean, did we . . ." My words failed me, my thoughts shattered. I felt naked before him—on display, begging for information I should have known.

He raised one brow but didn't respond. He ran his gloved hand along the top of the screen and waited for me to continue.

"Did you have sex with me?" I blurted out.

He blew imaginary dust from his covered fingers. "I completed the ceremony as necessary to keep you safe."

"So you did. You forced yourself on me!"

He crossed the room in large strides. I stepped backward, the back of my knees hitting the edge of the bed.

He stood so close that his body brushed against mine. The rough cloth of his trousers scratched my skin, and his belt dug into my stomach. He seriously had no understanding of personal space. I leaned backward, careful not to lose my balance and fall onto the bed.

"I have never forced myself on any woman," he said, eyes swirling with amber. "And believe me, I've had plenty of opportunities."

"You've not answered my question."

"Nor do I intend to." He took a step back and crossed his arms.

"But I want answers."

"You'll get your answers," he snapped. "But not until I get mine. We have lots to discuss."

"Such as?"

"Downstairs," he said, backing away from me and heading toward the door. "Get dressed and meet me downstairs. Or you can stay in that dead animal skin, but it does you no favours."

Odin fluttered across the room, and Erebus's gaze followed his path.

"He was Paymon's," I said. "And now he's mine. He stays with me."

Erebus nodded, but I saw a smirk pull at the edge of his mouth.

"Where's Bia?" I asked, sure she wouldn't have taken kindly to his arrival.

He stopped at the doorway and frowned. "Bia?"

"The infernal who lived here."

"Oh, her. She's dead." There was no remorse of any kind in his declaration.

"Did you kill her?"

He shot me a bemused look. "Don't tell me you and her were friends."

I shook my head.

"I told you earlier. I hate vampires. Vampires of any kind." He strode out of the room but left the door open, a beckoning tease for me to follow.

"Don't keep me waiting," he called as his footsteps drifted

along the corridor.

I sank onto the bed, my shoulders hunched. He wanted answers from me. About what?

I huffed before opening the cupboard door where my dresses were. He may not have any desire to see my flesh, but I wasn't going to wander around half dressed.

"Best do as I'm told," I muttered as I pulled a dull rusty brown dress over my head and slipped my feet into the matching shoes. The dress fastened up the front, and I laced it tightly, still smarting at his cruel words concerning my body. I pulled my hair into a high ponytail, securing it with a clasp from the dressing table, before venturing out into the corridor. Odin didn't follow. He'd settled on the wooden screen, preening and stretching his wings in the gentle heat of the fire.

I ambled along the corridor, noticing a quiet vibration in the air. There had always been heat, a warmth about the house when Paymon was here, but Erebus's arrival hadn't brought that. Instead, there was an unexplainable, hardly detectable buzz.

I wondered which room he expected me to head toward, but as I turned the corner of the stairs, I got my answer. He was leaning backward against the bottom staircase balustrade, inspecting his covered hands, and had one foot placed flat against the upright.

Without looking up, he said, "Go through to the lounge. Sit and wait for me."

My stomach churned, and I took an unsteady breath, trying to stay calm. I was worried about what he wanted to ask, and I certainly didn't want to anger him, not after I'd seen the way he attacked Livia.

"So, Athena." He was right behind me as I entered the

room, invading my personal space again, his body too close. "You have returned home."

I frowned as I sat on the sofa.

"You should never have left," he said, sinking into Paymon's favourite chair.

"But Paymon's dead," I said, not understanding his reasoning.

He sniggered. "As his wife, you were tied to Paymon, you should have stayed until I arrived."

"I had no ties to him or the house once he was dead. His presence here died with him. There was no reason to stay."

"Oh, but there was." He leaned forward, resting his elbows on his knees and pressed his hands together in front of his face. "You were married to him. He died, but not through old age. He died prematurely, but that is another matter. Now, you obviously seem confused by recent events, so I shall spell them out to you." He shifted even further forward. "If Paymon had died through old age, you would have been able to return to your village and live your years there as a free woman. But seeing as he was murdered, the marriage still stands."

"What, I'm married to a dead man?"

"Not exactly. You were his property and, like the rest of his belongings, they are passed along to the next demon. You are now my property. You are my wife. I completed the full ceremony whilst you were under my compelment."

"So you did have sex with me!"

"It will protect you if something happens to me. If Paymon had done as he should, Livia would not have come back for you." He shook his head. "I can't imagine why he didn't do it if you were his wife of choice."

I didn't offer a reply. I knew why Paymon hadn't completed

the full ceremony. It was because I asked him not to. He cared about me, wanted me to be happy. He was a demon, but one that seemed to have developed some sort of heart. I looked to my hand. The marriage symbol tying me to Erebus was already settling into the dark lines that I'd had before Paymon died.

Erebus sprang to his feet and stood in front of the fire, his back to me.

"I am not exactly pleased by the situation," he said. "I would have preferred to have found my own wife, not have my predecessor's forced upon me, particularly one as weak as you."

"Weak? Paymon said that he fed off my emotions without me having to do anything. I was a constant emotional charge for him."

"Really?" He turned his head to the side and raised his brow. "I find that hard to believe. I'm not impressed by you. Fortunately, I do not need to be constantly fed, but I warn you now, if you do not begin to satisfy me, I will send you to the Master. If you are no use to me, perhaps he could use you for something." His lips formed a scathing smirk.

I ran a shaking hand across my forehead as images of what could be flashed through my mind.

"Ahhh . . ." He breathed in deeply. "That's better."

I looked down, not willing to see the smug line of his mouth.

"Now, I need some answers from you." He walked to the chair he had only just vacated and perched on the side of it. "I advise you to be honest with me."

I straightened up, prepared to answer truthfully. I had no reason to lie.

His first question came quickly and was easy enough to answer. "When did you marry Paymon?"

"The night before the last Ascension Ceremony."

"Really? He left it a bit late." He scratched the stubble on his chin. "Had you been seeing him before then?"

I shook my head. "I only met him properly on my twenty-first birthday. That was two days before the ceremony."

"So you had only just turned twenty-one?"

"Yes."

He continued to rub his chin. "What was Paymon's categorisation of you for the Master's household?"

"A wife." I reminded myself what Paymon had saved me from, and even though I didn't want to admit it, what Erebus had also saved me from. Although I didn't yet know what the alternative was.

Erebus grinned. "A wife, interesting."

I hated that he found my categorisation even slightly amusing. "Why? What's so funny about it?"

He laughed quietly.

"Tell me? What would your categorisation have been?"

He shrugged. "I'm not sure, I've not spent years observing you in the village. Interesting though. He must have seen something that made you suitable. The wife of the Master is a difficult category to be chosen for. The Ascension Ceremonies across the country don't always provide him with wives. Some years there are none."

He crossed the room and closed the door before returning to stand in front of the fire. He kept his back to it as he continued watching me.

"I need to ask you about Paymon's death."

I sighed, staring at my hands on my knee.

"It's obviously upset you," he said, folding his arms across his chest. "Your emotions peak whenever he is mentioned."

"I liked him. He was kind to me."

"And you didn't kill him?"

"No." I lifted my chin, and pushed my shoulders back. "I didn't kill him."

"Tell me what happened."

I sighed again, not wanting to relive the last moments of his life. "We went to the village for the monthly feast. When we returned, he started to feel unwell. By the time we got home, he was struggling to stand and was in a lot of pain. He died in my arms." I sniffed, recalling the look in his eyes when I insisted he fed from my emotions, when I begged him to take everything I was feeling in order to save himself.

"He was poisoned," Erebus said.

"Poisoned?" I reeled backward. It was sudden, but I never once suspected that someone would want him dead. "Who would want to poison him?"

"I suspect it was someone at the feast last night. I presume he will have eaten, not wanting to upset the villagers by refusing?"

I nodded.

He turned around and picked an ornament from the mantelpiece, inspecting it closely. "Sometimes our humanity springs to life, and it doesn't always end well." He continued to focus on the red glass object in his hand. "He didn't need to eat at the feast, but he did so as not to upset the villagers. In return, one of them killed him." He paused for a moment. "Tell me more about your lover from the village."

I froze, this was the first question I was unwilling to answer.

"What makes you so sure I had a lover?"

He sighed but still kept his attention on the ornament. "Tell me, Athena. Don't make me compel you to tell me. I know it was the boy who tried to stop me taking you."

I swallowed hard, my upset at Paymon's death turned to panic. Why was he mentioning him?

"What do you want to know?" I failed to keep the shaking from my voice.

He cocked his head, and his gaze met mine. "How serious was it between you two? I want an honest answer."

I paused for a moment. "I'm not sure," I said, settling on the exact truth. "I thought he loved me until I caught him having sex with my best friend."

Erebus's eyes widened before he turned back to the ornament in his hands.

"And I thought I loved him," I added, lost briefly in happy memories. "But I'm not so sure now."

"What was his reaction to you being sent away at the Ascension Ceremony?"

"He suggested running away together."

Erebus shook his head. "Madness. You know you'd have got caught?"

"I didn't then, but I do now. Anyway, I refused. And that was before I found out about him and Hannah."

"Hannah?"

"My ex-best friend."

Erebus chuckled. He proceeded to remove his glove from his right hand and crouched in front of the fire. Without any hesitation, he reached forward and held the ornament in the flames.

"Why did you refuse him? Surely running away with a

lover was a better option than marrying an old demon."

"Better than marrying any demon."

"Indeed." Erebus twisted the ornament in the fire. It was glowing brightly in the flames, yet his hand remained untouched. "So why stay?"

"Paymon said a few things that made me stop and think about where my life was heading. I hate the cold, I hate the darkness, and I hate the rain."

"So life here was easy?" His cynicism was easy to hear. "Paymon showed you a life you desired?"

"No, not really, although I can't deny the appeal of the warmth that was around me whilst here. I made the best decision I could considering the options."

He straightened to his full height. "For what it's worth, I think you made the right decision."

His declaration stunned me, and while I remained silent, unsure of what to say next, he replaced his glove and walked to the old desk in the corner of the room. He sat on the chair and picked up a pen and a notebook.

"It's late," he said, scribbling away furiously. "You know where Paymon's bedroom is. Go there and wait for me. We need to get acquainted as husband and wife."

"But—"

"I won't be long. I have a few things to sort before I join you."

I swallowed silently, lifting a shaking hand to my forehead. I'd never been in Paymon's bedroom, and I certainly had no intention of going into it now that it was Erebus's. I tried to calm my shortness of breath and glanced at the seated demon across the room. Get acquainted as husband and wife? He could forget that.

"Go now, Athena," Erebus said, as if bored, "or do you want me to drag you there?"

CHAPTER 12

CONTEMPT

I SOMEHOW MANAGED TO STAND AND WALK ON SHAKING legs. As I left the room, I was acutely aware of Erebus's eyes resting on me, but he didn't speak.

With a stomach full of rattling nerves, I turned to the grand stairway. My racing heart sank even further when I climbed the stairs and caught sight of the dying rosebush through the hall window. I missed Paymon. And it didn't seem right that I'd never ventured into Paymon's bedroom when he was alive, yet now I was being ordered to go there by Erebus.

With a new resolve to ignore his request, I strode past Erebus's bedroom and into mine. I shut the door, knowing that he could enter at any time, but still felt the need to put every possible barrier between us. I didn't lock it, though; I saw no point. He'd just break it from its hinges.

I slumped onto the chair at my dressing table and watched Odin through the mirror whilst waiting for Erebus's inevitable arrival. Odin was still sleeping on top of the screen, hunched down and fluffed, like a black ball of feathers. I grinned as I looked at him. His proximity calmed me, and at this very moment, I needed to stay as calm as possible.

It had been strange seeing Thomas today. He'd stirred old memories, and not all of them were the ones revolving around his infidelity. He'd stood up to Livia, something I would never have thought him brave enough to do. He'd also stood up to Erebus, eventually, even though it ended in misery for him. I was glad he was okay, but recognised that any future life with him, whether I wanted it or not, wasn't possible. Not now. Erebus was a young demon, not old like Paymon. There would be no outliving him. He was here to stay, and as such, I was going to have to get used to him and his ways. I lifted my chin and made a promise to myself to stay as strong as I could around him. I wouldn't just let him boss me around.

As expected, he didn't knock when he came into my room. I jumped when the door flew open and banged back against the wall. Odin immediately woke up, squawked in alarm and flapped his wings as Erebus stood in the doorway staring at me. I didn't turn around to face him, but viewed him through the mirror as he approached.

He scowled. "I didn't tell you to come into your room. I told you to wait in mine."

"I have no desire to go into your room," I said, calmly turning to face him.

His eyes widened. "I don't care what you desire. You do as I say."

"Well, maybe if you asked me nicely, I'd do it."

"Ask you nicely?" He jerked his head back and stared at me incredulously.

I grinned at his reaction, and he instantly recovered his

predatory persona.

"Have you forgotten that I'm a demon? I don't ask nicely for anything."

"Well then, be prepared for me to ignore you."

I stood, intending to walk to the door and ask him to leave, but he grabbed my arm. Backing me against the bed post, he pressed his lower body against mine, pinning me in place. Once again I was reminded of his height and how easily he moved me to his will.

His gloved hand held my chin. My heart raced so much, I was convinced he'd see my chest pounding.

"I treat you how I want to, not how you want me to." He tipped my face to his. "If I tell you to wait in my room, you do it. If I tell you to get on your hands and knees and crawl at my feet, you do it. If I tell you to beg, you beg. If I tell you to eat, you eat. If I tell you to lie down and spread your legs, you do it!"

"No, I don't," I said as calmly as I could manage, although my words were not as strong as I'd have liked.

His eyes widened to a seemingly impossible width before he narrowed his gaze. His eyebrows practically met as he frowned.

"If you don't do as I say, I'll compel you. I've done it once, and I'll do it again." He held my chin tighter, the smell of his leather glove creeping under my nose.

But I wasn't going to let him scare me into accepting his orders so easily. My bravado, however ill-placed, leapt forward. "So that's your answer? If I don't do as I'm told, you'll compel me?"

He nodded, anger flashing across his features.

I straightened my back, and squeezed my arms between

us, crossing them over my chest. "What fun that must be for you. You told me that you'd never forced yourself on a woman, she was always willing. But if you compel me to have sex with you again, I'm telling you that in my mind I'll never be willing. You will only be fooling yourself!" I gripped his wrist and tried to move his hand away from my chin, but he held me firm, easily ignoring my physical attempt to move him.

He glared at me for an impossibly long time, not speaking whilst rich amber eyes surveyed me. Without any warning, he released my chin. His arm twisted from my grip, and he spun around before striding to the door. Odin squawked loudly, several times in succession, before the door slammed shut.

Left alone, I relaxed against the bed post. Odin fluttered onto my shoulder and leaned against my head. I rubbed my chin where Erebus had held me. His grip had been firm and strong, and I knew he could have compelled me to do anything he wanted. But I'd managed to fend him off with my words. My declaration of never being willing to sleep with him appeared to have struck a nerve, one I would never have expected. At least I knew what he expected from our relationship. I did as I was told, no questions asked, regardless of how unpleasant or derogatory it was. But I wouldn't be treated like that. He needed to know, and I intended to tell him.

The next morning, I dressed quickly, another front fastening dress so that I didn't have to ask him for his assistance. The less he came near me, the better. Odin flew to the window, and I let him out, watching until the darkness swallowed him.

When downstairs, I peered into every room to see if

Erebus was around. He wasn't, and I assumed that he was still in bed. Content that he was asleep, I headed to the kitchen hoping that there was some food. I was starving.

I opened the kitchen door hesitantly, recalling my only other visit to this room when Bia attacked me. Erebus had told me she was dead, but he hadn't mentioned whether there was another infernal around. An ensemble of lit lanterns was on the table, and whereas they provided enough light to see across the kitchen, I had to stretch onto my toes to see if there was anything curled up in the basket. A huge sigh of relief left me when an empty floor was revealed. There wasn't even a basket.

My peace of mind was quickly replaced by a streak of curiosity as a blast of cold air blew across my face. The door that led outside was ajar. My first instinct was to shut it, but the flicker of a light outside caught my attention. What was it? I wedged the door open with one of the wooden kitchen chairs, and stepped outside. The cold air made me shiver and I rubbed my arms with my hands as I headed toward the dancing light. I stilled when the normal endless silence was disturbed by a horse neighing. Erebus had arrived on a horse. Of course he would be tending to it, making sure it was fed, watered and brushed. Were there stables out here?

I crept closer, keeping out of direct sight by hanging to the limited shadows. The horse sniffed and huffed, but the voice of the man with it didn't sound like Erebus. It was too soft, too comforting to be him, but whoever it was, was brushing the horse quite vigorously.

"We need to go out every morning if you're going to run like that, Samael. Do you like it here? Free in the hills and the fields, running like there's no tomorrow? It wasn't just you,

you know. I felt that freedom as well. It was glorious."

Too curious to just walk away, I peered around the stable door, careful to stay hidden. The man had his back to me, and threw a blanket over Samael. When he stepped around the horse to straighten the covering I caught his profile. I shifted away from the stable door. It was Erebus. How could he have so much compassion and kindness in his voice when he spoke to his horse but speak to me the way he did? Every word he said to his horse, Samael, was edged with a tenderness I didn't think him capable of.

I stepped away from the stable and walked back to the house, my moves slow and careful, my mind racing with confusion over Erebus. Once in the kitchen I pushed the door back to the narrow gap it had previously been. Hugging myself, I stood in front of the lit stove and rubbed my arms furiously, tying to generate some heat. It was bitter outside, and I wondered if we'd get snow. I remembered it from before the demons came. Cold, white crystals that fell from the sky like tiny angel wings. I wondered if angels existed when I was a child, but never gave any thought to the others—the evil ones that walked amongst us now. It was strange how childhood prepared you for the best of things, never the worst.

Once I was warmed by the heat from the stove, I resumed my waylaid search for food. Nestled on a shelf in a small walk-in cupboard was a basket of eggs and a half loaf of bread. There was a small jug of milk next to a block of butter, but as I smelt the milk, I decided to leave it alone. Eggs and toast—it was a more than adequate meal.

I reached for the pan, cracked three eggs into it, and stirred them before placing it on the stand over the flames. I cut a thick slice of bread, speared it with the toasting fork, and settled it close to the flames before resuming my whisking of the eggs. Minutes later, the eggs were scrambled and the toast was burnt along the edges, just as I liked it. I pulled a chair out from under the table and found a space between the lanterns to put my plate.

Halfway through my meal, Erebus entered the kitchen. He closed the door before catching sight of me.

"Athena?" He jerked his head back. "What are you doing in here?"

I couldn't reply. Not only did I have a mouthful of food, but his appearance caught me completely off guard. His hair was wet, water dripping down his face. His clothes were also soaked, but even from where I was sitting I caught the bright amber of his irises. They were made even more striking by their contrast against his tanned skin tone and his dark stubble. I found myself thinking what a handsome man he was and then scolded myself for seeing him in such a way.

"Erebus," I managed to eventually reply, grateful that it didn't sound like a laboured breath after my shear ogling of him. "I was hungry. I made myself some breakfast."

His nose twitched, and a slight smile pulled at his lips.

"So you've made yourself some breakfast, but none for your husband?"

"I didn't think you'd want anything. Paymon never ate, well, apart from at the feast." I cut my toast with my knife, aware of his gaze resting upon me. "Do I have to cook you something?"

He pulled his gloves off and then his wet cloak. His coat underneath wasn't any dryer.

"No."

He removed his coat and threw it over his cloak whilst I

continued eating. I tried not to look at him, but as he unfastened the tiny buttons at the top of his smock, I found myself strangely mesmerised. When he pulled the garment over his head and discarded it the same way as his other clothes, I stopped eating and stared unabashed at his naked torso.

I swallowed loudly, glad to be sitting, as I was sure I would have swooned at the sight of him. Tanned, toned and sculpted, he was more an Adonis than a demon. He had lots of intricate designs drawn in ink on his upper arms and torso, and as he turned to lock the door, I tipped my head to catch the familiar design of the pentagram and the circle etched into the skin on his back.

He perched on the corner edge of the table near the door, no concern about his half-naked body, and watched me eat. I didn't like his scrutiny, but I was too hungry to care.

"You will need to go to the village today to speak to the old hag about providing you with food."

"Her name's Myrtle. And she's not a hag." I was about to place another forkful of eggs in my mouth, but halted my action. "Did Myrtle bring food here?"

"Someone must have done. I presume Paymon had the infernal cooking your meals. So now it isn't here you'll need to cook. I don't want you to starve, you're skinny enough. I like my women to be soft and curvy, not bony and angular." His eyes travelled down my body. Luckily I was sitting so his inspection was limited, but I didn't miss the curl of his lips as his gaze settled on the soft curve of my breasts.

"I can't help what I look like. Years of hardly having enough to eat made me this way."

"Perhaps, but you have no need to starve now, do you? Whatever you want, she will provide you with." He broke his greedy staring of me. "Which brings me on to my next point. When was your last monthly bleed?"

The heat in my cheeks increased, and I stopped eating.

"You're twenty-one. A woman. Have you never had one?" His brow rose as he continued to stare at me.

"A few months ago," I said.

"But you're not pregnant."

I shook my head. "No, as you've already pointed out, I'm skinny, all of us are. We don't have enough to eat. Our diet is basic. It affects all parts of the body." I wasn't prepared to tell him about the lace either. It was a secret.

Erebus nodded once, seemingly satisfied with my response. "In the future, you will eat in the dining room. When you cook your meals, you will also cook and set the table for me."

"You'll eat with me?"

He shook his head. "No, I will never eat what you cook, but as your husband, I demand that you cook for me."

"What? I have to ask Myrtle to provide food for both of us even though you'll not eat it? I can't take food from the village like that. It's a hard life, they need all the food they can get."

"That's not my concern. You will eat properly and you will cook for two." He cocked his head to the side. "I have to ask; do you think that living with me will be easy?"

I finished eating my mouthful of food, not answering him. Erebus grinned. "Maybe you should be rewarded with the best food available for having to endure what's to come?"

"I . . ."

"I'll remind you once again, shall I? You are my wife." He tilted his hand so the marriage mark was clearly visible. "And we will become physical at some point." He held his finger up to silence any response from me. "It will happen, and when it does, you will need to keep your strength up. I'm a demanding lover, and you will need all your energy to be able to satisfy me."

I lifted my brow, somewhat intrigued by his statement, but quickly covered my reaction. "I don't ever see it happening unless you compel me."

"Let me give you something to think about," he said, jumping from the table and catching my gaze. "I've yet to decide how long I'll let you play this game, but if it carries on for too long, I may send you to the Master and let him deal with you instead."

"I thought I was too scrawny, unattractive," I bit back, refusing to be intimidated by his threat.

He stepped nearer. "I never said you were unattractive."

My cheeks heated again, and I quickly looked away from his penetrating gaze.

"You are my wife, and as such I will enjoy your flesh. You belong to me, Athena, don't ever forget it."

"You make me sound like a possession, not a real living person. You showed more affection to your horse!"

"Were you spying on me? Or not able to keep away?"

"The door was open," I said, nodding to it. "And I saw the flickering of the lantern. I was curious."

He stood too close, well within my personal comfort zone. He smelt of outside, the freshness of the air and the rain clinging to his unique manly scent. I breathed in deeply and tried to settle on what the underlying scent was. It was intoxicating.

"You have a very curious nature," he said, crouching in front of me. His eyes searched mine, and I became lost in their rich burning amber. They were beautiful, but unfortunately, not black like Paymon's. I really didn't feed him. Erebus was telling the truth when he said my emotions were weak to him.

He unexpectedly rested one of his hands on my knee, and I jumped. Not from his touch but from a shock that ran through my knee and straight to my chest. He immediately removed his hand, sprung to his full height, and backed away. He scratched the back of his neck before gathering his clothes.

"Clean up in here when you've finished!" he said before leaving the kitchen.

I remained staring at the doorway after he left the room. What was all that about? I pulled the hem of my dress up and slipped my sock over my knee to inspect the stinging area. I frowned when I saw a red raised scratch on the skin. Had he caused that, or was it just a coincidence?

"Crazy demon," I muttered before rising from the table and placing my plate and the pan on the side. I attempted to twist the bronze-coloured pieces of metal that bent over the nearby sink, but they wouldn't budge. I stared at the strange design of the metal—taps. Gran had told me of the luxury of running water through the pipes. Hot and cold water, apparently. Life must have been so simple.

With no idea where the water was to wash the dirty pots, I resigned myself to finding Erebus to ask him. It was one thing giving me orders and expecting me to follow them, but if I had no idea how to do what he said, then he needed to tell me. He wasn't in the library, and I nearly missed his hunched figure in the lounge. The room was lit by a solitary candle positioned on the desk where he was sitting. He was writing, and his body blocked most of the light, although there was enough of a glow to confirm that he hadn't replaced the clothes that he'd removed in the kitchen. Unwilling to disturb his concentration, I crept quietly to the sofa and sat down.

He continued writing, either not aware of my presence or ignoring it. I stared unabashed, revelling in the opportunity to examine him without his penetrating gaze resting on me. He had high cheek bones, a straight nose and a strong jaw-line, and the muscle in his neck seemed to tense several times whilst he wrote. His hair was tied back, although lengths of it had escaped and gently curled over his ears. But it was his back that caught my attention, just as it had in the kitchen. It was such a large design, thick black lines carved into his skin, with blocks of text written in between them.

I pushed myself into a straighter sitting position when he groaned loudly and ripped a page of paper from his writing book. He screwed it up and threw it across the room. Only then did he become aware of my presence.

"Spying on me again?" He turned in his chair to face me. "This is beginning to become a bit of a habit."

"I need to ask you something, but I didn't want to disturb you." I inclined my head toward the desk. "You looked like you were doing something important."

His gaze followed mine to the book, and he sighed before standing and walking across the room to the unlit fireplace. He crouched in front of it and held his hands above the wood and tinder. As he rubbed them together, he created tiny white and blue sparks. The sparks instantly lit the tinder, and within moments the fire was a healthy glowing beast, lighting and heating the room.

Erebus straightened and stepped to the single chair be-fore sinking into the overstuffed seat.

"What did you need to ask me?"

"Water. Where is the water to wash the pots? Bia used to

cook and wash and clean. I have no idea where anything is kept or stored. And I need water."

"The water will be from the well behind the stables. I spotted it on my way to groom Samael."

"So you can't make the metal pipes work?"

He chuckled. "No, I can't."

"And what about the water in my tub?"

"What about it?"

"How do I empty it?"

He shrugged, but a smile still pulled at his lips. "I have no idea, but I can tell you how to fill it."

I waited for him to continue.

"You'll need to make a lot of trips to the well."

I sighed, not having the same sense of amusement as he did at the situation.

"And I expect you to bathe every day," he added, almost as an afterthought.

"What?" If the thought of trudging upstairs with countless buckets of water wasn't enough, I was now faced with the dilemma of how to get rid of the old bath water. "If you insist on me bathing every day, you could at least make sure the water is warm."

"You want warm water?"

"Paymon managed to keep the water at a nice steady temperature for me. Are you not powerful enough to heat water?"

His eyes narrowed. Did he not like the comparison?

"What is your power anyway?" I asked. "Paymon's was fire."

"So it would seem. But the power to create fire is an ancient one. Not many demons possess it nowadays."

"So what's yours?"

"That's for me to know."

I leaned forward, nearer to him. "Why won't you tell me?"

"It's of no concern to you." He sunk further back into his chair and stretched his legs out before crossing one ankle over the other.

I pursed my lips. I was determined to discover something about him. "You keep reminding me that I'm your wife, yet you won't tell me anything about yourself."

He didn't reply, and I waited for his expected cutting response.

"I'm thirty-one," he said, stroking the material on the arm of his chair. "I came above land when I was nineteen. I initially lived in the south of England, but moved further north with my sister about six years ago."

"You have a sister?"

"Olisha. She's thirty-four. I have an older brother, Narabus. He's a general in the Master's army. I also had an older sister, but she was murdered several years ago."

"I'm sorry," I said. I didn't like hearing of the loss of any member of a family. It reminded me too easily of my own.

"So what about your family?" he said, sitting upright. "Who have I dragged you away from?"

"No one," I said. "My parents and sister died when you all came. My gran looked after me until—"

"So you're all alone now? No one to save you from me?"

I composed myself after his interruption and tried to decide whether he was humouring me or about to unleash a vile demand, but he was too difficult to read. "Hopefully I won't need saving. I can look after myself."

He chuckled loudly and then leaned forward in his chair. "I think you kid yourself. Everyone wants to be saved from a demon. Well, maybe not those who are as twisted as us, but certainly nice, young girls like you."

"I didn't want to be saved from Paymon."

"Ahhh, yes. But he was hardly a true demon, was he?" He tapped his fingers on the arm of his chair. I saw the pull of a smile at the corner of his mouth just before he looked away. "So, what did Paymon do with you? He obviously didn't care for the pleasure of your body. So, how did you entertain him?"

"He respected me. Enjoyed my company."

"Respected you?" He began to laugh. "We are demons. We don't respect anyone, not even each other."

"Well, he did. Maybe when you get really old, you develop something of a soul, a conscience even."

He threw his head back and roared with laughter. "No, that's not what we are. We don't have a soul, and we certainly don't have a conscience. But I am intrigued to hear what you spent your time doing whilst you were with him. I know what we'd be doing if you were willing."

"Books," I blurted out, quickly steering the conversation away from his favourite topic. "I used to read to him."

"Read? What sort of books?" His familiar grin reappeared.

"Whatever I wanted." I quickly thought of a way to try and settle him. Show him how Paymon and I used to be with each other. "Do you want me to read to you?"

His eyebrows rose, and then he controlled his shock. "Only if you sit on my lap naked."

"I won't be reading to you then," I said, looking away from him. He was impossible. Everything I said he twisted.

"Oh, I'm sure you will. I see no harm in compelling you to strip and read to me. If I remember rightly, your little strop last night was all about sex and your unwillingness to cooperate.

I have no qualms about compelling you to read." He leaned back in his chair, and hooked one leg over the arm. "And as much as I'd like to get started on our reading session, I think a trip into the village is in order. I'm hungry."

"Hungry?" I asked, confused. But then I realised, food wasn't what he was referring to. Once again my weak emotions were not satisfying him enough.

He pushed himself from the chair and stretched his arms above his head before turning to me. "Yes, hungry. Unless of course, you've changed your mind." His eyebrows lifted and a hint of a smirk played on his lips.

I shook my head before standing up. I'd had enough of his games. "No. I've not changed my mind."

He surveyed me for a moment before speaking. "Pity. I think we'd have enormous fun together." He leaned forward, and I froze. I thought he was going to kiss me. But there was no kiss. His stubbled cheek rested against mine, and his hot breath blew on my ear. "I know that once you give in to me, your emotions will turn my eyes as black as the sky."

I swayed a little, and grabbed his arm to steady myself. What was wrong with me?

"Careful." Erebus chuckled, his breath fanning my ear. "I may think I'm beginning to break down these walls you seem to have put between us. Don't spoil all my fun."

My hand fell from his arm as quickly as I'd put it there, and I pushed him away.

"I'll just go and get changed," he said. "And then I'll go have some fun in the village."

"Am I coming with you?" I asked. For some reason I didn't want to be left alone, but at the same time I wasn't convinced that going with Erebus was the best idea.

"Of course. You need to speak to the h . . . old woman about food for the next few days. And you wanted to know what my power was. Well you'll get the chance to see it in action, won't you?"

"You'll use your power on them?"

"I need feeding, and the villagers need to know who they are dealing with." He strode to the door but turned back to me as he reached for the handle. "Oh, and try not to let your curiosity send you to spy on me whilst I'm getting changed." His brow rose and he shook his head. "I may not be able to stop myself from compelling you if you do."

Chapter 13

RESENTMENT

"**K**EEP UP WITH ME, ATHENA!" EREBUS MARCHED ahead, his strides long and confident.

"You seem excited," I said, lifting the skirt of my dress to stop it catching on the ground.

"Excited?" He stopped and waited for me to catch up with him. "I'm not excited, I'm starving." He winked before focusing ahead.

"Well you should have had breakfast with me," I said, recalling the way he sat across the table and watched me eat my breakfast.

"That's not the same, and you know it."

I stumbled on a small divot in the ground, and Erebus grabbed my arm to stop me from falling.

"Do you have to feed from them?" I asked, brushing his gloved hand off my arm.

"Of course. They are my villagers. They belong to me, and for providing them a safe place to live I expect them to keep me fully satisfied. A fact that you ignore."

"You won't hurt any of them, will you?" I lifted my gaze to him, but he didn't notice. He was fixed on his future meal ahead.

"Hurt them?" Erebus chuckled. "It depends how resilient they are. Fear is the easiest emotion for me to release amongst the villagers, and I need to make a point of them knowing that I'm not as easy to placate at Paymon. Start brutal, scare them, make them listen to me and respect me. I can always soften up when I get to know them." He flashed me a sinister smile, and I feared that whoever he selected today would be treated with no mercy.

I stumbled again, but quickly caught myself.

"Who does your old lover hang around with?" he asked as we approached the edge of the village.

"His name is Thomas." The hairs on the back of my neck bristled as I mentioned his name. Memories, too many memories revolved around him. Unfortunately, the one memory that constantly replayed itself was the one I'd never forget.

"Who does *Thomas* hang around with?"

I shrugged, unsure as to why he was interested in Thomas's friends.

"Oh, come now, Athena. Surely your ex-lover must have a few male friends who he joked with about your prudish behaviour."

My face heated so much I had no doubt I was the colour of the roses in the courtyard. I stopped walking, and Erebus spun to face me before stepping closer. He reached his gloved hand to my cheek and ran his fingers across it.

"Look how you colour when your sexual prowess is questioned."

"Stop it," I said, pushing his hand away.

His mouth twitched at the corners before morphing into a sneer. I fought the urge to cry when he began laughing.

"So, you're not a prude, but your standards are too high for a demon to enjoy your flesh?" He prowled around me, running his finger across my shoulders. I froze, not willing to answer him or play his games. "Let me tell you," he said, his mouth next to my ear as he stood behind me, "that you are nothing special. There is nothing about you that makes me crave your body. You would merely be a plaything, an object for me to satisfy my own sexual urges. And I'm twisted, Athena. Sick. Evil. Perverted."

My breath hitched as the heat from his breath blew across my ear. His unmistakable aroma wafted around me, and I closed my eyes to block the tightening in my stomach—it was too pleasant, too insistent. And it wasn't right that I reacted like this to him.

"Now," Erebus said, facing me. "A list of Thomas's friends. Names."

I shook my head, releasing myself from the drunken stupor he had created. "James is his closest friend, and Jacob."

"Only two? Let's find one of them, shall we?"

"They'll be at the field."

"Really? Why?" He strode forward, his focus on the centre of the village. "I've not restored the light. It's pointless them being there."

I rushed to keep up with him. "So when will you let the light return? You know they need the light for the crops to grow."

"Let it return? Athena, I don't just let it return." He glanced at the houses as we passed them. I'd become accustomed to

220

the women of the village hiding from me on the few times I'd been in the village, but many of the men also hid this morning. There were a few of them dotted between the houses, mending the thatch roofs or fixing walls where the rain and damp had rotted the wood.

"I need to see if the villagers deserve the light," he said. "A lot depends on my visit today. If I'm not satisfactorily fed, then I won't bother to grant them any favours."

"It's not a favour. They'll starve if the crops fail." Surely he knew this.

"Then they need to ensure I'm fed. You don't seem to be bothered about feeding me, but they will be desperate." He stopped walking as we arrived in the centre of the village. He turned in a circle before standing in front of me. "Are there any pretty girls in the village? Ones I could enjoy until you're willing?"

I screwed my nose up at his suggestion.

"If the villagers can't satisfy my hunger then we shall leave, find another village." He looked around, seeking out a potential victim.

"We? You mean I'd have to go with you?" It was then that I understood. There really was no escape from him.

He tucked a stray strand of hair behind his ear and pursed his lips. "Do I need to keep reminding you? You are my wife. Therefore, wherever I go, you will go too."

"What if I don't want to?"

"What you want isn't an option. It never has been, and it never will be. You'll do as I say." His words held no humour, he was serious, and not for the first time, I wished Paymon was still here. "Understand?"

I nodded, cursing his reminder of the control he had over

me.

"Go and find the old woman. Sort your food with her. I don't expect you to make journeys here unnecessarily. Your next visit will be at the feast, so ensure she knows what's expected."

As I turned away to head to Myrtle's he grabbed my arm.

"Athena, no kiss for your husband?" He cocked his head to the side and raised his brow.

I glared at him. Had I heard him right? He wanted me to kiss him? There was no way I'd let the lips of a demon taint mine.

He lifted his hand to his chin and rubbed at the stubble. "It may put me in a better mood, and I might not feed so voraciously."

I grimaced before taking a deep, pained breath. Stepping closer to him, I tipped my head toward his and planted a quick kiss on his rough cheek.

He grabbed my wrist as I backed away.

"Pathetic!" His fingers dug into my skin. "Totally pathetic. Remember you're—"

"Your wife." I shook my arm free from his clutch. "Yes, I know. You keep reminding me."

"Then start behaving like it! And don't talk to the old hag for too long. I don't want to wait for you. Come and find me when you've finished."

I rubbed my arm, still feeling the burn from his pincer-like grasp. Erebus was glancing around at the few villagers who hadn't fled into their homes. They all kept their distance, but their eyes were fixed on him. Their mistrust was easy to see and understand.

"Athena!" Myrtle called. She was standing in the doorway

of her home, clinging to the rough wooden edge of the frame. Her gaze drifted over me before settling on Erebus. Their eyes locked in a secret battle. But Myrtle didn't flinch, and it was Erebus who looked away.

Myrtle beckoned me forward with a curl of her bent fingers.

"So, he's Paymon's replacement?" She inclined her head at Erebus as he stood in the middle of the village, his arms folded, a twisted smile on his lips. He cast his heavy stare into the distance as if assessing the situation. When he puffed his chest out and straightened to his full height, I knew he had found his victim. I looked away, I didn't want to watch.

"I need to talk to you," I said, following Myrtle into her home. She shuffled to the window, keeping Erebus within her sight.

Myrtle's home was as basic as mine had been. There was a sickly smelling broth bubbling in a pan, the smoke from the fire billowing into the room.

"I presume you still need Bessie to take food to the house," she said. "Has the creature gone now he's arrived?"

"Yes, he killed her." I coughed and wafted the smoke away from my face. "I didn't know Bessie brought the food for me. I need to thank her."

"There's no need. You need to eat. How else will you get food?" She hobbled across the room, her steps as unsteady as the uneven legs on the chair in my old home.

"What's his name?" she said, sinking onto the wooden chair.

"Erebus."

Myrtle reached for my right hand. "Married already? The ceremony complete?" She inspected the raised black mark.

Her words could have meant many things, but somehow I knew exactly what she was referring to.

"Yes, very complete."

"You don't waste much time, do you? And you'll need more lace. I'll keep you supplied, send some every day with Bessie." She untied a pouch from her waist. "Keep it hidden."

I tucked the pouch between my breasts, pushing it under the material of my dress.

"He's powerful, Athena. You need to be careful."

As if to confirm what she had said, a loud, piercing shriek sounded from outside. I froze, as did Myrtle, before rushing to the doorway.

Erebus was standing over a man's sprawled body which was face down on the ground.

Erebus was lit by the glow from the fire, the flames throwing his features into a sharp mask of the demon within. He prowled toward the man on the ground whilst pulling his gloves off, one at a time, and tucking them into the pocket of his jacket. I clung to the edge of the doorway torn between not wanting to witness what was about to happen, but too curious about Erebus's power.

I jumped as a continuous bright zigzag of light crackled from Erebus's uncovered hand and hit the man in the chest. He flew backward, but the light continued to hit him as if connected to his body by an invisible force.

"Jacob," I gasped, seeing his body lit by the forceful surge of power.

His body shook, each limb trembling as he rose from the ground. Erebus walked toward him and grabbed him under the chin, holding him steady as his feet dangled in the air. He gargled wordlessly as Erebus's hand sent bright crackling bolts of power around his neck.

"Stop!" I gathered my skirts in my hand and ran across the mud splattered ground toward Erebus. "Stop it, now!"

I grabbed Erebus's elbow, pulling it with all my strength. He spun around, not releasing his grip on Jacob, and knocked me out of the way with his free hand. I stumbled and fell before looking back at them. Jacob's body has stopped moving. He now hung lifelessly in Erebus's hand.

Erebus viewed each villager in turn. "When I find out who poisoned Paymon, I will deal with them in exactly the same way. And I will find out."

He released Jacob, and he fell to the ground.

"No," I sobbed, crawling toward his crumpled body before looking to Erebus. "What have you—?"

My words faded, my mouth refused to move. My skin heated, and my vision swam. I knew immediately what had happened. Erebus had compelled me. I shot him a furious stare but he only returned it before pulling his gloves back onto his hands. Unwillingly, I rose to my feet and walked toward him. He stood with his arms open, ready to welcome me. And, as I stepped into his arms, I caught sight of his eyes—amber, edged with a thick rim of black. He was fed.

He pulled me against his hard chest and ran his fingers through my hair. As he gazed into my eyes I inched closer, feeling the heat of his breath on my lips just before I kissed him.

I didn't want to kiss him. Every part of me wanted to scream, tell him what a monster he was and how much I hated him, but my body wouldn't listen. Erebus's compelment was too intense, no room for my own decisions to be made.

As his lips met mine, I jolted as if every part of him

possessed some sort of charge. But a meeting of lips wasn't his only intention. He wasn't content with a simple kiss. His arm encircled my waist at the exact moment my mouth opened against his. My tongue swept forward with an urgency that wasn't my own. My mind hated him, but my body welcomed the demanding way he took control. A whimper built in my throat but wasn't released. My fingers tingled with the need to touch him, and I shivered with pleasure from his closeness.

He swiftly released me, staring into my eyes with a mixture of amusement and desire. I wanted to look away, not see his eyes when he looked at me with so much longing. But he didn't release his compelment. Even when I moved to his side, I was unable to take my eyes off him.

With an infuriating grin, he winked at me and then turned to the villagers. "The poisoner will not be as lucky as this boy." He pointed to Jacob who, thankfully, was alive, moaning and groaning. "I won't just torture them, I'll kill them. I will not tolerate any disobedience from my villagers, and if necessary, I will torture every single one of you. I have one less suspect to interrogate, but there will be more. I will return the light to the fields, but be warned, I can just as easily remove it."

I wanted to interrupt him all through his little speech, but I couldn't. My voice was held by the same force as my limbs.

"Come, Athena." He took my hand. "Time to go home."

CHAPTER 14

DETERMINATION

I T WASN'T UNTIL WE ENTERED THE HOUSE THAT EREBUS lifted his compelment. My steps became light, my head cleared of the thick fog that had clouded it, and I was furious.

"How could you?" The air buzzed with my outburst of anger. Candles flickered as if fighting to stay alight.

"Cloak, Athena." Erebus held his arm toward me.

"I asked you a question." I gritted my teeth and pressed my fingernails into the skin of my palm.

He ignored me and stepped forward, lifting his hand toward my neck.

I spun out of his reach. "Keep away from me."

His hand froze in mid-air and he cleared his throat with a small cough as if trying to hide a laugh. "I merely want to remove your cloak, seeing as you seem incapable of doing so."

I pulled at the fastening and swung the heavy item from my shoulders before hurling it at him. Part of the cloak landed over his head, and he pulled it away before hanging it up. Without looking at me, he strolled into the lounge. My footsteps sounded loud on the wooden floor as I followed him.

"Don't you ever compel me like that again!"

He crouched in front of the fireplace, removed his gloves, and placed more wood on top of the glowing embers. Extending his arms, he rubbed his hands together and created sparks to light the fire.

"And don't ignore me." I stood behind him, my arms crossed, waiting for him to explain.

When he stood and turned to face me, I backed away. The true demon was before me. The fire was already blazing and lit him from behind. His features were dark, more so than normal, and his eyes burnt with a brightness I had never seen before. Golden irises pinned me in place as he closed the gap I had just created.

"Your behaviour in the village was not acceptable," he said, slow and steady, bristling with controlled anger. "I will not have a wife of mine challenging me when in the company of others. I had to compel you, and I will do so again if necessary."

"It's never necessary."

"Yes, it is. You have a distinct lack of ability to appreciate who is in charge." His arms were at his sides, his hands curling and then uncurling into fists as he spoke. "Let me remind you that you are not the one who dictates what happens. Sometimes your outbursts humour me, but I will never allow you to challenge me the way you did in the village."

"You forced me to kiss you." I recalled the poisonous taste of his lips, and the hard contours of his body pressed against me.

Erebus scowled, and stepped forward. "I could have done so much more."

"I'm surprised you didn't. Nothing stopped you the night you forced me to marry you." My head buzzed with the sketchy memories I had of our marriage ceremony, and I covered my marriage mark with my unblemished hand.

"I could have thrown you over my shoulder and dragged you into one of the houses, let the villagers know exactly what we were doing by the sounds I could easily tease from your supine body. Or I could have backed you up against one of the huts and defiled you in the centre of the village where everyone could watch."

I stared at him, my mouth open as I stepped backward again, renewing the space between us. I blinked rapidly and ran my hands through my hair.

Erebus cocked a brow. "You like that thought?"

His obvious amusement only angered me further, and I tensed. "You disgust me."

He lifted his hand to his mouth and hid another laugh before running a finger over his chin. "I don't think I do. Somewhere underneath all your protesting is a fiery beating heart. You crave my touch on your skin. You just won't admit it."

"I feel nothing but contempt," I said through gritted teeth. "I hate you."

"I don't agree. I don't disgust you, I intrigue you. I set your heart racing in a way no other man has done before. I see desire in your eyes when you look at me. I hear your breath hitch when you think I'm not aware of you staring." He lifted his hand to my face, but hesitated just before his fingers touched me. With a quiet snigger he dropped his hand. "Just let me know when you've finished playing whatever game it is you're playing. I'm looking forward to what will be a most satisfying reward for my patience."

I caught his scent again as he sauntered to the desk. He smelt of the freshness of the forest pine trees and the muskiness of the earth and smoke. I closed my eyes fighting the powerful effect he had on my senses, and willed him to feel my eyes boring into the side of his head. My breath wasn't hitching, it was pounding out of me, sharp and angry.

"Now," Erebus continued, writing something at his desk, "I suggest you find yourself a book to read. I'll not be around for the rest of the day."

"Where are you going?" The only time Paymon had left me was when he went to the village to prepare Hannah and Julie for the ceremony.

He replaced his pen in the pot on the desk before leaning back in the chair. He lifted his arms in the air and rested his hands behind his head. "Worried about me?"

"No." My eyes wandered to his midriff where his shirt had parted to show a glimpse of flesh. "Just curious."

"I'm going for a ride on Samael. There are a few things I have to sort. When I return, I will need to rest. Do not disturb me. I'll be awake for our evening meal together." He dropped his arms from their raised position. "I'm looking forward to see what you'll prepare. Be ready for me, Athena. Bathed, clean dress, loose hair."

"If I'm not?"

"I'll bathe you. I'll dress you." He scratched his cheek and sniffed.

"And I suppose you'll compel me if I refuse."

His nose twitched, and he grinned. "No. I think I'd quite

like the fight you'd put up. Grappling with your naked body would be fun. The emotions you'd let loose would be most entertaining. I may even manage to feed from some of them."

I huffed at his infuriating assessment, but caught the excitement in his voice. "So you think you can feed from me?"

"No. I'll need to continue to visit the village and seek out others to feed from. Your emotions are too weak to be of any use. They will only become strong if I do something to cause an intense reaction."

"You didn't just feed when we went into the village," I said, stepping toward him and risking even more wrath. "What you did was horrendous. It was evil."

"What do you expect, Athena? You know I'm a demon. Did you think I'd sit down and have a chat with him, discuss the weather, ask him what he was planning to do with his dreary life?"

"You tortured him!"

He rubbed his forehead before replying. "I needed to feed. And I fed by using my power."

"And what is it exactly?" I waved my hands in his direction. "Some sort of spark?"

"My power is a surge through the palms of my hands." He lifted both his hands in the air and wiggled his fingers. "It's why I usually wear gloves. I can control it, but tend to let it run free when I lose the gloves."

"A surge of power, like electricity?"

He shrugged. "Perhaps. Having never known what electricity is I can't compare it. But whatever it is, it can kill."

My breathing faltered as I understood his true power. "So you could have killed Jacob?"

"Yes." He stood and walked passed me. "But I didn't."

As he reached the door he paused. "If you want me to stop torturing the villagers then you need to give some careful thought to how you can feed me. If you can manage to satisfy my hunger, I'll have no need to torture them."

"But you said I couldn't feed you." I was confused, he wasn't making any sense. Either I did feed him with my emotions, or I didn't, which was it?

"Not generally, no. Maybe you need to spend your time thinking of how you can feed me. What emotions are the strongest in a human? Fear, anger, lust?"

I folded my arms across my chest, and tapped my foot on the floor as he opened the door.

"I need strong emotions, Athena. Get thinking."

"Did you ever think that it could be your inability to feed from me rather than my inability to feed you?"

He strode from the room, ignoring my question.

I sank onto the sofa. He was infuriating. And even though he constantly told me how weak my emotions were, I didn't think they were as weak as he made out. They just weren't as strong as he needed.

The heat from the fire pulsed into the room and I stared vacantly at the agitated flames. I knew how they felt—trapped, burning brightly only to fade into dull embers when their spark had burnt out. I twiddled my hair, trying to work out what to do.

Was there any way to stop him torturing the villagers? Was it like he said? If I found a way to feed him then he would leave them alone. And his compelment was a worry. It was so easy for him to take over—my body became a mere vessel to carry out his silent orders.

Whereas Paymon had been old and more of a companion

than anything else, Erebus was young and handsome. I'd already witnessed his toned and muscular torso when in the kitchen yesterday. But he had a dark soul lingering just below the surface.

I threw my head back onto the sofa and closed my eyes. This house felt like my home, and whereas it had been warm and comforting when Paymon was here, it was now buzzing with excitement with Erebus prowling around. I lifted my hand to inspect the marriage mark. This was the symbol that proved we were married, but I didn't view him as my husband, and I never would.

As I glanced over to his desk I noticed dust particles swirling in the air, the fire lighting their slow restless descent. I scratched my head. The light—did Erebus know anything about the light? Would he part with information about their rise from below? Would he discuss it with me? I blew into the air, and the dust particles rose and swirled before settling into their new random descent. Could I get him to tell me? Could I appeal to him, persuade him? Could I trick him?

A tiny smile crept onto my lips. I knew the way to get information from him. I had to play my part well because if it all went wrong, I would be the one to suffer, and there would be no one to blame but myself.

When Erebus descended the stairs in the evening, I was waiting for him. I was bathed—having endured the icy water in my tub—wearing a clean dress, and my hair was loose. I'd also squirted some of my mother's perfume behind my ears, as well as pinched my cheeks to give them a healthy glow. Erebus looked like he'd given some attention to his appearance as well. A white smock shirt was tucked into a pair of black trousers. His shiny leather boots creaked as he walked. But he still looked ruffled. A dark waistcoat remained unbuttoned, and his hair was tied back, but not completely contained. His familiar dark stubble remained.

I gave him as genuine a smile as I could manage, and he cocked his head when he caught it.

"Dinner's ready." I nodded toward the open dining room door. "If you'd like to go through."

Erebus didn't reply, and walked straight into the room. His musky scent drifted around me as he passed, but there was also the scent of something else. A hint of cologne?

When he'd seated himself at the setting I'd arranged for him at the head of the table, I returned to the kitchen. The vegetable soup was simmering gently. Two chicken breasts were sizzling in the flat pan, and the carrots and potatoes were just coming to the boil. I spooned the soup into two waiting bowls and pulled two large chunks of bread from the freshly cooked loaf that Bessie had brought me.

Bessie's basket had also contained fresh eggs, butter, and cheese. The kitchen held every pot I needed to prepare whatever I was capable of cooking. In fact, there were far more pots than I'd ever need and, not for the first time, I wondered who had lived here before the demons ascended. The house was large and luxurious—there was the soft underfoot cushion of carpet in my bedroom, the large bed with posts to hold even more drapes, and the beautiful woven curtains at the windows. And the hall was stunning—polished floors, wood panelling lining every wall, and a dramatic sweeping staircase. The small square boxes on the walls amused me. How could a person just flick the switch on them and light fill the room? Gran called it electricity; to me, it was magic. But the demons wiped it out instantly when they rose from the depths. Strange then that Erebus's power matched what I thought electricity would be like. His surge of power reminded me of lightning, and I realised that the buzz I could feel in the air in the house was the same as the one I felt before a storm. Myrtle was right about one thing then—he was powerful.

Erebus stared at me as I placed the tray of food on the table. I positioned a bowl of soup and the bread in front of him before doing the same with mine.

"What is it?" he asked as I sat at the side of the table.

"Vegetable soup and bread." I picked up my spoon, ready to eat.

"Swap," he said, lifting his bowl and waiting for me to do the same.

I pushed my bowl toward him, wondering why he insisted on swapping them. He said he'd never eat with me, so why was this necessary? But I was hungry and didn't want to start another argument where neither of us ended as the victor. After taking his bowl from him, I began to eat.

Erebus leaned back in his chair, placing both hands behind his head.

"It looks impressive, Athena."

"Thank you." I swallowed another mouthful. The chunky vegetables were cooked just right—not soft and not hard. The stock was made from the bones of the chicken carcass.

"You look quite pleasant tonight," he said, watching me as I continued to eat. "I insist you don't tie your hair away from your face when in my company."

"Paymon didn't mind how I looked," I said.

"I'm sure he didn't. But I'm not Paymon, am I?"

I swallowed another spoonful of the velvety liquid, ignoring his piercing eyes.

He pointed at the dip between my breasts. "Why do you hide the necklace?"

"I don't hide it." My hand immediately covered my chest. My skin felt hot to the touch as I ran my fingers along the chain.

Erebus's lips twitched. "I noticed it at our marriage ceremony. It's not a normal necklace. You didn't bring it with you from the village, did you?"

I shook my head. "Paymon gave it to me."

"Hmmm . . . I thought as much." He tapped his chin and sniffed. "And do I detect the smell of roses? Perfume?" He leaned forward in his chair, sniffing the air in my direction.

I halted my eager consumption of the soup. "It was my mother's perfume."

"Ahhh . . . yes. You like roses?"

"I like the smell of them. It always reminds me of my mother." I looked down, determined not to let my memories flood my mind.

Erebus straightened up in his chair. "A rose is a very delicate flower, but has a strong, passionate scent. It suits you. You should always wear it."

A blush crept its way onto my face.

He banged his hand on the table. I jumped so much that I dropped my spoon and held my hand to my chest.

"That's what the rosebush is all about, isn't it?" he exclaimed.

"What rosebush?" I picked my spoon from the table and cautiously slipped it back into the bowl.

"Don't tell me you don't know. The rosebush in the courtyard."

"The dead one?" I said, scowling.

Erebus chuckled. "Did Paymon light the rosebush?"

I nodded.

He leaned forward. "You should have told me that Paymon planted a rosebush and watched it grow whilst he waited for you."

"He didn't. It was just there."

Erebus shook his head. "No, it wasn't, Athena. That rosebush isn't a normal one. It's a betroth rosebush. They're very rare, no thorns. Paymon must have planted it when he spotted you in the village." He tutted. "How old were you when you came here?"

"To the village?"

"Yes," he said before leaning forward and sniffing the soup.

I placed my spoon on the table, my appetite deserting me. "I was eight."

He growled, a low vibration from his chest. "But he never touched you or made any untoward advances?"

"No!"

"Good." He leaned backward and tapped his fingers on the chair arm before nodding toward my bowl of soup. "Eat, Athena. Enjoy your meal. It looks delicious."

I did as he instructed.

Erebus didn't talk to me any further throughout the meal, but he wore a stupid smile whenever I lifted my gaze to find him watching me. Only when I'd finished eating did he speak.

"I suspect you have something on your mind. Something you want to ask me?" He rose from the table and swept his hand in front. "Shall we go into the living room, make ourselves more comfortable so you can discuss whatever it is that is bothering you?"

"How do you know?" I asked as I left the table.

He grinned. "I can sense that you are nervous, apprehensive even. More so than I have noticed before."

I walked past him, unable to stop myself breathing in the woody cologne he was wearing. He followed, too close, as always.

I positioned myself on the edge of the sofa, placed my hands on my lap, and waited for him to sit in his usual chair.

He walked to the fireplace.

"So," he said, turning to face me. "Tell me what's bothering you."

This was where I put my plan into action. I'd thought about nothing else whilst he was out, but now I had to try to placate him, be nice to him, I found myself unnaturally nervous. I took a sharp breath before exhaling.

"I'd like to get to know you properly."

"Explain," Erebus said, stepping toward me. He loomed over my seated position. His hands on his hips.

I refused to curl away from him, and I straightened my back before looking him in the eye.

"As you keep reminding me, I am your wife. I want to get to know you. I don't want you to compel me. I'll behave."

A deep frown pulled across his forehead, and he scratched the side of his face. "Am I missing something here?"

"I won't sleep with you at the moment," I clarified, keeping my voice clear and strong. "But I'm hoping the idea won't be so repulsive when I get to know the real Erebus."

His mouth widened into a broad smile that twitched at

the corners. "What's going on, Athena?"

I'd practised my words this afternoon, speaking them to myself in front of the mirror, but now my nerves threatened to overpower me. I twisted the cuff on my sleeve and took a deep breath.

"We're stuck with each other. It's something neither of us want."

"At least we agree on one thing."

I stared at my hands. "We need to make the best of the situation. I'm going to try and make you happy. I'll do everything you ask. But in return, I'd like you to stop threatening me, and stop torturing the villagers."

He sank onto the sofa next to me and sighed. "I need to go to the village to feed. You really don't feed me as much as I need you to. Your emotions are weak. I only wish it was different."

I lifted my gaze. His eyes were golden amber, no sign of darkness clouding their surface. He was telling the truth. I really didn't feed him with my emotions.

He grinned and patted my knee. "But, I quite like having you around, so I promise not to send you to the Master."

The threat that I'd had hanging over me since Erebus's arrival lifted. A lightness flooded through me, and I released a huge breath, dispersing the fear and worry that had trapped me. Maybe he did have some kindness in his heart. The thought gave me hope. Maybe my plan to get information from him would work after all.

"What about the villagers?"

He pinched his nose with his fingers and closed his eyes. "I can see it means a lot to you, although I fail to see why."

"They're my family."

He shook his head. "No, they're not. The whole village has disowned you. Your lover has deceived you in the worst possible way, and yet you still want to protect them from me. Why?"

My attention drifted to the fire as Erebus's words sank in. I stared at the flames. He was right. Why was I trying to save them from him? I needed to save myself, not them.

"You need emotions to feed," I said. "I get that, I really do. And if mine are too weak for you then I understand you need to go to the village. But I'm asking you not to torture them. Your arrival will scare them enough to provide you with emotions. Isn't fear the strongest?"

I caught the grin that pulled at his mouth. "It's strong, but not the strongest. And you have chosen to deny me the only emotion of yours that I know would keep me a very full and well-fed demon."

I narrowed my eyes and turned to face him. I knew exactly what he was referring to. Even Paymon had mentioned the heightened emotions that flooded from a woman when she was making love. But that wasn't an option with Erebus. I had no intention of ever becoming physical with him, regardless of the open-ended promise I'd made.

"I can be awkward," I said. "I can fight you all the way, but it would be exhausting for both of us. Like I said earlier, we're stuck with each other."

"For a very long time," he added.

He sprung to his feet and wandered to the fire. His shoulders lifted and fell and then he chuckled.

"I've just realised . . . you're trying to make a deal with me."

I fixed him with my gaze. "No, I'm not. I'm trying to make

both our lives easier."

"Both of our lives or just yours?"

"Both." I pushed my shoulders back, confident in my statement.

He strolled back to the sofa and stood in front of me. Crossing his arms over his chest, he surveyed me for a few moments.

"I've never intended to kill anyone in the village, but I will when I find out who killed Paymon. That, you have to accept, but it will be the one and only time I will kill."

I opened my mouth to reply, but he held his hand up.

"I actually think I'm getting the better deal, even though you say it isn't one. You say you'll be nice to me, not argue, do as I tell you." His brow rose. "I may even like living with you, Athena, if what you're promising begins to happen. But I warn you now, if you do not do as I say, if you argue with me, if you annoy me in any way, I will have no hesitation in compelling you. I may do so just to entertain myself. Understand?"

I nodded. I'd expected him to make demands in return—sexual ones—ones where he would get what he wanted. My back prickled and I shrugged my shoulders in an effort to ease the uncomfortable reaction. Erebus hadn't dismissed my suggestion. He thought he'd got more to gain. But I knew I had more. It would take time for him to trust me, but that was what I needed to work on. I'd gradually earn his trust, and then he would start talking to me about his kind. Eventually I'd find out about the light, and my dreams about returning it would become a reality.

He crossed the room to the untidy desk. Rummaging through the drawers, he pulled out his usual notebook and a pen. It seemed that the conversation was over.

"What are you writing?" I asked, sidling up behind him.

"Notes." His tone was sharp, dismissive.

"Notes on what?"

He sighed.

"This is exactly the sort of thing I want to know."

"It's long and complicated and written in a language you have no knowledge of."

"Demon language?" I peered over his shoulder and caught a glimpse of the writing. "Teach me to read it."

He sucked in a quick breath. "I'm not going to teach you to read my language."

"Why not? I'm a quick learner. It can't be that difficult."

"You have no need to learn demon language." He continued writing with his illegible scrawl.

"I'd like to, and maybe I could help you with whatever it is you're doing." I reached for a sheet of paper he'd scrawled notes on.

He leaned back in the chair and sighed again. "Basically, I'm hunting vampires."

I jerked my head back and gasped. "Vampires?"

"Yes, ones like Livia, although, unfortunately, she's untouchable because she works for the Master. Such a pity."

I picked another sheet of paper from the desk. "So how do you hunt them, and why?" I asked, ignoring his scowl.

"Why is probably the easiest question to answer." He plonked his notebook in front of me. "I've never liked them or their feeding habits."

"Well, I'm not so keen on yours." How could he preach about vampires' feeding habits when he tortured people for their emotions?

"I don't kill, not unless I have to," he snapped. "They kill for fun." He slid the notebook away from me, and scratched the back of his head. "A vampire killed my mother shortly before we ascended."

I closed my eyes and inwardly berated myself for my insensitivity. "I'm sorry your mother was killed."

He nodded then ran his finger down a list of words written in demon language. "These are all the known places of unregulated covens. I'm working through them one by one."

"Working through them?" I bent over the desk, trying to decipher the words.

"Exterminating them." There was no remorse in his voice. The irony was that he was treating vampires no better than the demons treated humans, although I wasn't about to mention that I disagreed with him killing vampires. I felt like patting him on the back and congratulating him for his efforts to eradicate them from the world.

Erebus shifted sideways in the chair and patted the half empty space. I hesitated for a few moments but decided to sit next to him. He was working on something he was passionate about, and I'd asked to see it. Sitting next to him now held no ulterior motive as far as I could tell.

Several of the names had crosses against them and then a few words in demon writing.

"What does this say?" I pointed at words next to a cross.

"One member escaped." He tapped the paper, sliding his finger further down the page. "This says, 'whole coven killed, no survivors.'"

I viewed the words slowly, trying to remember letters from the demon text as letters that were the same in our language. "So a 'D' in demon language is also a 'D' in English? And an 'L' is an 'E'?"

Erebus cocked his head sideward. "Why the interest in demon language?"

I shrugged, slipping away from my seated position next to him, but decided to push him a little. "So your name in demon language begins with an 'L'?"

He nodded. "My name would be spelt L-G-L-F-P-I. But the pronunciation is very different."

"Go on."

"It's pronounced El-gee-el-ef-pee-i."

I giggled, and Erebus grinned.

"What's my name?"

"Em-hu-rur-el-jem. Maybe I should call you Gem for short?" He flashed me what looked like a genuine smile and then placed his pen on the desk. "Seriously, why all the questions?"

"I'm interested. I've always been curious about anything to do with your kind. Not just your language, but where you're from, why you're here."

Erebus sprung to his feet. "Come with me." He grabbed my hand and marched me into the library. He indicated with a nod of his head for me to sit at the central table. Picking a candle from the smooth surface, he rushed along one side of ceiling high books. The multitude of coloured spines glistened in the candlelight as he searched. He mumbled as he ran his finger along the books. I'd never seen him so animated and enthusiastic.

"Here," he pulled a large book from the shelf, "this should provide you with plenty of reading if you want to know where I came from."

"Why don't you tell me?" I ignored the book as he plonked it on the desk. "I'm sure your version will be more interesting than anything in a book."

"Depends what you want to know." He sat in the chair at the other side of the desk.

"What's it called, the place you come from?"

"Muspalta."

I drew my eyebrows together and concentrated on Erebus. "What's it like there? Is it like here?"

He shook his head. "It's a barren land, rocks and cliff faces, great expanses of dry, dusty desert."

"A desert? You have a sun?"

His mouth slipped into a lopsided smile, and he tucked a stray lock of hair behind his ear. "No, we don't have a sun. We have the bellies of volcanoes, though. Their red glow provides us with limited light."

"So it's dark, like it is here?"

"Not quite." He patted the book he'd placed on the desk. "It's all in here," he said. "Drawings, diagrams, text passages from thousands of years ago. Our previous attempts at trying to come above land and rise to power."

My mouth dropped open. "You'd tried to come before . . . and failed?"

"Each volcanic eruption that happened on land, each tsunami, earthquake, shifts in the ocean. All of those events were previous tests of our power."

"But why did you want to leave?" I edged nearer the desk, leaning on my elbows as I looked across at him.

"Human emotions." He eyed me wearily. "The strong ones, Athena."

I drew in a deep breath.

"We discovered long ago that we can feed from human emotions. We always did, even when below, but many of us

245

used to venture to land." He pulled the book toward him and started flicking through the pages.

"Paymon said he came to land before you all ascended," I said.

Erebus nodded. "Demons like him came back to Muspalta more powerful and ultimately stronger than those who stayed. It caused a divided world, until those that were in power decided that coming to land was what all of us should do—live on earth, rather than under it. There are thousands of years of history plotting our ascent. It really is quite interesting."

"Maybe for a demon," I muttered, quietly rejoicing at his permission to read all about their rise to power. This was what I wanted—information.

Erebus grinned and closed the book. "Take it, you'll learn all you need to from it."

I feigned a sigh and reached across the desk for it. "Can I take it to my room?"

He nodded. "It'll keep you busy whilst I'm out riding Samael. And I shall be out for the day tomorrow. Things to do."

I managed a polite smile, halting my question as to where he was going—I didn't care—and tucked the book under my arm before heading toward the door.

"Good night, Athena," he said just as I reached for the handle.

I bristled but managed to reply with a polite 'Good night' before leaving the room.

I trudged upstairs, weary and drained of constantly trying to keep one step ahead of him. He may not be feeding from my weak and pathetic emotions, but he was exhausting me with his endless dance of words and unexpected actions.

Odin was perched on the screen in my room when I entered. He opened one eye and then closed it again, letting out a quiet croak.

I threw myself on my bed before flicking to the beginning of the book. This would tell me things I didn't know, perhaps I'd find their weakness, maybe there'd be a way to send them back to Muspalta. I prayed there would be some reference to why they hid the light and how they did it.

I opened the first page and saw the all too familiar sign of the pentagram and circle. Placing my hand next to the diagram, I compared it to the mark on the back of my hand; they matched perfectly. I quickly turned the page.

I took a sharp intake of breath as I cast my eyes over the title on the next page. He hadn't done what I thought, had he? My suspicions were confirmed as I flicked through the rest of the book. The diagrams were the only useful thing for me to see as the whole book was written in demon language.

I rubbed at my forehead and suppressed a laugh that was building in my chest, but was soon laughing out loud. Erebus knew I couldn't read demon language and yet he had told me to enjoy reading it. He knew exactly what he'd done.

I was still chuckling when I reached to the end of the bed and felt for my book hidden under the mattress. It was still there, hiding itself as well as its secrets. I trailed my finger over the title on the front. 'DNMGO'

From what I remembered when I asked Erebus about the words written next to his list, the 'D' was still a 'D' in our language. The thought that this was a diary was confirmed even more in my mind. I chewed on my nails as I tried to remember any other letters he'd told me. An 'L' was an 'E'. Not much to go on, but it was a start. I recalled his nickname for me,

Gem, which was the demon pronunciation of the end of my actual name. Athena ended in an 'A'. So was the 'em' sound, an 'M', translated from an 'A'?

As I looked at the word on the front of the book in my hand, it all fit into place. The first letter of the title was a 'D', the third was an 'A'. This was a diary, and I was sure I knew who it belonged to—the woman who Paymon had killed all those years ago. Would she have known anything about the reason for hiding the sun? And who was she?

Its faded pages represented another part of demon history—a private one, one that could teach me so much more than a history book. Maybe it'd allow me to understand things from a demon's perspective. Whether I liked it or not, living with a demon meant I was in the right place to find out.

CHAPTER 15

WARINESS

I WAS AWOKEN EARLY THE NEXT MORNING BY ODIN HOPING around my dressing table and throwing hair clasps into the air. I pulled the window open, yawning as I shooed him outside. I was tired and my bones ached. I crawled back into bed and didn't wake until my stomach churned with emptiness.

Heavy drops of rain hit the windows, reminding me of the miserable weather that always hung around.

I knew I should get dressed, change from my short, flimsy nightdress into something more decent. But if Erebus was out, I saw no reason to.

Picking up the diary, I headed downstairs. All the rooms were lit, and I made a quick detour to the kitchen to grab some bread and butter before searching for Erebus's notebook.

I rummaged in the desk drawer, my fingers finding pencils, pens, a pair of gloves, and a pot of ink. But his notebook wasn't there. Huffing, I headed to the library.

I selected the shelf where Erebus found the book on Muspalta, reasoning that if there was a book on demon language it would be in the same place. I lifted a lit candle to the books and ran my other hand along the spines searching for anything that looked promising. The first three books I pulled from the shelf were all useless. But the fourth one was exactly what I'd been looking for.

"Perfect," I muttered as I rushed to sit at the central desk. I opened the translator and the diary and set to work on deciphering the foreign language. First, I swapped the letters that I'd learnt last night, 'L' to an 'E', 'M' to an 'A', and 'D' remaining as a 'D'. I had to concentrate, and when I'd written the letters on several pages, I found myself yawning. Switching tactics, I started to read the book I'd picked from the shelf and attempted the translation of other letters.

But demon language wasn't just a case of switching one letter for another. There were rules about each individual letter and how they sounded. I decided it was only a small step up from the way cavemen used to talk—a series of grunts and unpronounceable words. For instance, the book told me that the letter 'C' could be pronounced as a 'C' or an 'S' or even a 'K', and when a word had a 'W' in it, it wasn't spoken. This book was useful when translating English into demon language, but incredibly frustrating trying to do it the other way. Letters seemed to be missing, and I began to realise that a direct translation would be slow.

Some words became obvious, others fit into the context of the sentence. I had no idea how long I sat at the desk. But my eyes became heavy with the constant thinking and searching of words.

"We have been busy, haven't we?" Erebus's sarcastic voice trickled through my consciousness.

I lifted my head from the desk and focused on him. He was standing to the side of me, the diary in his hand. He flicked through the pages, frowning.

A heat rushed through me, and my stomach churned. "It's mine," I said reaching for the book.

He spun around before reading aloud. "Paymon knows not what he feels. His powers should be used fully. He should torture the villagers to feed from them and become the greatest demon that ever lived. And we shall rule together, where I belong."

I glared at him, grinding my teeth. I'd tried for hours to translate it and managed only a few words. I tensed and crossed my arms. Why had I fallen asleep and allowed him to discover my secret?

He'd obviously just returned from his ride on Samael. His hair and clothes were wet. Slithers of rain water pooled at his hairline, threatening to break loose and fall freely down his face at any moment. He scratched behind his ear as he read the diary. His hair became loose from the ponytail he wore, and I forced my eyes away from the muscle in his neck that a curl rested upon.

"This certainly isn't your diary," he said as he picked up the sheet of paper that I'd studiously worked the translation on.

"That word means 'fire,'" he said, "not 'flame.'" He chuckled for a few moments, inspecting my effort. "You're not very good at this, are you?"

I huffed. "I asked Paymon and you to teach me your language. You both refused. This is the best I can do."

"Whose diary is this?"

I shrugged, feigning indifference. "I think it belonged to a woman who Paymon lived with when he first came to land."

Erebus frowned and flicked to another page of the diary before shaking his head. "She was seriously deluded. She thought that Paymon and her should challenge the Master. Here . . ." He placed the book on the desk and read a sentence as his finger trailed beneath the words. "With our combined powers we will be invincible, no demon or vampire will be a match for us."

"What was her power?" I asked, not taking my eyes off the jumbled up letters before me. He had my full attention; I couldn't pretend otherwise.

He turned a few pages before sighing and then closing the diary. "She doesn't say."

I lifted my hand toward him, waiting for him to hand me the diary.

He grinned and then pulled it to his chest.

"Tell me all you know about this diary. It's not yours, how did you end up with it? Why have you got it? And why do you want to know what's in it?"

"So many questions," I said as snarkily as I could.

"I gave you answers to your questions last night. I think you could at least do the same for me." He raised an eyebrow. "It should be returned to her, whoever she is."

"Well, it can't. She's dead." I pushed the chair back and stood up.

"Dead?" His eyes narrowed. "Did you kill her?"

252

"Me?" I wanted to laugh at his question. "Just how do you think I killed her? I have no idea how you kill a demon." I wanted to add that if I knew, I'd have put my plan into action and killed him the morning after our forced marriage.

"We're not easy to kill," Erebus said as he perched on the edge of the desk and folded his arms. "Tell me what you know, Athena."

I let my shoulders sag and sighed. "Shall we go into the lounge and get comfortable? Then I'll explain everything."

He cocked his head. "What a sensible suggestion. I'll light the fire. You need to keep warm in that flimsy thing."

I resisted the urge to cover my chest with my arms and lifted my chin as an answer and acceptance of his suggestion.

He chuckled and then left the room, taking the diary with him.

I followed him to the lounge, my steps slow as I thought through the best way to play him for information.

When I entered the room, the fire was lit and Erebus was sitting at the corner desk, rummaging in a drawer. I didn't join him. I sunk onto the sofa and curled my legs underneath me, aware of my uncovered thigh showing.

"The diary belonged to a woman who lived with Paymon," I said. "She arrived in the village a few years after I did."

"Remind me again, how old were you when you came here?" he asked, still concentrating on finding whatever he was searching for.

I focused on him, wanting him to feel the weight of my stare, wanting him to turn and see how I was sitting.

"I was eight. The woman arrived when I was ten. She died when I was twelve. You'd have probably got on with her. She tortured the villagers, laughed at us for fearing her. She killed numerous times."

At last, he turned his attention to me. His eyes widened momentarily as he saw my thigh, and he swallowed before looking toward the fire. I suppressed a grin at his reaction.

"I was secretly fascinated by her. She often came into the village alone, sought out the men who were not at the fields to torture them." My pulse raced and I clenched my jaw, recalling the cries of terror that ricocheted around the village when she entered the house of her victim. "She reminded me of a princess in all her beautiful dresses."

"Like the ones you now wear?" Erebus returned his attention to me, although his eyes didn't meet mine.

"Sorry, do you want me to go and get dressed?" I asked, shifting on the sofa, ensuring more flesh was revealed.

He shook his head before standing and removing his jacket. I took a deep breath, steadying my nerves as he approached, and continued telling him about the woman.

"She was killed on one of the days she came to the village with Paymon."

Erebus sat down next to me, his gaze flitting from my bare thigh to my face, and I forced myself to continue speaking and not flee from his proximity.

"I followed them to the back of the village near the lake. They argued in your language."

"Then how did you know they were arguing?"

"Their raised voices and the way they stood. They were definitely angry with each other."

He rubbed his forehead with his hand. "They fought? And he killed her?"

"Not really. They didn't fight, he just blasted her with a ball of fire. It was quite unexpected. She never had a chance to retaliate. When Paymon left, I noticed the smouldering book on the ground, next to her dress. I picked it up."

Erebus shifted closer on the sofa, and my bravado gave out. I jumped up and stepped toward the fire, rubbing my arms with my hands. "I'm cold today," I said.

"I'm not surprised. I would suggest you put something warmer on, but I quite like what you're wearing."

I raised my eyes heavenward. So predictable. He may be a demon, but he was still a male, and I'd had years of dealing with Thomas and the way his brain worked. Seemed Erebus was no different.

But then he was behind me, his gloved hands on my shoulders, his body flush with mine, his stubble brushing my ear.

I froze. This was more than I expected. My aim was to tease, to get information from him. He'd shifted the power, and now I was the one caught out . . . or was I?

I turned around, taking my time with the movement. His hands dropped from my shoulders as I stood facing him. The top of his chest was at my eye level, and I stared at the smattering of fine hairs that peaked out from the top of his smock. With deliberate slowness, I reached for the loose ties of fabric at the neck of the smock and twisted them in my fingers.

"Did you have a successful day hunting vampires?" I asked, ignoring the powerful urge to pull the ties as hard as I could and strangle him.

His hands slipped along my sides and rested on the curve of my hips.

"Yes," he said, although the word was barely more than a whisper.

Desperate to hide my revolt at the heat of his gloved hands

through my nightdress, I continued twirling the ties between my fingers imagining the power shifting between us. It wasn't always about who had the physical strength, sometimes it was about a person's mental strength.

"So how are the vampires you hunt different to those that work for the Master?"

His hands tightened on my hips, his fingers digging into my flesh for a few moments before he seemed to realise. I looked up at him and was greeted by hooded eyes.

"The ones who work for the Master are controlled by him, they're nothing more than pets. They are grateful for the darkness that covers the land because it gives them freedom during the day. It's something they never had. But many of the vampires don't want to be controlled by the Master. Those are the ones I hunt."

I nodded, holding my breath, celebrating at this new found piece of information. I swayed against him, ensuring my hips brushed against his. "So the unregulated ones don't work for him?"

"No. They take advantage of the darkness but refuse to be controlled by his rules."

"So the Master controls the darkness?" My heart beat heavily in my chest.

"Yes. He promised the vampires the darkness in return for their allegiance."

As a final gesture, I leaned closer to him and let my breath fan his neck. "But they didn't all conform," I whispered, satisfied I understood.

"Athena," he breathed.

I removed my hands from his shirt and shrunk backward out of his grasp. "I'm tired," I said, as I headed for the door, not waiting to see or hear his response. "Good night."

I ran up the stairs, praying that he didn't follow me.

Cruel, I'd been so cruel in the way I'd treated him. But what did he expect? That I'd fall at his feet and beg him to sleep with me? Had he believed that I was genuine, that I was attracted to him?

I strode to the window that I used to let Odin in and out of the house and lifted it open before leaning outside. The rain was still falling, odd flashes of lightning illuminating the surrounding forest. If I screwed my eyes half-shut, I could see the distant twinkle of the lanterns in the village. It seemed years since I'd left, not just weeks, and even though it had been a hard life, living with Erebus was proving to be just as tough, just in other ways. I ducked my head back into the room and waited for Odin to return. He wasn't usually long when the window was open for him.

I startled when a soft knock sounded on my bedroom door.

"Athena?" It was Erebus. He didn't shout, it was more of a question than a call for my attention. I headed to the door but didn't open it.

"What do you want?" I said through the wooden barrier.

"Can I come in?"

I grinned but composed myself quickly. Since when did Erebus ask if he could come into my room?

"No," I said, rushing my answer. "I'm just about to get in the tub. I'm naked."

Odin chose that exact moment to flutter into the room, and I kept my eye on him as he landed on the screen and croaked his greeting.

"Are you okay?" Erebus asked.

"Yes . . . just tired."

"You're sure?"

"Yes." I suppressed another grin. My acting skills were very good this evening. He seemed concerned, and my thought that he believed everything that had happened downstairs as genuine gave me renewed hope. "Good night, Erebus," I said before wandering away from the door.

I was telling the truth when I said I was tired. Not physically, but mentally. I'd discovered why the light had been hidden, I'd discovered who'd hidden it, and I understood the reason for the vampires' existence in our world. I also knew that Erebus hated vampires. Next, I needed to find out how the darkness had been put there. Did Erebus know how to get rid of it?

CHAPTER 16

FRUSTRATION

I HARDLY SLEPT. MY DREAMS HAD MADE ME RESTLESS, AND I'd woken many times during the night. Only this time, I'd not had nightmares. Erebus had featured in all my dreams, and each one had finished the same way—him and me together. All of them had replicated the events of the previous night, only I didn't back away when I'd got what I wanted, I didn't escape his company. I willingly pushed him further.

When I woke up properly, I was eager to wash and scrub every patch of skin to rid myself of the imaginary feel of his fingertips.

"Nightmares," I muttered to myself as I sank below the surface of the water. "Stupid nightmares." I ignored the coldness, desperate to be clean.

I took my time drying myself and getting dressed. I wasn't in a hurry to see Erebus and deal with the fallout from last night. After filling several buckets of water and throwing them from my window, I faced the task of fetching more water from the well for my next bath.

I huffed and chuntered to myself as I made the trip to the well several times. At least Erebus wasn't around, laughing at my repetitive journey. I assumed he had gone out for the day on Samael again, hunting more vampires, but as I approached the well for the tenth time, I heard the snort of a horse. The sound came from the stable, and welcoming a break from my laborious task, I changed direction.

I tiptoed toward the stable, not wanting to disturb Erebus when he was with Samael and not wanting him to know I was there. But there was no talking, no vigorous rubbing down of the horse after a run, just the agitated snorts of Samael. When I poked my head around the stable door, I was surprised to see him alone.

"Hi there," I said as softly as possible. I didn't want to frighten him, and I knew horses were easily scared.

His ears pricked up and turned forward. He snorted and stamped his hoof.

"It's okay." I said, remembering the times I'd tended to the few horses we used to have. They were well looked after as they were the only form of communication we had with other villages. But over the years, we'd lost the riders and the horses. They'd ride off with a message and never return. We never knew whether they'd reached their destination or perished along the way.

"I'll bring you a carrot later," I promised him as I slid the lock on the stable door.

Samael's tail swished, and he stepped backward. I stayed at the stable door, letting him get used to my appearance and my scent. Horses were such nervy animals. I stayed where I was for several minutes, watching his movements, taking in the small signs of his gradual acceptance. I spoke calmly to him, chatting at a level tone, guessing what he got up to with Erebus. When one of his ears turned to the side and his head dropped from its upright position, I moved forward, my hand outstretched. Samael didn't flinch when I touched the side of his head, and as my confidence grew, I stepped even closer. He whinnied and lifted and dropped his head but then stepped toward me knocking my arm. I stroked his nose, patted his neck and generally fussed over him, all the while talking nonsense so he became used to my voice. I stayed with him for a long time; he was good company, and his proximity calmed me in the same way that Odin's did.

"I need to go," I eventually said, nuzzling up to him before backing away. "I've got to get some more information from Erebus. See what else he'll tell me."

Samael snorted and stepped to the stable door.

"I can't take you out for a ride," I said. "And I'm sure Erebus will make sure you have a run at some point today."

I glanced at the saddle and riding tack hanging on the far wall. I could remember how it all fit together, but I didn't think Erebus would take kindly to me stealing his horse and taking off with it.

"Later," I promised and unlocked the stable door before stepping outside and relocking it.

I fetched four more buckets of water from the well before deciding the tub held sufficient water for my next bath. Breakfast beckoned, and with my stomach rumbling loudly, I headed to the kitchen. After cooking some bacon and toast, I intended to head to the library to continue with the translation of the diary, but raised voices from the lounge waylaid me. I crept along the corridor, listening intently to the guttural demon language. Erebus and another man. The unknown voice was talking quietly, but I jumped when Erebus responded. As the sound of rustling clothes and jangling belts became louder, I backed up the corridor and hid under the arch of the stairway. But I couldn't resist peeking out to see who the stranger was who was arguing with Erebus.

A tall man, with straight grey hair flowing from under a black hat, stepped into the hall. He sniffed the air and turned sharply my way. I ducked backward, completely out of view, praying he hadn't seen me.

With only a few more strange words spoken, the front door opened and then slammed shut.

"You can come out now, Athena," Erebus called. "Sebastian's gone. He won't be coming back."

I shifted from my hiding place. Erebus was waiting outside the lounge.

"Come, come," he said, beckoning me forward with a wave of his hand before moving into the room.

"Who was that?"

"Sebastian, an old friend. Well, he was a friend in the loosest of terms. Now, perhaps he is an enemy."

"He's a demon."

Erebus settled himself on the chair at the desk and nodded. "It seems that word has got around about your intended categorisation for the Master. Like I told you before, there are not many females selected for that category. I still fail to see how Paymon thought you fit for him, but he must have seen something. Unfortunately, now others are finding out about it, they all want to meet you, or rather, take you to him."

My legs weakened, and I fought a feeling of dizziness. "No!" I rushed over to him and placed my hands on the side of the desk. "You promised you'd not send me to him. You promised."

Erebus frowned and rubbed his chin. "Why are you panicking? I told Sebastian what he can do with his offer. I have no intention of letting you go to the Master or anyone else. I will keep my promise."

I released a huge breath and threw my arms around him. "Thank you." I pecked him on the cheek before backing away. My cheeks heated and I dipped my chin, unable to meet his gaze.

"Your gratitude is most welcome, but unnecessary."

I opened my mouth to speak, but couldn't think of what to say.

Erebus tilted his head to the side and pursed his lips. "We are married, Athena, and whether the Master wants you or not, our marriage bond is unbreakable. If he wants you as his wife, he has to kill me."

"He'd kill you?" My fear for myself was suddenly replaced with one for Erebus.

He scoffed. "He could try."

"But . . . but . . ."

"But what, Athena?"

"You're risking your life for me."

He chuckled, but I didn't see anything humorous about what he was saying.

"I see it more as I'm looking after what's mine. Have you eaten this morning?"

I nodded, my relief and shock giving way to contempt as he stated his reason for not letting me go to the Master. I'd thought, just for a second, that he cared, that he wouldn't let me go because he wanted me here with him. Everything that had happened last night blurred into a confusing memory. Who had been playing who?

I moved away from the desk and sat on the sofa. Erebus followed.

"Sebastian offered me my freedom," he said as he sat beside me.

"Your freedom?"

"Well, the opportunity to return to my old way of life. Before I came here, I travelled a lot. I never stayed anywhere for long. I liked my life as it was, hunting vampires, no ties to anyone or anything. Sebastian has known me for years, our paths crossed regularly. He thinks he knows me, and he offered me my old life back. He was prepared to take on the village as his. But there was no disguising his real desire, which was to be here with you. And who knows whether he would have kept you or sent you to the Master and reaped the reward."

"But wouldn't he have to kill you first?"

Erebus shook his head. "Sebastian knows better than to threaten me. I could kill him easily. I'm powerful, Athena, more powerful than other demons. My gift is rare, only my brother and sisters possess the same power. We know of no others."

I nodded, taking in another piece of new-found information.

"Now," he said, patting my knee. "What shall we do for the rest of today?"

"Can you help me translate the diary?" I didn't want him to know how desperate I was to uncover everything the woman had written, but it was impossible to hide my enthusiasm.

"Not today. I think we have other things to discuss."

"Such as?" My shoulders dropped, and as I looked up at

his all too knowing eyes, I feared his response.

"I want to know what happened last night. What was going through your mind when you attempted to seduce me?"

"I did not!" I was on my feet, leaving him alone on the sofa. "You must have compelled me." How the lies flew easily from my lips.

"I can assure you I didn't. I'm not complaining about any of it, but you need to be careful. I don't know what game you're playing, but it could end in a way you don't want. Don't tease me, Athena, don't try to get the better of me. It won't work."

I gritted my teeth, refusing to let him intimidate me with hidden threats. "I wasn't teasing you. You must have compelled me."

He shook his head, a grin pulling at his mouth. "Whatever." He threw his arms in the air. "Go find a book you can read to me. Let's have a quiet day today. A day to reflect on what's happened, and a time to think about what's still to come."

I left the room without a second request. I needed to escape his overly confident gaze. He knew what I'd done last night. Damn and blast the stupid demon. But I wouldn't let him win. I'd find out what I wanted to know one way or another. And at least he hadn't second guessed why I was trying to seduce him. He hadn't made the connection with me gaining information. I just needed to be extra careful about how I approached the subject of the dark and how the Master controlled it.

My first month living as Erebus's wife was full of surprises. Whereas I'd fit into an easy routine with Paymon, with Erebus,

I never knew what he'd do or say next. He'd kept his word about not torturing the villagers, or so he said. Sometimes I'd watch from my bedroom window, squinting through the darkness to try and see if there were any familiar sparks lighting the sky. There never was. But other times, I used his absence to visit Samael.

Erebus often left me alone for the day, pursuing his obsession with catching and killing vampires, and I began to be able to read his mood when he returned. If he'd killed even one vampire, his mood was light, almost carefree, and he was quite pleasant to be around. They were the times when I questioned him, allowed myself to relax a little in his company. They were the times it was easy to forget he was a demon. We often found ourselves laughing at the same things, but one of us was always quick to change the subject and halt the merriment. Neither of us could forget the situation we were in. Neither of us wanted to be here.

By contrast, when he'd had an unsuccessful day, found no vampires to kill, he'd be moody and sarcastic. He'd throw things around, sometime shooting his power at them so they exploded in the air, before settling at the desk and writing. I'd learnt not to question him when he came home on these days. But I couldn't escape to my room. He wanted me in the room with him, ready to taunt and belittle me if the mood so took him. At those times I didn't need to be reminded that he was a demon. And at those times my hate for him grew.

Whenever he was out riding Samael, I took the opportunity to translate the diary and search through the library for books that could tell me anything about the Master and the darkness. But I never found anything of any use, and the translation of the diary, one line at a time, still with lots of guesswork, was a long drawn out task. When Erebus was in a good mood, he promised to help me with the diary, and when he was in a bad mood, he threatened to burn it. And so now I kept it hidden in my room, under the deep mattress on my bed, the same hiding place as when I lived in the village.

The end of the first month of living with Erebus also marked the night of the village feast. But I couldn't settle. I'd read the same page of my book several times. I fiddled with my hair, drawing out the long strands between my fingers. I smoothed and rearranged my dress, fidgeting on the sofa to get comfy. Erebus ignored me, he was too busy chuntering and swearing as he wrote notes.

"It's the village feast tonight," I said, looking up from my book.

"And?"

"You should be there."

"Why? So one of them can poison me?" He carried on writing, not showing any interest in moving.

"It's their chance to thank you for providing the light over the fields and protecting them from the beasts in the forest." I shuddered, my nostrils flaring as I remembered the vile heated breath of the creature I'd faced. I lifted a trembling hand to cover my nose, and squeezed my eyes shut, blocking out the terror induced scent and memory of when I'd faced one of them.

"I don't need to go every month, surely? Wasn't that something Paymon did? He set the monthly occasion. Strange really, I never viewed him as a demon who liked to party."

I fixed him with a withering gaze, angry for so many reasons. "They'll have killed a pig, cooked all day. All of it's for you."

"Athena." Erebus laid his pen on the desk and swung around in his chair to face me. "They can still enjoy all their hard work. They can eat the food they've prepared. I actually think they'll enjoy themselves a lot more with me not there."

"You should still go."

He chuckled before turning back to his desk. "I'm beginning to think you want them to poison me. You go if you want. I'll not stop you."

I curled my legs up underneath me. "I don't want to go by myself." It would feel weird going back to village when I'd not been there for over four weeks, never mind traipsing out into the cold that seemed to have grown in intensity over the last couple of days.

"Then you'll have to stay here, with me." He shot me an amused smile and then continued writing.

"I'd go if I could see the moon," I said, risking an attempt at small talk.

"The moon? Why the moon? It doesn't protect you from anything, regardless of what the old hag in the village says."

"Myrtle," I corrected him.

"Whatever."

"I'd just like to see its white glow through the darkness that the Master put there. Do you like the darkness?"

"Not particularly." He placed his pen on the desk and stood up, rubbing the back of his neck.

"So get rid of it."

He laughed, the sound loud to my ears. "I don't know how, not that it's an option. It was the Master who created the shield of darkness that covers the land."

"A shield? He can do that?" I uncurled my legs, straightened my back and angled myself toward him.

Erebus nodded and walked across the room to his usual chair.

"But how does he keep it there?"

"He'll have used ancient and powerful spells that upset the balance of the world we both now live on. Demon magic is strong, Athena, and the Master is the strongest demon in the world."

He leaned back and closed his eyes. He looked tired, the darkness under his eyes seemed to be deepening every day.

"You said you were powerful." I leaned forward. "Can't you fire your power at the shield and break it?"

He ran his hands over the arms of the chair before opening his eyes and laughing. "I never knew you were so bothered about the light. Do you seriously want me to part the sky so you can see the moon?"

I nodded but gritted my teeth. I hated that he was laughing at me, belittling my hopes and dreams.

"Come here," he said, curling his finger at me.

I didn't move.

"Come here, Athena, and I'll tell you a secret."

I pondered his request for a moment, and then crossed the room to where he sat. He patted his knee. "Sit down, and I'll tell you all I know about the shield of darkness."

His offer was too good to refuse, and I lowered myself across his knee.

"You should have told me earlier that you wanted to know about the darkness, we could have come to some arrangement about what I'd tell you."

I straightened up, prepared to jump from his knee, but his arm wrapped around my waist, and he held me steady. "I don't know whether the shield can be broken," he said. "They say that the magic used to create it was so powerful that the magic to destroy it also had to be created. Apparently the Master hid the magic needed to destroy the shield."

"Where?" He had my full attention, and I would do anything, within reason, for him to part with more information.

"There are rumours that only his children know where it's hidden. They keep its secret safe."

"I didn't think he had any children. Paymon said they all died."

"Not his demon children. The offspring he has successfully bred with humans have died within hours of being born. But he has sired children with other demons."

"And they know where this magic is?"

"So it is believed."

I sighed, leaning into him as I contemplated his revelation. "Is there any way to find his children?"

He shook his head. "Not that I am aware of." His gloved hand rested on my thigh, and his other arm continued to hold me with a firm grip. "And what do you intend to do if you find the rumours to be true? Hunt down his children? Demons? How many would you need to find, and then how do you expect to get them to share their secret?"

I glanced away from his penetrating eyes. My heart felt like it was shrinking, and my chest tightened. I'd found out about why the darkness was constantly around us; I'd found out how it was put there. I even knew how it could be destroyed. But the irony was that even though I had all the information, I was still no further in my quest to return the light. I bit my lip, attempting to stop it from shaking.

"We all dream, Athena, even demons." Erebus's voice was low. "But sometimes our dreams are too impossible to ever become reality."

I swallowed hard as tears built behind my eyes. This wasn't what I wanted. This wasn't what I'd planned. I pushed against his chest, determined to leave him and go to my room. I wanted to cry in privacy, not in front of him.

Erebus pulled me against his chest, and both of his arms curled around me.

I sniffed, unable to halt my tears. I hadn't had the simple affection of a comforting cuddle for months. And even though my head screamed at me not to, I shifted closer to him and placed my arm around his waist, twisting the soft cotton of his tunic top between my fingers. Now the tears had broken free, I couldn't stop them.

"I didn't mean to make you cry," he whispered, squeezing me as if to accentuate his words. "Is life really that bad?"

I sobbed even more. How could my life be any worse? I sniffed again, trying to control my emotional outburst. "I hate the darkness," I said against his chest. "If the sun came back, life would be much better."

"Is this all about the darkness?" His hold on me loosened, and he placed a finger under my chin to lift my face.

I nodded, and he dropped his finger. I tightened my hold on him. I didn't want him to let me go—not yet. His hold was reassuring, comforting and slightly possessive. My breathing became steadier, slower, matching Erebus's as he rubbed my arm.

"I can't part the sky for the moon," he said. "It moves, and it would be impossible and exhausting for me to constantly keep it within sight. But I can part it to let the light through for the rosebush."

"You can?" I lifted my head to catch his expression. His

eyes were soft, swirling amber irises devouring me.

"I can, and I will."

I hugged him, wanting him to know how much I appreciated his gesture. It was something I'd never thought him capable of.

But as he tightened his hold on me even more, I froze. What was I doing? I needed to get away from him. He was confusing me. If I didn't know any better, I'd have said he had compelled me, but I was confident he hadn't.

I pushed my arms against his chest and slid from his knee. He didn't try to hold me back and just held me in a steady gaze as I left the room to seek the solitude of my bedroom.

CHAPTER 17

CONFUSION

I KEPT OUT OF EREBUS'S WAY FOR THE NEXT FEW DAYS, ONLY venturing to the kitchen to eat when he was out. I wrote endless notes about what I'd discovered about the light and about what Erebus had told me. But by the end of three days of self-imposed solitude, I was desperate for company. Odin was a pleasure to be around, but he was no substitute for conversation, or even an argument. Erebus had never knocked on my bedroom door, never even spoken to me through the thick wooden barrier, although I was sure I'd heard him pacing the corridor outside on numerous occasions.

I hadn't kept hidden from him just because of my disappointment at the impossible task of getting rid of the darkness. I'd also stayed away because of the rumbling and simmering emotions I was beginning to feel toward him. I still wanted to hate him, and it was easy to categorise him as a heartless, uncaring demon, but he'd shown me a different side to his character over the last few weeks. He'd rarely made any threats to me about our future together. He seemed concerned about my general well-being, and he appeared more . . . human. I kept pushing my thoughts aside and regularly took to writing out my frustration, listing all the things he'd done that classed him as evil. But even when I read through the list, I found myself making excuses for him, either for the way he'd behaved or the way he'd responded.

I dressed in the dullest dress I had and left my long hair loose and wild before making my way downstairs to the lounge.

Erebus was seated in the old chair at the desk, and I raised my eyes at his obsession with tracking down the vampire covens. It was all he ever did. Whenever he was at home, he'd be hunched over the desk, scribbling away, sighing and huffing.

As I sat down, he stopped writing. His back straightened, and he placed his pen in the ink pot before turning sideways in the chair. He hadn't tied his hair back, and it hung in twisted wavy lengths, dipping across his face. "Athena, what a pleasant surprise. Finished sulking yet?"

"I wasn't sulking."

He sniffed and ran his hand through his hair, pushing it away from his face. I tensed, and, for a split second I held my breath. Even from across the room, I could see the dark circles under his eyes.

"Hiding then? From me? Why?" He rubbed the back of his neck, and pulled at the collar of his top.

"I just needed some time alone to think." I leaned forward, eager to see him properly, not in the dimmed light of the flickering candles. "You look tired. Not sleeping?"

He guffawed and then shook his head.

"What's wrong?" I left the sofa and moved toward him.

He turned away. "Nothing."

I leaned on the side of the desk. "Liar."

His knuckles whitened as he gripped the chair arms.

I reached to tip his chin toward me, and his dark stubble scratched the softness of my fingertips. "Look at me."

He shook his head, keeping his gaze downcast.

"Erebus. Look at me!"

As he turned, golden irises locked with mine. There was no darkness about them, none at all, and the sunken pallor of his skin alarmed me.

"You're ill," I said, placing my hands on either side of his face and then resting my palm on his forehead. He was cool to touch, but nothing untoward.

"No, I'm not."

"You are. You shouldn't be this pale, and look at the state of your eyes. When did you last feed?"

He shrank away from my hands and laughed, but the sound held no humour.

"When?"

"A week ago."

"Madness. You need to go at least every other day."

"I'm saving for a big feed," he said, a grin appearing on his face. "I'm going to go later today."

"But why make yourself weak? What would you do if Sebastian came back? Is your power as strong now as when you're fed?"

"And the questions begin again." He sniffed and scratched the bridge of his nose. "Are you really concerned about me or worried that I may not be able to save you if Sebastian comes looking for you?"

I tensed, immediately knowing my answer. I was

concerned for Erebus, not myself. Where had this come from? Why was I suddenly concerned for him?

"What are you thinking?" Erebus asked, his words clipped, excited.

"Nothing."

"Now who's the liar, Athena?" He stood up and leaned over me. His face was mere centimetres from mine. "Look at my eyes? What colour are they?"

"Amber," I said, hypnotised by the swirling colour. "They remind me of the sun, well, what I remembered of it."

His expression became serious. His features softened, and he closed his eyes. When he opened them I gasped.

"Now what colour?"

"B . . . black," I stuttered, seeing nothing but dark solid irises.

"Athena, what are you thinking about?"

"Nothing."

"Don't lie. I need to know." His hands held the tops of my arms as he questioned me. The sparks of his power rippled and danced along my arms, leaving a tingling sensation all the way down to my wrists. "This is the first time I've being able to freely feed off your emotions. What's going on in that head of yours?"

I struggled against his too warm hands, trying to shrink away from his hold, but he only held me firmer. The sallow grey colouring under his eyes disappeared, and his warm olive skin tone returned. He was so close. My gaze dropped to his mouth, and I realised that if I moved forward, our lips would touch. I closed my eyes, and breathed in his woody, musky scent. My heart beat loudly against the side of my rib cage, and I struggled to not move my head forward—to make our lips meet.

"Athena, it's strong. Really strong. You must know what you're feeling. Tell me."

I snapped myself free of the cloud of lust that had overwhelmed me. "I don't know. But if I'm managing to feed you, you don't need to go to the village." I pushed his hands away from my shoulders and headed back to the sofa.

Erebus followed. "You think it's that simple? We've lived together for over a month and this is the first time you've provided me with emotions of any strength. If you won't tell me what you're feeling, then I can't rely on it." He drew his hand across his face and groaned. "Just tell me, and we can work something out."

"I can't tell you because I don't know." I tried to gather my thoughts, but couldn't. The blazing fire caught my attention, the flames licking high into the chimney breast as the burning wood crackled and spit. There were only a few candles lit in the room, not the usual multitude decorating every available surface. The room felt warm, welcoming . . . seductive.

"If we can keep creating whatever emotion it is your feeling I won't have any need to go to the village." Erebus's voice was soft. "It was very strong, but short-lived. It's already dwindling."

I dared to cast my eyes his way. The dark irises were already swirling back to the normal amber colour I was used to seeing. I pulled at the neck of my dress, a sudden heat making me uncomfortable. His eyes had turned black when I'd thought of kissing him. Was that it? Was that all it took?

"Come closer," I said, fighting my instinct to move further away from him. The crackle of the fire didn't seem as loud as it had a minute ago, and the dappled light cast by the candles softened Erebus's sharp facial features.

He walked toward me before sliding onto the sofa, never freeing me from his line of vision.

I dipped my gaze to the smooth, soft plump outline of his lips partly hidden by his whiskers. I trembled and moved closer. My fingers tingled with the need to touch him. I breathed deeply, once again catching the earthy muskiness of his cologne, and wet my dry lips with my tongue.

He narrowed his eyes and then backed away from me. "Are you seriously thinking of kissing me? Where's this coming from? Another game?"

"No."

"I've had enough of this. You seem to enjoy toying with my emotions whereas yours are a mystery to me." He marched to the fire before spinning around. "I stayed away from the village because you don't like me going there. And what do I get for my compassion? You, playing with *my* emotions, trying to get the better of me. I'm not a fool, Athena. Don't treat me like one!"

"That's not true." I ignored his building anger. He'd got it all wrong. "And how dare you speak to me about compassion. You don't even know what the word means."

"Really? So why have I left you alone and not insisted you act like my wife in all ways, even physical? Why haven't I sent you away and found myself a willing, loving wife? Why didn't I hand you over to Sebastian and return to my previous lifestyle when it was offered to me? My list is long, Athena."

"Let me go then, if I'm such a disappointment to you. Free yourself of me."

He dipped his chin and shook his head. "I can't. You'd not survive out there without me. Not now everyone knows you were categorised as a wife for the Master. It's a heavy title to carry. And despite what you think, I do care about you. You are far from a disappointment."

My teeth dug into the skin of my lip, and I winced as the coppery taste of blood swept into my mouth. This was the first time he'd admitted any feelings for me. I had to gather my thoughts.

"I lit the rosebush for you," he said, approaching me with slow steps. "I just wish you would drop all this hate you pretend you have for me. I know you don't hate me. You wish you could, but you can't."

I narrowed my eyes and looked at him. "Oh, I can, believe me. I just think back to the first day we met." I lifted my hand and flashed the marriage mark at him. "Remember?"

"I saved you from Livia!"

"Just so you could have me instead."

His hands clenched at his sides. "I didn't even know who you were when I arrived in the village. And I certainly wouldn't have brought you back here if you hadn't been Paymon's wife."

"This is all about me belonging to you. You looking after what's yours. It's not compassion. It's ownership."

His jaw tensed, the vein in his neck pulsed. "You don't want to believe me, do you? You have no intention of even trying to see me as anything other than evil."

I shrugged. "You're a demon. It's what you are. It's how you exist."

"How I exist? You have no idea what you're on about." His voice was loud and raw, and his face flushed. But I refused to shrink away from him.

"All demons are evil. You torture purely for entertainment."

He jerked his head back. "That's how you see me? How

you think of me?"

I didn't reply.

A sneer formed across his lips. It was an expression I hadn't seen since those first days we were thrown together. I drew away from his penetrating glare, wishing more than ever, that our paths in life had never crossed. Underneath all his seemingly niceness was a demon, and that would never change.

"I'm going to the village," he said, striding into the hall. "You stay here. I'm not just going to feed tonight. I intend to torture someone. And this time, it's all your fault!"

"But—"

"I'm a demon, Athena. It's what I am, it's how I exist. I'll do what you expect."

He swirled his cloak in an exaggerated spin before positioning it on his shoulders.

I ran to the door and stood with my back resting on the cold wood.

"No, you can't go. You can't torture them. You promised you wouldn't."

"Worried I'll find Thomas? Concerned for your old lover?"

Images of Thomas flashed in front of me. I'd hardly given him any thought lately—he was part of my past, and I had no intention of him being part of my future, whatever happened.

"Do you want me to bring him back, let you have one last look at him before I kill him?"

"Stop it! You're not going anywhere when you're like this." I held my arms out to my sides, letting them rest on the door, creating a visual barrier for him to pass. I tensed as he approached, slipping his hands into his gloves.

"Move." His teeth were gritted. "If you don't move, I'll compel you."

"Another promise broken. You promised never to compel me."

"Only if you behaved. Seems you're incapable of that tonight. First seduction, and now defiance. What's next, Athena?"

A sudden heat hit me, sinking deep into my bones, and before I had time to voice my repulsion, I froze. I tried to fight the overpowering influence his compelment had on me, but it was too strong, too intense. With no will of my own, I moved swiftly to the side of the door. Erebus strode forward, his sneer still fixed on his lips. I didn't know who I hated the most at that moment, him, or me, for all the lustful thoughts his lips brought to mind. I was angry that he hadn't let me kiss him. Maybe it would have confirmed what emotion was feeding him. Was it lust, desire? It was only recently I'd felt any slight stirrings for him that way, and the thought filled me with dread.

He loomed over me, tilting his head to the side, and tapped his lips as if deep in thought.

"Yet again, your emotions flow from you. What is it, hmm?" His gloved hand stroked the side of my cheek, and I was powerless to move away from him. Bottomless pits of darkness mirrored my fixed stare. He moved nearer, edging his face closer to mine. I was fixed in place by his compelment, unable to control even the slightest of movements, and he knew it.

When his lips hovered over mine, I felt the movement of them as he spoke. "So you want to kiss me? Experience what it's like to lose yourself in the deep, dark fantasy of kissing a demon. We've kissed before, remember? But you were compelled then. To kiss me of your own free-will will be completely different."

I managed to whimper. The heat of his compelment built with the heat of my own lust-fuelled thoughts. I didn't know if what I was thinking was real, or if Erebus was playing with my mind.

He breathed heavily, the warmth of his breath caressing my slightly parted lips. I could taste him. Raw. Dangerous.

"But a kiss is never enough, Athena. You'll always want more. Always." He trailed his mouth across my cheek, a whispered touch of his heated lips. If his compelment hadn't held me in place, I was sure I would have grabbed him to stop myself from falling. He rested his cheek against mine, his stubble scratching me. "You'll crave the strength of my body over the curves of your naked flesh. You'll experience what it's like to be loved completely. And after me, you'll never want any other man—not a human nor another demon."

His teeth nipped at my ear and jolted me back to reality. My skin felt like it was crawling with a thousand insects, and my throat burnt. Everything I had felt had been his compelment, but it had weakened, leaving me free to fight the remnants of its hold. I screwed my nose up in disgust.

"I wish you were dead," I hissed, finding my voice.

He stepped backward, his eyes wide.

I hoped my stare conveyed all I was feeling—hate, contempt, and revulsion at his suggestion. He huffed, and then with no further words spoken, picked a lantern from the side of the doorway. He pulled a glove off and lit the candle with a small spark from his finger. "We'll continue this conversation when I get back."

When he pulled the door open, an icy blast of air flooded into the hall.

He didn't close the door, and I clung to the edge of it, not finished with my insults. There was no need for us to discuss anything when he got back. I wanted him to know exactly how I felt about him right now.

"I hate you!" I yelled after him. "I hate everything about you!"

He didn't turn to face me, just carried on walking, laughing as the darkness wrapped around him.

I slammed the door shut and reached for my cloak. Odin flew downstairs and perched on the end of the bannister.

"I'm leaving," I said. "You coming with me?"

He ruffled his feathers and croaked.

I ran along the hallway and into the kitchen. Odin followed, and as I opened the back door, he flew outside. Together we headed to the stables.

"Stupid demon, stupid emotions, stupid darkness!"

How dare he compel me? I wouldn't let any man, or demon, treat me like that.

Samael whinnied as I opened his stable door. "We're going out. I promised you a ride several weeks ago. Tonight's your lucky night."

He stamped his foot several times and then waited patiently as I tacked him up.

"Good boy," I said, rubbing his neck. "Now, I know I'm not Erebus. Just be patient with me. It's been years since I've ridden."

I ran through all the times I'd ridden the horses around the village—a slow trot, nothing more, and realised that I wouldn't be trotting on Samael, we'd be galloping. Swallowing my apprehension and still running on adrenaline from my heated argument with Erebus, I moved a bale of straw to the side of Samael and stepped onto it. Securing my foot in the stirrup, I sprang up into the saddle. Samael shifted around the stable, and I leaned forward and stroked his neck. "Shhh . . . I'm sure I'm lighter than Erebus, but it's okay."

Once mounted on him, the times I'd ridden in the past came flooding back. I clicked my mouth and squeezed my legs against his side. He walked forward and out of the stable.

"Good boy," I repeated, grasping the reins.

Odin was watching us from the fence just outside the stable, but took off into the sky as Samael turned and faced the forest. My smugness at managing to get Samael saddled and obeying my simple command to walk didn't last long. As if sensing the freedom on offer, and that Erebus wasn't controlling him, he took off. I straightened in the saddle, leaned backward, and pulled on the reins, but he carried on running. I was jostled in the seat as his trot turned into a cantor and then a gallop.

"Samael!" I screeched, but he still didn't listen. He ran as if I wasn't there. I tugged on the reins, but he still ignored my command. Needing more to hold on to than a leather strap, I wrapped my hands in the long hairs of his mane, leaning forward to keep my balance and to avoid the low hanging branches that threatened to knock me from the saddle. The wind whipped my face, and I called out several times, begging Samael to slow down as he headed deeper into the darkness of the forest. It was thick with restless evil, the stench of rotting flesh carried on the bitter wind. Maybe that was what had panicked Samael, but as he continued into the forest, and the unearthly howls of creatures I had no desire to face again rang out, I feared that he was running toward danger rather than away from it.

"Slow down, slow down." I renewed my hold on his mane, fearing that I'd fall from the saddle and be left in the middle of the forest by myself. Samael changed direction, the shift so abrupt that my fear of falling nearly became a reality. But as he continued in this new direction, his pace slowed to a comfortable trot.

I gulped in air as a shakiness in my limbs developed. My adrenaline had spiked, and I was dealing with the result. My knuckles were white against the darkness of Samael's mane, and I blinked rapidly, trying to make out the shapes around us. There was only a smattering of trees, not the thick forest we had just charged through. There was the sound of running water, and it increased in volume on each step that Samael took. After a short, calm walk, we arrived at a stream. Samael stopped, and I took the opportunity to dismount.

Standing on shaky legs, I looked around, seeking out any signs of danger, or anything familiar. I didn't recognise anything. My heart thudded loudly in my ears, and my lips and chin trembled. I pulled my cloak around myself, shivering as a breeze hissed through the forest. I'd been so stupid.

Why had I fought with Erebus? Why had I angered him so much? And why had I run away?

"Where've you brought me?" I said, glancing at Samael who was still drinking from the stream, his tail flicking as if agitated. "Can you get us back home?"

Home.

How could one word create such a knot in my stomach?

Home . . . to Erebus.

A loud chorus of laughter disturbed the quietness of the

forest and I turned my head in the direction of the joviality. Relief flooded through me when I spotted a twinkling light in the distance. Was there a house nearby? Were humans living there or another demon? If it was a demon's house, did that mean we were near another village?

"Come on," I said, grabbing Samael's reins and pulling him away from the water. "Let's see if we can get someone to take us back."

I walked toward the light, my steps tentative and slow. But as I neared the hypnotic welcoming beam, the sound of many voices and general laughter swept my way. Was there a party going on? I halted my advance, and hid within the remaining trees as I assessed the situation. As I watched the house, a rider arrived. He jumped from his horse and tied it to a wooden rail at the side of the house. Another rider arrived shortly after and strode to the door before walking straight in. Moments later, a man left, swaying sideways as he made his way into the forest.

It was then that I realised this wasn't a house; it was a tavern. My heart raced at the thought of entering such a place. Gran had told me they were always full of people enjoying themselves. There was always a friendly smile and a general atmosphere of wanting to help. The building certainly looked welcoming: flickering lights, smoke billowing from the chimney, and the sound of general merriment. Surely someone would be willing to help me get home.

When the man left on his horse, I hurried forward with Samael, desperate to feel the warmth of a roaring fire. I duly fastened Samael's reins around the wooden bar. The two horses already there were smaller than him; they looked bedraggled and underfed. Samael was a large and proud black stallion, and even in the dimmed light coming from the house, his coat shone like it was lit by tiny crystals.

"I won't be long," I said before adjusting my cloak and pulling the hood up. "Hopefully we'll be leaving here soon. You'll be back in your stable with fresh hay for the night."

As if to remind me of the coldness of the April air, another breeze picked up and swirled around me. I pulled my cloak even tighter before entering the tavern.

CHAPTER 18

FEAR

THE HEAT FROM THE INTERIOR STUNG MY EYES AS the door swung shut behind me. I looked around the room, hoping for a kindly face, or a sympathetic smile. None were offered. In fact, no one even looked up as I crossed the room to the area where a tall female stood behind a counter.

There were no hanging lanterns in the tavern, and it appeared to only be lit by the ones the visitors had brought with them. It was gloomy and cheerless, and the air hung with a thick scent of unspent powers.

"What can I get ya?" the woman asked.

I shook my head, once again taking surreptitious glances at the occupants of the tables.

She leaned forward, resting her elbows on the counter, and revealed the majority of her ample bosom. "You looking for someone or hiding from someone?"

I cleared my throat, which was suddenly dry. "Neither."

"Really? We don't get many of your kind calling on us."

I glanced around the room again, spotting a few females, but the majority of people were male. "Are there any humans in here tonight?"

She smiled, and in doing so revealed two prominent fangs.

I took a step backward and swallowed loudly. My hand flew to my neck, covering the spot where Livia had bitten me. Turning my head toward the door, I resisted the urge to run from the room and never look back. If I ran, she could follow.

The woman twisted her fingers in her dark hair, surveying me with greedy eyes. "There's no humans, 'cept you."

"H-how do you know?"

"I can smell ya."

I wanted to scream at the top of my lungs and curse everything about this frightening and miserable life. I didn't want to be here, I wanted to be back home.

I needed to leave. No one had shown any interest in me so far, and if I was calm and slow with my movements, no one would notice.

The door to the tavern creaked open. "Where's Erebus?" the man at the door shouted. "His horse is outside."

Nobody responded.

My elbow was knocked as the newcomer stood next to me. "One mead please, Giselle."

"My pleasure." She selected a metal tankard, filled it with an amber coloured liquid and handed it to the man next to me. "So, Erebus's horse is outside, but Erebus isn't here."

The man chuckled. "Maybe he's out for a romantic walk with his new love."

I stiffened.

"The man's gone soft. I still can't believe he refused my offer to free him from the responsibility of that damn village. It's not like him, you know. Twenty years I've known him, and he looked me straight in the eye and told me to never cross his path again."

"She must be special." Giselle's eyes wandered to me, and she grinned. "What's her name?"

"Athena."

"Well, maybe you should try and ask him again. See if he'll change his mind. Maybe things aren't as you think, Seb."

"I doubt it."

Giselle laughed. "Well, maybe you should ask her what she wants. Could be she ain't happy with him."

I slid further along the counter. I needed to get out of here.

The man guffawed. "It doesn't matter what she wants. Erebus will have her nicely under his control. She'll be completely under his compelment. I doubt she'll even know her own mind by now. You know demon wives don't last very long, not the human ones, and she certainly won't. She looked weak." He chuckled, but there was a sinister edge to the sound. "He's one of the most ruthless demons I know."

"You've met her?"

"Caught sight of her briefly. She's nothing special."

She leaned forward over the counter toward the man. My eyes darted around the tavern for another door that would lead me to safety. I pressed my elbows into my sides and tugged at the hood of my cloak. I wanted nothing more than to disappear and be back at the house waiting for Erebus to return. I didn't care that he was a demon, not now. Hearing what Sebastian was saying made me realise that Erebus had treated me differently than others expected him to. I hadn't lived under his constant compelment. I'd lived as free a life as I could expect, and he had shown me compassion. I'd just not allowed myself to acknowledge it. I'd fought him on everything since we'd been thrown together and only concerned myself with getting information that would help me uncover the truth about the darkness. I'd told myself again and again that I hated him, he was a demon, he was evil. And yet he'd done nothing to substantiate my thoughts. Even the marriage ceremony, which was the one thing I fiercely hated him for, was done for my protection. Life with him wasn't all bad; when he was in a good mood he made me laugh; he talked to me and showed a general interest in me as a person. He'd cared for me when I was upset, ensured I was fed, and the fires in the house were always lit to keep me warm. He'd parted the darkness to light the rosebush—just for me. He'd not forced me to sleep with him. And how had I treated him? I'd teased him, led him on, played with his emotions without a thought for how I was making him feel. No wonder he'd exploded with rage tonight when I'd tried to kiss him. What had I done?

"Well, well, well."

I held back a cry as I was tapped on the shoulder and then held firmly by a hand. I was spun around and my hood pushed away from my face.

The man grinned as I was revealed to him. "Athena!"

I recognised him instantly from his tall hat and his long grey hair.

"Sebastian." His name slipped from my lips as a rush of air.

He slipped his hand into mine and held it with a firm grasp. "What are you doing here?" He looked around me, peering into the background of the tavern. "Is he around?"

"It's just her." Giselle beamed at me and then Sebastian. "You owe me, Seb. Don't disappoint." She wandered away from the bar, shooting him a flirtatious smile over her shoulder.

"Just us then," Sebastian said. His lips were shaped like those of a woman, too perfect a pout for a man. His skin was smooth, pale, as if never exposed to anything but the darkness. And he smiled, sickeningly so.

I tried to pull my hand away from his, but he only tightened his hold. He sidled next to me so his body was touching mine. I could feel the heat of his body through our clothes, and I shifted away, jerking my head backward.

"He'll be here soon," I said, hoping that somehow Erebus would find me. I didn't allow myself to think that he was still at the village and didn't even know I'd run away.

"Really? Well then, I think we need to get moving pretty quickly."

"I'm not going anywhere with you."

My raised voice caught the attention of other demons in the tavern, and several of them looked my way.

Sebastian sniffed and then leaned toward me. "You'll do as I say. Now, I have no idea why you are here without Erebus, how you managed to escape his compelment, but I do know that it's not safe for you to be alone. I'll look after you."

"Until Erebus arrives?"

He sniffed again, grabbed my arm with his free hand and, whilst still holding me in a tight grip, twisted my wrist.

I gasped as pain shot up my arm.

"I'm not like Erebus," he said, giving my arm another sharp twist. "I don't go all lovesick when I meet a human. I don't tolerate disobedience." He bent his head to my level and stared into my eyes. I looked away, quietly satisfied that they weren't black—I wasn't feeding him anymore than I did Erebus. "But I'm curious about you. What's so special that it's got him putting you before anything and everything else, huh?"

I cocked my head to the side, my bravado winning through in a moment when my head was telling me to be quiet. "That's for me and him to know. Not you."

Before I had chance to even recognise that he had released his tight grip, the hard palm of his hand met my face. I was knocked sideways and stumbled to the floor.

"Hey!" One of the other demons in the tavern sprung from his chair and came to my assistance. "What's your problem?"

"Back off, Cresil." Sebastian stepped over to me and bent down. He gripped my chin, and I scrambled to my feet as he lifted me from the floor. Other demons were showing more interest in the unfolding events, but I didn't see any of them as my means to escape.

Sebastian must have also noticed their attention. "Do any of you know who this is?"

A sickening feeling churned in my stomach. What would their reaction be when they knew? Erebus had told me that news had spread about me being intended as a wife for the Master. Was I about to see what that meant to them?

"Seems Erebus, the mighty demon, can't control his wife!"

The pub fell silent. Every demon and vampire turned my way and greedy sets of darkened eyes and crimson ones surveyed me.

"Yes." Sebastian gloated as he twisted my arm behind my back and forced me to face the shocked and more than interested demons. "This is the woman who should have been sent to our Master. She was categorised as a wife for him."

The demons chatted to each other, disapproving noises, ones of excitement, whispered words behind raised hands. But it was hard to tell their overall reaction—it was too mixed. I tensed in Sebastian's hold, and swallowed the sour taste in my mouth. What would they do, what would they say? I shut my eyes to block out the unwanted stares, and silently screamed for Erebus. I needed him. I wanted him, no one else. Where was he?

"Erebus didn't want her to go to our Master, so he married her himself."

"Liar!" I shouted, twisting in his hold. "Paymon married me, not—"

My mouth stopped moving, it was as if I'd chewed on sticky dough. I fought to speak but made no sound. Even though there was no accompanying heat, I knew what had happened. Sebastian had compelled me.

"Now, we all know that the only way to keep a woman from going to our Master is by marrying her. That's what Erebus did. But I'm here today to give you the opportunity to either keep this rather interesting human for yourself, or hand her over to our Master, reaping the reward for taking her to where she should have originally gone."

All the demons cheered, apart from Cresil, who viewed Sebastian with a furrow of his brow. He scratched his jaw and tilted his head as Sebastian continued talking.

"Now, who'll start the bidding? What are you going to offer me?"

Cresil tapped his chin. "She's not yours to offer, Sebastian." He approached us from the corner of the room where I'd fallen. "She belongs to Erebus."

"Back off."

"Let me see her hand. If the marriage mark has faded or is fading, then what you say may be true. But if her marriage mark is dark, she clearly still belongs to Erebus."

Sebastian growled, but Cresil reached for my hand. "See!" he said, holding my hand in the air for the others in the tavern to witness. "She is not Sebastian's to offer. And I pity any of you that fancy upsetting Erebus. Sebastian may fancy his chances against his power, but do you?" He glanced around at everyone before addressing Sebastian. "Let her go. I'll return her to Erebus."

Sebastian laughed. "You fool. You think I'm going to let an opportunity like this slip through my fingers?"

Cresil stepped in front of Sebastian, invading his space. "Erebus will kill you."

"He has to find me first, and I intend on being a long way from here when he comes looking for her. Anyway, what makes you think he's bothered? You know what he's like. He'd have not let her escape if he wanted to keep her."

Cresil switched his attention to me. His gaze drifted over my face. "Let me take her," he said. "She'll be safe with me. I'll return her unharmed." There was a softness in Cresil's voice, one that hinted at safety and security. I believed that he'd keep me safe, I trusted him.

"What's this?" Sebastian shouted, grabbing the front of Cresil's cloak. "You dare to try and override my compelment. You seek to force your way through my barrier to speak with her."

I screwed my eyes shut, and the peaceful calm of safety with Cresil disappeared. I breathed heavily, swaying against the edge of the counter.

"She's not yours." Cresil lifted his hand and wrapped it around Sebastian's wrist.

Sebastian dipped his head, focusing on the floor. "I'm not playing this game."

The ground beneath Cresil split open and tiny green shoots emerged from the cracks. The tendrils shot around his feet and ankles, moving so fast up his body that he was quickly wrapped in a green writhing mass. Sebastian released Cresil's cloak and stepped back, surveying his victim. Cresil didn't scream or shout, but his eyes—wide and glossy—betrayed his fear, moments before his mouth was filled with the same flowing shoots. He fell to the ground, his flesh unseen beneath the mass of green, killing, creeping vines.

Tears threatened to break free from my eyes, but I couldn't wipe them away. I was still held firm in Sebastian's compelment, trapped in my own body, unable to speak, unable to move of my own freewill.

Cresil had been prepared to help me, and now he was dead. A new fear crept through me and nausea pulled at my stomach.

"Let's get back to what we started, shall we?" Sebastian turned to the demons, some of whom viewed the lifeless body of Cresil with a mix of horror or amusement, others still had their greedy eyes on me. "What will you offer me for this woman?"

"My sword!" A demon stood up, brandishing the large silver weapon so Sebastian could see it.

"My wife!" another shouted. "She's old and not much use to me. This pretty one would be a welcome addition to my home." I fought the revulsion in my stomach as I caught the intention behind his offer.

Sebastian had a captive audience. "Come closer, all of you, come and see her properly."

Several demons surrounded me, unknown hands touched my face and my hair. Tough calloused fingers stroked the side of my face, eager, forceful hands turned me first one way then another. I was nothing more than a prize to the highest bidder. If I'd not been compelled I would have slapped their hands away, verbally snapped at them and told them to back off. I was no prize for them—I already belonged to someone, and he would never part with me.

One demon's breath wafted over me and his dirty pock-marked face inched too close. I closed my eyes and blocked out the constant churn of sickness in my stomach as his fingers smoothed my hair behind my ears. My chest hurt, and my ribs felt as though they were squeezing together. A raspy breath shuddered from my mouth as tears flowed freely down my cheeks.

Sebastian tutted. "Not too close, Verin. She's not yours, yet."

"My horse," he offered, his finger wiping away my tears. "And I'll take her to the Master."

"Two horses!"

"My village—all the emotions you could ever want."

Sebastian shook his head. "None of them are enough. Offer me more!"

"Your life," a voice shouted from the doorway. Silence shot through the tavern and everyone spun to face the new-comer. He wore a hood over his head, pulled down over his eyes and nose. "I'll take the girl, and in return, I'll not kill you."

The general excitement my auction had created was ripped open, and malice filled the air.

"In fact, I'll save all of your lives in return for the girl."

Sebastian laughed. "Against all of us, stranger, I don't think so."

The man approached Sebastian, his hood still in place, his face still a mystery. "My offer is the one and only one you should be concerned with. I don't give second chances."

My heart leaped as he spoke his final sentence. I'd heard exactly those words before, and even though this newcomer didn't sound like him, I knew who it was.

The stranger seemed unconcerned as he addressed Sebastian. "I told you several weeks ago that I wasn't interested in any offer you made. But I seriously think you need to consider mine." He slipped his hood away from his face. *Erebus*.

The demons in the tavern shrank into their seats, some even headed for the door, fleeing what was to come.

Sebastian's compelment left me, and I stumbled, reaching my hands out to the counter to stop my fall. Emotions crashed through me, all ones concerning Erebus, all ones I realised I'd held back. And now he was here, I let them flow—how much I cared for him, how much I wanted to be with him, and how much I wanted to be his wife—in every possible way.

Erebus's black eyes caught my eyes briefly and then he looked away. There was no softness to his appearance. His usual frown was etched deep into his forehead. Dark shadows hollowed his face making his cheek bones prominent and angular. His lips were curled back, as if ready to rip the flesh from anyone who questioned him. At that moment he didn't look like Erebus. He was a frightening demon, an unknown, letting all his basic instincts pull to the surface to create a terrifying mask of evil.

Whilst I stood in a state of relief, shock, and some-what adoration for him, Sebastian's face drained of colour. "E-Erebus. What a pleasant surprise. I was intending to bring Athena back to you when I'd seen just what these reprobates were prepared to offer for her."

"Liar," I said, rounding on him. "You had no intention of returning me. The only demon willing to help was Cresil." I glanced to the lifeless body on the floor.

"Your handiwork?" Erebus asked, not looking away from Sebastian. "I always found your flower power to be a little primitive."

Sebastian edged his back along the counter, putting space between himself and Erebus. But his journey was stopped when Erebus thrust his hand out to grip the counter, halting his escape.

"I warned you to not bother me, or my wife, when you visited." Erebus leaned forward, his head nearly touching Sebastian's. "But never did I think you'd try to steal her from me."

"I didn't. I didn't steal her. Erebus, please believe me." Sebastian shrank away from Erebus, his shoulders hunched and his head dipped.

"This little party of yours seemed in full swing when I arrived. My wife the centre of everyone's attention." He shook his head and stepped back before removing his gloves. He cast his gaze around the room, silently challenging every demon and vampire. "Let it be known that Athena is my wife. If any of you even so much as look at her again, I will kill you. You all keep away from me, and you keep away from Athena."

"Or else what?" Sebastian lifted his chin.

Erebus smiled so serenely I though he mustn't have heard

him, but with a quick flick of his wrist and a lunge forward, he had hold of Sebastian around his throat. Blue sparks flew from his hand, crackling and buzzing, illuminating the dull, unknown corners of the tavern.

The ground below Erebus shifted and the beginnings of green shoots began to unfurl.

"His power!" I pointed to Erebus's feet.

Erebus twisted his arm, and Sebastian was lifted off his feet, held only by Erebus's hand.

"I lied when I said I would save your life," he said, ignoring Sebastian's gurgles and frantic attempts to free himself. "You're not worth it."

The sparks flying from Erebus's hand increased and Sebastian's face scrunched up as his body convulsed. I stared, transfixed by the power surging from Erebus into Sebastian's neck. Last time I had seen this was in the village when I'd tried to pull Erebus away from Jacob. Now, I recognised that the power he had used on Jacob was nowhere near as strong as what he was inflicting on Sebastian. And this time I had no intention of attempting to save the man Erebus was torturing.

Within a heartbeat of time, as the glow from Erebus's hand became too bright to look at, Sebastian's gurgling stopped. The green shoots that had been threatening to wind around Erebus's feet turned brown and died.

Sebastian fell to the floor, heavy and unresponsive, a canvas of black clothes and grey hair.

"Is . . . is he dead?" I asked, staring at another body as lifeless as Cresil's.

"I hope so."

Erebus pushed his shoulders back as if stretching out his muscles and then replaced his gloves. Taking a lit lantern from the nearest table, he held his other arm in my direction. "Now, Athena, time we went home." I reached for him, desperate to have contact. My hand trembled as I gripped his arm, and I struggled to walk on wobbly legs as we left the silenced demons behind.

Once outside, Erebus turned to the right and pulled me alongside him.

"Samael's tied up at the other side of the tavern," I said.

"We're walking. Samael's not here. He'll find his own way home." He lifted the lantern in the air, guiding us into the darkness of the forest.

I nodded, rushing my steps to keep up with Erebus's fast pace.

I was so relieved to be back with him that I wanted to throw my arms around his body and tell him how grateful I was that he came looking for me. I wanted to tell him what a fool I'd been, not just for running away, but for everything where he was concerned. I'd been wrong about him, so wrong, and I wanted his forgiveness. But his stiff posture and his tense shoulders, coupled with his fast pace and forward fixed gaze, made me think that now was not the time.

"Can you slow down?" I asked, bunching my skirts in my free hand.

"No, just shut up, concentrate, keep walking."

"But I need to talk to you."

"Really?" His word was clipped, angry. "Maybe you should have thought about that before you ran away."

His pace increased rather than slowed, and I had to jog to keep by his side.

"I'm sorry," I said, the words slipping easily from me.

He released my hand and stopped. His chest lifted and

fell several times before he held the lantern to his side and faced me.

"What on earth possessed you to run off? Did you not understand the danger that you put yourself in? Not just from other demons, but from the creatures in the forest?" He gritted his teeth. "Madness. What would you have done if Odin hadn't alerted me to your disappearance and where you'd gone?"

"Odin?"

"Yes. I was in the village. I hadn't even fed when he started squawking."

"You hadn't fed?"

"Athena! What part of this are you not grasping?"

I bit my bottom lip, halting a wave of tears. I didn't want to argue, not again.

Erebus threw his free hand in the air. "And your emotions are all over the place. I have no idea what's going on in your head."

"You said you didn't feed in the village, but your eyes are black."

"Yes. This is all you." He pointed to his eyes. "It hit me when I entered the tavern, and it's not left me since."

"So you weren't fed when you came looking for me? You were weak, yet you were prepared to fight other demons?"

"Yes." He looked to the ground before stepping closer to me. His gloved hand cupped the side of my face. And for the first time ever, I willingly leaned into his touch. "Athena, I don't know what you've done to me, and part of me doesn't care. But I didn't just want you back because you belong to me. I wanted you back because I didn't want to lose you. I truly care for you, and I hope, given time, you'll feel the same for me."

I was about to tell him that I did feel the same, perhaps more, but as he finished speaking, he spun his head to face the direction we'd come from. "Shhh . . ."

Not far away, I made out a moving light. It disappeared from view for a few moments and then came back, brighter, nearer.

Erebus scratched the back of his head. "It seems we've been followed. It's not surprising, but unwelcome all the same."

"You're not surprised we were followed?" A chill swept up my back as I made out Erebus's expression. The limited light from his lantern cast faint and random shadows across his features, his brow was furrowed and his mouth set in an uncompromising straight line. He huffed before hanging the lantern on a nearby overhanging branch.

"It seems they have tracked us, or rather, you. There's no point in hiding." His teeth were gritted as he practically spat the words out. "Let's give them a show to remember."

Without any warning, he pushed me away from him, the force so strong that I stumbled and fell sideways onto a tree trunk. I winced as my shoulder crashed against the hard wood, and turned my head in Erebus's direction, about to tell him exactly what I thought of him. But I kept quiet when he stepped forward to confront the demons who had followed us. He removed one of his gloves and tucked it in his pocket.

I didn't know why I kept quiet, whether it was fear, annoyance, or even self-preservation. Was it an inane curiosity about Erebus's removal of his glove? His bare hand meant one thing and one thing only—a repeat of what I'd just witnessed in the tavern.

"I see you've followed us," Erebus said in greeting,

although the words were said without friendly meaning.

"Naturally."

I squinted, struggling to see the features of the demons.

"We were hardly going to let her slip through our fingers, were we?" The other demon hung back and let the one who'd spoken take the lead.

"You were in the tavern. Did you not see what I did to Sebastian?" Erebus stood his ground, not moving, not backing away.

"It was impressive. But, you see, I've had a taste of your pretty wife—her tears are like nectar. I rather fancy keeping her for myself."

Heat flooded through me and my stomach wretched. It was Verin, the demon who'd wiped my tears away. He'd tasted them? Why?

"You shouldn't have told me that." Erebus blocked my view of the demons, keeping himself between us.

"I just did."

Erebus lifted his hands to his side and shrugged. "You're not very good at this, are you? I could have let you go, let you pass without an unfortunate accident. But now?" He tapped his chin. "Let me think for a moment. Oh, yes. I'm going to kill you."

"You're outnumbered," Verin said, his confidence soaring. "And we'll make sure she's taken care of properly when we've finished with you."

Erebus sniggered. "I don't think so. Not today."

I sunk to the ground with no thought from myself, and knew instantly that Erebus had compelled me to move. He was still doing so as I crawled behind the tree trunk I'd smashed into only a few moments ago. When I was hidden behind the tree my actions became my own again.

The ground shook, tremors vibrated against my skin. The dirt around me jumped into the air like tiny insects dancing a private jig. Snaps of splintering wood drew my gaze to the canopy of branches above me.

"I would be very careful if I were you," Erebus said, standing with his feet apart, several metres away from the smug, challenging demons.

"We have powers," Verin said.

"Like most demons," Erebus replied, removing his other glove and carefully folding it before tucking it in his pocket.

A sharp crack echoed through the forest followed by a false silence. It was like the calm before a storm, the thunder before the rain. All around me the air buzzed with a powerful charge.

The silence shattered, and the canopy above me shook. Leaves fell from the trees, and a branch thumped to the ground behind me. I crawled to my feet, leaning on the tree trunk for support as branches cracked and snapped all around.

As I focused into the distance, a large branch flew through the air, aiming for Erebus's back. Behind it were several others. All of them rushed toward Erebus's static body, their broken splintered ends pointing at him.

I wanted to shout out, warn him of what was happening, but my voice failed. Damn his compelment—he'd released his control over my limbs, but kept it over my voice.

Erebus spun around, and raised his hands in front of his body. The familiar blue surge of power shot from his palms and hit the first branch. The noise was deafening, the light blinding, and the power his force unleashed reverberated through the forest. The blast whipped the air into a frenzy, and I fell backward as if I'd been hit by a physical force.

When I lifted my head and squinted at the point of impact, all I could see was a smouldering pile of sawdust on the forest floor.

The attacking demons didn't give up. Their cocky, smug smiles remained.

"Let's see what you do with this one!"

Erebus stood straight, his arm raised, armed and ready to respond to whatever was about to come his way. This time there was no sudden movement, just a low hissing noise. I looked to the ground, shifting from one foot to the other, and pulled my skirts tight around my ankles as I looked for the expected snake.

Shadows sprung forward from where the two unwelcome demons stood. A ribbon of black mist rolled along the forest floor before rising and swirling toward Erebus.

"You seriously think this will stop me?" Erebus laughed as the mist rose in front of him.

I placed my hand over my mouth and nose as a pungent smell crept around me. I was so busy watching Erebus, keeping him within my sight and ensuring nothing untoward happened to him, that I didn't see the mist crawling up my body and wrapping itself around my neck. I gasped as a tightness pulled around it. I tried to call Erebus's name but his compelment still had a hold on my voice. Each breath I took became more urgent, and I clawed at the mist with my fingers, trying to loosen its hold, but I met no resistance—there was nothing to grab. With a desperate determination I flung myself from behind the tree, eager for Erebus to see what was happening to me. He had to stop the mist, stop playing games, and get rid of these demons that were attacking us.

"Athena!"

As soon as he saw me he roared. There was no pause as he focused on the source of the mist, and sent bright zigzags of power through the air. The surge hit the demon who had sent the broken branches, and he shot backward. He landed against a tree trunk, speared on the remnants of one of the branches that he'd hurled at Erebus.

Verin, the demon who had sent the black mist, ran into the thick darkness of the undergrowth. But he wasn't fast enough. Erebus lit the forest in another blinding light. His power once again whipped the air and the force crashed into me, flinging me onto my back. I knew the exact moment Verin had died. I breathed deeply, filling my lungs with gasped breaths of air as I lay on the damp ground, looking up at the angular branches above me.

"Get up," Erebus said, replacing his gloves and releasing his compelment on me. "We need to go home, quickly."

He stepped toward me and roughly took hold of my arm. I tried to shake him off as I stumbled to my feet, but he wasn't letting go. No sooner was I standing then Erebus was marching forward with me. I struggled to keep up with his demanding pace, and each time I slipped or fell slightly behind, his tight fingers dug into my arm even more. But the bruising throb his fingers caused was nothing compared to the ache in my stomach. It wasn't a sickening feeling though, it was a fluttering of nerves, excitement and the urgency for something more. Each time he shifted his hold on my arm, or sighed or huffed, my breath quickened. My nerves tingled and I craved more of his touch however harsh.

The time had come for me to be honest with him about my feelings.

chapter 19

DESIRE

A S WE STEPPED THROUGH THE DOOR OF THE HOUSE, Erebus removed his gloves.

"I have to tell you something," I said, prepared to admit how wrong I'd been about everything.

"Me first."

Before I had chance to speak, he grabbed my shoulders and slammed me back against the wall.

"I know what emotion of yours is feeding me." His face was mere inches from mine. "And I want you to be honest."

He pushed his body against mine, trapping me between the wall and his muscular frame.

"I will," I gasped, my voice a rushed breath of air.

"It's not pain. It's not anger. And it's definitely not hate. Those are nothing to me." His voice was no more than a whisper. He lifted an ungloved hand to my face. I flinched when tiny sparks tickled my flesh. "Nothing compared to what they are when you laugh, when you talk to me as though I am the only man in the world who has your attention."

His fingers gripped my chin, and the ensuing sensation of his crackling power nipped at my skin causing me to whimper. "Only one emotion of yours feeds me, Athena." He paused and then looked me right in the eyes. Once again I was greeted with black orbs. "Love."

My mouth dropped open at his interpretation. "I don't love you." It was only this evening that I'd admitted to myself that I liked him. It certainly wasn't love.

"Really? I beg to differ."

"How can I love you? You're a demon." My argument was weak. Being a demon wasn't a reason to not love him, not when he'd shown me how human he could be.

He released me and took a few steps back. I rubbed my chin where he'd held me, easing the raw sting.

"I've been asking myself the exact same question." He removed his cloak and hung it up, beckoning for mine. When I'd handed it to him he prowled to the living room door and leaned on the frame. "How can a human love a demon? It's practically unheard of. But somehow you've managed it."

I stepped away from the wall, prepared to argue my case. "I can't love you. I don't!" My voice shook with emotion.

He stormed across the hall, stopping directly in front of me. "Don't lie to me! Stop lying to yourself." His warm breath blew across my face, and I found my gaze resting on the smooth outline of his lips.

"I'm not," I murmured. "You're impossible to love. Who could ever love you?"

His eyes darkened even more. Molten black fluid swirled across his pupil, like oil spilling onto water.

"You love me," he said, quiet, as if in disbelief at his own words.

About to shake my head, I stopped the action as his eyes cleared of the blackness. His irises returned, bright amber with a black circle outlining his pupils. It was easy to lose myself in such hypnotising brightness and clarity. He was fed—completely full.

His already close face moved nearer to mine.

"I'll ask you again to stop lying." His words were soft in their delivery, caressing my ears, soothing my frustration.

With a movement so slow, but too fast, he pressed his lips onto mine. Heat, almost impossible heat, burnt my lips. It was like kissing a burning coal—scorching and white-hot.

He didn't stop.

I didn't want him to.

The burning increased as he pushed me back against the wall, although now the rest of me became consumed by the heat. The simmering embers in my stomach were building into a fire, one that was coming to life just for Erebus.

His hands gripped my wrists, and he lifted them above my head, pinning them together with one hand in an easy grasp. He curled his other hand around my waist and pulled my lower body against his. We moulded together perfectly—his hardness complemented my softness.

I gasped at his increasing forwardness, and he slipped his tongue into my mouth. There was no hesitancy, no long preliminary tenderness. Erebus was in charge, a demon who took what he wanted. But this wasn't all him. I eagerly responded.

I pressed myself against him, matching contours, sighs and moans. A sudden light-headedness would have made me stumble if Erebus hadn't had me locked in position. I whimpered as the first signs of his compelment took hold. Forcing my lips away from his, I gasped for breath.

"Don't compel me," I begged.

He rested his forehead against mine. "I'm not. I promised I wouldn't, and believe me, you'd know if I was. You'd be half-naked, crawling all over me, begging for me to defile you here and now."

Through a moment of clarity, my humour suddenly returned. "Only half-naked?"

"Makes life more interesting."

I drew in a deep breath, and my stomach clenched with jolts of pleasure at his teasing words.

"So the demon gets his wicked way." I grinned at the easy way we sparred.

"I always get my way." His free hand stroked the side of my face, venturing down my neck and across to my shoulder before slipping under the fabric of my dress. "Whether you know it or not."

His lips crashed onto mine with an urgency that fanned the flames in my belly into a raging fire. I wanted him. It was no use trying to hide my primal instinct any longer.

With my hands still held above me, I hooked one of my legs around the back of his thigh and pulled him flush against me. A low growl sounded within his chest at the same time that he released my hands. He grabbed the skirt of my dress and pushed the hem up my legs. I held his shoulders, supporting myself as his warm hands rubbed up and down my naked thighs.

"I want to devour you." His warm breath blew on my neck as he gripped my thighs with possessive hands. "But I also want to take my time."

My breath hitched as he placed a soft kiss on my neck.

The skin his lips covered tingled as if he'd latched on to every nerve I possessed.

"Do whatever you want," I whispered. My voice was not my own; it was the voice of the woman who wanted Erebus as much as she needed every single beat of her heart. I slid my hands around the back of his neck before pulling him closer for another demanding kiss.

"Oh, I intend to," he said before my mouth covered his.

His urgency spurred me on, and I pulled at his jacket, wanting it off his body. He pushed a leg between my thighs, replacing the position of his hands, and assisted my removal of the cumbersome coat. All the time we kissed, fast, demanding, possessive. Our pace dictated our rhythm, and both of us were in a rush. I wanted him to claim me as his, to make me his wife in the most physical way possible. He knew my body, he'd seen it at our marriage ceremony, but this was different. Very different.

"Trousers," I said, breaking our kiss and reaching for the buttons below his belt. He duly obliged and assisted my eager fumbling fingers in releasing them. I smiled as I slipped one of my hands into the gap of his trousers. He was already hard and smooth. His jaw clenched and his eyes closed as I wrapped my hand around him, stroking him, marvelling as he grew even firmer.

I breathed deeply, trying to calm myself, but the fire within me roared. A pleasant ache throbbed in my lower belly when Erebus's hand slipped back to the top of my inner thigh. I gasped, a short intake of breath that stuck in my throat as his fingers slipped inside me. Dropping my head onto his shoulder, I tried to breathe out slowly, but a shuddering sigh escaped my lips.

Erebus chuckled before adding another finger to his slow thrusting. "You've made me wait, Athena, and now see how impatient you are."

I kissed his neck and squeezed his erection. What he said was true. Why had I missed feeling like this? I wanted him—now. The delicious ache was spreading through me, matching the raging fire, one he would continue to feed, and one only he could smother.

"Please," I whimpered, needing the full force of him inside me.

"Lean back." He removed his hand and stepped back. "Shoes off."

I moaned at the loss of his body but when I saw the eager glimmer of lust in his fully fed eyes, I did as he said, kicking my shoes off, and resting my back against the wall.

He pushed my legs apart with his foot, and then stepped between them, bending his knees. Realising his intention, I gripped his shoulders. My skirt was pushed around my waist as his hardness nudged at my inner thigh. And then he slid effortlessly into me.

My world stopped.

I exhaled deeply, revelling in the sensation of him inside me and of his demanding ownership of my body.

"Wrap your arms around me," he said, slipping his hands under my bottom.

I did as he asked and was rewarded with him lifting me from the floor.

"Ohhh . . ." All my weight was centred on our deep connection, and I instinctively wrapped my legs around his waist.

I pressed my back firmly against the wall as he began to thrust. His speed wasn't slow; there was no build-up, no increase in depth or vigour. He immediately rammed into me—quick, deep, and consistent; stroke after stroke he stretched me fully each time he thrust.

My mind clouded, lost in a haze of dreams and fantasies. He was fulfilling every one of them as he defiled me in the most glorious way. I was trapped between the wall and him, vulnerable in my confinement, but never feeling safer. My movements were restricted, but my feelings weren't. Each thrust caused his pelvis to rub against mine, increasing the throbbing heaviness that built within.

As our actions became steady, his lips searched mine. I eagerly welcomed his invasive tongue and matched his vigorous exploration with my own. I nipped his lips with my teeth, and he returned the favour. I sucked his lip, drawing away before releasing it. Grunts escaped from him, whereas an uncontrolled sharp intake of breath flew from me each time he thrust.

The slow burn of pressure morphed into something else. Something I'd caught a glimmer of before, but never quite found. Then it wasn't a glimmer anymore. Erebus increased his pace, and my thighs quivered. They didn't stop. I whimpered as the trembling in my thighs spread up my chest and along my arms and the fire inside me exploded. My whimpers turned into loud moans as I became lost within my own body. I bit into his shoulder, trying to silence my cries of crashing pleasure.

Erebus shifted, leaning onto me fully as he pressed me back into the wall, and I gasped for breath, squashed between the cold wall and his burning body. He broke the steady rhythm he'd dictated from the start. His hips thrust harder, erratic and forceful. A low growl sounded from deep in his chest before he groaned loudly. And after one last deep thrust, he stilled.

He rested his head at the side of mine, and his heavy breathing blew across my forehead. My thighs were not gripping him anymore; they were limp, wrapped around him with no muscle strength left. He kissed the side of my forehead and ran his fingers through my hair.

"Unbelievable," he said before kissing my ear. "Why did you make us wait so long?"

"I . . . I had no idea . . ." My words were lost in a fog of contentment. I was calm, satisfied.

"No idea about what?" Erebus nudged my head with his, requesting my full attention.

"That it could feel like that."

"Really?" Erebus chuckled. "Oh my, Athena. You're in for a treat this evening."

I grinned stupidly, inwardly rejoicing at his promise.

"Let's get more comfortable," he said against the skin on my neck. "I'm nowhere near finished with you."

He slipped from me and lowered me to the floor before tucking himself away. I screamed when he grabbed me around my waist and threw me onto his shoulder. As he marched up the stairs with me locked in position, and my skirt scrunched around my waist, I couldn't contain the excited giggle that escaped me. His hands were firmly planted on my thighs, and I could sense the tingle of his power though his fingers. The whispered crackle of blue sparks lit the upstairs corridor as he strode to the door before mine—his bedroom.

He kicked the door open and carried me inside. The room was only lit by the glow from the fire and a few random candles, and my eyes struggled to adjust to the dim light. The bed had a canopy like mine, posts rising at each corner to support the structure above. The curtains were closed, blocking out the night outside. A powerful scent hit the back of my throat, and I drew in the taste of it. It was Erebus's smell, the one that seeped into my senses and calmed but excited me at the same time. Musky, woody with a hint of pine—an intoxicating mix of pure masculinity.

He threw me onto his bed, and as I bounced on the thick mattress, he walked backward to the door, not taking his eyes off me. Crossing his arms in front of his chest, he continued to stare at me.

I shifted to the edge of the bed, returning his scrutiny. My heart beat fast as I concentrated on him. I wanted him next to me. I already missed his touch.

He spun around as if suddenly remembering something and turned a key in the lock of the door. I frowned as he resumed his position.

"Locking intruders out?" I pushed myself off the bed, and rested my back against the bedpost, mirroring his position at the door.

"There'll be no intruders. There's no one around to break into the house, never mind my bedroom."

"Then why—?"

"To keep you in. I don't want you running off again."

My breath caught in my throat, and I curled my fingers around the wooden post behind me.

"Undress," he said. The command was simple, concise. His voice had deepened to a breath—smooth, silky, and laced with desire.

"I thought you'd like to undress me," I said, craving his touch on my skin.

"I want to watch. I want to see every inch of your skin revealed to me. Don't go all shy on me after what's just happened downstairs." He paused, and his lips twitched before he continued. "Besides, if I attempt to undress you, I shall fail. The dress will be ripped and on the floor within a heartbeat."

His deep, searching eyes drank me in, desperate to devour, but eager to savour the moment. With a wicked curl of my lips, I turned my back to Erebus and lifted my hands to the base of my neck. Collecting my hair, I placed it over my shoulder so it trailed across my front. I twisted my right arm, reaching for the lace tie on the low v-back of my dress. With a few tugs, it unfastened easily to the base of my spine. Attempting to play the seductress as well as I possibly could, I looked back over one shoulder at Erebus.

"Continue." He was still at the door, his arms crossed over his chest.

I wriggled my shoulders, and the dress slipped from the one I had looked over. A quick tug on the bottom of the sleeve was all that was needed to release my arm. I repeated the action with my other arm, and the shift caused the weight of the dress to slip lower. I turned to face Erebus, my arms across my chest, holding the dress in place.

Erebus lifted a questioning brow before nodding toward the floor.

Taking an unnecessary deep breath, I dropped my arms to my side and let the dress fall.

I was naked, apart from my long socks.

He didn't move or show any expression other than his transfixed gaze, which greedily devoured each and every part of me.

Did I disappoint him? Had his initial statement, when I

awoke after our marriage ceremony, about me not impressing him been true? I lifted my chin and met his eyes as they eventually focused on mine. Finding my voice, I uttered words that I feared the answer to. "Will I do?"

"Will you do?" Erebus strode toward me, covering the distance in a few quick strides. He loomed over me, but didn't touch me. "You'll more than do, Athena."

He spun me around with his hands and gripped the top of my arms. My skin tingled, and small blue sparks fizzed where he touched me. I welcomed the reminder of his power, of how strong he was.

"You're perfect," he whispered against my ear before kissing the base of my neck. I groaned when the softness of his lips met my skin. "Perfect for me." He ran his hands down my arms, and I leaned back onto him, relishing the solid muscles of his body. I arched my back and lifted my arms behind, reaching around the back of his neck and pulling his head next to mine. I twisted my face toward his, wanting his lips on mine, craving the kisses we'd shared downstairs. His stubble scratched my skin as he gently sucked my neck.

"Slow down, Athena. We have all night."

"Not long enough," I said before grasping him even tighter and trying to turn to face him.

He chuckled against my skin before planting further gentle kisses along my shoulder.

"Lie on the bed. On your back," he said. The words were spoken quietly but were an order.

I reclined on the bed, my head on the pillows, with no embarrassment about being completely exposed to him. I ached delightfully from our union downstairs, and the fluttering fire within my belly yearned for more of the same.

I bent one of my knees, raising it a couple of inches into the air, and lifted my arms above my head. Erebus drew in a sharp intake of breath before stepping toward the foot of the bed.

"Your skin glows in the light from the candles. I always thought a fire burnt within you, Athena, but it has grown into a glorious monster—it rages within you now."

I smiled at his assessment of my character and the burning beast within me. Had it always been there, or had he unlocked it?

Erebus finally began undressing. His fingers worked deftly on his shirt, slipping the top buttons open with ease.

"Can I help?" I propped myself up on my elbows.

He shook his head. "If I want you to move, I'll tell you. Stay where you are."

He lifted his shirt above his head before throwing it to the floor.

Standing before me in just his trousers and boots, I realised that it was the fire within him that had attracted me. He knew what he wanted and took control. I was surprised he had been prepared to wait for me when it meant missing out on this burning crescendo of our feelings. And why had I made him wait? What would it be like if I had my time with him again? I'd certainly be awake during the marriage ceremony, not compelled and half-asleep. I'd insist he complete the full ceremony, enjoy the moment we came together whilst surrounded by flames and his demon chanting. My breath caught in my throat as the images flashed before me.

Erebus cocked his head to the side. "Now what are you thinking? It's something strong."

"I'm just wondering why I didn't jump on you the moment

we met."

"Because you're stubborn." Erebus's mouth curled at the side. "And you have principles and rules that you live by. I don't want you to ever forget who you are or where you come from, but now we are truly a couple, married and joined together in every sense of the word. I demand that you remain true to me and only me."

"There'll never be anyone else," I said, my voice strong. I didn't want anyone else.

He nodded, his eyes narrowing as he stared at me. His scrutiny was becoming easy to take, not like it was when we first met, when I shied away from his penetrating, all-knowing eyes.

Candles lit his torso, giving flickering teases of the designs inked on his body. I'd seen them before, but I had never let myself stare. I'd never wanted him to catch me watching his naked torso, but now I didn't care, and tipped my head as I tried to study the designs in the limited light.

"What do they all mean?" I dipped my head at his bare chest, ignoring the urge to crawl to the end of the bed to take a closer look.

"Various things."

"Tell me."

He grinned. "Which part do you want me to translate?"

I tilted my head to the side, catching a block of text written between two curved symbols. "That one," I said, pointing to his left side over his rib cage.

He glanced at the text before returning his intense gaze back to me. "May my life be a wondrous opportunity to seize the powers bestowed upon me."

"Your surge of power?"

"It's very rare," he said before diverting his attention away from me and pulling his feet free from his boots. With the translation forgotten, he stepped to the edge of the bed. "Athena, how many lovers have you had?"

His words snapped me back to the moment, to what was happening and to my nakedness. "One," I said. I wasn't the village whore. "Only one before you."

"Thomas?" The name was spat as he placed one knee on the bed and proceeded to crawl toward me.

I nodded, my breathing already increasing in pace.

"So you've never been loved by a demon." It wasn't a question—it was a statement.

"O . . . only downstairs, with you."

He shook his head. "That wasn't what I meant. What we shared downstairs was perfunctory, necessary. We both needed the release. But now . . . now I will make love to you properly."

He wrapped his hand around my ankle and lifted my foot onto his shoulder. With steady hands, he rolled my thigh length sock down my leg. Soft kisses were immediately placed along the inner edge of my foot, trailing to my calf, before he paid attention to my other covered leg. Once I was free of the woollen coverings he edged further up the bed, teasing me with his languid movement. His hands parted my thighs as he kissed higher. The touch of his fingers was as electric as his mouth, and I moaned, wanting more of the same and yet eager for what was to come.

He inched higher, slipping his mouth to the front of my legs. "Has any man ever kissed you here?" he said, lightly pressing his hand between my thighs.

"No," I whispered, a word that sounded far louder in the

silence of his room.

"Thomas was a selfish lover. Every woman should be worshipped here." Once again, his hand pressed against me, but this time his fingers slipped further. I instinctively lifted my hips from the bed, wanting more contact, more pressure.

"Would you like me to kiss you here?"

I nodded frantically, imagining the warmth, the wetness, and the soft contours of his mouth.

"You are so eager, Athena. And to think that you have denied me your body since the day you met me."

"I wouldn't have if I'd known," I uttered as his stubble scratched my inner thighs.

"Known what?" Erebus's warm breath blew across me.

I moaned as I waited for his promised kiss. I would surely explode, come undone as easily as I had downstairs.

His lips covered me.

"That you . . . could make . . . me . . . feel . . ." I shattered as the tightness in my stomach unfurled.

My words were lost to a scream of pleasure, and I reached for him, grabbing his hair, urging him on. I continued to climb the dizzy heights of saturated bliss that Erebus teased from me, losing myself in his lascivious worship of my body.

Time after time, he pushed me over the edge. And each time, I begged for more. My mind cleared of all that had happened over the past few months, and my thoughts centred on Erebus and only Erebus.

And as the darkness of the evening raged into a loud storm outside, Erebus and I continued to explore each other's bodies. Many times we came together, and each time he ensured I reached my peak before he followed.

Selfless, demanding—he was all I required from a lover.

Insatiable, possessive—my husband loved me and proved it repeatedly.

CHAPTER 20

ELATION

"Time to get up," Erebus said as he moved across the bed.

"I want to stay here." I rolled over and reached my hand in his direction. "Come back to bed."

He was already pulling his trousers on. The crumpled material stretched out over his muscular thighs. He smiled at me before crouching, about to pick his shirt from the floor.

"I've got something I want to show you," he said seriously, although he chuckled when I raised my brow.

"Well, come back to bed. I've got something I want to show you."

Leaving his shirt where it was, he sidled to the bed before leaning over me. His lips were instantly upon mine, urgent, searching and demanding a response. He growled before straightening up and heading back to his shirt.

"Seriously," he said. "Get dressed. We're going out."

"Why?" I wanted to spend the rest of the day in bed. I'd

only just discovered the intensity of shared love-making, of a man worshipping my body and ensuring my pleasure before his own. I didn't want to go anywhere.

"Like I said, I want to show you something. It's already midday. We'll miss it if we don't get a move on." He pulled his shirt over his head, ending my lust infused haze.

I sighed in defeat as I sat up. "Is it far? Are we walking?"

"Far enough." He pulled one of his boots on, and then the other. "That's why we're going on Samael. It'll take us most of the afternoon to get there."

"Samael is back?"

"He came back last night. I told you he would."

"Where's Odin?" I needed to thank him for helping last night. The bird was more intelligent than I gave him credit for.

"I let him in last night whilst you were sleeping. He slept in your room on the screen."

"Can he come with us today?"

Erebus smiled. "Of course. But even if I didn't want him to come, I suspect he still would."

"And you're not going to tell me where we're going?"

"No. It's a surprise."

"I think I had plenty of those last night." I pulled the furs up over my head and flung myself backward on the bed, hiding my flushed, heated face.

Erebus chuckled. "Well, prepare yourself for another. Get dressed, something warm, and I'll meet you downstairs. You'd best hurry, I'm going to try and cook you some porridge." He fled the room, whistling as he wandered along the corridor.

He had to be joking. He'd never cooked for me. And now he was going to attempt to make porridge? It wasn't difficult, but the oats needed to be soaked overnight, and I was sure he'd not have done that.

He was happy, though, a smiling demon, a man who was as content as the woman with him. My heart threatened to burst from the confines of my chest whenever he held me close. I loved the tingling touch of his fingers, the ticking jolts of his power tracing my flesh. And when he loved me . . . there was no other male in the world who could love me the way he did.

I rushed to my room to select the warmest dress I had, but rummaged in my bedside drawer before dressing. I'd built up quite a supply of lace since I'd been here. Bessie regularly brought some with the food, and I'd never informed her the seeds weren't needed. I grinned as I popped a handful of the seeds in my mouth and chewed them. I'd be needing them every day now.

Odin wasn't in my room, and I missed his early morning chatter waking me up. I grinned. Someone else had woken me this morning and he hadn't stirred me from my sleep by talking to me.

I searched through my dresses for the thickest one I had, but stopped moving as I spotted several small finger sized marks developing into deep purple bruises on my arms. I twisted each arm in turn, systematically inspecting them. Erebus had marked me. I inhaled a deep breath and closed my eyes. I'd never felt him hurting me last night. His hold was comforting, commanding and possessive, and I would have told him if his grip had caused any pain. I frowned, once again inspecting the bruises. Paymon's words about demons been strong, sometimes too strong, rushed through my head. Erebus needed to be careful.

When I ventured downstairs, Odin's loud squawks

sounded out from the kitchen. I followed their noise and the distinctly unpleasant smell of something burning. Erebus was stirring a small black pot over the stove, his back to the room, and Odin was hopping from the back of one chair to another. I silently walked around the table and wrapped my arms around Erebus.

"Let me sort this," I said.

He turned in my arms to face me. "I don't think I'm doing a good job of it. I did try." He grimaced at the creamy liquid spotted with dark brown burnt pieces.

"I'll just have toast," I said, squeezing him. "And a few eggs."

It seemed strange to be eating breakfast at midday, but there was no way I'd have willingly left the comfort of a warm bed, and an equally warm man, just for food.

I made my way to the pantry and picked two eggs from the straw filled basket. When I returned to the kitchen, Odin had settled on back of the chair next to Erebus who had his legs crossed and resting on the seat next to him. Erebus was scratching Odin under his beak. "He's quite a sweet little chap when you get to know him."

I smiled. Seeing Erebus and Odin together wasn't something I'd ever thought would happen. They only just managed to put up with each other, and I hadn't forgotten the times Odin had pecked Erebus.

"How are you feeling this morning?" Erebus asked. "Tired?"

"Bruised," I said, honest with my response.

He narrowed his eyes. "I was too rough. I shall try to be more considerate in the future, but I can't promise."

"Did you hear me complaining last night?"

327

He looked away. "No, but I need to be careful. Women have been known to die whilst demons have sex with them. Sometimes we forget our own strength. And you would make any man forget his mind when he is consumed with passion and buried deep within you."

My cheeks burnt, the usual redness sure to follow.

"Is there anything I can do to help?" I asked, skewering the bread on the fork ready to hold it in the fire pit.

"To help?" He shook his head. "No. It needs to be me who controls myself. Although my pleasure may be diminished if I try to control exactly what I'm doing."

"Have you ever made love to a human before me?" I had to ask even though I didn't want to know the answer.

His gaze lifted and his eyes hit me with their full black force. "I'm not prepared to hide my past from you, Athena. I've had a few female demons share their bodies with me . . . and one vampire." He shook his head as if trying to rid himself of the memory. "But they are nothing compared to you. And to answer your question, no, I have never made love to anyone apart from you."

His words made my heart leap, stutter and race, seemingly all at once.

"You mean I . . . I'm the first?"

Nodding, he offered me a lazy grin.

I froze, unable to speak. Had he just told me he loved me?

The toasting fork dropped from my hand as I repeated his words in my head.

Erebus sprang to his feet and was upon me instantly, pushing me back against the old sink. I squealed with surprise at his passionate attack. His lips covered mine with his usual urgency—hard demanding kisses that scorched. I matched his vigour with that of my own, but when his hand grasped at the skirt of my dress and his hips pressed against mine, I reached for his hand, entwined my fingers between his and held him still. His fevered kissing stopped and he sighed before pressing a single chaste kiss on my mouth. We both breathed heavily, our foreheads touching. His hand slipped from mine, and he stroked my cheek with his fingers. "Later," he promised before pressing another soft kiss on my lips.

He stepped backward and smiled. "Get some food into you, Athena, we need to leave as soon as possible."

Erebus never told me where we were going. He was calm to-day, relaxed, but moments of bristling excitement kept creep-ing through his serious façade. When we left the house and rode through the forest, Odin followed us. He occasionally cawed, alerting us of his presence as he swooped low in front of Samael. Erebus laughed every time Odin made an appear-ance, enjoying his company as much as I did. There was no rain today, but there was a bitter wind, one that nipped at my exposed face and threatened to tear the hood of my cloak off my head. We travelled most of the afternoon, stopping only twice at the side of streams to let Samael have a drink. Erebus showed no fear of the thick forest around us or for travelling on the deserted clover covered roads. But I was on edge, fears of what the darkness hid were never far from my mind. The times I heard a distant howl or caught the movement of the hedgerow as we raced passed on Samael, I tightened my hold around Erebus's waist and buried my face in the back of his cloak. If anything jumped out at us, I was sure he would kill it.

His gloves were tucked in his coat pocket, and the deadly power he could unleash from his bare hands was unquestionable.

"How much further?" I asked, my voice raised to a volume he would hear above the constant beat of Samael's hooves.

"Nearly there," he shouted, nodding forward.

I peered into the darkness ahead of us, and for the first time in my life I noticed a brightness in the sky over the horizon. I stared in awe at the sight as we travelled toward it.

"What is it?"

Erebus slowed Samael to a steady trot. "I've brought you to see the true beauty of the light."

My mouth opened, and I stared in wonder at what lay ahead.

"The light? You mean I'll be able to see the sun?"

"There are areas where the sun isn't blocked. That's where we're heading."

"Really?"

Erebus nodded before urging Samael to gallop.

A few minutes later, he pulled Samael to a halt and quickly dismounted. "Come on, jump down." He held his arms up to me and assisted with my dismount. "We'll go on foot from here, and I'll try to explain the situation with the light."

I reached blindly for his hand as we walked forward. I couldn't tear my eyes away from what we were heading toward. The darkness still covered us, but ahead, like a candle glowing with an incredible beam, the sky lightened.

"I thought it was all hidden," I said, watching the brightness, scared it would disappear if I turned away. "Will we be able to see the sun when we get nearer?"

"I hope so," Erebus replied. He was as serious as I was curious.

"How is that possible? How did you know it was here? And why didn't you tell me?"

Erebus chuckled and removed his hand from mine before placing his arm around my waist. "So many questions, Athena. Which one shall I answer first?"

I shrugged, still concentrating on what lay ahead.

"Yes, I have seen the light before, that's how I knew it was here. I stumbled upon it one day when riding Samael." He sighed and his arm tightened. "I decided to not say anything, even though I knew of your obsession with finding it, but I always intended on telling you . . . eventually."

"Eventually?"

"When we were married properly, in all ways."

I turned to face him, and he stopped walking.

"I wanted to tell you about it," he continued, lifting his hand to my face. He pushed several loose strands of hair behind my ears, concentrating on the action. "But I wanted the moment to be special. As we walk closer, you'll see what I mean. The sun will soon set and the sky will turn a beautiful colour." His eyes fixed on mine. "I wanted to share this with you when the time was right."

"And the time's right now?"

"The time is perfect. I know how much this means to you. I wanted you to see it."

I leaned into him before reaching to kiss his cheek. "Thank you."

"My pleasure." He held close, wrapping his arms around my waist and hugging me. "Let's get closer."

We strode toward the clear sky, Samael on one side of Erebus, me on the other.

I gasped loudly when something else came into view. Not

only was the sky changing colour, I could see water.

"We're at the coast!" I ran forward before spinning to face Erebus. "You brought me to the seaside!"

He chuckled, watching me with an intense gaze. "The seaside? What exactly is that?"

"You don't know? Ice creams, donkey rides, penny arcades, sand castles, and the sun!" I spun on the spot as I listed my childhood memories. My heart lifted at the thought of those special lost moments.

Erebus's lips twitched as he tried unsuccessfully to hide his amusement. "Well, you've had a ride on a stallion, not a donkey, but I'm afraid the rest will not be possible."

I ran off again, desperate to see the sand on the beach and hear the waves crashing ashore. It had been so long since I'd seen or heard either. It was years, too many years since that life had been stolen from me.

"Athena!" Erebus shouted, marching to catch up with me. "Don't go too far ahead. Stay close."

I stopped running and waited for him to walk in step beside me. "Sorry. I guess I got carried away."

"Just a bit." He took my hand again and held it tightly. "It's very appealing to see you relive your childhood, your enthusiasm is contagious, but I selfishly prefer the woman. I have no interest in imagining you as a young girl." He lifted my hand and kissed the back of it.

"Whereas I'd love to meet the young Erebus." I giggled, imagining him with his cherubic curls and cheeky dimples. My quiet giggle turned into a laugh as I caught myself imagining him as angelic. A cherub indeed. He was a demon. Why did I keep forgetting?

"Look over there." Erebus pointed to the sky to the right

of us. "The sun is just beginning to set."

I followed the direction of his hand and nodded. I couldn't see the sun, but it was affecting the sky. It was turning a soft yellow. The edge of the dark sky over the land framed the changes over the sea.

Erebus squeezed my hand. "Let's go onto the beach and watch it."

A small ridge of sand dunes separated us from the beach, and as we ploughed through them I caught my first smell of the salt water. The rumble of the sea, the quiet crash of the waves, and the squawk of a bird disturbed the silent, eerie background of my normal life. And the one thing I was taking for granted suddenly became very apparent. I could see properly. There was no grainy vision of subdued and artificial light from candles, lanterns, or fires. This was the light we'd had before; this was the light I longed to return to our world.

As we strode onto the sand, I pulled my boots and socks off and carried them. The gritty texture rubbed between my toes, and I shrieked with excitement at such a simple but pleasant feeling. Erebus watched me with fascination.

"Take your boots off!" I shouted at him as I made my way to the water's edge.

The wind was stronger here than over the land, but it wasn't like the wind that rushed through the village, or like the one we'd battled against whilst travelling; here it was invigorating and fresh. It brought with it a sense of freedom, one I hadn't experienced since the demon's ascent. The urge to run and not stop until I was exhausted flooded through me, but as I caught sight of Erebus removing his boots, I realised I didn't want to run—it would only take me further away from the man I was beginning to love. I spun on the spot instead, taking in the views around me. There was no one around apart from us. No sound apart from the roar of the sea and the boisterous buffer of the wind.

Odin swooped over the swirling ocean before rising high in the sky. He dipped and turned, playing in the currents of the wind that blew over the water. He was silent, enjoying himself.

"Don't go in the water," Erebus said as he came to my side. He took my hand and indicated with a sweep of his arm for us to walk along the beach.

"You now know that the darkness isn't everywhere," he said. "Where the land meets the sea you can see into the brightness that once existed. The Master only created the shield of darkness over the land."

"So did the Master put the shield of darkness over the whole world or just England?"

Erebus looked to the ground before answering. "It covers every landmass around the world."

I inhaled, shock and disbelief crashing through me. This was worse than I feared, or was it? When Erebus told me about the cloak of darkness I assumed it covered the whole world. I'd just found out it only covered the land.

I unwillingly turned away from the vision of the sun and looked at Erebus. "We should all go and live on boats, and then we'd have the beauty of the sun above us."

He shook his head. "The sea is not safe. It's why I warned you to keep out of the water, however tempting it may be. When nighttime comes and the light disappears over the oceans, the vampires can enter the water and feed freely if they so wish."

I shivered and cast my gaze toward the beach behind us. "I know demons walked amongst humans before the world literally split open. Paymon did, but did vampires?"

Erebus nodded. "Of course. But, like demons, they had to keep a low profile."

"Were you around?"

Erebus chuckled. "Around?"

"Yes, were you on earth . . . or in Muspalta?"

His humour disappeared and was replaced by what I could only describe as a death stare as he narrowed his eyes and held me in his gaze. "I was in Muspalta. And I would prefer not to return. Living on earth is far better. Even with the darkness, it offers a beauty that cannot be found in Muspalta." He smiled, his fleeting earlier anger disappearing. "And also . . . *you* are not in Muspalta."

I smiled at his tender words before glancing over the water into the distance. I breathed deeply. If I saw this every day, I'd never want to leave. The sun was peeking out from behind the darkness as it slipped toward the horizon. The yellow tinge of the sky had been replaced by a bright orange and deep red edged the darkness. It was an angry looking sky that promised nothing but goodness to me.

I stopped walking, and Erebus wrapped his arms around me from behind.

"It's beautiful," I said, devouring the sight. "I don't suppose we can stay here. Is there a village nearby you can look after?"

He rested his head against mine, looking at the same vision as me. "I wish there was. I'd love to continually see the brightness of your face and feel the happiness that this visit has awoken in you. I knew the light was something you craved."

"It's the one thing I'd change if I could."

He turned me in his hold so I was facing him. "Athena,

the light will never return as you wish it to." He pulled his cloak around me, wrapping us in its warmth. "But I promise we will come back here, maybe once a month, so you can see the light and catch a glimpse of the sun."

"I'd like that," I said, grabbing a fistful of his cloak in my hand. I rested my head sideways on his chest so I could continue to look over the sea. The sun was already dipping below the horizon, festooned in a ribbon of colours as it disappeared. I held on tightly to Erebus, fearing the loss of the light more than normal. I'd been given a glimmer of what it used to be like, and I didn't want the moment to end.

When I'd originally found out that the Master controlled the shield and his children held the power to destroy it, I'd given up on ever discovering more. But a renewed hope surged though me as I watched the sun sink below the horizon. This was too important to just forget. I couldn't just give up—I wouldn't give up.

If there was no darkness over the sea, maybe the Master wasn't the all-powerful demon that everyone believed. I clung on to that hope. I imagined life in the village with the light returned and the sun heating the ground. We'd have proper seasons. We'd have a summer. The light had always been important to me, an obsession even, but now it became important for other reasons. If I found a way to destroy the shield, then I'd also reduce the number of vampires that dared to walk amongst us.

And I knew just the man who'd want to help with that.

Erebus.

Together, we'd find a way to destroy it.

CHAPTER 21

ANXIETY

SINCE OUR TRIP TO SEE THE SUN SETTING OVER THE ocean, and with all the books in the library at my disposal, I'd tried to discover even more about the darkness. Erebus continued to trace the unregulated vampire covens. We worked together, sitting at the same desk, him on one side, me on the other as we investigated our different obsessions. His foot often rubbed my leg under my skirts, and I'd catch him staring at me when he thought I wasn't looking. Whenever I caught his gaze, he'd smile before continuing with what he was doing. I often studied him as well, but usually on the few times he fell asleep at the desk.

He was nothing like the demon I'd first met; he was more concerned about my happiness and well-being than anything else. His face had softened slightly, and he wasn't as wild looking as he used to be, although his hair was still an unruly mop, but his jaw wasn't as angular, not as tight—as if he'd eventually found a way to relax and keep calm. The most significant change about him, though, was his eyes. He fed from me constantly, completely unwillingly. When there were emotions flooding from humans, a demon couldn't shut them down—the only thing he could do was sit back and feed or leave the company of the person feeding him. Hence, Erebus was a very full demon. My growing love for him left him with either solid black eyes or bright amber irises with an outer black rim. Although, recently, they'd made another development, and I was often left staring into fully fed eyes with an additional outer red rim. The central amber colour was like looking into a kaleidoscope of multiple shades that swam and merged over the surface. I much preferred it to the black.

Odin had accepted Erebus. There'd been no sneaky pecks, and he didn't squawk at him or leave the room if he was in it. He was like a family pet, albeit a mischievous one.

A loud knock at the door of the house had both of us looking up. No one ever called at the front door.

Erebus sprang from his chair, his head cocked to the side as he strode into the hall.

"Who is it?" I asked, remembering that the last visitor, Sebastian, had caused nothing but trouble for us. I closed the book I was reading and ignored the unease in my stomach. I was determined that whoever it was wouldn't spoil the life that Erebus and I had created.

"Unexpected visitors," he called back. "Go into the lounge, Athena. Let's see what they want." Erebus waited at the unopened door. "Go on. I'll not open it until you're in the room."

I ambled into the lounge, stood next to the desk, and listened for the lock being turned. I smoothed my shaking hands across my dress, waiting for an introduction that I was sure wouldn't end well. My fingers and toes tingled as I recalled my last meeting with unknown demons. I took several deep breaths and tried to convince myself that everything would be fine.

"Unbelievable!"

I jumped at the deep booming voice coming from the hall.

"When were you going to let us know?" A female, her voice accusatory. She didn't sound happy at all.

I placed one hand in my other and wrung them together, trying to control my need to run from the room and lock myself in my bedroom. Surely Erebus could deal with the man and the woman, send them away with threats about what he would do if they didn't listen to him.

Erebus entered the room followed by a man and a woman. Both of them wore riding clothes and knee-high boots; gloves covered both of their hands, and neither of them removed them. The woman had striking features; midnight-black, short and spikey hair, alluring almond shaped eyes, and bee-stung, heart shaped lips. The man had a pointed face, one that didn't show any emotion other than that of annoyance. His rat-like, narrow eyes surveyed me and his barely existent lips tightened. I clung to the edge of the desk behind me, trapped by his constant glare.

Erebus moved next to me and placed his arm around my waist. "Athena, allow me to introduce my brother and sister, Olisha and Narabus." He squeezed my waist, a reassuring gesture that I more than needed. "And, Olisha, Narabus, this is Athena. My wife."

Olisha shrieked, her hands flying to her mouth.

Narabus huffed and looked away before slumping into the single chair. His long hair was neatly tied back, although I could still see the curls that were so familiar to me on Erebus.

Erebus kissed my cheek, and it was only then that I released my grip on the desk.

"Let me see," Olisha said, directing her words at Erebus. He lifted my right hand, turning the back of it upward before presenting his in the same way. Olisha's gloved hands held both mine and Erebus's as she inspected the identical marriage marks. Wordlessly, she looked at Erebus's eyes, her own widening as she focused on him. "Oh my, Erebus. Look what she does to you."

Narabus growled from across the room and crossed one leg over the other. "It's more than that though, isn't it?"

I slipped my hand away from Olisha and hid it behind my back, out of sight from Narabus. He was brimming with hostility I had no understanding of.

"What's that supposed to mean?" Erebus shot him an angry stare, and moved toward him.

Narabus stared at me, his gaze burning. I looked away, not comfortable under his scrutiny. It wasn't easy to tell that Narabus and Erebus were related. Narabus was tall, thin, smartly dressed, whereas Erebus always looked crumpled, as if he'd just crawled out of bed. Erebus had stubble, whereas Narabus was clean-shaven, in fact he was too perfect, too pristine. He didn't have one thing about him that looked soiled or used. His long riding jacket wasn't mud splattered, neither were his boots, but the handle of his sword caught my attention more than anything else. In the centre of the cross guard, between the handle and the blade, was a mercury-red stone or gem. It caught the light from the candles in the room and glistened vibrantly whenever Narabus moved. My attention was quickly diverted as Olisha took my hand again.

"So, where did he find you?"

"In the village," I said, surprised by her forwardness.

"And you've just married? How did he win your affections?"

"He married me the day he arrived." I said, sidetracked by the raised voices of the two brothers.

Olisha sighed as Narabus lowered his tone.

"I didn't come to discuss your marriage." He ran his hand down the buttons on his coat, and dusted imaginary dust from the fabric. "I came because of the death of two demons. They were killed by a violent surge of power. One very like the one that we all have. Seeing as you live nearby, I wondered if you had anything to do with their deaths."

I held my breath, knowing that he meant Verin and the other demon who followed us into the forest a few weeks ago.

Erebus's forehead creased into a deep frown line. "You know it was me. We are the only three who have such a power. Why come all this way to check?"

"I have to ask why, although now I am here, I can guess at the reason." He tapped his chin and leaned forward as he glanced at me. I froze. I'd seen that look before, the night Erebus killed the very demons his brother had mentioned. It was the same look they'd given me. My hand rose to my chest, and I fought the new panic building within me. Narabus was older than Erebus—did that mean he was stronger?

"Did they show too much interest in Athena?"

"They showed more than interest in her."

Narabus nodded. "I understand. I only hope Valafar does."

"Valafar?" I'd never heard the name before.

"The Master," Erebus said. He seemed unaffected by the

341

mention of this name and beckoned me forward with a wave of his hand. "Sit down, Athena. This is your home. You have more right to be relaxed in it than my brother does."

Narabus sniggered as Erebus sat next to me. "You always make me feel so welcome. Although, I must say I wasn't expecting to find you like this."

"So this visit was purely to confirm me as a killer?"

"Hey, I came," Olisha said. "I was desperate to see my little brother. It's been too long." She pointed at both of them in turn. "You two sort your business out, I'll sit quietly whilst you do, but then I want to know everything about Athena."

"Just the one human?" Narabus asked, raising his brow at Erebus.

"Yes, I don't keep a harem like you."

"Maybe it would have been better for you to have several girls here," Narabus said. "Not just this one. Although, she is rather pleasing on the eye. Does she satisfy you? Humans are usually too weak for me."

Erebus's posture changed. His shoulders lifted and his back straightened.

"Too weak for what?" I asked.

Narabus chuckled, cold, uncaring and dismissive. "Sex," he said, placing his hands in a prayer like position on his knee. "I break them."

"You treat them like toys!" Erebus sprang to his feet. "You play with them for a while and then get rid of them when you're bored."

"What an intriguing analogy. Toys . . . yes. I suppose that is how I treat them. You should do the same. Humans are weak, pathetic really. You should enjoy the flesh of the vampires; they are more than willing to entertain us."

Erebus hissed and Narabus waved his hand at him. "My apologies. I forgot about your private vendetta." He paused. "Has Athena any friends I can take back with me?"

"No!" I was on my feet, desperate to stop him. "You don't take anyone from the village."

Erebus placed his hand on my shoulder.

"There is no one suitable," he said in reply to his brother. "The carriage came only three full moons ago. You will not take anyone from my village."

"Not even one? A gift for your brother."

"There are no girls suitable for you," Erebus repeated as he guided me back to the sofa. He sunk down next to me.

"I feel responsible for this ridiculous situation," Narabus said. "I was the one who suggested you as Paymon's replacement. Valafar thought it a good idea as well."

"I'm well aware of that. I received his order."

Narabus snorted. "I thought it'd do you good, give you a grounding in your crazy nomadic lifestyle. I thought you may tap in to your true nature and live as we are supposed to. But what do I find? My brother . . . in love . . . with a human!"

"You make it sound like it's an impossibility," I said.

Erebus drew in a long breath and then sighed. "It's rare, very rare." He took my hand in his. "There aren't many humans who can genuinely love a demon. Why do you think the Master asks the village demons for the women when they turn twenty-one? He is seeking the love of a human woman. A love like ours. He believes that if the woman truly loves him then she will be able to produce a strong and healthy child with him. One that will survive."

"That's crazy." I shifted closer to Erebus. "Love has no bearing on whether a healthy child will be brought into the world."

"You and I know that, but it's not what the Master believes."

Narabus leaned forward in his chair. "You do realise what she's done to you?"

"What do you mean?" Erebus looked as confused as I felt.

"Your eyes," Olisha said.

Erebus huffed and released my hand. He folded his arms across his chest.

"I don't understand. What about his eyes?" I asked.

"The red circle. He's too powerful," Narabus said, straightening up in the chair. "At the moment, he's more powerful than the Master. If he were to find out—"

"I have no intention of him finding out," Erebus snapped.

"I will have to tell him. I can't ignore this."

"Will someone tell me what's going on?" I pushed my hair away from my face and looked to each of them in turn.

Erebus cupped my chin in his hand. "Athena, I am too powerful. Your love is feeding me, making me strong."

"But I thought fear was the strongest."

Erebus shook his head. His familiar amber eyes, edged in the black and red rim, stared back at me. "Fear is the easiest emotion for us to feed from, but it seems love is stronger. At the moment, I am incredibly powerful."

"The Master will not tolerate you," Narabus said. "And he will want Athena as his own."

"What?" I was on my feet again. "No! He can't have me. I'm married to Erebus. A demon's marriage is unbreakable." I couldn't just be taken to the Master. I belonged here, with Erebus.

Narabus strode to the fireplace and warmed his gloved

hands. "When the Master knows you have fallen in love with Erebus, he will seek you out and expect you to love him, just as you do my brother. He will also expect you to have many children. His children."

"I'll never love him." I crossed my arms over my chest and willed Narabus to turn and see my defiant stance. Who did he think he was?

Narabus ignored my outburst. "And because a demon's marriage is unbreakable, as you so rightly pointed out, he will kill Erebus to have you. I suggest you leave him. Don't be responsible for his death."

"Enough!" Erebus snapped, standing by my side.

"I can hide her," Narabus offered. His words were rushed, excited. "I can ensure she is safe and well looked after."

Erebus laughed. It was hollow, empty. "Athena is going nowhere. She stays with me." Erebus shoulders were back, stiff, and his voice had rediscovered its threatening tone. "If you think for one moment that I'd let you take her away with you . . ." His words trailed off as he shook his head. "It will never happen."

"It's the only possible option." Narabus's features darkened, his face appeared even more angular as he sensed victory.

Erebus gritted his teeth. "No. She will not become part of your harem. You wouldn't hide her. You'd treat her like all the others—"

"I wouldn't. I promise I'd not treat her like my other females."

My stomach twisted and turned as I imagined the unspoken words behind his statement, and I shivered as his gaze hit me. His lurid amber eyes swirled with the storm of darkness as he fed from my fear.

Erebus stepped in front of me, blocking Narabus's uncomfortable scrutiny. "And do you think that hiding her will stop the Master wanting her? As soon as you tell him of her existence, he will use all his powers to find her. And I know you'll tell him, your ties to him are far greater than they ever have been to your real family."

"That's not true!"

Erebus growled. "Athena is going nowhere with you. I will never trust you with her well-being. You'll not keep her safe, you'll either keep her in your harem and subject her to . . ." He stopped talking and rubbed his face with his hand. "Or you'll hand her to the Master, rise even further in his army rank. What are you now? A major? A lieutenant? What's next?"

Narabus sighed. "The Master would treat Athena like a princess."

"A princess? I've heard how he treats his human wives." Erebus's voice reduced to a hissed whisper. "He's worse than you."

Narabus shook his head. "If he wants Athena's love, he will not treat her like he treats his other wives."

Erebus snorted, and I reached for his hand, desperate for contact with him.

"We can't alter what's happened," Erebus said, holding my hand tightly. "I wouldn't want my life any other way. Not now. I am no threat to the Master. I merely wish to live a peaceful life with Athena."

His words made my heart glow. They mirrored how I felt.

Olisha, quiet throughout their interaction, tutted loudly. "I wish you two would get on."

"Well, he missed his calling, didn't he?" Narabus snarled,

nostrils flaring. "And so did you."

Olisha's hand flew to her chest, and she stared at Narabus incredulously. "I had no desire to work for the Master."

"Nor did I," Erebus added.

"But you should have. You know how strong and unique our power is."

I frowned, confused by their words. Erebus must have seen my confusion, and he guided me back to the sofa. "When we came above, Narabus, Olisha, Kitra, and myself were invited to join the Master's household. None of us wanted anything to do with him, apart from Narabus. Although Kitra was tempted, wasn't she Narabus?"

He snarled, but offered no other response as he turned his back on us and faced the fireplace.

"We'd been trapped all our lives beneath this world," Erebus continued. "We wanted to experience the freedom it offered and not be under his command. Narabus was keen to show his commitment to Valafar and ran to him as soon as we were free. I have no desire to be controlled by anyone."

I nodded, understanding.

"You say you don't want to be controlled by anyone, but what about Athena?" Narabus said, still not turning to face us. He picked an ornament from the mantelpiece. "It seems that she, although unaware, is controlling you. Now, faced with the Master, would her love for you diminish? He is a striking looking demon, worthy of any woman's love."

"I've seen his portrait, he's not my type," I said, desperate to quieten Narabus and his threats.

He placed the ornament back on the mantelpiece and turned around slowly.

"What category did Paymon select you for at the Ascension

Ceremony?" Narabus asked, his gaze widening as my discomfort became apparent. His hooded black eyes caught mine. My hands shook and I sensed the rising beat of my heart.

"His wife."

Narabus laughed. "Seems it has always been your destiny."

"Enough," Erebus said, his head down, unfocused. "Leave Athena alone."

"She should have been taken to him at the last ceremony." Narabus shouted, his face reddening. "The Master will be furious when he knows she was destined for him to begin with. You know how rare it is to find a female suitable to be his wife. Paymon should have sent her to him, not wed her himself." His anger was switched to Erebus. "And it's not like you to want another's cast-offs!"

Erebus sprang from the sofa, his hand raised. I shrank backward, fearing the power that I knew all of them possessed. One wrong move, one stray surge, and I'd not survive.

The desk chair shot backward as Olisha ran between them and faced Erebus. "Stop it. Both of you! Let's all calm down. Drop your hand, Erebus. You will not attack your brother."

Erebus snarled before resting his arm at his side.

"All this does is prove my point, and my concern," Narabus said, prowling around the back of the chair he'd originally sat in. "You're too powerful, and you are blind to all sense and reason. You know what you should do, but you refuse." He perched on the chair arm, casual in his demeanour, but never taking his eyes off Erebus. Erebus wasn't wearing his gloves—he never did when we were in the house. He could easily fire his power at Narabus; there'd be no warning.

"I wasn't completely honest with you when I arrived," Narabus continued, his eyes flicking to me then Erebus. "Yes,

I came to see you, despite what you think, and yes it did coincide with my orders to investigate the death of two demons. But it was also slightly more. The power that killed them was so forceful that the Master was alerted. Neither he nor I have seen such extreme force, yet I bet you only blasted them as you always do. There was no extra force, no sudden surge that you were aware of?"

Erebus shook his head.

"Too powerful, without even knowing." He resumed his predatory prowl at the side of the room. "You're dangerous, Erebus, not just to the Master, but everyone around you."

"Why is he a danger to the Master?" I couldn't grasp what Narabus was implying. But the snarl that sat on Erebus's face confirmed he knew.

"Well, we could have found out just how powerful I've become if our sister hadn't got in the way."

"Stop it! Now!" Olisha ordered.

Erebus returned next to me on the sofa and reached for my hand. The low buzz of his power tickled my palm. "The Master does not like anyone to be more powerful than him. He will see me as a threat to his position. I have no desire to challenge him or his army." He cast a sideways glance at Narabus before dipping his head and focusing on me. "But I will not lose you just to keep the Master happy." He leaned forward and kissed me on the lips. It was a chaste kiss but more than I expected from him considering the presence of his brother. I released a shaky breath and squeezed his hand.

Olisha returned to the desk. She picked up the notes that Erebus had been researching and flicked through them. "Are you still hunting vampires?"

Erebus twisted his head to face her. "Yes."

The tension in the room eased with Olisha's attempt to divert the anger flowing between the brothers. And I breathed deeply, filling my lungs, freeing them from the constricting tightness that had wrapped around them since Narabus's arrival. But the air was still charged with a pulsing power, one that oscillated around me and made the hairs on my skin vibrate.

"It's a waste of time," Narabus said, returning to sit in the single chair. He leaned back and breathed deeply. "Unlike the situation we need to sort here."

"There's nothing to sort," Erebus said. I slid my fingers between his, locking our hands in place.

"What about you, Athena?" Narabus asked. "Are you content to leave things as they are?"

Erebus shifted. "I won't warn you again," he said. "Leave Athena alone. Back off."

Narabus ignored him. "My brother will be killed because of you."

"Seriously. Stop it!" Erebus was on his feet, although his hands were by his side.

"Let her speak," Narabus said. His piercing eyes met mine. "How do you feel about all this?"

A wave of confusion hit me, my breath quickened and the floor rose and fell around me. I lifted my hand to my head and tried to focus. I struggled with my thoughts, not because I didn't know how I felt, but it was like my brain had hit a foggy road.

"I . . . I . . ." My answer wouldn't form the way I wanted it to. Words drifted in my head—words that I needed to say, words that would ensure Erebus's safety, words that would see me as the Master's wife. They weren't true, though, and I fought the overwhelming desire to speak words that were not mine.

"Athena?" Erebus placed his hand on my shoulder. The heavy fog lifted. My mind became my own. I knew what had happened.

"How dare you?" I shouted at Narabus as I sprang to my feet. Heat rushed through me and my muscles quivered. "How dare you compel me!"

A surge of crackling light hit Narabus in the chest. The force of the blow sent the chair skidding backward. With Narabus still seated, the chair crashed into the wall.

Erebus stood beside me, his hand held in front of him, his palm facing his brother.

Narabus quickly recovered. "Is that the best you can do, little brother?"

Erebus moved slowly and deliberately toward him, the muscles and veins in his neck straining against his skin. I didn't hold him back. What Narabus had just tried to do, to make me turn away from the man I loved, was unforgivable. I was still shaking, my anger brimming quietly, along with the frustration at not being able to resist his initial compelment.

"No!" Olisha was across the room and between them again.

"Move," Erebus growled quietly, lowering his arm. "I lied earlier. I know how powerful my surge is. I hit those demons with its full force. I intended to kill them. I made sure I didn't give our brother the full force. Let's hope he doesn't make me wish I had."

Olisha stepped aside. "You kill him, and I'll never forgive you."

My gaze flicked between the brothers. Narabus's sword

still hung in its sheath at the side of his leg, but it was the surge of power that would kill, not a blade.

As Erebus approached his brother, I moved backward, toward the desk. I didn't look away, I needed to be alert, ready to duck out of the way of a stray blast of power from either brother.

Erebus placed an uncovered hand on Narabus's chest on the exact spot where his surge of power had hit him. Blue sparks fizzed at his fingertips.

"How dare you compel Athena?" Erebus was controlled, quietly angry. "You've overstepped the mark, and you've definitely outstayed your welcome. Get out of my house."

"You need to be stopped," Narabus said, brushing Erebus's hand off his chest. "You are too powerful and cannot continue like this." He straightened as Erebus stepped away. "I have to alert Valafar of your power. Whether you intend to act on your strength or not, you are a threat, and it will not be tolerated."

"Then why don't you just kill me now? Get it over with?" Erebus stood with his arms outstretched at his sides, inviting Narabus to attack him. My eyes widened at his open suggestion, but I hardly had time to register the full meaning as Narabus, with a movement so fast, I momentarily questioned whether he was a demon or a vampire, withdrew his sword from its sheath.

"I'm warning you now," he said. "I will use it. I will kill you if I have to."

Erebus tapped his foot on the floor. "I think not. As much as you love to play the fearless warrior, you will not kill me, your brother. Just as I did not kill you a few moments ago."

Narabus edged forward. "I will if I have to."

"Really? Then I can play this game as well." Erebus lifted

both hands in front of him, ready to unleash another surge of power. "Try to kill me, Narabus, and you will be the dead one. No sword is a match for me now."

"It could be."

"Try it. Come on, try it!"

Narabus stared at him before shaking his head and replacing his sword in its sheath. "I will be informing Valafar of your power, and of Athena. He will come after you, Erebus. Every single member of his army will be sent to kill you and take Athena to him."

I swallowed hard; this wasn't the outcome I wanted. Erebus would be hunted, killed even, and I would be caught and taken to the Master. I pulled at my lip, my hands shaking. Why couldn't we just be left alone?

Erebus lowered his arms but took another stride toward Narabus. "Then let it be known, *brother*, that if he sends an army, I will kill every single one of them. I will not sit here quietly and let Athena be taken from me. I have no desire to challenge the Master, but if he comes looking for me or Athena then this becomes personal. I won't just kill his army. I will kill him as well."

Narabus remained where he was, not flinching at his brother's threat. "Then I bid you farewell, Erebus, for I fear this may be the last time I see you. Just remember that this has been your choice."

Erebus shook his head. "No. There were no choices. And there never will be where Athena's concerned."

Narabus glanced at Olisha then me. Taking one last look at Erebus, he nodded and then left.

As the door slammed shut, Erebus rushed to my side. He tilted my chin with his fingers. "You won't ever be taken from me. I promise. You're not going anywhere without me." He kissed my lips and pulled my shaking body to his. "Now, if I am truly as powerful as my brother seems to think, I will be able to keep you more than safe."

"But how? A whole army. You heard him. They'll kill you." My chin quivered as I grabbed the cotton of his smock and pulled him even closer, needing the comforting warmth of his arms around me.

"They won't. As long as you are with me, I'll be the most powerful demon on earth." He chuckled and kissed the top of my head. "Not that I'm interested in power. Olisha was always the one who craved being in charge."

"Because I could do a far better job than any man." She huffed and fidgeted with the papers on the desk.

Erebus kissed my forehead, keeping me cocooned in his arms. As my breathing became steady, my fear about what could happen turned into anger that our lives could be ruined by something neither of us wanted. How dare Narabus come into our home and demand we live separate lives. We fought, so, so hard to be where we were, and our relationship didn't belong to anyone but us. Humans had been ruled by demons for far too long and I refused to have my life dictated by them anymore.

"Erebus?" Olisha said, breaking the silence of the room. "Where did this book come from?"

"Which one?"

"This one." She held the diary in the air.

"It belonged to a woman who lived with Paymon," I answered as I raised my head from the comfort of Erebus's warm chest. "She was a demon. Paymon killed her."

Olisha took a deep breath.

"Now what?" Erebus sighed. "More rubbish to deal with?"

"I read some of it whilst you three were deciding what to do about true love."

"And?" Erebus snapped, impatient.

Olisha waved the diary in the air and then placed it on the desk. "This is Kitra's diary."

Erebus released me and strode to the desk.

"How do you know?" He stood behind Olisha, and she slid the diary his way, tapping repeatedly on an open page.

"She mentions her siblings," Olisha said. "Narabus, you, and me. I think we can assume she's our sister."

"She was delusional," Erebus said, picking the diary up and flicking through the pages. "I read some of this when Athena showed it to me. Somewhere in here she says that she and Paymon were powerful and should challenge the Master."

She nudged him. "Seems you weren't the first then."

Erebus opened his mouth to respond but started laughing instead.

I moved to the sofa, suddenly feeling like an intruder. Siblings had strong connections, and I wasn't jealous of their apparent closeness, but it made me think about what I'd lost when my sister was killed alongside my parents. I'd give anything to have her at my side and be able to laugh and joke with her. My vision blurred as tears built within my eyes. Once again I was reminded of the loss I suffered when the demons ascended, of the pain everyone suffered, and the life we had endured for thirteen hard years.

"Athena?" Erebus was back at my side. "What's wrong?"

I shook my head, wiping my tears with my fingers as he sat beside me. "Sorry. Just remembering my sister."

"You had a sister?" Olisha perched on the arm of the sofa.

I nodded. "She was three years older than me. Helen."

"Same age gap as Erebus and me," Olisha chirped. She paused for a few moments and then jumped up to retrieve the diary. "Can I keep this for a while? I want to read it to see what else she has to say. I know she was our sister, but she was an absolute witch to me when I was little."

Erebus nodded, another smile gracing his features. "She wasn't particularly nice to me either."

"Strange how she always got on with Narabus," Olisha said.

"You have until tomorrow morning to read it," Erebus said, his serious tone returning. "And I want to know exactly what she says."

"I'd best start now then," Olisha waved the book at Erebus. "I'll be in the library if you need me."

She left the room, shooting both of us a sideways grin.

Erebus pulled me to his side, and I sighed with a juddering breath.

He hugged me and kissed the side of my head. "I'm sorry about all this. I never expected Narabus to visit. And I certainly didn't expect him to say what he did."

"It's not your fault." I lifted my head to catch his eyes. "Is it true, though? The Master will come looking for you and me?"

"Yes." His face set with concentration as he smoothed my hair away from my face. "Unfortunately, due to his reaction today, we need to get away from here. We have to leave this house and the village. And we'll leave tomorrow."

CHAPTER 22

HOPE

I SNUGGLED INTO HEATED FLESH. MY FACE RESTED ON Erebus's shoulder as I lay sideways, trapped in the comforting hold of his arm.

I stretched, curling my hand around his waist, and his arm tightened around my shoulder before he kissed the top of my head.

"How are you this morning?" His voice was heavy with sleep. "Did you sleep well, or did you have nightmares about my nasty brother?"

"Don't remind me," I said, attempting to wriggle away.

His hold on me tightened. "Don't try to escape. It's a pointless waste of energy."

"I don't like you joking about him." I hadn't slept well. Nightmares about Erebus being killed so that the Master could marry me were too fresh in my mind.

Erebus sighed. Twisting onto his side, he looked into my eyes. "You'll be fine. I promise."

"It's you I'm worried about, not me."

He cupped my face in his hand. "Don't be. No harm will come to me, and I promise that no harm will come to you."

"I wish I felt as confident about this as you do." I sighed. We'd been so happy before his brother called, and now . . . now what happened?

His smile faded and became a serious line. "If I fail with my promise and he does confront us . . ." He dipped his head. "I will kill any man, woman, demon, or vampire that tries to take you from me." He brushed a stray strand of hair away from my face. "I love you, Athena."

My skin tingled and my heartbeat raced. It was like a sudden rush charging through every part of me. I had no doubt of his feelings for me, but he'd never said the words by themselves, never solidified his feelings so precisely. And as I gazed into amber swirling irises, edged in the beautiful red circle I was so used to seeing, I slipped my arms around his neck and pulled him closer, about to tell him how much I loved him.

"Erebus! Erebus!" Olisha's shouting came moments before the bedroom door was flung open. "You'll never guess what I've found out!"

Erebus released me and yanked the furs and blankets over our naked bodies. He scowled at his sister as he sat up. "Do you ever knock?"

She ignored his sarcasm and plonked herself on the end of the bed. Kitra's diary was in her hand. She wasn't wearing the black gloves that covered her hands yesterday, and I noticed a fairy-tale-green stone ring on one of her fingers. It reminded me of the necklace Paymon gave me, and I cocked my head to the side, taking in the silver leaf-work design around the gem.

"Did our sister write all her secrets in her book?" Erebus said, scowling at the diary.

Olisha nodded, a nervous smile pulling at her lips.

"It better be good."

"It is."

I sat up next to Erebus, pulling the blankets even higher, and concentrated on Olisha.

"And . . .?" Erebus waved his hand in a circle, encouraging her to tell us what she'd discovered.

"You'll never believe me."

Erebus raised his brow, waiting.

"I didn't think it possible, but . . . seriously, even I'm finding it hard to believe."

"Olisha, if you don't tell me what it is that has you behaving crazier than normal, then get out of my bedroom. Athena and I were enjoying our morning before you burst in."

Her cheeks flushed and she cleared her throat. "Valafar is our father."

Erebus didn't say a word. I, on the other hand, gasped loudly.

Olisha stared at Erebus, her eyes widening and then narrowing to slits of frustration. "Did you hear me, Erebus? Valafar, the Master, is our father."

His eyes fixed on the diary. "Let me see." He held his hand toward her.

Olisha thrust the diary into his hand.

"What does it say?" I asked, leaning closer to him. I caught sight of the sea of words, but demon language was as much a mystery to me now as it had been several weeks ago, despite my early attempts to translate it.

"Near the end," Olisha said, "I've folded the corner of the

page."

Erebus flicked to the page and quickly scanned it. He took a deep breath and leaned backward. "I've read it, but I don't believe it. You know how delusional she was." He ran his fingers through his hair, scrunching it back at the base of his neck. "I mean, look at what happened between her and Narabus."

"What did happen between them?" I asked. There was still so much to discover about Erebus. I knew snatched moments of his life, ones he'd told me about, but they were like short versions of the whole picture. I wanted to know everything, and that included Kitra.

"We don't talk about it, do we, Erebus?" Olisha stiffened, and she narrowed her eyes at him.

"You maybe don't," he snapped.

"There's no point in bringing it all up again."

"Why not? I'm sure Athena would like to know what happened. And I think it seems even more relevant after this revelation, which I have to admit, I'm finding very hard to believe."

"But it's there, written, in her diary." Olisha tapped the book, but Erebus didn't respond. He scanned more pages before huffing.

"Just because she's written it, doesn't mean it's true. Her head was always full of wild ideas. I mean, Valafar, our father? It's crazy talk."

I shifted closer to Erebus. "What happened between Narabus and Kitra?"

He glanced at Olisha before turning to me. "You heard yesterday that when we first left Muspalta, Narabus immediately joined the Master's army. Neither Olisha nor I were interested. As we said last night, we'd spent years below the earth's surface—we wanted freedom, not to be under the control of anyone."

"Kitra visited," Olisha said.

"Narabus introduced her to Valafar's head demon, Zagam. She stayed at the Master's to be with Zagam. She witnessed and contributed to the depraved way of living that the demons there seem to enjoy. She saw the way Narabus lived and the luxury surrounding him and wanted it for herself. I'm sure that Narabus introduced her to Zagam in the hope that he would sweep Kitra off her feet and persuade her to join the army."

"Did she join?"

Erebus scratched the stubble on his chin. "No, she fell in love with Zagam. But instead of him persuading her to join the army, he persuaded her to help him overthrow the Master. Zagam didn't love our sister, he used her. He'd seen Narabus's power and knew Kitra had the same. Zagam was a formidable demon, and with Kitra, he thought they'd be invincible."

"Narabus found out about the plan," Olisha said.

"And he killed Zagam." Erebus scowled at the diary as if the book was responsible for everything that had happened. "He didn't kill Kitra, though, and he should have."

"Of course he didn't. She was his sister." Even though I'd met Narabus yesterday and seen how he squared up to Erebus, I'd doubted whether he would actually kill him. This just proved my hopeful theory.

A sudden thought hit me. "Do you think Valafar knows you are his children?"

Erebus lifted his head and turned to me. He shrugged. "I'm not convinced we are his children. He's never bothered about us. I think it's Kitra being her normal crazy self. And even if Valafar is our father, it doesn't mean that he'll have any qualms about stealing you from me. That's what's important here, and that's why I'll protect you."

I rubbed my arms, at a loss of what to say.

Olisha shook her head. She jumped from the bed and wandered to the side of the room before leaning back against the wall. "From what I read in the diary, Paymon must have seemed very placid after Zagam. Maybe she wanted a safe option—someone who wasn't a risk?"

Erebus waved the diary at her. "But she didn't want to be safe. She tortured the men in the village, and she still plotted to overthrow Valafar. With her powerful surge and Paymon's power of fire, she thought like Zagam. She thought them invincible and capable of challenging him. She obviously never mentioned it to Narabus."

"He'd have killed Paymon," I said, outraged that her behaviour would have ended Paymon's life. He was a good demon, kind and patient. Why on earth had he got involved with Kitra?

"Did you read any further?" Erebus asked. "Does she say how she found out that Valafar is supposedly our father?"

She shook her head. "I was so stunned when I read that bit that I immediately came to tell you."

"Well, don't ever expect me to call him father. He'll always be the Master or Valafar to me." Erebus turned the pages and continued reading.

"I still don't think she'd write something like that if it wasn't true. I mean, why?" Olisha walked to the window. She peered through the thin opening watching the world that lay outside. The village would be visible from the window, but only if the early morning fog had cleared.

Both Erebus and I looked up when Olisha gasped and jumped back from the window. She placed her hand over her chest, and pointed to the glass with her other. I was just about to ask what was wrong when I heard the familiar sound of tapping.

Odin.

"There's a raven outside," Olisha said. "It's huge."

"It's Odin," I replied. "You can let him in."

"Let him in? He'll destroy the place."

I shook my head. "No he won't. He knows how to behave."

Odin's insistent tapping of the glass continued.

Erebus tutted. "Just let him in, or he'll drive us all mad with that noise."

As soon as Olisha opened the window, Odin flew inside. He fluttered to the top of the chest of drawers before squawking several times in succession at Erebus and me.

"Nice of you to pay us a visit," Erebus said before concentrating on the diary.

"It's good to have you back." I smiled at Odin as he tipped his head to the side. He'd kept away from the house since Narabus's visit yesterday, and whereas it wasn't unusual for him to fly off for a day or two, I always preferred it when he was around.

"Athena, you need to hear this." Erebus looked at me, his eyes wide with wonder.

"Why, what does she say?" I moved even closer, as if seeing the words he wanted me to hear would make the writing understandable.

Olisha strode across the room and hopped onto the bed. She crossed her legs and waited for Erebus to continue.

"I'll translate this for you. This is what you've been

searching for," he said, his hand resting on my arm.

My heart jumped, as if receiving a shock.

Erebus cleared his throat and began:

"*And the magic to remove the shield of darkness is kept by Valafar's pure-born children, those born by Liami.*"

I focused on the words he was reading. "Who's Liami?"

"Our mother."

My breath hitched, and my hand flew to my throat. "Carry on," I encouraged, nodding at the diary.

"*The magic is kept in weapons for his sons, jewellery for his daughters. Gifts bestowed on them when they were born.*"

I stared at Olisha's ring again, instantly knowing its importance. "Your ring," I said, nodding at her hand. "And the necklace." I turned to the nightstand where it lay.

Erebus's jaw tightened. Olisha reached for the necklace and handed it to me.

"Oh my, do you think . . .?" Her words were laced with an excited trill. "Where did you get this from?"

"Paymon," I said. "When he was dying he gave me the necklace. He told me to put it to good use. I had no idea what he was on about."

Olisha scratched the side of her head. "But why did he have it?"

Erebus pinched the bridge of his nose, and cleared his throat. "It would have been Kitra's." He sighed heavily. "It seems that she was right then. It looks like Valafar is our father."

I rested my hand on his shoulder and rubbed his tense muscles. "Have you never known who your father was?"

"No." Olisha shook her head. "Mother would never tell us."

"But Kitra knew," I said.

"Or she found out." Erebus waved the diary in the air at Olisha. "She was out of control. You've read most of this, what did she sound like to you? Balanced and reasonable? I said when I first read parts of this that she was a temptress, someone I was surprised Paymon fell for. You said she was horrendous to you when you were young. I don't remember her all that well, thankfully. She didn't stick around much in Muspalta or when we came above land. She forged her own fate with Zagam by being as she was. I'm surprised Paymon didn't kill her sooner than he did."

Olisha folded her arms across her chest and huffed. "Sometimes you sound like Narabus."

"I can live with that—just don't you dare start acting like Kitra."

"So, we have the jewellery he gifted his daughters," I said, desperate to bring the conversation back to the items Kitra mentioned. "I think the magic is in the gems. Look at how the colours swirl." I held the necklace toward Erebus. "I think Narabus's sword is one of the weapons. There's a red jewel in the crossbar. I noticed it straight away when he arrived. What do you have, Erebus? And does Kitra say what you need to do with them to break the shield?" I spoke fast, impatient to know more.

"I have a dagger. I never use it, but I'm sure it'll be what Kitra's referring to." He turned his attention back to the diary and continued reading. "*Valafar guards his own magic. But when together, they hold the power to destroy the shield.*"

"His own magic?" I caught my frustration at the half riddle. "Does she say what it is and what we need to do?"

Erebus shook his head as he continued to read. "Nothing.

She just goes on to list what she did with the human men." His eyes widened before he frowned. "I think Zagam had more of an effect on her than we realised. She wasn't just power crazy, she was barbaric and iniquitous."

He placed the book on the bed and stared at it.

I huffed and crossed my arms over my chest. "Where's this dagger you mentioned? I've never seen it." My initial excitement was dwindling. I knew where the magic was kept, split into five, but I had no idea what the fifth item was, the one Valafar guarded. And I had no idea what to do with them to destroy the shield.

Erebus opened the drawer at his side of the bed and lifted out what looked like a dirty old rag.

"I hardly ever use it. I have no need to, not when I can do all the damage I need with my hands."

He unwrapped the rag from around a leather sheath. Protruding from the cover was a silver handle, and he carefully drew the dagger free.

The hilt of the dagger was carved in an intricate leaf pattern that matched both the design around my necklace and the one around the ring. Just below the hilt, swirls of silver held the amber jewel in place before merging into the blade. It was highly polished, like a mirror, and as Erebus lifted it in the air, the blade caught the flickering images of the lit candles around the room.

"That's where the magic is," I said, pointing to the amber gem. I reached for my necklace and placed it next to the dagger. The swirling turquoise of the gem in my necklace glowed, as did the gem in the dagger.

"Ring," I said, snapping my gaze to Olisha who quickly pulled the ring free from her finger.

When I placed it with the dagger and necklace, the gems in them all glowed brighter. The ring vibrated, dancing against the dagger handle. I couldn't tear my eyes away from the items. All beautiful in themselves, they were magnificent when together. And with Narabus's sword, they were only one other item short of having the power to rid us of the darkness and return the light to this dreary world.

"Kitra says these were gifted to you when you were born," I said, puzzled.

Erebus replaced the dagger in its sheath, and wrapped the rag around it. "Maybe they were, but our mother only gave them to us the day before we ascended."

Olisha nodded. "She said that they were gifts from our father, and we were to keep them safe." Lost in a sea of memories, her eyes clouded.

"Now we know why," Erebus said, sliding the dagger into the drawer.

I continued looking at the ring and the necklace. "But if he gave you these when you were born, how do they hold the magic to return the light? The light was still here when you were all born. It only disappeared when you ascended." I scrunched my nose, something else didn't make sense. "And how did Kitra know Valafar was your father? How did she make the connection?"

I concentrated on Erebus, but Olisha answered. "Maybe she saw something during the time she lived at the Master's? She always stuck her nose in where it wasn't wanted, always interfering, always inquisitive."

Erebus straightened his back. "I think the magic was set many years ago. Remember, our ascent has been planned for hundreds of years. We've had failed attempts in the past, but none with our current Master. It would make sense for him to plan for the day when we ascended, particularly if he wanted his children to unknowingly guard the secret. I think the main source of the power and magic is the one that he guards. That will be the most powerful item, and the one that ultimately keeps the darkness in place."

"The item that we have no idea about?"

"Yes."

I handed the ring back to Olisha. My mind was buzzing with information, and I tried to make sense of everything that we'd just discovered.

"What else does she say?" Olisha nodded at the diary that Erebus was flicking through.

"Is there anything else about the light or the shield?" I asked as I fastened the necklace around my neck.

He continued reading. "I don't think so. But it seems she had as deep a mistrust of vampires as I do. She's rambling about killing them with the brightness when it's restored." Erebus ran his finger down the page and turned it over. "Ha! She even says how much she hates the darkness, that it's no better than the depressing colours in Muspalta." Erebus shook his head and chuckled as he read. "She really hated Livia. Glad to hear I'm not the only one who wants to rip her scrawny head off."

I shuddered when he mentioned Livia. Her wild, grinning face regularly appeared in my nightmares. I prayed that I'd never actually see her again.

"Are vampires easy to kill?" I asked. "I mean, you told me they can't be in sunlight. Why? What happens to them?"

"They combust." Erebus's whole face lit up in a huge grin. "And they're not too good with fire either. They're pretty

INIQUITY

flammable."

I pursed my lips. "So I could kill Livia?"

Erebus closed the diary and placed it on the bed. "Yes, I think you could, with some training, and if you had some sort of flame or fire to throw at her." He placed his hand over mine. "But you also need to learn how to protect yourself. Perhaps when we've left here and find a safe place to settle I can train you to use my dagger."

"I'll help," Olisha said.

"Not that you'll need to fight." Erebus tightened his hold on my hand. "Both of us will blast anyone that comes near you."

"Including Narabus?" I had to ask the question. I was certain that he would be leading the army that would come after us.

"Including Narabus," Erebus said as he leaned toward me and kissed my cheek.

"I'll leave you two alone." Olisha reached for the diary, but Erebus placed his hand over it. She stared at his hand as if willing it to disappear, but after a few moments she straightened her back and left the room, closing the door with a soft click.

With Olisha gone, Erebus threw himself backward on the bed. He placed his hands over his eyes and sucked in a large breath of air.

"I can't believe that Valafar is my father. All these years . . ."

"Have you never tried to find him? Did you never ask your mother?"

Erebus removed his hands from his face and rubbed my arm. "We all asked, many times. She refused to tell us who he

369

was, only letting us know that we all had the same father."

"I'm sorry," I said.

"What for?" Erebus shifted into a sitting position.

"That you've never known who your father was? It must have been hard for you when you were growing up."

Erebus shook his head. "Not really. And can you imagine what life would have been like if we'd known who he was?"

I frowned, not sure whether Erebus's easy dismissal was the truth. Did he really not care?

"Come here," he said, opening his arms to me. "Let's enjoy our time together before we have to leave."

I shuffled across the bed before lying next to him.

"It's not going to be easy keeping one step ahead of Narabus. I think the safest places to go will be the old cities."

"But don't infernals live there?"

"Yes. And the renegades will also be there. But if we can get them onto our side, it will confuse Narabus and the army he brings with them." He kissed the top of my head. "I'll keep you safe, don't worry."

This house had become my home, this room my sanctuary, and I never felt safer than when I was in Erebus's arms. But as his grip on me tightened, my worry tumbled through my mind. We were going to be running away and hiding from an army of demons. How did Erebus expect us to keep ahead of them? We were going to be heading into cities, ones like the one I'd lived in. We'd face infernals like Bia, and the unknown renegades—humans, warriors, that had stayed in the cities. How long did he think we could survive?

I hid my face against his chest, and tried to stop the unwanted tears slipping from my eyes. I was stronger than this—I was a survivor and a fighter.

Even if Narabus found us, I wouldn't let him steal me away from Erebus. And I certainly wouldn't be going to the Master's to become his next wife.

We left the house later that morning with our few personal belongings tucked securely into two strong bags. I wore my boots and a pair of Olisha's trousers, as well as a long woollen tunic that belonged to her. Erebus had wrapped me in his spare jacket, and I pulled Paymon's old cloak over the top.

The horses were saddled, and within minutes, we were ready to go. I was on Samael with Erebus, Olisha was on her own horse, Malachi. I wrapped my arms around Erebus's waist as he encouraged Samael to trot out of the stables. Looking skyward, I caught site of Odin circling above us. The darkness swallowed him every so often, but his white breast feather helped me keep track of him. I hoped he'd follow us, just as he did when Erebus and I went to the coast.

"Remember to hold tight," Erebus said. "We'll be travelling a lot faster than when we last rode Samael."

I did as instructed, leaning into the warmth of his back.

Olisha pulled up beside us on her matching black stallion. Samael's ears twitched and Erebus sighed, dipping his head.

Olisha reached her gloved hand out to him and patted his arm. "You know Narabus's ties to the Master have always been strong. He seeks his approval no matter what the cost."

"He is ultimately betraying me because of my love for Athena. He would betray my strength, of which I have no desire to act upon, to the Master. And now, he himself seeks her. He is no brother of mine. Not anymore."

Olisha shot her gaze to me. "We'll keep you safe. Both of us."

"I'll die before they take you to the Master," Erebus said.

I nodded my understanding of his ultimate commitment. "I know. But let's all try to keep living."

"Indeed."

With a sharp kick of his heels, Erebus encouraged Samael to move. Once we were away from the stables Samael charged forward—a demanding pace that never diminished. I closed my eyes, ignoring the bitter sting of the rain, and clung to Erebus, the demon who had managed to steal my heart in a way I'd never thought possible.

We were heading to a city, one where infernals and renegades lived. The Master's army would be looking for us, aiming to steal me away from Erebus.

The future appeared grim, but for the first time in my life, I had hope—more than hope. There was something else, something so strong that my own bravado frightened me. I knew where the magic was hidden to break the shield of darkness. I had access to three of the sources already, and I knew where another was—Narabus's sword. I only had one more to find.

I'd eventually destroy the shield and make sure we saw the sun again. I'd never give up. I'd do whatever I had to do to restore the light to this world.

THE END

Thank you for reading.

I really hope you enjoyed reading INIQUITY. It was a story that wouldn't stop talking to me—the characters demanded I tell their story, and we still have another book or two of this dark world to discover.

If you have a minute to spare, please leave a short review on the retail site where you purchased the book. Reviews are incredibly important to authors because they help more people discover our books.

Acknowledgements

It's taken many people to help shape INIQUITY into the growling beast it now is. As my first self-published novel I've reached out to many new contacts including cover designers, formatters, editors, and writing friends who have spent their precious time reading/making suggestions/screaming at me/ proof-reading.

Amalia Chitulescu, cover designer. You took my brief idea and once we selected the figure of Athena you delivered what I think is a truly beautiful cover. It captures the story so perfectly, hinting at the fantasy and darkness within. And I LOVE Odin!

Stacey Blake, formatter at Champagne Formats. You took the stress out of formatting for me. You made INIQUITY look amazing on the inside.

Katelyn Stark, editor and old friend, at Stark Contrast Editing. We have known each other for years, when we were both dipping our toes into the world of writing for the first time. We formed a great friendship across the miles back then, and recently it's been wonderful to pick up where we left off. You 'got' INIQUITY, and through your development notes and fantastic editing we've arrived with a monster of a book. I'm looking forward to throwing ADVERSITY at you, and have every faith that we'll whip the second and third books in the series into something just as great as the first.

There have been four special friends who have held my hand during INIQUITY's journey. **Denise Hall** and **Barbara Reichwein** have been by my side since the very first glimmer of the story appeared in my fuzzy brain. We grew the story together, twisted and turned it, pulled it in every direction to end up with the first draft. And then we attacked it again. When the story was as complete as I could get it I entrusted **Michelle Hoehn** and **Kathleen Palm** with my words. They have worked so hard to help iron out the kinks: alert me to word choices that were suspect (to say the least), pointed out repetition of words, and highlighted paragraphs that needed more oomph! They were all there, and you spotted them. Your support has been amazing. You are wonderful people, and INIQUITY would not be what it is now without your help. Thank you all so, so much.

There are always other people, those who silently cheer you on from the side, and I'd like to thank those people for their seemingly never-ending support: **Nicki Tailby, Claire Davies, Lorna Jones, Tammy Farrell** (and **Finn Farrell** because his cute little face always makes me smile), **Julie Hutchings, Katie Teller, Ashley Hudson**, and **Emma Adams**.

My family still put up with my random need to shut myself away whenever I'm 'in the zone'. Cups of tea, Baileys, wine, and many, many gin and tonics are kindly provided by my husband, **Pete**, when I plant myself at my desk. My teenage children, **Joe and Matt**, still humour me when I throw random questions at them about the world I've created. My **mum** and **dad** still enjoy telling their friends that I've written a book (or two), and I'm eternally grateful that when I was young, they never tried to quash my imagination. Thank you all.

About the Author

Growing up, Melody showed a natural ability in art, a head for maths, and a tendency to write too long English essays. Difficult to place in the world when she graduated, she pursued a career in teaching, but ended up working in finance. Melody is convinced the methodical times she spends working with numbers fuel her desire to drift into dream worlds and write about the illusory characters in her head.

Melody Winter lives in York, North Yorkshire, England with her husband and two sons. When not dealing with football, rugby, and a whole plethora of 'boy' activities, she will be found scribbling notes for her stories, or preparing for another trip to the nearby beaches at Scarborough and Whitby. With an obsession for anything mythical, Melody revels in reading and writing about such creatures, and creating her own.

Website: www.melodywinter.com

Twitter: @melodywinter

Facebook page: Melody-Winter-Author

MORE FROM
MELODY WINTER

THE ASCENT SERIES

CALAMITY (a prequel)—Coming soon
INIQUITY—Available now
ADVERSITY—Available now

THE MINE SERIES

SACHAEL DREAMS—Available now
SACHAEL DESIRES—please contact the author
SACHAEL DISCOVERY—Available now
SACHAEL DESTINY—Coming soon

THE LOVE IS SERIES
LOVE IS EVERYTHING—Available now
LOVE IS INTENSE—Coming soon

STAND ALONE BOOKS
STARSHINE—Available now
PROMISE (a Christmas Novella)—Available now

Printed in Great Britain
by Amazon

83663605R00223